W9-AQC-051

The Prince of Broadway

"Wrong. I barely know anything about you," she said. "For instance, I haven't the first clue on how well you can kiss."

He paused, but only for a second. "Are you asking for me to rectify that?" He reached out to slide his hands up her arms, past her shoulders, until rough fingers trailed under her jaw. "Because you'll find I'm very amenable to requests."

She shivered as he traced the skin of her throat with his knuckles, his gaze never dropping hers. It was as if the simple touch was a test. As if he expected her to push him away.

She didn't.

The touch had the opposite effect, the backs of his fingers mesmerizing as they swept back and forth. Tingles followed in his wake and she was quickly realizing that, yes, Clay could be quite gentle with her. And she liked it. A lot. The air grew heavy in her lungs, each breath filled with expectation, and she leaned in ever so slightly.

He bent his head, his hands shifting to cradle her jaw. She could see the whiskers on his face, the bow of his upper lip. Dark lashes that framed his eyes. Tiny lines and creases in the skin that signified a life well lived. Every inch of him was fascinating, each mark and scar another facet of his mysterious past.

His mouth hovered just above hers, their noses almost touching. "Change your mind yet?"

By Joanna Shupe

Uptown Girls
THE ROGUE OF FIFTH AVENUE
THE PRINCE OF BROADWAY

Coming Soon
THE DEVIL OF DOWNTOWN

The Four Hundred series
A NOTORIOUS VOW
A SCANDALOUS DEAL
A DARING ARRANGEMENT

The Knickerbocker Club series
MAGNATE
BARON
MOGUL
TYCOON

ATTENTION: ORGANIZATIONS AND CORPORATIONS
HarperCollins books may be purchased for educational, business, or sales promotional use. For information, please e-mail the Special Markets Department at SPsales@harpercollins.com.

UPTOWN GIRLS

3 3210 2710958

This is a work of fiction. Names, characters, places, and incidents are products of the author's imagination or are used fictitiously and are not to be construed as real. Any resemblance to actual events, locales, organizations, or persons, living or dead, is entirely coincidental.

THE PRINCE OF BROADWAY. Copyright © 2020 by Joanna Shupe. All rights reserved. Printed in the United States of America. No part of this book may be used or reproduced in any manner whatsoever without written permission except in the case of brief quotations embodied in critical articles and reviews. For information, address HarperCollins Publishers, 195 Broadway, New York, NY 10007.

First Avon Books mass market printing: January 2020

Print Edition ISBN: 978-0-06-290683-0
Digital Edition ISBN: 978-0-06-290684-7

Cover illustration by Jon Paul Ferrara

Avon, Avon & logo, and Avon Books & logo are registered trademarks of HarperCollins Publishers in the United States of America and other countries.

HarperCollins is a registered trademark of HarperCollins Publishers in the United States of America and other countries.

FIRST EDITION

20 21 22 23 24 QGM 10 9 8 7 6 5 4 3 2 1

If you purchased this book without a cover, you should be aware that this book is stolen property. It was reported as "unsold and destroyed" to the publisher, and neither the author nor the publisher has received any payment for this "stripped book."

For the girls who play hard

Chapter One

The Bronze House
Broadway and Thirty-Third Street, NYC
1891

There was a special place in hell for men who attempted to cheat at cards.

Clayton Madden stood in a back room inside his casino, scowling at the man kneeling on the carpet. Tears and snot leaked all over the man's face, his pleas for mercy echoing off the bare plaster walls. The words meant nothing to Clay. Cornered rats always begged for their lives when trapped. He'd seen it time and time again.

Clay had a reputation as unfeeling, a cold monster. And it was absolutely true. He'd long turned hard in the face of this world's cruelty, growing up poor in a city that worshipped money and prestige over kindness and faith. Where graft, bribery and violence ruled. He'd learned . . . and thrived. Climbed up through the ranks of the criminal underworld until he'd accumulated enough power to wield it on his own behalf. Darkness had settled in his soul years before he'd opened the city's poshest casino.

He loved the Bronze House. It was his pride and joy, the culmination of all his scraping and scrapping. The city's richest and most privileged men came here nightly. Eager to wager large sums of money, which Clay was only too happy to pocket. Some men, however, thought they were smarter than Clay. That they could steal money from him and get away with it.

Clay hated those men worst of all.

They were dealt with swiftly, harshly. He let them live, of course—but just barely. Dead men could not spread tales to warn other potential cheaters that Madden's casinos were off-limits. Not to mention killing men brought about questions Clay would rather not answer.

"P-please, Mr. Madden." The man was trembling, his voice cracking. "Please don't hurt me. I won't ever come back, I swear."

Same song, different rat. Did he really believe Clay was stupid enough to let him walk out, unharmed?

Clay shook his head. "You're right. You won't ever come back, not when I'm through with you."

Sweat coated the man's brow, his eyes growing impossibly wide. "No, please. I have a family—"

"What would you like to do?"

Clay turned to the source of the question. His assistant and longtime friend, Bald Jack, waited in the shadows. Jack was a former pugilist and a crack shot. He was also loyal, intelligent and good with people where Clay faltered. Clay trusted him with his life. "How much?" In Clay's mind, everything was measured in terms of dollars and cents.

"One-twenty before we stopped him."

Not an exorbitant amount, but it was the point of the matter. "The usual, then."

"You got it. Want to talk to him first?" The edge of Jack's mouth kicked up, as if he anticipated Clay's answer.

"Yes, I do." No cheater walked out of the Bronze House without a "talk" from Clay.

"Then, before you get blood on your suit, I should also tell you that she's back."

Clay's spine straightened. *Now* Jack was telling him? Jesus. "How long?"

"Strolled in as we were bringing this piece of filth back here."

Goddamn it. Why had she returned? He dragged a hand down his jaw. "Take care of this here," he said and gestured to the man sobbing on his floor. "And don't ruin my carpets."

Jack jerked his chin toward the two staff members hovering nearby. "Take him to the meat shed," he instructed the men. "I'll deal with him in a moment."

Clay left the room and hurried to the balcony, focused on *her*, already forgetting the past few minutes. All that mattered was getting to his hidden perch. He had to see her for himself.

She shouldn't be here. Her family was one of great wealth and privilege. Old money and small minds. The kind of people Clay exploited for his own gain. Her father was legendary, a bombastic blowhard who rolled over anyone who dared to get in his way—including less fortunate families trying to eke out a modest living downtown.

What would her father think about his middle daughter's late-night visits to the Bronze House? Clay almost wished he could tell him merely to witness the reaction.

Hard to say why Clay allowed her entry. After all, the Bronze House had strict rules for gaining entrance. Men of a certain class congregated here, men with deep pockets and little sense. Women were forbidden, per his explicit order. He didn't even permit prostitutes here, as many casinos did.

Yet, she flouted his rules. On more than one occasion. Not only that; she also walked out a winner. Every time.

He admired that about her. And so, he tolerated her presence.

It was irresponsible of him—and Clay was nothing if not responsible. He prided himself on the solid judgment that had saved his life time and time again in a city full of danger and retribution. Those sharp instincts had helped him rise to the top of New York's underbelly, the places catering to the voracious appetite for vice. And his current instinct screamed for him to kick her out.

He took the stairs to the balcony two at a time, his shoes slapping on the old wood. She was becoming a problem, one he needed to solve. Her attendance was disruptive. Not in a loud, destructive way, but nearly every man in her vicinity would leer at her or angle somehow for her favor. It was disgusting. Worse, if the men were leering and angling then they weren't *gambling.* Another reason why women had no business inside these walls.

He reached the balcony and paused to take in the sprawling casino floor. *Ah, glorious.* His kingdom. The place was flooded with men in dark suits, oiled hair gleaming in the gaslight while they spent money on frivolous games they had no hope of winning. The sight never ceased to please him.

Except, this evening, it didn't. Because *she* was here.

He spotted her right away. The light glinted off her blond hair and creamy skin. Full red lips revealed white teeth when she smiled or laughed, which was often. She was a lone beautiful flower in a field of dirt and sticks. Why in hell was she here, at his casino? What was her end game?

A nearby door closed and the soft thud of footsteps approached. Clay didn't bother turning. Only one person dared to come up here.

"She's alone again tonight," Jack said. "Want me to show her out?"

"No," he answered quickly. Too quickly.

Jack chuckled. "I see."

Clay shot a menacing look over his shoulder. "Shouldn't you be dealing with our other problem?"

"The boys'll handle him, don't worry. I thought you might need help with *her*."

"I don't need help. I need her to stop distracting my patrons. They're ogling her instead of losing money."

Jack eased toward the railing and peered down. "Can't blame them. She's a pretty one."

Pretty? No. *Pretty* was too tame a word to describe her. Too superficial. Birds were pretty. A shiny gold piece, the sky at dusk. A royal flush. Those things were pretty.

She was *radiant.* A feast for the eyes. With a gaze that sparkled with mischief. A sly smile with hidden secrets. She was sunshine in a stormy sky. Warmth and light in the midst of the very worst element. Namely, him.

"I *can* blame them," Clay growled. "It's as if they haven't seen a woman before. She's nothing special."

Jack remained quiet, the word *liar* hanging between them in the shadows. Lucky for Clay, Jack didn't bother to say it aloud. Instead, his friend said, "Do you plan to stand up here and loom over her all night like a specter? Or should I bring her to your office?"

"And why would I meet with her?"

"To find out why she keeps comin' back."

"I assume it's because she continues to win. Have we spoken to the staff? I want her to lose money, not gain it."

"What happened to 'the house has no need to cheat because the house always wins in the end'?"

"The house is clearly failing when it comes to her."

Jack paused. "I'll speak to them."

"Good."

"I suppose that means you'll continue to admit her."

"I haven't decided." It was untrue and they both knew it. She had intrigued him . . . and he was not a man easily intrigued.

You're acting like a fool. Just tell her not to come back.

Not yet. He needed insight into her actions. This was her third night visiting the Bronze House in ten days, and the house's take on those three evenings had dipped significantly. How long could this go on before her presence ruined his business?

Jack was right. It was past time to find out what she was up to. "Fine, bring her to my office."

"Finally," Jack said. "Now maybe you'll stop making everyone miserable around here."

"I'm the owner," he snarled. "Anyone who is unhappy with me may find employment elsewhere—and that goes for my second-in-command, as well."

Not bothering to smother his laugh, Jack walked away. The sound grated over Clay's nerves, but instead of lashing out, he kept his gaze trained on the woman below. He'd noticed she liked roulette and mostly bet on red. Funny color, red. Brought to mind hearts and flowers, flesh and blood. He preferred black, like mud and coal. Rot and ruin. Like the stain on his soul.

Had she any idea of his history with her father?

He doubted it. If she had, she'd stay very far from the likes of Clayton Madden.

The crowd soon parted to make way for Jack's hulking form. She looked up from her chips, a flash of annoyance on her face before she masked it with politeness. Jack said a few words and, without missing a beat, her head swung toward the balcony, eyes locking with Clay's. He sucked in a breath, the impact of her greenish-brown irises like a blow. A ridiculous reaction, he chided himself. She couldn't see him, not where he stood in the shadows.

Even still, he took a step back then turned on his heel.

He gave himself a mental shake. He would not be cowed by her. No one, man or woman, had ever gained the upper hand with Clay. A beautiful uptown debutante certainly wouldn't be the first to succeed.

It was past time to put Florence Greene in her place.

FINALLY, FLORENCE HAD gained Mr. Madden's attention.

She followed Jack, the casino's manager, deeper into the darkened corridors, anticipation crawling through her veins. She hadn't come to the Bronze House to win money, though she'd done that quite handily.

No, she'd come here to *learn.*

Not the games, of course. Those she knew. Nor had she wanted to observe how a casino operated. Rather, she'd wanted to observe how the city's *best* casino operated. From one man, the casino's enigmatic owner, Clayton Madden.

Anyone who'd played a hand of cards or thrown a pair of dice in this town knew his name. Madden owned poolrooms, policy shops, craps games . . . He was the ruler of all gambling activity in town. It was said that everything he touched turned to gold, an empire that neither the police nor Tammany Hall could topple.

The Bronze House, however, had turned Madden into a legend.

Renowned as the most exclusive and fairest of all the casinos, the Bronze House was where the elites went to drink champagne, eat caviar and gamble. All the games were aboveboard, the dealers too well compensated to skim. Madden treated his staff and patrons well—unless they double-crossed him. Those who dared to work against Madden's interests were dealt with swiftly, irrevocably. In manners so horrific they were merely whispered about. Florence had heard stories about bones broken, houses burned. One enemy had supposedly been weighted down with cement and chains, and then dropped into the East River.

As a woman, she'd known her presence here would attract attention. Had planned for it. Embraced it. Part of her had expected to be tossed out within moments of arriving. Yet, she'd been allowed to stay. More than once.

And he'd watched her.

Somehow, she had sensed him up there, in the dark balcony, staring down at her, despite not knowing what he actually looked like. Not many did, apparently, as he never left his club unless absolutely necessary. While the casino operated, he remained in the shadows and Jack handled the problems on the floor.

Now Madden wished to meet her. Even though this was what she needed, Florence had to admit it terrified her.

Daddy liked to tell all three Greene sisters, *Show no fear. Men are afraid of women they cannot intimidate.* So she stood a little taller and pressed her shoulders back. She would face him bravely or not at all.

A large wooden door with a single brass plate loomed at the end of the corridor. Embossed on the plate, bold lettering read Do Not Enter. She suppressed a shiver. *No fear.*

Jack stopped and turned. The smooth, dark skin of his forehead creased slightly as he studied her. "Do you scare easily, Miss Greene?"

"Certainly not." At least, she was trying to appear that way.

A slow smile spread across Jack's face. "Yes, indeed. You might be just what we need around here." Before she could ask what he meant, he threw open the door and swept his arm out in a courtly gesture. "After you."

Playing along, Florence gave a royal dip of her chin. "Thank you, sir."

The room was brightly lit, a cheerful fire crackling in the grate. Eastern rugs covered the floors, and dark wainscoting adorned the walls. A large desk sat at one end, two small armchairs opposite. It was a cozy space, one well used.

And it was empty.

She glanced over her shoulder at Jack. "Is he . . . ?"

"He'll be along shortly, miss. Just wait here." Jack gave her a brief nod and departed, leaving her alone in Clayton Madden's office.

His *office.*

So this was where he oversaw his gambling syndicate. She would have thought it more . . .

decadent. After all, he was one of the richest and most powerful men in the city. Yet, this was a simple space, not one designed to show off his considerable wealth. What a fascinating contradiction.

Papers were neatly stacked on his desk. She longed to flip through them, discover what matters awaited his attention. Credit he'd extended to patrons come due? Bills from his champagne and caviar suppliers? Reports on dealers and club operation?

Her mind whirled with possibilities, her heart full of giddy envy. *Someday. Someday you'll have an office just like this.*

The door behind her opened and she spun toward it. A large man stood in the doorway, his wide shoulders taking up nearly the width of the entry. He was dressed entirely in black with no hint of color anywhere on him. Not a collar stud or silver button in sight. Dark hair framed his face, the strands a bit longer than the current style, and two scars marred his skin: one through his eyebrow and the other along his chin.

He was not conventionally pretty, like the society swells who slept all day and caroused at night. No, this man was handsome, but in a rough-and-tumble, unforgiving way. He oozed confidence, as if he never failed, never let anyone tell him what to do. A warrior, scarred from years of battle, someone who'd built a kingdom with his two bare hands.

She wished that didn't appeal to her, that she didn't feel a strange pull in the pit of her stomach . . . but she did. It wasn't every day she encountered a man so dangerous and shrewd, interesting and complex.

She met his gaze and it was clear he was not-so-patiently waiting for her to finish her assessment of him. Had she been staring too long? Clasping her hands, she wiped any hint of expression off her face. *Don't react. Give him nothing.* After all, she'd perfected a blank look over the years, thanks to hiding her misadventures from her parents. It worked every time.

Madden's lips quirked as if he instantly saw through her ruse. Impossible. She'd perfected that blank stare at each ball, dinner party and social gathering since the age of eighteen. No one had ever suspected otherwise.

"Miss Greene." He stepped forward and closed the door behind him. Trepidation slid along her spine, a cold chill of warning. She was alone with him, a man reportedly no stranger to violence.

He wouldn't be stupid enough to hurt Duncan Greene's daughter. Would he?

Florence didn't care for being afraid. She lived her life boldly, outside the lines of what society considered normal female behavior. Tea parties and sewing circles were not for her. She had more exciting plans in her future. Dice and roulette wheels. Cards and craps games. Fear was some other woman's problem.

She lifted her chin. "I presume you are Mr. Madden."

"Have a seat." Now behind his desk, he indicated one of the armchairs.

"Not until you answer my question."

He paused and stared at her just long enough to make her uncomfortable. His eyes were dark and unfathomable, no hint to his thoughts whatsoever. "Was there a question, Miss Greene? Because I didn't hear one."

"Are you Mr. Madden?"

"I am, which means this is my casino. And you are trespassing." He lowered himself into his large leather chair without waiting for her to be seated.

"No one has asked me to leave."

"You are aware that women are forbidden from crossing our threshold. Yet, you've flouted that rule. Many times. Care to tell me why?"

"I assumed your policies had changed." A lie. Her first visit she'd entered through the kitchens, sneaking into the main casino. On subsequent visits, she'd flashed a smile and pressed a large bill into the hand of the man at the door. The staff recognized her now, though she knew Madden's benevolence was the reason for her continued admittance.

"Let's do away with the pretense. My curiosity is the only reason you've gained access to the Bronze House. I'm requesting you satisfy that curiosity now."

Though he spoke politely, it somehow sounded like a threat. "Or?"

"Most people are smart enough not to refuse my requests."

"You won't hurt me." It came out with more confidence than she felt. Inside, doubt twisted her stomach into knots.

One dark brow shot up. "Won't I?"

"I don't intimidate easily, Mr. Madden."

A flash of something passed over his face, a glimpse of appreciation, perhaps. Had her answer *pleased* him?

"I'm beginning to see that. After all, someone nearly drugged your sister here and yet you return."

Florence waved her hand. Mamie hadn't been fooled. The man's clumsy attempt at pouring an unknown liquid into her champagne had been as obvious as the heat in Hades. Besides, Florence felt eyes on her every time she visited the Bronze House—a protective presence that wouldn't dare allow anything terrible to befall her within these walls.

Had it been Madden looking out for her? Watching her?

She wasn't certain if the idea excited or frightened her.

"I'm perfectly safe inside your casino."

He didn't bother to confirm or deny it. Instead, he said, "You show a remarkable skill at the tables. How did an uptown debutante learn such things?"

She lifted a shoulder. "Practice."

He threw his head back and laughed. The sound was rough and genuine, the mirth transforming his face into something . . . lighter. Younger. She hadn't realized. He couldn't be more than thirty or thirty-one years old. Tingles coursed through her, as if she'd been dealt an ace and a king while playing twenty-one.

Goodness. Was she *attracted* to him?

She recognized the feeling. There had been various young men in her life over the years. Florence liked kissing and touching and all the things that went with it. She hadn't ever considered saving herself for marriage, not when a whole wide world awaited her. She was a modern woman in charge of her own destiny—and her future did not include being under the thumb of a husband. She wanted an equal, not a jailer.

But an attraction to Clayton Madden would *complicate* things.

Madden collected himself, shaking his head as if to clear it. "I can see you're no novice. You've walked out a winner each time you've visited. Yet, your presence here is disruptive. My patrons are unaccustomed to seeing a woman in their midst. You are . . . distracting."

It would seem a compliment if not for his frown. "That is not my fault. Admit more women and they won't notice me."

"Impossible. No man would miss you, even in a crowd."

Her throat dried out. That was most definitely a compliment. However, she didn't think he was flirting with her, merely being honest. Clayton Madden didn't seem like a man who *flirted*. "Your policy is antiquated. You should allow women to gamble."

"Not a chance. If men are watching the women then they aren't losing money to me."

She bit back a smile. His attitude served her plans perfectly. Let him ignore half the population of New York, the women who were bored and looking for entertainment. Florence would soon take their pin money in *her* female-only casino. Still, she couldn't resist adding, "So women must suffer for the stupidity of men. Again."

He blinked, his expression full of both confusion and admiration. "I see you are a woman who speaks her mind. That's a quality I appreciate. So let's answer this once and for all. Why do you continue to visit the Bronze House? What are you after?"

It's now or never, Florence. "I'm here for lessons. I wish for you to teach me how to operate a casino."

Chapter Two

Clay paused, certain his ears had failed him. "I beg your pardon?"

She strolled closer, her silk skirts rustling with every step, a whisper of femininity that slid over his skin. Florence Greene was even more stunning up close. She looked like a blonde angel, only with teasing eyes and a wicked mouth. Long, elegant limbs combined with a proud bearing born of privilege and wealth. He desperately wished to dislike her . . . but quite the opposite. She was provoking and intelligent—a dangerous combination.

Especially when Clay planned revenge on her father.

Duncan Greene had sealed his fate twenty years ago when he'd razed an entire block of homes on the east side to build a factory. One of those homes had belonged to the Maddens. They hadn't received fair market value for the property—Greene was a greedy bastard—and therefore hadn't been able to locate equitable lodgings. Their family had ended up in a slum, where Clay's younger brother died of cholera and his father walked out.

A family destroyed. Lives changed for the worse. Clay would soon repay that favor and move on with the next phase of his life. But not if Florence kept distracting the House's patrons. He had to find a way to get rid of her for good.

She lowered herself into the armchair across from his desk and met his gaze. "I plan to open my own casino. I would like to learn from you on how to do it."

A rough sound escaped his throat, a weak chuckle of sorts. Christ, that was twice she'd caused him to laugh. He couldn't remember the last time before tonight. She really was remarkable. "Miss Greene, women of your . . . status don't go into business for themselves. They get married. Have children. Summer in Newport and the like. I think you should return home and—"

"Please do not use that condescending tone with me. Believe me, I'm aware of my status and what girls my age are *supposed* to do. But I have absolutely no interest in marriage and children and Newport. I wish to open a casino for ladies."

Now he knew she was cracked. "Gambling is illegal."

She gave him a bland look. "Anything is legal for the right price."

So true. He tried another tack. "Ladies don't gamble. Lower-class women might occasionally dabble at cards or lottery, but ladies do not."

"You're wrong. Ladies most definitely gamble."

Her stubbornness was beginning to grate on his nerves. "No, they don't," he snapped.

"Really? How many ladies do you know?"

Admittedly, not many. None, actually. "Even if you're right, this is not a school. I have neither the time nor the inclination to mentor someone."

"Why not?"

"Because my time is valuable and I'm not running a charity."

"So I'll pay you. Whatever hourly rate you set."

Frustrated, he drummed his fingers on the arm of his chair. Was she so eager to enter the lion's den? This was no place for her. Gambling made men desperate, stupid. Just last evening a man who'd lost everything tried to strangle a croupier. It was dangerous here, and his staff needed to pay attention to their jobs, not watch over this woman.

"It would be a waste of your money. You'll never get past the police and politicians to even open your doors."

"Precisely why I need guidance from you. The type of casino I wish to open is exactly like the Bronze House."

He wanted to roll his eyes at her naivete. It had taken him fifteen years to achieve something as grand as the Bronze House. He'd scraped and hustled for half his life in alleys and taprooms to sit here. His scars were a daily reminder of his struggles. And she thought to snap her fingers and get whatever she wished?

Unbelievable, this woman.

He ought to throw her out. Refuse her request and bar her from ever returning.

And yet . . .

The idea of helping Duncan Greene's daughter descend into the city's underworld was appealing. Her father would hate it. The family would be humiliated, their social credibility ruined. Perhaps that might sour some of Greene's business deals, cause him to lose money. That Clay would help to orchestrate the Greene downfall made the proposition all the sweeter.

It wouldn't satisfy Clay's need for revenge, but it was a good start.

"I would require only two to three hours of your time once or twice a week," she said, her voice impatient. "I hardly see how that is an inconvenience for you."

He didn't answer right away. Negotiating was much like gambling. One had to possess patience. Otherwise, you never got what you wanted.

And what he wanted right now was to see how far she'd go. To discover just how badly she wanted this casino of hers. What was she willing to trade for it? Because he'd decided he liked her enough to keep her around. If she planned to ruin herself, then he would be more than happy to assist her in the endeavor.

"Name your price, Mr. Madden."

He threw out an obscenely high amount. "One hundred dollars an hour."

"Done. When may we start? Tonight?"

"You didn't even attempt a negotiation. Perhaps I'm wasting my time in trying to teach you anything."

Her lips twisted into a wide smile, her eyes sparkling from across the desk. The effect was an arrow through his chest to steal his breath. Goddamn, she was beautiful. He stared at her so often from a distance that he hadn't prepared himself for witnessing her joy up close. He was destroyed. *Slain.* Unable to speak as his brain struggled to take it in.

"You won't regret this, Mr. Madden. I swear."

He wouldn't regret it, but he would bet anything *she* would. Other people's regrets weren't his problem, however. Someone wished to bet their fortune on the turn of a card? Go ahead. Someone offered up their home as collateral only to then lose it? Hand over the deed. In the end, he was a selfish man who looked after his own interests. So the consequences of Florence Greene's actions were hers alone to bear.

Though there was something else he should mention. "You should know a few things before we finalize any apprenticeship."

She leaned in, all eagerness and devotion, hanging on his every word. A sudden fantasy crossed his mind, one where he tutored her in more than card games and ledgers. Dark, passionate games with punishments and rewards. Where he would bend her over his desk when she was bad and pleasure her within an inch of her—

Fuck. He dropped his gaze and dragged air into his lungs. "I'll put my cards on the table. I'm attracted to you."

Her brows shot high on her forehead, her face slackening. "W-what?"

"I find you attractive, Miss Greene. Surely a woman as beautiful as you understands what that means."

"I understand what it means but *why* would you tell me?"

Simple. Because he had nothing to hide.

Because he hated liars and cheaters.

Because she was dangerous to his peace of mind.

God knew it would be better for both of them if she reconsidered and tutored elsewhere. "Complete honesty," he said. "Understand that my motives are never pure. I'm as selfish as they come, and if there's an opportunity to get you in my bed I won't hesitate to take it."

"I . . . cannot believe you are telling me this. Are you planning to force me to—?"

"Absolutely not," he said with deep conviction. "I would never hurt you or force you to do anything against your will. However, I often have goals that don't line up with society's standards of propriety. If you expect me to play the gentleman here, you'll be sorely disappointed."

She studied him, her hazel gaze contemplative. "I'm more than competent with a pistol. If you hurt me, I will come here and put a bullet in your chest."

"Fair enough, but I won't hurt you. Neither will anyone else in this city while you are under my protection."

"Was there anything else?"

"Yes, actually. I plan to bring about your father's ruin."

"My father's *ruin*? Duncan Greene?" Her mouth worked, then she said, "You must be joking."

He folded his hands behind his head and

watched her absorb this news. "I'm quite serious. I won't bore you with the details but you should know I'm agreeing to this scheme of yours because your father would absolutely hate it. Anything that causes him the least bit of aggravation entices me."

"You don't like him."

An understatement. Duncan had taken everything from Clay's family. And soon, Clay would take something that mattered to Duncan. "No, I don't."

"I cannot decide if you are trying to scare me off or if you are telling the truth."

"If the truth scares you then you have no business opening a casino. The world is full of hard decisions and uncomfortable choices. You cannot be softhearted. What will you do when a friend with an outstanding debt comes crying to you that she cannot pay? Pat her on the head and tell her not to worry, that you trust she'll give you the money eventually?"

"I am not completely sheltered, Mr. Madden. I know running a business won't be easy."

"Gambling is more than a business, Miss Greene. It is a way of life. A burning obsession for some. If you want safe, then procure a position at a department store."

She rubbed her forehead. "Let me understand this. Agreeing to help me has nothing to do with the money I'm paying you, but rather revenge against my father."

"Wrong. Everything I do is about money. The revenge is a nice side bonus."

"As selfish as they come," she muttered, repeating his words from earlier.

"That's right—and you'd be wise not to forget it."

Wait, Madden was trying to *ruin* her father. What did that mean? Bankrupt him? She didn't think that was possible. Her father was careful with money and they were more than comfortable. Not to mention her father's intelligence. No one pulled anything over on Duncan Greene. Except for her, of course. "Exactly how are you trying to ruin my family?"

Madden cocked his head and seemed to contemplate the question. Florence stared at him through her lashes. The casino owner was unexpected in so many ways. Yes, he was intimidating, but he didn't treat her like a silly girl with the intellect of a housefly, as most of the men her age did. Instead, he listened and bantered back and forth with her. It was refreshing.

In truth, she'd been ready to pay more for his help. The Bronze House was the exact model for the casino she wished to open for ladies. Nowhere else came close, not in New York City. Furthermore, Madden was a reported genius, a shrewd businessman and excellent with numbers. Choosing someone else felt like settling.

And she needed to learn fast. She had less than two years to open her casino and build an independent future. Her father had recently begun pressuring Florence's twenty-three-year-old sister, Mamie, to marry. At twenty-one, Florence was next in line for marriage. Duncan Greene's patience for unmarried daughters would only last for so long, and Florence had no intention of handing over her life to some strange man. She intended to support herself instead.

Her plan had started six months ago. For years she'd gambled with her grandmother and her friends, who wagered jewelry and other baubles over weekly euchre games. The competition could get quite fierce and Florence realized that proper ladies love to gamble just as much as proper men. Unfortunately, there was no place women could safely do so.

She began wondering, why not? Why couldn't ladies have a casino just for themselves, where no men were allowed? Hire female dealers and servers, provide employment to those who needed it. Things were changing rapidly for women in the city. Jobs, apartments, bicycles, independence . . . The old ways were dying off, changing. And she liked the idea of going into business for herself.

Where she could be her own person, live by her own rules and never be made to feel like she wasn't good enough again.

So she'd started visiting the seedier parts of downtown to learn the games, a tiny pistol tucked in her bag for safety. Roulette in the West Village. Craps and fan-tan in Chinatown. Twenty-one near Wall Street. Without fail, she turned over her winnings to her sisters, who used the money to help the needy in the tenements.

Now she was here, in the poshest, most exclusive casino in the state. Though gambling was illegal, the Bronze House was never raided because Madden had the police force and a few politicians in his pocket. How did one *do* that? Florence had no idea, which was why she needed Madden's assistance to learn the business.

But he was planning to ruin her *father*? How could she work with a man under those conditions?

He finally answered, "I'd rather not share my plans. They have nothing to do with you directly."

"They do if they affect my family."

"You might tell your father. I can't risk it. Besides, he'll learn of it soon enough."

She blew out a frustrated breath. Was she actually considering this? Yes, because there were no other options, not in such a short amount of time. And shouldn't she stick close to him in hopes of discovering how he planned to ruin her family? Then she could warn her father.

"I feel as if I'm making a deal with the devil," she muttered.

"Indeed, you are." His dark eyes glittered in the gloomy gaslight. "I never claimed to be a nice man."

Her skin prickled with awareness. God help her, but that appealed to her even more. "You won't scare me away."

"Oh, but give me time, Miss Greene." His voice was low and husky, a tone one would use with a lover. The man was clearly trying to run her off.

Which showed he had a lot to learn about today's modern women. She was tougher than she looked and not about to quiver in fear before him. "You might as well call me Florence."

The side of his mouth kicked up. "What would you have done had I not noticed you in my casino?"

"Keep coming back until you did."

"I knew you were bribing my men at the door. I could have stopped you at any time."

"And yet you didn't. Was it because of my father?"

"Definitely not. I do not make allowances for anyone connected to Duncan."

"Are you certain you won't tell me your plans regarding him?"

"Absolutely positive." He tapped his fingers on the desk. "So what will it be? Lessons on how to operate the Bronze House for one hundred dollars an hour, or back to visiting the poolrooms?"

She nearly shuddered. The idea of never returning here, of going back to the poolrooms—seedy, filthy gambling haunts in rough neighborhoods—was depressing. Sitting here, she was closer than she'd ever been to her independence. She couldn't leave.

She'd just find a way to thwart his revenge plans later on.

"Fine. I'll pay for mentoring."

"Call me Clay, then." He pushed out of his chair and started toward the door.

When he turned the knob, she quickly stood. "Wait, where are you going?" They hadn't settled on a tutoring schedule yet.

"Come along. It's time to begin your first lesson." He disappeared into the corridor, and she was left staring at the empty doorway. *Oh*. She hadn't expected to start tonight.

Lifting her skirts, she hurried after him.

"WOULDN'T YOU RATHER hear what I am interested in, what I need help with?" she said to the wide shoulders draped in black wool. "You don't even know what I am planning."

He began to climb a small set of stairs, clearly ignoring her. Huffing out a frustrated breath, she started up behind him. "Are you going to answer my question?"

"There's no point. You need to start at the bottom."

"What does that mean?"

He came to the landing and turned to wait for her. "It means the pace and content of each lesson is at my discretion. And if I need to cancel or cut our time short, you'll respect my decision. This is not up for debate. Now, go left and around the corner."

God, he was so frustrating.

She continued along the scarred wooden floors and into a corridor. Noises from the casino—shouts and curses, dice and chips—rose up and jolted her like a shot of energy into her veins, as if she'd touched a live electric wire. Men took this for granted, their ability to wallow in vice and sin at will, while women were tasked to uphold society's virtues. Any slip meant failure and ruination, the damnation of one's soul and confinement to spinsterhood.

Bollocks to that, as their cook liked to say when she thought no one was listening. Florence craved the danger and freedom in every part of the city, especially the ones off-limits to her. Why should she be cast out of society's good graces for occasionally doing what every man her age did nightly?

Her casino would change that. An illegal gaming hall where society ladies could lose their pin money and jewelry without fear of recrimination. *No men permitted* meant no judgment or gossip. The women would be free to enjoy themselves, to live their lives without men ruining everything.

If only she could unionize the entire female race . . .

After following his directions, she found herself on the balcony overlooking the casino floor. She sucked in a breath. He would be able to see *everything* from up here.

"I knew you were watching."

He came to stand shoulder to shoulder with her at the railing. "When there's a potential problem in my casino, yes."

"Is that what I was, a potential problem?"

"An innocent woman in a lion's den is always a problem."

"I am not innocent." She froze. The words had escaped her mouth like a locomotive traveling at high speed. All because she'd wished to counter his opinion of her as a sheltered uptown schoolgirl.

Idiot. What did she care if Clayton Madden thought her green? Unfortunately, there was no taking the sentence back. Perhaps he'd act a gentleman and let it go.

"Fumbling kisses from boys between waltzes

hardly counts," he said, and her hopes of gentlemanly behavior died right then. No need to mention she hadn't stopped at fumbling kisses. God knew she'd already said too much.

He gestured to the floor. "Men who gamble here are often drunk or high on the thrill of a win. An unescorted woman can prove a temptation some men cannot resist taking, regardless of whether she agrees or not. You saw what nearly happened to your sister."

"You needn't worry about me. I'm able to handle myself."

"Oh, indeed."

His tone implied he didn't believe her, but she let it go and took in the scene below. Patrons were clustered throughout the casino floor, every table full. The crush of well-dressed men, with their black evening wear and thick billfolds, was a thing of beauty. How had Clay managed to build this up so quickly? The Bronze House wasn't even a year old.

The minutes ticked by and he said nothing. Her impatience got the better of her. "Is there a point to standing here or are you fleecing me out of one hundred dollars?"

"I was waiting to see how long it would take before you asked. Yes, there is a point. Close your eyes."

"What?" She cast him a sideways glance. "Why?"

"Because I am your mentor and I'm telling you to do it. If you'd rather learn from someone who cannot teach you a fraction of what I know, then by all means refuse me. I've lots of other tasks I should be doing."

Heat washed across her neck, an anger that spread to the roots of her hair. His employees must absolutely hate him. If this was how he treated people, no wonder his assistant handled everything below during club hours.

She forced her eyes closed. The sounds from the casino floor sharpened, as did her awareness of the man next to her. He smelled . . . manly, like faint cigar and a forest. Was it pine? The unusual combination appealed to her, dash it. She heard his shoes squeak ever so softly as he moved closer. His elbow brushed hers.

"What do you hear?"

"Voices."

"What else?"

She didn't understand. Was this a test of some kind? If so, was she already failing? "Lots of voices."

"Florence, try harder. You need to hear all of it. Take a moment and *think.*"

She exhaled and cleared her mind. She and her sisters had often hid outside from one another in the summers. The first person to find the other two would win. Florence had triumphed nearly every time. She'd keep perfectly still and listen until the familiar sounds fell away and she could discern the unnatural ones. Then she'd hurry to where Mamie and Justine hid and reveal them.

The same thing happened tonight. The voices drifted to the background and she could hear the underlying noises. "Dice, more than one set. From directly below us. One roulette wheel spinning, a ball dropping in another." A tiny ivory ball clanged against the metal. "Champagne cork popped. The stacking of chips."

"Is that all?"

"Cards being shuffled." She held her breath, hoping for more. "A scraping of some kind."

"Now open your eyes."

She blinked in the dim light and let her eyes adjust. "How did I do?"

"You tell me."

Refraining from frowning at him, she glanced at the floor. A waiter poured champagne in one spot; roulette players collected their winnings in another. Craps games rolled on. An older man with one lame leg slowly made his way toward the exit, his foot dragging on the wooden floor. She cast Clay a satisfied grin. "I'd say pretty well. It's not hard when you put your mind to it."

All of his attention was now focused entirely on her mouth. The intensity of his stare sent a bolt of heat through her, rooting her feet to the floor. What was he thinking? Something to do with his attraction to her? Her heart pounded as the moment stretched, the surroundings drifting away in their darkened and secluded spot. His features were sharper at this distance, angles and scars that fascinated her. They told a story of a life much different than hers.

Stop it. As compelling as she found him, she could not become distracted from her purpose. Men wanted only one thing from women: to control them. To take away their choices.

No one was taking away Florence's choices. Ever.

Clearing her throat, she averted her face and studied the craps game beneath them.

"You must learn to filter out the noise at any given moment, concentrate on what's missing or out of place. You have to know the sounds, grow familiar with them, until they're like the sound of your own breath. Then you know when someone is stealing from you." He pointed toward a poker table on the left side of the room. "Watch."

One of the players was casually glancing at a man at the neighboring roulette table. From his position at the roulette wheel, the man could see the cards of the other poker players. He was subtly tapping his arm with his fingers, giving clues to his friend on his opponents' cards.

Florence exhaled. "He's cheating. How was I supposed to hear that?"

"You wouldn't. The man at the roulette table isn't betting. He's not even watching the wheel. It's what is *missing* in this case that counts." He lifted his hand and caught the attention of Jack, who was dealing with a drunk and disorderly craps player. Some quick hand motions followed then Clay took her elbow and began leading her to the stairs. "Jack will meet you at the bottom of the steps. I have another matter to attend to."

"The cheaters?"

"Yes, my second occurrence just this evening. It must be my lucky night."

The words were terse and angry, but there was a hint of anticipation there, as well. She almost pitied those two cheaters. "Wait, are you kicking me out?"

"Those are the terms we agreed to, yes. Anytime I must cut a lesson short you'll respect my decision. And we are cutting this lesson short."

"Well, when should I return for my next lesson?"

Impatience radiated from his hurried gait, the stiff movements of his arms. He wrenched open the door at the top of the stairs. "Why not surprise me? You seem to enjoy doing that."

He disappeared, leaving her to descend alone. As she reached the bottom, she realized he was right. She did like surprising him.

What worried her was how he'd come to recognize it before she did.

Chapter Three

Clay pressed the block of ice to his knuckles and strode toward his office. Two attempts to cheat the House in one night? That had been unusual.

Not as unusual as Florence Greene, however. The girl was surprising. He hadn't met many society women but he had to assume that opening a casino for ladies put her in a class all by herself. She'd never pull it off, of course. Duncan Greene would lock her up and throw away the key before he allowed that.

But it would be damn fun to watch her try.

Clay would assist her in any way possible. If it meant aggravating her family, Clay was fully on board. The past twenty years had been about two things: making money and ruining Duncan Greene. The groundwork had been laid some time ago but, in another six months, Clay's plan should come to fruition. When the dust settled, Duncan's family home would be obliterated. Destroyed. Just as Clay's had been.

Eye for an eye. Like for like. That was Clay's way—and there was nothing Duncan could do to stop it.

A dark smile twisted his lips and he threw open the door to his office, ready to get back to work. He paused just over the threshold. A red-haired woman was perched in his chair, her booted feet propped on his desk, a lit cigar in her mouth. Sighing, he continued inside and shut the door behind him.

Annabelle Gallagher. One of Clay's few friends and investors. She owned the brothel next door to the House, providing a service to the fancy fat cats that Clay was unwilling to undertake himself. He did not peddle in flesh, though Anna's girls were willing and well cared for. It was her business, one he did not judge. God knew she'd never judged him for the way he'd earned his money over their decade-long friendship.

A secret tunnel below ground connected their buildings, providing access in case either business was ever raided by the Metropolitan Police. Hard to imagine that happening at the Bronze House, however, considering the second-highest officer in command was also an investor here, but Clay liked to be prepared for anything. He hoped the tunnel remained permanently unused, except for trips by Annabelle.

She exhaled and let out a stream of smoke. His good Cubans, damn her. "Hello, Clayton."

"Slow night?"

"No. We're quite busy, actually. I did hear an interesting rumor, though. Thought I'd come over and see for myself."

He dropped into the armchair across from his desk and reached for the humidor. Normally he enjoyed visiting with Anna, but he was edgy tonight. Two cheaters in his casino and lusting over Florence Greene had soured his mood. Bearing the weight of an empire certainly could wear a man down. "And what rumor was that?"

"That you let a woman gamble in your club tonight."

"Wrong." He took his time to select a cigar and snipped off the end with a silver cutter.

"I knew it had to be a lie. You'd never bend your intractable rules for a pretty face."

"I let her gamble here *three* nights this week." He enjoyed the way her mouth slackened, her jaw hanging open. "You're a bit behind, Anna. Surprising, as your customers love gossiping almost as much as they love getting their cocks sucked."

She smirked. "Almost. My girls are the best in the city, after all. Tell me about this woman. Who is she?"

He took a few puffs on his now-lit cigar. "Florence Greene."

"Florence . . ." Her eyes widened almost comically. "Surely you don't mean *that* Florence Greene. Duncan Greene's daughter?"

"I do. She's the middle one. The troublemaker."

Anna's feet hit the floor as she straightened. "Why on earth would you let her in?"

Clay exhaled smoke and tried to come up with an answer. Only, there was none. "Curiosity, I suppose."

Anna closed her mouth and narrowed her eyes, studying him. After a long minute, she nodded. "Oh, I see. This explains why everyone's been extra terrified of you this week."

He had no idea what she was implying. "That's ridiculous. This week has been no different than any other—except that I've dealt with two cheaters in one evening." They were getting bolder. His reputation must've slipped.

"No, I think it is Miss Greene. You like her."

"Bite your tongue," he snapped, though it came out halfhearted and they both knew it.

"Clayton Madden, gone soft for a fancy uptown debutante." She grinned and shook her head. "Never thought I'd see the day."

He ground his back molars together. If this rumor gained legs, he'd never hear the end of it. "I have work to do and no doubt you have clients next door. As much as I've enjoyed this visit, I think it's time to cut it short."

"Is she pretty?"

"Anna!" He came to his feet. "Get the hell out of here."

Chuckling, she rose. "Here is your chair, Your Majesty." She waved a hand and edged away. He stalked over and sat, the well-worn leather creaking under his weight.

Instead of leaving, she went to the sideboard. He ignored her and concentrated on the stack of papers on his desk. These were financial reports from various operations all over the city. He owed quarterly payments to his investors, including Anna. The net profits would determine how much to pay out, if he could ever find the time to balance the books. His attention had been sorely distracted as of late.

Maybe you have gone soft.

No, never. The idea was laughable. He remained focused on what truly mattered: money and revenge.

A tumbler half-filled with spirits was placed on his desk. "Drink this," she said. "It's your favorite and it'll sweeten your mood."

"My mood needs no sweetening," he clipped as he set down his cigar and reached for the glass. "And I do not like her. I merely wished to learn why she was so desperate to gamble here."

She lowered herself into an armchair. "And?"

He took a long drink and let the smooth bourbon warm his insides. "She plans to open a casino. For ladies."

Anna hooted, a gleeful grin overtaking her delicate features. "Oh, I like her. I approve, Clay. I approve."

"Whatever you're thinking, stop it. She's hired me to give her lessons on how to run a casino. That's all."

"And you agreed? It cannot be for the money. God knows you have enough of that."

No, he didn't. One could never have enough money, especially in New York City. "It . . . pleases me to assist her down the path of debauchery and vice. Mostly because I loathe her father and I know how much it will irritate the old bastard."

Anna sobered, her brows pinching together. "I don't like you using her. Men and their hidden motives. Women have it hard enough without being lied to—"

"I haven't lied to her about a thing. In fact, I told her how much I hate her father."

"You did?"

"Yes. I also informed her that I was attracted to her."

That caught his friend off guard. "How did she take that news?"

"Not as expected," he admitted. "I thought to scare her off by telling her, actually. She merely asked if I planned to force her. When I said no, she threatened to shoot me if I hurt her."

Anna's lips pressed together like she might be fighting to hold in laughter. She hid her face by taking a long drink of bourbon. "So you're not planning on bedding her?"

"It would be a terrible idea. Women of her ilk get ideas after intimacy."

"Know a lot of fancy uptown ladies, do you?"

"I know enough. And even I would not fuck a woman purely as revenge against her father." *An eye for an eye.*

"What if she's attracted to you, as well?"

He shook his head. Florence Greene had her pick of men in Manhattan. Why on earth would she settle on a man like Clay, who lived in the shadows? "She isn't, nor will she be." Not after spending a significant amount of time with him. He wasn't capable of romance and warmth. Of long walks and picnics in the park. He preferred the nighttime, with its damp fog and anonymity.

Anna tossed back the remaining liquid in her glass. "I'd best return next door." She rose. "Shall I send over a nice young woman to keep you company tonight?"

He thought about it. The problem was Anna's people were being paid. Clay didn't like feigned passion. And he knew his face wasn't the kind to draw admirers. "No, that's not necessary."

"Clay." Her voice gentled and he braced himself. "You've been alone far too long. What's it been since that pretty widow, a year?"

Eleven months, but who was counting? "Stop wasting your pity on me. I'm perfectly fine. Go see to your business."

"I'm not going to drop this. You deserve happiness."

No, I didn't, he thought as he watched Anna leave. He was not a good man. His entire life he'd traded on fear and violence to get what he wanted. Namely, money, power and Duncan Greene's ruin. Only after he succeeded would Clay turn his eyes toward a legitimate venture—one that might turn him into someone deserving of a slice of happiness.

Until then, he was more than happy to embrace the darkness.

Florence Greene had said it was like making a deal with the devil. She wasn't that far off.

"AND WHERE WERE you last night?"

Florence tore her gaze away from the passing buildings to cast a bland stare at her younger sister, Justine. It was midmorning and the three Greene sisters were traveling a few blocks south to visit their grandmother. "I don't know what you mean. I was home."

"No, you weren't. I came to see you around eleven-thirty and your bed was empty."

"I have a good idea where she went," Mamie said. "And I bet it starts with the letters *b* and *h*."

"The Bronze House? *Again?*" Justine's brows nearly touched her hairline, they were so high. "Did you at least win?"

"Of course." As if she'd lose. "And I'll donate the money to your charity, as usual. Why is no one asking Mamie about where *she* went last night?" Florence knew full well that her older sister had gone out to see a man. Why was a trip to the Bronze House more interesting than Mamie's tête-à-tête?

"Now, that is interesting. I know she wasn't meeting Chauncey," Justine said, referring to Mamie's almost-fiancé. "Because he's with his family in Boston."

"How do you know that?" Mamie asked with a frown. "He didn't tell me he was leaving town."

Florence rolled her eyes heavenward. "The only way you two could care less about one another is if you were perfect strangers. Lord, Mamie. Why are you marrying that man?"

"I don't wish to talk about Chauncey . . . or any other man," she added, her tone harsher than usual.

This merely piqued Florence's interest further. She had a good idea who the other man was in this case. The air fairly sparked whenever Mamie and Frank Tripp were in the same room together. Yet, Florence knew that pushing her sister would not help the situation. Stubborn as a mule, Mamie had to make up her own mind on matters. Florence sent Justine a look, a slight shake of her head to indicate they should switch topics.

"So the Bronze House," Justine prompted with a nod in Florence's direction. "Tell us everything."

"I finally met Mr. Madden."

Both sisters stared at her in astonishment. "You did?" Mamie's voice was a whisper even though they were alone.

"I did. He summoned me to his office and demanded to know why I kept returning to his casino."

"What did you tell him?" her older sister asked.

"Forget that for a moment," Justine said. "What did he look like?" Justine was the romantic one, always seeing the good in people. She thought anyone could be redeemed, if only shown enough love.

"Sturdy, with shoulders like—" Florence held her hands out wide to indicate the breadth of Clay's shoulders. "And handsome, in a rough sort of way." She didn't tell her sisters of his two admissions, that he was attracted to her and had designs to ruin their father. He'd soon get over the first and she'd dissuade him of the second.

"Did he hurt you?" Mamie lowered her brows, her shoulders hunching. "Because I will—"

"Settle down, big sister. He didn't hurt me. And, he's agreed to tutor me."

"Tutor you?" Justine glanced between Mamie and Florence. "Do not tell me this is about that casino for ladies again."

Florence had confided in her sisters about her idea months ago, and Justine had predictably disagreed about the need for a ladies-only casino. Mamie liked the notion, only commenting that it was impractical. Florence didn't care. She'd show everyone that a woman could succeed in business as well as a man. "Yes, this is about the casino for ladies. And you're wasting your breath if you think to talk me out of it."

Justine's lips tightened but she said nothing more. The carriage swung around the corner to start along Seventy-Ninth Street and Florence tried to shake off her morose mood.

Lord, she was tired of this, of feeling like the odd sister out. Mamie, the self-assured and strong one, not to mention Daddy's favorite. Justine, their mother's favorite daughter, was the righteous and kind one. Florence was . . . nothing. The daughter they rolled their eyes over; the girl no one understood. She hated society, while Mamie and Justine tolerated it. She wanted to explore the city, while her parents insisted they stay north of Forty-Second Street. She had no interest in marrying and turning her life over to a man, while Mamie was practically betrothed, the understanding arrived at years ago.

Florence had always been the problematic one.

Florence, be a good girl in church today.

Florence, do not say anything outrageous during tea.

Florence, stop encouraging the housemaids to unionize.

So she'd learned to play the part. To lie and pretend. Whatever the situation required, Florence adapted to blend in. Mamie had once called her a chameleon. Florence rather liked the comparison. Changing was certainly easier than fighting to be noticed all the time.

Only her grandmother seemed to comprehend Florence's real nature, the burning need to do something *else* with her life. Which was why Florence loved their grandmother like no other person on earth.

"Look, they've torn down those two houses over there, the ones up the street from Granny." Justine pointed out the window. "Who lived there?"

"The Turners and the Hoffmans, I think," Mamie said. "The houses were stunning. I wonder why they were torn down."

Florence murmured in agreement, though it wasn't that unusual. New York City was forever building up and tearing down. Old and new. Outdated and modern. And some of the people who lived up here had more money than sense. Why, there was a castle with an actual moat a few blocks north.

And in less than two years there would be a casino just for ladies. Wouldn't that send Knickerbocker tongues wagging? She'd be an independent business owner, relying on no one other than herself.

The carriage slowed to a halt in front of a large four-story stone house in the middle of the block. The house's front door cracked before the wheels even stopped rolling. Granny appeared on the front stoop, her tall frame clad in a smart purple silk morning gown. Her hair was mostly gray, with only a hint of the dark brown from her youth. She was a handsome woman, still fit and sharp as a tack. A formidable society matron, Granny held the annual Forsythia Ball each spring, which made Mrs. Astor's Patriarch Ball look like a child's tea party.

The three sisters piled out of the carriage and stepped to the ground. Florence let Mamie and Justine precede her, as she always preferred to enter her grandmother's home last.

"You look tired," Granny said when Florence finally climbed the step. "Should I be worried?"

She melted at her grandmother's concern. That was one of the hundreds of reasons Florence loved this woman. "Hello, Granny. I'm fine, just out late causing trouble."

Granny patted Florence's cheek, her expression filled with understanding and affection. "I'd expect nothing less from you, sweet child. We are alike in our restlessness, I'm afraid."

"And beauty," Florence added with an exaggerated wink.

"Not to mention our fondness for cards. Speaking of, we missed you at the weekly game yesterday. I won a diamond brooch."

Florence hated missing her grandmother's weekly euchre game. "I hope you weren't cheating again."

Granny chuckled. "As if I need to stoop to such antics. Come in and you may catch me up on your week."

Florence smiled and nodded. As they went inside, she caught a glimpse of another empty lot farther up the street. "Why have all these houses been torn down recently?"

"Probably for another tall office building. Dashed things are a blight on our city. They offered to buy me out of this house."

"Buy you out?" Florence closed the heavy wooden door, one that still had an indentation from her shoe. At nine years old, she'd been furious with Mamie and thrown a boot at her sister—thankfully missing—only to hit Granny's front door. Her grandmother had laughed over the damage, telling Florence to work on improving her aim. Florence knew every inch of this house. She'd practically been raised here. "You didn't sell, did you?"

"Goodness, no. They keep sending me letters with offers and I just let them pile up. I do not even bother to open them any longer."

"That's a relief. I love this house." Granny's home had been Florence's refuge during her childhood. She'd spent nearly every weekend here. Now the entire Greene family gathered at Granny's for each holiday.

"I know you do. That is why I left it to you in my will."

This was not news. Granny had been saying as much for years, ever since Florence's debut. "But you are never allowed to die."

Granny's mouth softened. "It happens to all of us, I'm afraid. I have such fond memories of this house, though. You know, your father terrorized his younger sister and brother right in these very halls."

"He did?" Florence asked.

Granny took Florence's arm and began leading her to the sitting room. "Oh, I have stories about your father that would make your toes curl. Maybe I'll share them one day."

"Can't you tell us just one for today?"

"Oh, let's see. There was the time he put a garden slug in your uncle Thomas's slipper . . ."

Chapter Four

Heart pounding, Florence didn't know what to expect when she knocked on the now-familiar bronze door that evening. Clay had agreed to mentor her, yes, but they hadn't decided on a schedule or discussed the topics to cover. Would he turn her away? Or would he make time for her?

It didn't matter, she realized. He'd agreed not to bar her from the casino, and just walking inside was an education. So if she didn't see him tonight, she'd still find the experience beneficial.

And any disappointment over that possibility needed to be quashed.

The young man at the door lifted his brows when he spied her. "Looks like I owe Bald Jack twenty dollars. Thought for certain you'd change your mind about lessons from Mr. Madden."

Ah, so word had gotten out amongst the staff. "You bet against me because I'm a woman?"

"Name's Pete," he said as he waved her in. "And my bet had nothing to do with you being a woman. I've seen grown men piss themselves at the idea of spending time with Mr. Madden." His expression grew sheepish. "Beg pardon, miss."

"Oh, I've heard worse. No need to censor yourself on my account."

"That's what Mr. Madden said. He told the staff no one should make allowances for you or change their behavior when you're about. I can't see how that's proper, though. We don't have any other women in the club, except for Annabelle, and she don't mind a bit of bawdy talk."

Annabelle? Who was that, Madden's relative? An employee she hadn't met? His *paramour*? She put that thought aside for the moment. "In this case, Mr. Madden is correct. I don't require any special treatment. Now, where shall I go? To the floor?"

"Up to the balcony with you." Pete pressed a flat panel behind him. It clicked then popped open. This must be another secret passage. "Mr. Madden wants you up there first."

She ignored the flutter in her belly as she climbed the narrow stairs to the second floor. The dim lighting swathed the shabby interior in gloomy shadows. Clay clearly hadn't bothered to spend money where no one would see it. The public part of the casino was lavish and elegant. This portion was . . . not.

The balcony was empty. No doubt Clay would be along when it suited him, so she stood near the rail and waited, observing the action on the floor.

"There you are."

She started at the deep voice behind her. Whirling, she found Clay there, dressed in all black again. His face appeared impassive, almost forbidding, but his eyes said something else entirely. Light danced in the dark depths as he stared down at her, almost as if he was glad to see her.

"How do you manage that?"

He cocked his head. "Manage what?"

"Walk without making a single sound?"

"Practice."

"Were you a thief at one time? Breaking into homes and stealing jewels?"

"No, I prefer to steal outright." He waved a hand at the casino floor. "It's much cleaner that way."

Hard to argue with his logic. "Busy evening. I think this is the most crowded I've seen it."

"A bit busier than normal. See that group near the back, the gents at the roulette table? Some sort of pre-wedding bacchanal."

She searched where he indicated—and then gasped. Good Lord, she knew every man at that table. Had danced with many of them at various parties and balls. Fought off advances from two at a particularly rousing costume ball.

She instinctively took a step back into the shadows.

"Ah. May I assume you are acquainted with these young men?"

"One or two," she lied. "I'd rather not be recognized, if I'm able to avoid it."

"Then tonight we best begin our lessons off the floor. Follow me."

"Off the floor? But what about—"

"My casino, my rules," Clay said as he started down the long side of the balcony. She hurried to keep up, remaining close to the wall and shrouded in the darkness. Where was he taking her?

They twisted through several corridors to a set of stairs. Without telling her what he was about, he started climbing. His feet made no noise, as if he were a ghost. Meanwhile, her heels clicked loudly on the old pine, alerting anyone in earshot of her presence. *Another trick I need for him to teach me.*

He held open a door at the top of the stairs. "Welcome to the training room."

Training room? She stepped inside . . . and froze. Tables were spread out in the large space, each one a different game. Roulette. Craps. Card tables. It was a veritable feast of chance.

He came to stand at her side. "You look like a child in an ice cream parlor."

"You have a miniature casino on your third floor."

"Yes, I do. As I said, it's the training room. You don't think those dealers and croupiers come to us fully trained, do you?"

That made sense. "So you teach them the games here."

"Wrong. Most have an understanding of how roulette or craps works. What they don't know is how the games work in *my* casino."

"But I've played in your casino. It's no different than anywhere else."

He walked toward the closest card table. "Isn't it?"

She thought back to her nights here as a guest. "I . . ." She trailed off, unable to come up with an answer.

"Florence, if gambling here was like anywhere else, then why would anyone choose to patronize the Bronze House? The overpriced champagne?"

"Because the Bronze House has the fairest games in the city."

"Exactly. There's no need to cheat guests when the very nature of the game is leveraged for the house to always come out ahead."

"Every game?"

"Yes." He picked up a deck of cards from the green baize and began shuffling, his thick, blunt fingers moving deftly.

"But I won every time I played here."

"You are a rare exception, Miss Greene." He flicked his eyes over her face. "But then, you are an exception in many ways."

Was he calling her exceptional? With any other man, this banter would come across like flirting. With Clay she couldn't tell. "I was lucky."

He gave a dry, hoarse laugh, a sound torn unwillingly from his throat. "There is no such thing as luck. No, you are extremely talented."

Warmth suffused her chest. She didn't know why his praise affected her like this, but her insides were quickly turning to jelly. *If there's an opportunity to get you in my bed I won't hesitate to take it.* Was this part of his effort? If so, she feared it might work. Flowers and jewelry from admirers hadn't ever wooed her, yet a man who noticed her gambling skills? That was dangerous.

She might end up dragging *him* to bed if he kept it up.

"Now," he said, "you've always looked at the games from the guest's perspective. I am going to teach you to look at the games from the house's perspective."

Why was he so appealing like this, with his stern voice and exceptional card-shuffling skills? His hands were nimble and steady, the cards moving swiftly through his fingers. He bent them, flipped them, spun them around. Cut the deck with just a flick of his wrist. Clever man. She could watch this for hours.

"Which game has the best odds for a guest to win?"

She cleared her throat. "Poker."

"Wrong."

"Roulette?"

"Wrong again. Twenty-one has the best odds for winning, at about fifty-fifty. It's also an easy game to learn."

Light moved over his harsh profile, the scars dark slashes in the gaslight. She liked listening to him. Watching him. Soaking in his vast amount of knowledge. *Pay attention, Florence. You're here to learn, not to ogle.* "Should I be writing this down?"

The side of his mouth hitched as he cut her a glance. "Having trouble keeping your attention on the topic at hand? Is that a female problem . . . or am I too distracting for you?"

* * *

"FEMALE PROBLEM?" FURY sparked in Florence's gaze, just as Clay had known it would. He liked seeing her riled up, a cool blond beauty instantly transformed into an avenging angel. Fierce. Ready to eviscerate. A lesser man might even cover his balls at that look.

Not Clay. He preferred his women with a backbone.

He paused, muscles locked in disbelief. *His* women?

Clayton Madden, gone soft for a fancy uptown debutante.

He frowned at the reminder of Anna's words. He was better than this, a man slavering after a woman he'd never have. Yes, he was attracted to her, but any man of a certain age would find himself feeling the same after spending a few moments with Florence. She was magnetic. However, she was also young and from a class that forbade casual liaisons.

Clay had nothing but casual liaisons.

Get this over with. Teach her and then send her home. "It was a jest," he told her. "Do you know how to play?"

"Of course." She appeared affronted that he'd even asked.

He hid a smile as he moved behind the table to stand across from her. He dealt them each two cards, one down and one faceup. "Then let's play. Those chips are yours." A wooden box of Bronze House chips had been placed on the table, per his instructions.

"If I win, will you abandon this idea of ruining my father?"

Cocky girl. "No, that's not up for discussion. However, if you do end up besting me, the house, then the money you win is yours."

"What if I lose?"

Thoughts of her naked, spread out on his bed, her golden hair like a halo around her head, flickered in his mind. Holy Christ, he wanted that. His skin heated just imagining it. But he wouldn't take her quickly. He'd torture her for hours until she begged—

Jesus, what was he doing? He had to be at least ten years her senior and much too rough for the likes of an uptown heiress. Perhaps he should've taken Anna up on her offer last night. That way, he could have fucked off some of this . . . steam and kept his wits about him tonight.

"No harm if you lose," he forced out.

"Even better." She rubbed her hands together. "Come now, dealer. Don't keep me waiting."

The cards moved quickly. She won the first two hands then lost the next six, down in her stake by twelve dollars. "What will you do now?" he asked.

"If the odds are nearly even, I must be due for a winning hand." She pushed a twenty-dollar chip into the pot. "There."

Biting off a comment, he dealt the cards. Dealer had sixteen. She ended up with twelve. She took two more cards and busted at twenty-two. She drummed her fingers on the table, irritation on her face. "Dash it. I'm normally better than this."

He put the deck down. "Your mistake is trying to reason each hand based on the last. Each hand has the same odds, no matter what came before it. You're never 'due' for a win or a loss. Now, how might a player gain an advantage over the house in twenty-one?"

"Tracking the cards."

"Yes, but that takes considerable skill and is rare. How else?"

"A dealer on the take?"

"Good, yes. That is why we have several men walking the floor at all times. They watch the games to ensure our dealers and croupiers are on the level and that players are not working in conjunction with another guest. Anything else?"

She stared at the cards, an adorable crease deepening on her forehead. "I don't know."

He dealt himself two cards, keeping one facedown. "Stand there." He pointed to the seat farthest to the right. "Watch the bottom card." When she was in position he lifted the hidden card to check it.

"I saw it," she exclaimed. "Six of clubs."

"Correct." He flipped the card over. "Some dealers are sloppy and check their cards before the betting ends. It's not malicious, just idiotic. Now, let's move on to the craps table."

Over the next two hours, they moved between the other games. She was an adept pupil, asking all the right questions and giving him her full attention. He stopped thinking of her as Duncan Greene's daughter, a rich Knickerbocker princess, and more like a comrade. A confidante that understood the inner workings of a casino. He hadn't been this frank with anyone other than Jack in a long time.

When they finished, he wasn't quite ready to end their intimate lesson. He propped a hip against the roulette table. "I'm curious. What do you do with your considerable winnings? Buy a new dress or hat or diamond?"

Delicate fingers curled around the edge of the empty roulette wheel and flicked it. The wheel spun, a mesmerizing blur of red, black and metal. "No, I donated it to a charity that helps families in the tenements."

His jaw fell open. A . . . charity? Of course. God knew she didn't *need* the money. Her family was obscenely wealthy. No doubt Duncan spoiled his three daughters.

Only, Florence didn't seem spoiled. A spoiled girl didn't go into business for herself—a dangerous business that certainly would cause her ruination. A spoiled girl didn't donate her casino winnings to charity. And a spoiled girl didn't hire the king of the city's gambling trade to corrupt her.

A rare exception, indeed.

"Have you always wanted to own a casino?"

Her question caught him off guard. He hadn't expected her to return his personal inquiry with one of her own. "No, but I had an aptitude for it. My uncle operated one of the most popular saloons east of the Bowery. When my family moved to Delancey Street, I spent a lot of time in that saloon, learning numbers and doing the books. I started organizing games on the street around thirteen. At sixteen, I expanded to poolrooms and policy shops. By twenty-two, I'd found Jack and the two of us went into business together."

"And the rest of your family?"

Clay paused, unsure how to respond. His mother now lived in Philadelphia, away from the filth and bad memories of Manhattan. His father had walked out when Clay was eleven, after their house had been stolen and destroyed by Duncan Greene. A year later, cholera stole Clay's brother, Franklin, from them. But he didn't wish to share that with anyone, especially not Florence Greene. To her, gambling was a lark. Something exciting and forbidden to dabble in.

For Clay, gambling was everything. His very lifeblood. Hundreds depended on him to keep the games running, the drinks flowing, the cards turning. And he'd done it, happily, for more than a decade to gather wealth and power. Soon he'd have enough of both to ruin Duncan Greene.

Once he did, he'd be free of his need for revenge. Free to pursue a future just for himself, perhaps one not so dangerous.

Absolutely *free*.

The possibility of it was dizzying.

"Clay."

Clay's head snapped up to find Jack in the open doorway. "What is it?"

"Big Bill is here."

"Shit." Why would the assistant superintendent visit tonight? Payouts had been taken care of yesterday, Clay's network of coppers and politicians well compensated for looking the other way on his empire. This was the very last thing he wanted to deal with now. "Where?"

"I put him in your office."

"Any ideas?"

He and Jack had been friends for so long they were able to communicate in a few words. Better for Clay, as he'd never been exactly loquacious. Jack shook his head. "None. No reports of any trouble yesterday."

So all the payments had been made, no complaints shared by their couriers. "I'll come down."

"What would you like to do . . . ?" Jack tipped his chin toward Florence.

Clay clenched and relaxed his hands, thinking. If she was going to open a casino, she'd need to know how to deal with those in power. New York City was a cesspool of corruption and one must wade through the muck to get anywhere here. There was no downside to giving this lesson so early. Hell, it might even scare her off this entire venture.

"Let's give her the eyehole."

Jack's gaze widened then he scowled. "Are you certain? That seems like a bad idea."

"I know what I'm doing."

Jack cast a pointed look at Florence, then back at Clay, as if to comment on how close the two of them were standing. "Yes, I can see that."

"Fuck off."

"What are you two talking about?" Florence asked.

"Allow me to apologize for Mr. Madden," Jack said to her. "He sometimes forgets his manners."

"That's quite all right. I've heard worse."

Jack's expression held a note of warning as he looked back to Clay. "I'll return to the floor, if you don't need me."

"No, you've done enough." Clay waited for Jack to leave before glancing at Florence. "Do you still plan to open a casino in the city?"

"Of course." Her brows drew together. "I'll not change my mind."

Time would tell on that. "Then you'll need to learn the most important lesson, one that isn't taught in any book."

"Oh? And what lesson would that be?"

"How to successfully bribe the police. Come along. You're about to get a demonstration right now."

Chapter Five

Florence shifted on the uncomfortable stool then looked up in Clay's general direction. She couldn't see him, but she knew he was there. She could feel the heat of him, smell the cigar on his clothing. He was large and intimidating, and they were all alone in this tiny dark closet. A shiver went through her.

But not from fear. Oh, far from it.

Stop. Lord, her imagination was getting away from her around this man. She needed to focus. Her increasing lust would need to wait until she was back home, undressed and under the covers. Right now she had to learn about the inner workings of a casino.

Though she definitely looked forward to that under-the-covers time.

Clearing her throat, she folded her hands in her lap. *Look the part.* She could do whatever was required, even pose as a respectable uptown lady when necessary.

Without making a sound, Clay shifted something on the wall and a tiny sliver of light was revealed. The eyehole, he'd called it. She leaned forward and pressed her eye to the opening. Goodness, it was Clay's office. She could see his desk and the chairs quite plainly. A large man in a brown suit occupied one of the chairs. Bushy red sideburns covered most of his face, a matching mustache drooping over his lip. Big Bill, Jack had said. She tilted her head toward Clay. "But who—"

A large hand covered her mouth, his skin rough against hers. These were not the hands of an uptown swell used to yachting and horse racing. These were a man's hands, thick and toughened from hard work. Capable hands. Her heart pounded, and a rush of excitement caused her nipples to stiffen inside her underclothes. As if he sensed her reaction, his fingers tightened on her skin, the tips pressing slightly deeper into her flesh before easing off. A huff of breath gusted over her temple, the sound remotely like frustration. Was he annoyed with her?

She suddenly longed to see him wild and unbuttoned, his cool demeanor ruffled for once. What did it take to rattle this enigmatic man?

His lips met the shell of her ear. In the faintest of whispers, he said, "No sound in here. You must remain absolutely still and not speak." She jerked a nod and he released her. "Good girl." Then he disappeared into the corridor and Florence sagged, the air leaving her lungs. Sakes alive, he was potent.

Perhaps knowing he found her attractive made her more comfortable around him. There were no secrets, his motives entirely transparent. He saw her for exactly who she was . . . and hadn't judged her. When was the last time that had happened, if ever?

Clay's office door opened and the man himself walked in. Florence pressed her eye to the hole, not wishing to miss a moment of this interaction.

"Bill. This is unexpected," Clay said on his way to his desk.

"Evening, Madden." The man rose and she immediately saw why they called him "Big Bill." He was well over six feet and the buttons of his vest strained around his torso, as if he had gained weight but hadn't bothered to adjust the size of his clothing.

They shook hands before Clay settled himself in his desk chair. She could see his face clearly and Bill's profile. "Was there an issue with yesterday's payment?"

"You know the issue. When I agreed to invest in the Bronze House we had an understanding about the profits."

"That's correct. I agreed to revisit your percentage after the first year based on how the casino performed."

"And I still haven't received that revisited percentage. This is the most profitable casino in the city, possibly the state, and you're holding out on those profits."

Clay reached for a humidor on the desk, flipped open the lid and offered Bill a cigar. The other man selected one then Clay took a cigar for himself, and soon they were both exhaling smoke. "Bill, if I had intended to swindle you I would've done it already."

"Not when you need the city's police department to look the other way. If it weren't for me, you'd have been raided and shut down already."

"And if it weren't for me your wife would not have that new vacation house in the Poconos."

"How did you . . . ?"

"I know everything about you." Clay pointed at Bill with his cigar. "You bought her the house in the Poconos and renovated your old brownstone in Brooklyn off our money. The problem is that she's now clamoring for another vacation house, this time down in Virginia, which you don't quite have the sawbucks for, do you?"

"Jesus. Do you have a spy in my house?"

Clay's lips twisted in what Florence suspected was satisfaction. "Bill, you don't seem to understand how this works," he said. "You were brought on as an investor to protect my casino from the police and political meddling. Which makes you *my* investment, one that I watch over very carefully. Because the second you are no longer useful to me, or you work against my interests, I will replace you with someone else."

"I'd like to see you try," the other man shot back. "There's only one man higher at the entire department and he'd never sell himself out to the likes of you."

Clay shook his head, as if Bill wasn't understanding. "There's also the commissioners. Do you honestly believe I don't already have influence there, as well?"

Clay had bribed one of the police commissioners?

"And that's not even touching City Hall and the

judges. I need you, Bill, but you are not irreplaceable to me. No one is."

Gooseflesh broke out on Florence's skin. He was so cool. Calm. Threats rolled off his tongue the way society men doled out compliments. *And why do I find that so appealing?* She was riveted, more excited than she'd been in eons. What was *wrong* with her?

"I don't believe you. Without me, you'd be out of business within a week."

Clay smiled coldly at that, the look so full of dark menace that Florence couldn't understand how Bill wasn't cowering in a corner. "That sounds like a threat. Are you threatening me?" He sounded positively gleeful at the prospect, as if he hoped the answer was yes.

She licked her lips. The air was stifling in the tiny closet, and a trickle of sweat rolled down her chest and between her breasts. Still, she couldn't take her eyes off Clay. He was utterly fascinating.

"You don't want to make an enemy of me, Madden."

"Or . . . ?"

"Or you can kiss this casino goodbye. You'll find yourself sitting in a nice cell in the Tombs instead."

Prison? Goodness, the idea of Clay behind bars felt wrong, like those wild bears chained up at circuses.

Clay reached inside a drawer, flipped through some papers, then tossed a packet onto the desk. "And what do you think will happen to that nice renovated brownstone if the Bronze House folds?"

Bill leaned in but she couldn't see his reaction to whatever was on the papers. "You . . . You hold the banknote on my house?"

A sound of surprise erupted from her throat, so Florence covered her mouth with her hand. *Checkmate.*

"I consider it an investment in my investment." Clay took a drag on his cigar and blew out a long stream of gray smoke. "Now, you're going to stand up, walk out of here and we're both going to forget this conversation ever took place."

"I want a higher percentage, Madden. I deserve it." Bill pounded a fist on the armrest. He wasn't backing down, apparently. The fool.

Clay rose, the cigar clamped between his teeth. "You won't get it."

The policeman hefted himself out of the chair. "We shall see about that, won't we?"

Clay said nothing, his expression stoic as Bill stormed from the room and slammed the door behind him. Quiet descended, yet Florence couldn't move, her breath coming short and fast, her skin feverish. That had been . . . astounding. Like listening to Mozart compose a symphony. Or watching Michelangelo sketch. She wasn't familiar with any other casino owners but Clay was clearly a master, a brilliant manipulator focused on getting what he wanted and protecting what he had. Rumor held him to be the best and she'd now witnessed it firsthand.

A hum coursed through her veins, a very inappropriate tingle between her thighs—all symptoms she recognized. Viewing this encounter had affected her, left her shaken and, God help her, aroused. For Clay. A man who intended to ruin her father.

Attraction had no part in this—it couldn't—at least not on her side.

She'd been burned by lust before, making questionable choices when desire took over her brain. Like showing Billy Palmer her drawers in an alcove at the Metropolitan Opera House. Kissing the Webster twins in the Vanderbilt gardens. Sleeping with Chester McVickar at the Astor Place Hotel . . .

Florence had thought it all harmless fun, a rebellious form of experimentation. The men, however, had formed assumptions based on her actions, and had pursued her. Doggedly. Daddy still couldn't understand why Florence had turned down several marriage proposals.

Because I cannot allow someone else to control my future.

Indeed, try getting a father to understand *that*.

Just then, Clay's gaze locked on the peephole, as if he could see straight through the wood and into her soul. Her breath caught, the blood rushing in her ears.

Oh, my. Would he notice? She nearly shook herself at the ridiculous question. Of course he would notice. Nothing slipped past Clay.

She had to get out of this place. *Right now.* Before he discovered what she had been thinking.

Shooting to her feet, she lunged for the door. The light in the corridor stung her eyes as she stumbled in the opposite direction from Clay's office. A hand suddenly wrapped around her arm and she smothered a squeak.

Bald Jack stood frowning at her, his brows knitted. "Miss Greene, everything all right?"

"Fine, fine. Everything is just fine. I'm fine. I need to leave, though. Will you tell him . . . ?" She drew in a steadying breath. "Please tell him it was late and I had to return home. I'll visit again in a few days."

Jack nodded and released her. "Stairs are around the corner, behind the third door. Boys at the front will fetch you a hack. Don't wander the streets alone at this hour."

"I won't. Thank you." She hurried along the hall, eager to find some peace and put her thoughts back together. Because the next time she faced Clay, she had to be in control of herself.

CLAY HEARD THE keyhole door open and he paused, waiting. Had he driven her away for good? Half of him prayed that yes, she'd been appalled at the nature of his business. God knew it would make his life easier. Florence's presence in his club only complicated everything.

And yet . . .

Well, there was no reason to finish that thought. Only fools wished on stars.

He exhaled a long stream of smoke, enjoying the sting to his eyes, when the outer door opened. Only, it wasn't who he expected.

Jack strode in, his face thunderous. "What in Hades did you say in here?"

Clay hadn't a clue as to why Jack was so angry. "Bill demanded a larger share. Thinks he's got me over a barrel."

"I assume you set him straight."

"Of course. Showed him the banknote." He took a long puff. "He was displeased."

Jack lowered himself into the armchair vacated by Bill. "No doubt that's true. He's been spending money as soon as it comes in."

"You mean his wife has been spending money."

"She does love to shop, apparently. Add her store bills to the renovations and the vacation house, and Bill's skating on thin ice."

"Well, I've made our position clear. I suspect he'll calm down."

"And if he doesn't?"

"Let's worry about it if the time comes. Was that why you stormed in here like you wanted to punch me? Because of Bill?"

"Hell, no. I saw Miss Greene tear out of here like the building was on fire. Couldn't imagine what you'd done to affect her in such a manner."

He braced himself. This was the part where Jack relayed how much Clay had scared her. "Horrified, then."

"No, it didn't seem like it. She didn't come across as scared. Just anxious to get out of here."

Clay picked through the papers on his desk and tried to sort out the jumbled mess inside his brain. "So she's not coming back."

"Wrong. Said she'd return in a few days."

Clay couldn't wrap his head around it. He hadn't scared her off? At every turn she had surprised him.

"The two of you certainly were cozy in the training room."

Clay leaned back in his chair and glared at his friend. "Worried for her virtue, Jack?"

"Seeing as how you've sworn off women, no, not particularly. But that doesn't mean it's right."

"She's asked me to mentor her. I cannot do it by letter or telegram." He shrugged. "No one's forcing her to come here."

"I know there's no convincing you to do the right thing and refuse her entry, so I won't even try."

"Good. Let's move on and discuss more important matters. Where are we with the architect?" On the advice of one of the city's top attorneys, Clay had decided to carry on building his casino on East Seventy-Ninth Street, whether Mrs. Greene sold her house to him or not. Surely once construction started, she would wish to escape the neighborhood—at which point Clay would swoop in and buy the house for far below what he'd first offered.

Then he'd smash the house to the goddamn ground.

Everything comes full circle, Duncan, you miserable bastard.

Jack said, "He's bringing the final plans over the day after tomorrow."

"Excellent. The sooner those plans are filed, the sooner I get my hands on that house."

Jack came to his feet. "And the sooner Miss Greene finds out what you're up to. Something tells me she isn't going to like it."

Clay stubbed out his cigar in the tray and reached for a stack of paperwork. "It's none of her business."

"You keep telling yourself that." He started for the door. "Listen, Mike has everything under control downstairs, and it's mostly cleared out. I'm headed over to Anna's for the night."

"Ah. Mrs. Gregson?" Jack had been seeing Anna's widowed cook for the better part of six months.

"Yes. If you need me, you know where to find me."

Enjoying the tender attentions of his lover, no doubt. "I won't. See you tomorrow." Clay would cut off his own arm before disturbing Jack's tiny slice of happiness.

When they met, Jack had been traveling on the boxing circuit. Clay had offered Jack three times his yearly boxing earnings to quit and oversee the poolroom's security, back when Clay operated just the big one on the Bowery. Jack agreed, and the two had soon become business partners. It was the best decision Clay ever made. Jack was smart and fair, respected by employees and good with customers. Clay had no patience for dealing with either; he scared just about everyone. Helpful when taking on corrupt coppers and cheaters, but undesirable in every other situation.

He couldn't help his prickly nature, though. He'd been burned too many times by associates, customers—even bed partners. Elizabeth, his only longtime lover, had presented herself as a widow, eager for some fun with a younger man when Clay was nineteen. But she'd been jumpy around him. Even after seven months of seeing her she'd tensed each time he made a sudden movement. She hadn't stayed for conversation, either. Once they got off together, she would dress and hurry from his apartments.

Then he'd found out her secret. Elizabeth wasn't a widow. Her husband was quite alive . . . and one of Clay's investors. Curiosity had driven Elizabeth to Clay's bed, where she'd told him lies about her background and family. Clay didn't hate her for it, though. Most marriages were unhappy, and unhappy spouses tended to stray. He owed no loyalty to the husband, even if the man was an investor. Clay turned away investors weekly. Finding money was never a problem.

But he'd learned a valuable lesson about trust. People lied to get what they wanted, if they wanted it badly enough. And Clay hated liars.

From then on, he never slept with married women. The hassle wasn't worth it, not in a city where beautiful unattached women were every which way one turned. Moreover, he made damn certain he knew exactly who came into his bed. He wouldn't get fooled twice.

I am not innocent.

Jesus, that was not an image he needed right now. What had Florence meant by that? Had she lost her virginity to some straw hat–wearing imbecile who probably couldn't find a clitoris even with directions? He almost felt sorry for her if that were the case.

I could show her real pleasure.

Clay swallowed hard. Yes, he certainly could . . . but where would that get him? No place good, that was for certain. Better to return to the business at hand.

There was a haven of vice and sin to oversee, and it had no place for a Knickerbocker princess.

Chapter Six

God, would this dinner party never end?

Florence stifled a yawn and tried not to fall asleep in her plate of roasted duck. She'd accompanied her parents to the Van Alans' for dinner and the crowd was positively ancient, full of Daddy's cronies and Mama's charity ladies. The only single man near her age was her sister Mamie's almost-fiancé, Chauncey. And there was dust more interesting than Chauncey.

Mamie was supposed to attend this evening, as well, but she'd backed out at the last minute with a headache. Stupidly, Florence hadn't done the same. She assumed there would be at least *one* young man here. The Van Alans must have planned for Chauncey to fill that position and hadn't bothered to invite anyone Florence actually *wished* to talk to.

Everyone had been polite, even if she could tell they all wondered about her. It was no different than any other event she attended. She never fit in with high society, mostly because she didn't *care* what they thought. Their strict rules and traditions were ridiculous. Two girls Florence had debuted with four years ago had already been ostracized by society: one for divorcing her philandering husband and the other for daring to criticize Mrs. Fish's hat within earshot of the older woman. Florence wanted no part of a world where women were not free to speak and do as they pleased.

If only I had been born a hundred years from now.

"A penny for your thoughts." The older gentleman on her right, Mr. Connors, had leaned in to ask the question. Cologne assaulted her nose with the subtlety of a charging elephant.

She angled away and tried not to draw a deep breath. "Merely enjoying the duck."

"You haven't taken one bite that I've noticed."

Why was he watching her so closely? Connors was in his late forties or early fifties, his wife having died some fifteen years prior. She had met him many times since her debut, as New York high society wasn't that large. Everyone knew everyone, really. This was the first time she had been seated next to him at dinner, however. *Thank you, Mamie.*

She put down her wineglass and picked up her fork. "It's impolite to call a lady a liar."

"Fair enough," he said through a chuckle. "Are you enjoying yourself?"

"Of course. Are you?"

"I've been observing you, Miss Greene. Though you appear beautiful as always, I don't believe you're having much fun this evening."

"I just have a lot on my mind, is all." What else could she give as a reason? Certainly not the truth, as Mr. Connors matched the age of almost everyone here.

"And what would a young woman like you need to worry about?"

She didn't care for his patronizing tone. "Oh, I wouldn't wish to bore you."

"That's just the thing." He angled toward her and lowered his voice. "I find it hard to believe anything about you would ever bore me."

"I . . ." Her voice trailed off. Was he *flirting* with her? Coming from a man her own age the answer would be yes. But Mr. Connors was much older. Perhaps he was merely terrible at making polite conversation.

She cleared her throat. "My father certainly wishes I were more boring."

If she thought the mention of her father would put a stop to this awkwardness, she was proven wrong when Connors said, "Well, I'm not your father and I find you rather refreshing."

"That is kind of you to say," she mumbled and snatched her wineglass. The man on the other side of her was in a deep discussion with another guest, and Florence had no way out of this interaction short of bolting from the table. She tried to catch her mother's eye but she was listening to Mr. Van Alan. When Florence's gaze swung to her father, she found him watching her closely. She lifted her brows meaningfully, hoping he would understand her need for rescue.

Duncan shook his head once, as if to say, *Whatever it is, do not make a scene.*

The little kernel of hope in her chest popped. Why on earth had she thought anyone would help? Her parents had instructed her time and time again to fit in. Not to offend or be impolite. *Be someone else, Florence.* Wasn't that really what they meant?

When her casino opened, she wouldn't have to worry about all of this nonsense. She'd support herself, without the need for a father or husband to dole out pin money each month.

Ages ago she'd considered causing a scandal to ruin herself, therefore ending the need to attend any of these events. Two things had stopped her. First, a scandal would hurt her mother and sisters. Neither Mamie nor Justine was married yet and Florence hated the idea of ruining their prospects. Second, Florence needed the women of society to patronize her casino once it was finished. If she offended all of them by flouting their conventions now, she hadn't a prayer of getting some of them in the casino later.

"I'm quite serious," Connors was saying. "You are different than the other girls your age. I see a spark in you that they lack. I've always admired that in a woman."

She took two swallows of wine, nearly gulping the contents of her glass. "Thank you."

"You've turned down three proposals, haven't you? I cannot blame you. Men your age are nothing but boys. Silly and immature. Perhaps that's why you haven't found someone yet. Perhaps you'd prefer someone older instead."

A heavy leg pressed against hers and Florence didn't wait to hear any more. She pushed back from the table and stood. "If you'll excuse me," she said to no one in particular and hurried into the corridor. When she was alone she leaned against the far wall and put a hand on her chest, hoping to ease her racing heart. Connors was her father's age. The idea of marrying him caused her stomach to turn over.

And had he touched his leg to hers intentionally?

"Florence."

Her head snapped up at that familiar voice. "Daddy, what are you doing out here?"

Duncan approached, his frown fully in place. "I was about to ask you the same thing. You bolted from the dinner table as if you were ill."

"I'm fine. I just needed a moment."

He shoved the sides of his dinner jacket apart and put his hands on his hips. "Why?"

"It's nothing."

"I should hope it's something after you just put yourself at the center of everyone's attention. Again."

She hadn't done anything but excuse herself and come into the hall. How on earth could that disappoint her father so fiercely? Anger slid across her skin, radiating from deep inside. She was tired of being a disappointment, of feeling so *wrong* all the time, especially when it was undeserved. Daddy wished to know what happened? Fine, she would tell him. "Mr. Connors made me uncomfortable. I wanted to get away from him."

Brows knitted, her father rocked back on his heels. "Connors? I've known him forever. What on earth would he say to make you uncomfortable?"

"I don't know—"

"Tell me exactly, Florence. None of your dancing around a topic this time."

Another barb. She mentally brushed it aside. "That he admired me, that I'm different from the other girls my age. That perhaps I'd prefer an older husband, one more mature."

"And?" her father prompted when she stopped.

"And that he's been watching me."

"That's it?"

Her father's expression was stern and forbidding yet she forged ahead. "His leg brushed mine under the table."

"Which could have been an accident."

She blew out a long breath. "Combined with what he said?"

"Let me understand. He complimented you, made an observation about the possibility of an older man for you—a possibility I happen to agree with—and accidentally brushed your leg under the table. Because of this, you caused a scene by bolting from the table."

"I did not cause a scene, Daddy."

"Don't argue with me, young lady. It's always the same with you. You're not happy unless you're causing a stir or the center of everyone's attention."

Florence pressed her lips together and folded her arms across her chest. He wouldn't listen to her anyway, he never did, so why bother trying to explain herself? No one cared how she truly felt on the inside.

"Now, get back in there and sit down," her father ordered. "I expect you to be quiet and polite for the remainder of dinner. Ignore Connors if what he says bothers you. He's harmless, and I won't have you snubbing our friends."

She lifted her chin, impotent fury burning so brightly in her chest that she couldn't speak.

"Do you understand me?" he asked in his sternest voice, one she'd heard a thousand times.

"Yes, Daddy."

She marched past him and headed to the dining room. From behind her, she heard him mutter, "I swear, that girl'll be the death of us all."

CLAY PICKED UP his fists and continued smacking the heavy bag hanging from the ceiling. Jab, punch, hook, repeat. Sweat poured off his forehead, down his bare chest. His lungs struggled to pull in air but he kept going.

The casino was half-full tonight. A decent crowd, from his early calculations. The plans for the east side casino had been to his liking, which meant the architect would file them with the city to get the permits. Things were moving forward. Thriving.

Still, he felt restless. Unsettled. He knew why; he just didn't want to admit it. But the truth kept staring him in the face.

She hadn't returned in two days. He told himself it was for the best, but he couldn't help thinking about her. Wondering what she was doing. Probably attending some fancy dinner party where a young buck groped her thigh under the table.

He hit the bag so hard pain radiated up his arm and into his shoulder.

No doubt she fended off suitors everywhere she went. A woman like her, beautiful and vivacious, would attract attention at every turn. *I am not innocent.* Christ, why would she tell a man like him such information?

"Here you are."

Anna strolled into the cellar, her skirts rustling as her heels clacked on the hard floor. How had he missed her coming down the stairs?

She's got you distracted. Get your head right, Madden.

"I'm busy."

"Sorry to interrupt, but I had to see you right away. Jack told me I could find you here."

He wrapped his arms around the heavy bag and leaned against it, his chest bellowing to bring in enough air. "Oh?"

Anna perched on top of a wooden crate. "Do you remember Charity? William Coogan, from the police commission, is a regular of hers."

Ah, one of the few commissioners not on Clay's payroll—but only because Coogan was already on Mulligan's payroll. Mulligan ran everything in town that Clay didn't. "I know him."

"He told Charity tonight that the Bronze House would soon have a new owner."

Clay made an exasperated noise. "That's ridiculous."

"You aren't selling, are you?"

"If I intended to sell, don't you think you'd know about it?"

She studied his expression. "I'm not certain. You've never kept secrets from me, but there's a first time for everything, I suppose."

"You have my word that I would tell you, Anna."

"All right, you're not selling the Bronze House. So do you have a clue what this is about?"

He bent and grabbed the cloth he'd placed on the ground earlier. He used it to wipe the sweat off his face. "I might."

She waited a beat then rolled her eyes. "And?"

"Big Bill is a prick. Nothing I can't handle, though."

"I see." She glanced down for a long moment. "Should I be worried?"

"Not in the least. I've got him locked down."

Anna absorbed this information then slid off the crate. "I'm glad to hear it. I don't need to remind you what my investment in this place means to me. It's my chance at a retirement, at living in some nice house upstate, away from the filth and disease in this city."

"I am perfectly aware, and I won't fail you or any of the other investors."

Her expression instantly softened. "I didn't mean it that way. You're more than an investment to me. You're my friend. And I can't be worried about you, too, in addition to the other multitude of worries in my day."

He tossed the cloth to the ground. "You don't need to worry. I have everything under control here."

"Yes, I can see that."

He flicked a glance at her before lining up for another swing. "What does that mean?"

"It means you never come down here unless you're upset or bothered."

"That's not true," he lied. Yes, this was one of the outlets he used to let off steam. These days, without a regular woman, it was either hitting baseballs or boxing. "And how would you know? You're hardly here."

"You are not the only one who gathers information, Clay."

"In this case, your information is wrong."

He continued his series of punches and hooks. When he finally stopped and turned, she raised an eyebrow.

"Does this have anything to do with your missing uptown debutante?"

"Fuck no. And she's not missing."

"What was it Shakespeare said about protesting too much?"

"I never read *Hamlet*," he snapped, "and whatever he said was wrong."

"Then how did you know the reference was from *Hamlet*?"

Growling, he faced the bag once more. "Aren't there men next door, customers who need coddling?"

"They can wait. I'm too busy coddling a man over here."

"I do not need coddling. Leave me alone. You're as bad as Jack."

She shook her head and started for the door. "I hope Miss Greene returns soon, for all our sakes."

"No doubt your spies will inform you the instant she reappears."

"No doubt. Of course, there is the possibility that she won't. Jack said she left in quite a state."

Clay's chest squeezed, unwanted emotions burning at the idea that he might never see her again. It was an absurd reaction. He didn't care whether she returned. There were more important things to concern himself with, like expanding his business. Getting revenge on Duncan Greene. Ensuring Big Bill fell in line. Discovering why the casino had experienced a flurry of cheaters in the past two weeks.

So, yes. He had far more pressing concerns than Florence Greene.

He forced himself to relax his shoulders. "Unless she's changed her mind about opening a casino, she'll be back."

"I admire your confidence, Clay. And I'd almost believe you meant it if I hadn't been watching your face when I said she might never return. You looked as if you'd been punched in the stomach."

"Get the hell out, Anna." He pummeled the bag with a left and right hook combination, her laughter ringing in his ears as she departed.

"HURRY, MAMIE." FLORENCE tugged her sister's elbow. She was full of energy, unable to calm down. Like there was a buzz under her skin that couldn't be ignored. Whenever she got this feeling she knew she had to escape and find some excitement. Distract herself with dance or cards, music and raucous laughter. *Live*. Usually Mamie was game to accompany her on these outings, though tonight Florence had used a little blackmail. "We must get there before they switch to the watered-down alcohol."

"I don't understand," Mamie said as they trudged along Thirty-First Street. "Why are we not going to the Bronze House?"

Because I am a coward.

Florence hadn't visited the Bronze House in two days, during which time she'd tried to wrestle with her fascination over Clayton Madden. Her feelings were complicated and twisted, like an ever-tangling knot she couldn't straighten. It was embarrassing, really. He probably had scads of women at all hours in the upstairs chambers, serving his every whim.

I'm attracted to you.

Was that why she couldn't get her mind off him? No, she discounted that idea straightaway. A few men had professed their desire to her over the past few years. Goodness, Archibald Warner had begged to "shag her silly" at Granny's last ball. Such words had never affected her before—so why would Clay's?

"Florence, are you even listening?"

"I heard every word, and we're not going to the Bronze House because I want to win some money tonight. I cannot gamble there any longer. We must go somewhere else."

"I'm just uncertain why we are racing to this place as if we're being chased. I wish you would slow down."

"Stop complaining," Florence said. "You owe me for skipping out on the Van Alans' dinner. Headache, my foot."

"I've already apologized for stranding you alone at that event. There's no need to torture me with a sprint across town, Florence."

At the corner stood Donnelly's saloon. A side door led to the upstairs rooms, where the gambling took place, away from prying eyes and police notice. Florence had played here twice before. A few women frequented Donnelly's to play roulette, cards, dice and other games, so the Greene sisters likely wouldn't stick out as the only females. Though, despite dressing down this evening, they would gain notice as the only ladies.

That couldn't be helped.

She slipped the man at the door a dollar and he allowed them in. Mamie followed her up the stairs and into the single large gaming room. Tables were spread out on the bare wooden floor, the cracked plaster on the walls giving the place a haunted appearance. Rough-looking men walked the perimeter, their keen eyes on the tables. The place smelled of sweat, perfume and damp. Florence nearly rubbed her hands together, eager to get to it.

"Well, this is charming," Mamie drawled under her breath. "How did you ever find this place?"

"Never mind that. Let's play."

Mamie started for the roulette tables but Florence paused. She thought about her lessons with Clay. If she wanted to win, perhaps she should stick with twenty-one. After all, that game had the best odds. She touched her sister's arm. "I'm going to play over there."

"Not roulette? You love roulette."

"I know, but I thought I'd test my skills at cards instead."

"I'm sticking with roulette."

They split up, Mamie walking to the far side of the room toward the roulette tables, and Florence to the card tables. Two older men were currently playing twenty-one. Florence took an empty chair, withdrew a small pile of bills from her handbag and turned them over to the dealer for chips.

The play went at a steady pace. Florence recalled Clay's advice, that each hand had its own odds and never to think beyond what was in front of her. It was relaxing, the shuffling and dealing, the watching and betting. Easy to lose track of time. She won more than she lost, and soon found herself in possession of an enormous stack of chips.

"You're doing well," one of the men playing at the table said. "You must tell us your secret."

Florence smiled as she peeked at her cards and discovered a total of nineteen. "There is no secret. I'm just lucky, I guess."

The dealer observed her carefully, paying more attention to Florence than the other players. Unsurprising, as Florence was the player consistently winning. The other two had hardly any chips left. "Another card, miss?" he asked.

"No, I'll stay."

The other two players both asked for cards and ended up busting out. The dealer took one card and totaled over twenty-one. Florence won again.

As the dealer counted out her winnings, she noted the way his gaze searched the room. What or who was he searching for? When he seemed to find his quarry, she glanced over her shoulder. The man who'd been pacing the floor, overseeing play, was staring at the dealer, some message communicated between them. Florence paused in stacking her chips, uneasiness skittering down her spine. She'd done absolutely nothing wrong. What reason had she to worry?

After another hand, the same man appeared at Florence's elbow. It was the floor manager. "Miss, come with me."

She blinked at him. "Me? Whatever for?"

"You're counting cards and we don't allow that here. You need to get up and follow me. Now."

"Counting cards!" Her voice went high, carrying over the cavernous room. "I am not counting cards. It's pure skill. I have no need to cheat."

He took hold of her elbow and roughly pulled her to her feet. "No woman has this much skill, not without cheating. I've been watching, remember. Come along."

"But you're wrong." She tried to grab at her chips, but the floor manager nodded to the dealer.

"Take those chips back. She won't be needing them."

"Those are *my* winnings!" Now she was shouting, digging her heels into the old pine to prevent him from towing her out of the room. Only, he was stronger and her resistance meant little more than an annoyance. Where was her sister? Swinging her head about, Florence searched for Mamie.

"Stop right there!" Mamie yelled, closing in quickly. "Unhand my sister."

"You're her sister?" The man turned and waited for Mamie. "Then you can come along, as well. Both of you."

Mamie exchanged a concerned glance with Florence before lifting her chin in that imperious way she had. Mamie was downright regal when she chose to be. "Where are you taking us?"

"You'll see."

Florence struggled to free her arm from the man's grasp. "Let me cash in my chips and I'll leave, I swear."

"Afraid I can't do that, miss."

"Dash it, release me." She tried to kick his leg but her damned skirts hampered her. "This is outrageous. I haven't done anything wrong."

"Tell it to Donnelly."

He dragged her over the threshold, a locomotive sweeping her along for the ride. Her pleas and attempts to get free were for naught. When they reached the end of the hall, he opened the door and practically tossed Florence inside. Mamie came in right behind her, thank God. Florence didn't think these men would hurt her, but she was grateful to not be alone.

"What do we have here?" A man stood up from behind the desk. Large stacks of money were spread out over the surface, more bills than Florence had ever seen in one place.

"Donnelly, we got ourselves a card counter."

"No, I never—"

"This little thing?" Donnelly drew closer, a slow smile emerging as his dark gaze raked Florence from head to toe. His lips were dry and cracked, with dried spittle around the edges.

His nose spoke of overindulgence in spirits. Fear sprinted along her veins. "I don't care much for cheaters in my club."

"I wasn't cheating." Why would no one believe her? "I just happen to be very good at twenty-one."

"So good that she was up four hundred on Biddle."

Donnelly's smile faded as his brows flew up. "Four hundred? Jesus fuck, that's a lot of money."

"It's how Biddle knew she was cheating."

"I wasn't cheating," she ground out.

"Sirs," Mamie said as she stepped forward. Logical, reasonable Mamie, ready to save Florence from another disaster. Even as Florence appreciated it, she resented the need for rescuing all the same. "Let's remain calm. My sister is quite accomplished at cards. I have never seen her cheat, not once."

"Just because no one notices don't mean it ain't happening," Donnelly said. "I've never known a woman to win that much from Biddle, even one as fancy as you."

"Well, you've never met anyone like my sister." Mamie sounded almost proud. "She's been tutored by—"

"Mamie, no!" Florence said, but it was too late.

"Mr. Clayton Madden," her sister finished.

Donnelly's jaw fell as he crossed his arms over his chest. "Wait, this little blonde thing right here has been tutored by Clayton Madden? *The* Clayton Madden? Of the Bronze House?"

Florence closed her eyes. The last thing she wanted was to drag Clay into this mess. It was mortifying enough that she'd been accused of cheating. To have Clay witness this humiliation would multiply her misery tenfold.

"Yes, that same Clayton Madden. Tell them, Florence." Mamie elbowed Florence in the ribs.

"She's mistaken," Florence told Donnelly. "Clayton Madden doesn't know me."

"Why are you lying?" Mamie asked. "You told me that the other night he agreed—"

Donnelly held up his hand to the sisters and addressed his guard. "Send a note over. Let's see if this story holds water."

"That's not necessary," Florence told them.

"Oh, I think it is," Donnelly said. "It'll prove if you're a liar as well as a cheater. Have a seat, ladies. You're going to be here awhile."

Chapter Seven

The wait was unbearable. Florence and Mamie sat in Donnelly's office, silent, speaking only with their eyes, as Donnelly counted money at his desk. Mamie was apologetic for evoking Clayton Madden's name and Florence let her know she wasn't upset. The wheels had already been set in motion and now they had to see how the night played out. Florence apologized for leading them here in the first place and Mamie waved that away. It was amazing how much the two sisters could say to one another without words.

Florence wanted to die from embarrassment. Clay would admonish Florence for being careless. She should've paid more attention to the dealer, keeping her winnings reasonable so as not to attract notice. Stupid, stupid, stupid.

Finally, after what felt like years, the door opened. Jack walked in, a derby held tight in his fist. She blew out the breath she'd been holding. At least it wasn't Clay who'd arrived.

Jack's gaze swept the room until it landed on Florence. When he saw her, his shoulders relaxed just before he gave her a quick nod. Had he been worried about her?

"Bald Jack," Donnelly said as he crossed the room. "Thank you for coming."

"Hello, Donnelly. Madden sends his regards."

Florence cringed at the mention of Clay's name. He must think her an idiot, even though she'd done nothing wrong.

"What seems to be the problem?" Jack asked as the two men shook hands.

"I caught the blonde cheating at cards. Sister says she's been tutored by your employer."

"She did, did she?" Jack cast Florence an enigmatic look. "What makes you think she was cheating?"

"I wasn't cheating—"

"She was up four hundred on my best dealer. No one wins that much off Biddle."

"Ah. It's her skill you're questioning."

"Do you expect me to believe this girl could win four hundred dollars? Off Biddle? Even if she had been tutored by Madden, it's impossible."

"This is ridiculous," she said. "I am an excellent card player."

"She is," Mamie put in. "I've seen her."

"Madden has taken a shine to the girl," Jack said. "She's quite talented."

"Are you . . . She and *Madden*?" Donnelly's face slackened. "Are you pulling my leg?"

"No, I most definitely am not."

Florence almost spoke up to deny it. After all, she and Clay were teacher and student, not lovers. They would never act on the attraction between them, not if Florence could help it. However, if

Donnelly believed her under Clay's protection then that could aid in her release. Surely Donnelly would not wish to anger Clayton Madden.

Donnelly frowned at Florence as if trying to figure this all out. "He didn't send her here to steal from Mulligan, did he?"

"Careful," Jack said, his voice laced with menace. "Think before you go making accusations. You know my employer has only the highest regard for Mulligan."

Mulligan? Florence had no idea who they were speaking about.

Donnelly pointed at Florence. "Then what's she doin' here, counting cards in one of his clubs?"

"There we are, back to your accusations." Jack folded his arms and rocked back on his heels. "Tell me, have you ever heard of Madden taking someone under his wing, especially a woman?"

"No, definitely not."

"Correct. He's not the charitable sort. Now, considering he has agreed to mentor her, does that not say something about the young woman's skills? Do you honestly think he'd take on someone who *wasn't* skilled?"

Donnelly rubbed his stubbled jaw. "Well, no, I suppose he wouldn't. But I still can't believe she won four hundred dollars off my best dealer. No woman is that skilled."

She was tired of them speaking about her as if she wasn't in the room. "Let me show you. I'll prove my skill."

"Good idea. Shall we test it?" Jack gave her a quick wink.

"How?" Donnelly asked.

"Bring in Biddle," Jack said, "or whichever dealer you prefer, and let's see her play. You can watch to make sure she's on the level."

"And what happens if I see her cheating?"

"Then Madden will pay out five times what she supposedly swindled. But . . ."

"But what?"

"Well, if she wins outright without cheating then you let her take her winnings home."

Florence perked up at that. She could do it, no matter who dealt the cards. She didn't need to cheat to win.

"Fine." Donnelly strode to the door and ordered someone outside to quickly retrieve Biddle. "Now we'll see if she possesses these skills you speak so highly of. Come on, girl."

Florence stood and walked to the desk, which Donnelly promptly cleared off. All the money disappeared into the safe in the corner. Mamie positioned herself at Florence's side, while Jack stood at the end of the desk. Florence tried to calm her racing heart. She hated that she'd been put in this position, but at least Donnelly was giving her the chance to prove herself.

Biddle soon arrived and unboxed a new deck of cards. Even still, Jack asked to see them. He flipped through the cards and counted to make certain the deck hadn't been altered in any way. Satisfied, he passed the deck back to the dealer. Mamie reached out to squeeze Florence's hand as the cards were dealt. Florence gave her a small smile. They had nothing to worry about, not with Jack here and Florence's skill at twenty-one.

The first deal gave her a total of twelve. Not ideal. The dealer's up-card was a three. Again, not ideal. However, she knew from Clay that odds were slightly better if she took a card in a situation like this, so that's what she did. A six, for a total of eighteen. The dealer took two cards and busted out at twenty-three. First hand to Florence.

For the next ten minutes, the cards were dealt and no one in the room spoke. She lost two hands, one when she stupidly didn't split a pair of nines and another when the dealer had twenty-one. The rest were all hers, and Jack began to chuckle when she won with an ace and a ten. "Has she impressed you enough, Donnelly? I'd say you're lucky she was only up four hundred."

Donnelly exhaled long and slow as he withdrew a stack from his pocket. "Damn it. Go on, take your four hundred. I better never see you return, miss."

Florence stood and accepted the money. "You won't, Mr. Donnelly. I promise."

Jack and Donnelly shook hands, but Florence grabbed her sister's arm and started for the door. She wanted to get out of this place as soon as possible.

"You were amazing," Mamie whispered. "I knew you were good but that was astounding."

"Let's talk about this later." Florence crossed the threshold and ended up in the hall. The two of them continued toward the main entrance then down the front stairs and out onto the street.

"Hold up, miss." They turned and found Jack hot on their heels. He pointed to a sleek black carriage waiting on the street just a few doors down. "Hop in. I'll give you a lift uptown."

"Oh, we wouldn't want to impose," Florence said. "Thank you for coming, Jack."

"Let me rephrase that, then. Mr. Madden asked that I see you safely to your door, Miss Greene." His expression remained firm, letting her know that he meant to carry out this order for Clay. Florence's shoulders sagged.

"Jack, you remember my sister, Mamie?"

Jack tipped his derby. "Indeed, I do. Pleasure to see you again, Miss Greene."

"And you, as well. Thank you for saving us tonight."

"Oh, I did nothing of the sort." He started walking them to the carriage. "Miss Greene did that all on her own. You should have split those nines, by the way."

Florence nearly rolled her eyes. "I know. It was a stupid mistake."

"The only one you made, actually." He flipped open the latch on the carriage door. "At least during the game."

"Are you going to tell me how idiotic it was to come down here?"

"No. Mr. Madden plans on doing that himself tomorrow. He said to tell you be at the club by nine o'clock."

She paused on the step. The words had a portentous undertone. "Am I in trouble?"

"I've stopped trying to read his mind, miss. But I've never seen him quite so worked up as when the messenger arrived to tell us of your predicament tonight. He was mighty unhappy."

"Because I was accused of stealing?"

"I couldn't say exactly why. If I had to guess, though, I'd say it had more to do with putting yourself in danger. This isn't a safe place for ladies."

"I can take care of myself," she grumbled as she adjusted her skirts and sat.

Jack was shaking his head as he sat across from the two sisters. "You're Madden's now—and he takes care of his own."

SHE WAS EARLY.

This pleased Clay, probably more than it should. He watched Florence from the shadows, observing her as she stood on the balcony overlooking the casino floor. She was gorgeous, in a midnight-navy silk evening gown that was probably sewn by the city's most expensive dressmaker. Her hair was perfectly styled on her head while diamonds hung from her ears, both designed to show off her elegant throat. He longed to place his lips along that milky skin, to test its softness with his mouth and tongue.

He was still angry over her foolishness last night. To gamble elsewhere was a slap to his face, let alone choosing one of Mulligan's spots to do it in. Had she any idea of the danger, how terribly wrong it all could've gone without Jack to intercede on Clay's behalf?

He'd nearly worn a hole in the floor, pacing, until he'd learned of her safety. The relief he felt at the news told him all he needed to know about the way she had gotten under his skin.

Clayton Madden, gone soft for a fancy uptown debutante.

He was beginning to think it was true.

No, he couldn't let it be true. Duncan Greene's daughter was off-limits for so many reasons.

Making no sound, he approached and halted directly behind her. He saw her breathing hitch, knew she was aware of his presence.

"I had an inkling you were here somewhere, observing." She threw him a quick glance over her shoulder. "Hello, Clay."

He said nothing. His thoughts were an amalgam of anger, relief and lust, none of which he was ready to voice quite yet.

She sighed and spun around. "Let's have it, then. No doubt you are brimming with recriminations about last night."

He thrust his hands in his pockets and studied the perfect skin, the delicate features of her face, questions buzzing in his mind. Why would she risk her reputation—not to mention her person—at one of Mulligan's dives? Had she truly been repulsed by Clay's interaction with Bill? Was that why she'd gone gambling at a seedy casino last night? What would she have done if Jack hadn't intervened with Donnelly? What would she do if Clay kissed her?

It was that last question that had him clamping his lips tighter.

"Fine." She threw up her hands. "You're clearly angry with me. It was stupid, of course. I wanted to win some money and test out the advice you'd given me, so I went back to Donnelly's. I didn't go alone, however, and took my sister with me. I never should've stayed so long at that table. I wasn't paying attention to the amount I'd won and soon it attracted the wrong kind of notice." She dragged in a long breath and kept right on going. "I did not bring up your name. My sister did that, despite my efforts to get her to shut up. I never wanted you or Jack involved. But thank you for sending him to help us."

He let her words sink in and contemplated them, remaining silent. The two of them obviously had differing views on what the issues were, because the tightness behind his sternum didn't dissipate one bit after her diatribe.

"Aren't you going to say anything?" she asked when the silence stretched.

He cleared his throat. "I hear you didn't split a pair of nines."

Her jaw fell open before she quickly recovered, a chuckle escaping her lips. "I thought you were furious with me."

"Oh, I am furious. I nearly put my fist through a wall when Donnelly's man showed up here, saying a woman claiming me as a mentor had been caught cheating there."

The muscles in her neck worked as she swallowed. "That reaction seems a bit extreme, considering."

"Considering what?"

"Considering I'm only paying you to teach me about running a casino. We hardly know each other."

Irritation crawled along his skin, though she wasn't altogether *wrong*. Yet, it seemed there was more he needed to teach her. "Florence, being under my tutelage means that you are under my protection. We are linked, whether you like it or not." She started to speak, so he held up a hand. "Furthermore, your decision on where to play last evening was an unfortunate one. Do you know who owns Donnelly's saloon?"

"A man named Mulligan, I think."

She showed no reaction so his suspicion was confirmed. "You obviously haven't heard of Mulligan. What I don't run in this city, Mulligan does. We are . . . associates of a sort."

"Rivals?"

"Not quite. I've risen above the type of places Mulligan runs. We're not enemies—but we're not friends, either. More important, Mulligan allows the men running his properties a fair amount of latitude to do as they see fit with patrons. Even if you hadn't been accused of cheating, you were in danger just by being there."

She waved her hand. "I've been all over the city and never encountered any problems. I'm perfectly safe."

"Don't be naive, Florence," he snapped. "You're far from safe in casinos, dance halls, saloons and other two-bit dives. Even if rape or personal injury doesn't scare you, the possibility of being kidnapped for ransom certainly should. Your last name puts you at risk. God knows your father has made any number of enemies over the years."

"Including you."

"Yes, including me, although I don't need to use you to gain retribution against him. Not all men would feel the same, however."

"No one would dare."

"Yes, they certainly would. Mulligan wouldn't think twice about using you as a pawn to gain power in this city."

She worried her lip and he hoped his words were getting through to her. "You speak of him as if he's some sort of bogeyman."

"He's no one to trifle with. Mulligan rose through the ranks in the Five Points gang. When he got older, he realized how much more money everyone could make by consolidating all the gangs under one leadership—his. He oversees a vast criminal empire from his New Belfast Athletic Club. He's likely the only person in the city who knows as much about gaming as I do."

"Hmm." She stared out at the patrons below as the games carried on. He said nothing, let his information sink in. Instead, he watched the money exchanging hands as patrons lost at the tables. The sight warmed Clay's heart.

Finally, she turned back to him. "What if I wished to play somewhere else, a place where no one knows who I am?"

"Then ask me. There are several small places I own where you'd be safe and could remain anonymous."

"Were you truly worried about me?"

Hadn't he already said as much? Was Florence digging for compliments? "You know that—"

A sharp piercing whistle cut through the air like a sword. Every eye swung toward the exit, where Jack stood, his eyes wild. He whistled once more then circled his arm over his head, which caused all the dealers to begin moving at a breakneck pace.

"Goddamn it," Clay growled.

"What's happening?"

He moved toward the stairs. "We're being raided."

Chapter Eight

Everything happened so quickly.

One minute, she and Clay were on the balcony, arguing, and in the next the place was thrown into chaos. Though it was *organized* chaos. The staff had rehearsed this, obviously, because everyone knew what to do to hide any evidence of gambling. Chips and money were shoved in locked boxes. Tables flipped and secured into place. Jack opened a panel of wainscoting to reveal a secret passage, and patrons quietly streamed through the door like rats scurrying off a sinking ship.

"Florence!"

Clay's hiss reached her ears and she hurried after where he'd disappeared. He was waiting for her at the bottom of the stairs, a frown on his face. "Were you going to stand there and wait for the police to question you?"

"No. I was watching your staff remove any traces of a casino. It was fascinating."

"It's an annoyance," he snapped. "And we need to get out of here." He pushed open a door and ushered her down a long corridor. Just as she was about to turn the corner, he stopped. The section of wall here was brick, not plaster. Feeling under a sconce, he flicked what must have been a release mechanism because the bricks separated from the wall. Another secret passage.

He pulled open the wall and she slid through. When he followed, she asked, "Are you not going to stay and talk to the police?"

"No. Jack is far more reasonable in situations like this. If I stay, I'm likely to punch a copper."

He closed the wall and darkness descended. Before she could grow concerned he took her hand. "Come along. It's not far. Watch, these are stairs."

Down they went. At the bottom of the steps, he held her hips briefly to steady her. Almost as soon as his touch appeared, it vanished and another door opened. A few steps later he closed them in. Then she heard a pull chain. Soft yellow light illuminated a tiny passageway, one so small that Clay had to bend over to fit. She plucked a cobweb off her sleeve and followed him steadily through the gloom. His large shoulders shifted under his black topcoat, his movements lithe for a man so large. It was a routine he was well familiar with, clearly. "Where are we going?"

"To the brothel next door."

A brothel? Excitement simmered in her veins. This was turning into some remarkable evening. "Do you go back and forth often?" She held her breath, unsure why his answer mattered. Yet somehow, it did.

"No, not since I had it built. Annabelle uses it often, however."

Annabelle. There was that name again. Florence's lungs deflated like a popped balloon. Of course he would have women come to him. The great Clayton Madden wouldn't visit a brothel like a common plebeian.

Why do I even care?

She didn't. Just because her heart beat a little faster in his presence didn't mean there was anything between them. She wasn't foolish enough to develop an interest in him—or any man—when her goal was in sight. In less than two years her choices would disappear, along with her independence. So good that Clay had a paramour. The information would help her maintain perspective throughout her tutoring.

"If you do run your own casino," he said, "remember to build in an escape route just in case."

"Of a raid by the police?"

"That or anything else that might require a quick getaway. You'd be surprised the number of people who'd rather not part with their money—even after losing it fairly."

Another set of stairs awaited. At the top, he gave three short raps. A click sounded just before the wall opened. "Took you long enough," a feminine voice said.

Clay grabbed Florence's hand, his skin rough and warm against hers, and pulled her into what turned out to be a tiny closet full of clothing. A woman with a gorgeous head of red hair and large blue eyes shut the panel behind them. "So much for having Big Bill under control," she muttered before facing Florence. "Miss Greene, a pleasure. I am Annabelle Gallagher, the owner of this fine establishment."

Florence blinked at the familiar greeting. How did this woman know her name? Had Clay been speaking about her? "It is nice to meet you, Miss Gallagher."

"Just Annabelle will do. Now, follow me and let's get you two safely hidden away." She waved them into the hall.

"We can get out through the alley," Clay said.

"Not tonight. Police are all over the neighborhood. You'd best hide here." At the end of the hall she swung open a painting to reveal a handle, which she turned. The bookcase on the other wall popped open.

"Clever," Clay murmured and widened the opening for Florence to slip through. Darkness enveloped her once again. She had no idea where they were, but she was grateful to be safe. Getting questioned or arrested in a casino would certainly not go over well with her father.

"You aren't the only one with secret rooms," Annabelle said. When Clay followed inside, Annabelle whispered, "Be quiet in here and enjoy the show."

"Wait, is this—"

"I'll come and fetch you when Jack says it's safe." Her hand flicked near Florence's head and a wooden panel the size of a small painting slid on the wall. Goodness, it was an opening. Was this like Clay's peephole?

Before Florence could ask, the door closed and latched shut. Soft yellow light in the opening caught her attention and she leaned in.

"I wouldn't look in there, were I you."

She ignored Clay and peered into the rectangle of light. *Good God.* She could see into the bedroom next door. And there were people in there. She jerked back, startled.

"I warned you," he said, his voice laced with superiority. He reached to close the partition. "Those activities aren't for a lady's eyes."

The fine hairs on the back of Florence's neck stood up. How dare he decide what she could and could not see? Her hand darted out to catch his wrist, stopping him from closing the slat. "You said you wouldn't play the part of a gentleman around me. Don't change your mind now."

"Florence," he said on an exasperated sigh, "there are people fucking in there. Do you really want to see that?"

Yes, she sort of did, actually. "I suppose it's rude to watch them."

"Not from their perspective. They want others to watch. If they didn't, the partition on their side would be closed."

Oh. "You mean . . ."

"That some people like to perform sexual acts while others observe? Yes, that's what I mean."

"Then you are concerned for my delicate sensibilities."

He paused. In the soft glow from the partition she could see his features, which now appeared etched in granite, as he considered what she was saying. She'd visited casinos, poolrooms, tenements and dives all around this city. Any delicate sensibilities she'd possessed had long disappeared. Furthermore, she didn't need him to shelter her from the unsafe or unsavory. God knew her parents had tried to do that for the majority of her life—and it hadn't worked then, either.

He moved out of her way, shifting to stand behind her. "If I tell you no, you'll watch out of spite. So go ahead. But don't say I didn't warn you." He knocked twice on the glass, presumably to let the occupants know they had an audience.

Out of habit, Florence ducked. "Can they see us?"

"No, it's too dark in here."

"Oh." Feeling foolish, she straightened. The window was rectangle shaped, roughly the size of a piece of paper. Just big enough for Clay and her to watch at the same time. She moved closer to see what was happening.

A man and a woman stood in front of the fire, kissing, the man in trousers and shirtsleeves. The woman was dressed in a corset, chemise, drawers, stockings and boots, with her brown hair piled on her head. Their mouths moved feverishly, lips parted slightly to reveal how their tongues rubbed against each other. The man moved his hands to the woman's breasts, cupping them, his fingers digging into the plump flesh rising above her corset. Warmth slid through Florence, her skin prickling at the scene in front of her.

The man loosened the laces of the woman's corset and she helped him, the two of them continuing to kiss as they worked together to get the piece off. When she was down to her chemise, the man began kissing her throat, his hands cupping her heavy breasts. Her hand went to his groin, where she stroked him through his trousers. Florence's nipples tightened behind her corset, her breasts growing heavy with want. Her own amorous sessions hadn't been this . . . carnal. They had been civilized. Almost polite.

Boring.

This was something else altogether, wild and raw. Desperate. Her body reacted with blood pulsing in her veins and gathering between her legs. Clay's scent, the outdoors and faint cigar, filled the small space, making her quite aware that she wasn't alone. He stood behind her, not speaking, a potent hulk of masculinity she couldn't ignore. Yet, she didn't take her eyes off the couple in the next room.

Now the man tore off the woman's chemise and immediately began sucking the tip of one breast, and she threw her head back, eyes closed in ecstasy. Florence could hear her own breathing, rapid exhalations that gave away her arousal, but she didn't care. She could neither look away nor could she leave. Her feet were rooted to the floor, her body both hot and cold as desire dug its claws into her flesh. She remembered the sweet tug, the pressure of what it felt like to be suckled by strong lips.

Heaven. Pure heaven.

Then something unexpected happened. After untying the woman's drawers, the man lay down on the floor and brought her atop him. Just when Florence thought the man might kiss the woman's lips, he wriggled lower until the woman straddled his face. "What on earth . . . ?" Florence whispered.

A soft chuckle sounded behind her. "Say goodbye to your delicate sensibilities."

Florence swallowed. The woman was . . . sitting on the man's face, his mouth and lips feasting between her legs. Florence had never dreamed anything like this was possible. Her one serious lover, Chester, certainly hadn't kissed her *there*. Was this . . . Did everyone do this?

The woman rocked her hips, her hands molding her breasts, squeezing them, as the man pleasured her. Her eyes were closed tight, her face slackened in bliss. Florence had never seen a woman in such a state of euphoria before, like she'd been drugged. Her own core was slick and swollen, jealous of the attention, throbbing insistently between her legs as she observed the couple.

I'm aroused just from watching.

Actually, *aroused* was a tame word for what she was experiencing. She was on fire. Burning alive. Sweat rolled between her shoulder blades, her clothes confining and uncomfortable. Her chest heaved, each exhalation pushing her breasts against the hard whalebone of her corset, cloth dragging across her nipples. *God, I'm dying.* They would find her here weeks from now, expired from lust.

Soon. She'd soon leave, return home and ease this awful craving with her own hand under the covers. Until then she had to keep a level head.

"Do you like what you see?"

Clay was behind her, his voice a dark whisper in her ear. She shivered and tried not to melt into a puddle on the floor. "I had no idea," she rasped.

"He's eating her. Licking her juices. Sucking on her clitoris."

Florence gasped for air, the raw words sinking into her bones to weaken them. Her knees nearly buckled. She was dying to ask him if he'd ever done the same but her mouth had gone dry. Speaking felt like too much effort.

"There's nothing like the taste of a woman's arousal," he continued. "Sharp and spicy, utterly delicious."

Oh, sweet Lord.

A buzzing built in her ears, as if she could hear the blood coursing through her body. Craving gnawed at her, and she wondered what Clay would do if she spun around and pressed her mouth to his.

"Or when her thighs shake around your head," he said. "When her tiny bud hardens and swells on your tongue right before she comes."

Florence placed a palm on the wall to steady herself. The pounding of her heart echoed between her legs, a steady beat of desire that only grew stronger. Needier. *Hotter.*

"She's climaxing. Watch."

As if she could look away.

Florence pressed her thighs together and stared as the woman began quaking, the shouts clear through the wall. The woman trembled until she nearly fell over, but the man steadied her as he moved a hand to his trouser fastenings. When she recovered, she helped to free his erection. The flesh was hard and thick, capped with a round head. Florence had seen a penis, of course, but not for any length of time. With Chester, the unveiling had happened mere seconds before the instrument was put to use. There hadn't been a pause for her to take it all in.

Now, she took it all in. What a marvel this piece of anatomy was, so tall and proud. Designed to give and receive pleasure. The man stroked it, using his hand along the shaft as the woman shimmied down to align their hips. She lined up and he angled himself toward her core, preparing to penetrate her.

Florence nearly crumbled. *Oh, my God. How will I possibly last?*

"Had enough? Shall I close the partition?"

"No," she wheezed and he gave a soft chuckle. She didn't care. Let him laugh at her, if he chose. This was too . . . educational to resist.

The man's cock slowly disappeared inside the woman's body—and Florence heard herself whimper. It was faint, a sound of pent-up frustration and hunger, but no chance Clay missed it. And she was beyond caring. The scene was the most arousing thing she'd ever watched. Her body was tight, on edge. If she rubbed her thighs together, she might possibly combust. If only Clay weren't here . . .

"Would you touch yourself right now if you were alone?" he whispered.

Heat burned her skin. Was he reading her mind? Or was her desire so obvious?

She couldn't answer, partially due to embarrassment. But more likely because her brain was too busy processing what she was witnessing.

The woman rose up on her knees then lowered once again. The man reached to toy with her nipples, pinching and petting them. Their eyes were wild, movements frantic, like mindless creatures of pleasure. Two nymphs in a secluded wood working toward mutual satisfaction. The woman was bold. Confident. She steadily rolled her hips to work the man's cock in and out of her body.

"So would you?" the devil asked over her shoulder. "Would you lift your skirts and make yourself come?"

"I . . ." Florence cleared her throat. "Stop trying to embarrass me."

"I don't want to embarrass you. I want to know you. It's obvious this arouses you. And, as you said yourself, you're no innocent."

"Would you?" she threw back at him.

"Yes, were I alone I might pull my cock out and tug on it until I spent."

Her lungs froze, unable to function at his confession. God above, why would he say such things to her?

"But we're discussing you. And there's no reason to deny yourself, seeing as how we're trapped here for the time being."

"No reason other than your presence."

"I could turn around."

Her sex pulsed, liking the idea very much. But that was too wild, too deviant . . . even for her. "I couldn't."

"Yes, you can. Just pretend I'm not here."

"But you are here. I can't forget it. And what you're asking of me? It's private."

"Where is your spirit of adventure? The woman who enjoys taking risks, who wants to be treated equally? You have nothing to fear from me. I won't touch you. I swear on the deed to the Bronze House."

"I . . ." The woman in the next room curled forward until the man could suck on a nipple, his feet braced on the floor to give him leverage as he thrust upward. Florence briefly closed her eyes, her body a wire pulled taut. My God, how much more could she take? "This is different. I cannot undo a lifetime that tells me it's wrong."

"Then undo who you are."

"What?"

"Be someone else, if only for a moment. Physical pleasure is not evil. Whoever tells you it is has an interest in keeping you ignorant or chaste. Perhaps both."

"Who would I be, then, if not myself?"

"Anyone. A hedonistic creature seeking self-fulfillment. A woman I've brought here as my guest. A young girl who snuck in to see what all the fuss was about. There's any number of choices."

On the other side of the wall the man rearranged the woman on her hands and knees and quickly shed his remaining clothing. Naked, he mounted her from behind. His buttocks clenched as he pushed in and out of her, while her breasts swung with each thrust. It was raw and earthy and utterly mesmerizing. Florence's body screamed for relief.

Could she do it? Could she pretend to be someone else while easing this insane need? Clay promised not to watch or touch her. What was the harm?

Embarrassment, that's what.

When she paused, he asked, "What if I do the same but face the other way?"

She bit her lip, nearly moaning at the idea. That would certainly ease her mortification. If they were both pleasuring themselves then she wouldn't worry about the aftermath. Clay, stroking himself, hand flying over his shaft? *Yes, please, yes.* God forgive her, but her resistance weakened at the image.

She surrendered. "Turn around."

Glancing over her shoulder, she waited until he'd angled toward the opposite wall. When all she could see was his back, she said, "You start first."

He made a strangled noise in his throat. "Fine, but I expect you to soon join me."

She could see his shoulders shifting as his hands went to his waist. Clothing rustled and after a few seconds he groaned. "Oh, fuck," he whispered. "That's good."

Now, now, now . . . She spun toward the window and her fingers couldn't gather her skirts fast enough. Desperation caused her to fumble but she kept going, moving fabric out of the way, tugging, shifting, until she could hold all the layers of cloth in one arm. Air rushed over her stockinged legs, and she dove to find the part in her drawers. When her fingers brushed through her folds, her eyes nearly rolled back in her head. She was soaked and swollen, delirious with need, and she didn't waste any time, focusing directly on her clitoris.

"I can hear you," he said, then grunted. "You're dripping, aren't you?"

Words eluded her. She panted, air bellowing harsh and fast, as the pads of her fingers circled the taut nub. Her lids fell and she envisioned she'd snuck inside the brothel, an innocent young woman eager to discover the carnal delights two people could find together. Shocks of pleasure streaked up her legs, pressure building in her muscles.

He was right. Imagining does make it easier.

Noises came from Clay's side of the tiny room. Distracting noises that heightened her arousal. Skin moving over skin, cloth rubbing. His rough exhalations. She bit her lip, picturing what he looked like, with his fist gripping his hard penis, stroking, pulling, his eyes dark with pleasure . . . . Was he thinking about her?

"Christ, Florence. I wish I could see you right now. I bet you're slick and flushed, so goddamn beautiful. I—" He bit off whatever he'd been about to say and cursed instead. His breath stopped for a few seconds before he let out a long moan.

Oh, mother of mercy. Clay was spending. In the same room with her. Right behind her.

It was too much, too fast. Her limbs tensed, everything tightening as if to fly apart. Before she could prevent it, the orgasm was there, overtaking her in a burst of electricity and heat, obliterating all thought. She trembled and shook, the strength of it causing her to lean her forehead against the wall. On and on it went, so satisfying and necessary. Like nothing she'd ever experienced before.

When it finally ended and her brain righted itself, disbelief and shame started to creep in, burning her skin. What kind of woman pleasured herself in front of another man, a dark and dangerous man who wished to ruin her father? She'd never been exactly shy, but this was more than she'd ever imagined. Good God. What had she done?

She cleared her throat and rearranged her skirts. When she peeked over her shoulder, she saw that Clay was fully dressed, no trace of what just occurred anywhere except the handkerchief he was tucking into his jacket pocket. Was that—?

A knock sounded at the door. "Clay?"

Annabelle. Panic filled Florence, and she couldn't meet Clay's gaze. The brothel owner would surely know what had transpired in this tiny room.

"We need a minute," Clay said to the woman on the other side of the door.

"There's no rush. Jack said you can return next door whenever you're ready."

"Thank you."

Annabelle didn't answer and silence descended. Florence needed time and space to think about tonight. She didn't know how this would change her relationship with Clay, if at all, but going back to the House was out of the question right now. "I should return home," she said, still not looking at him.

His big shoulders shifted. "Are you . . ." He sighed and rubbed his eyes. "I apologize for bringing you here. And I shouldn't have pressured you into doing something you weren't ready for."

The apology surprised her, which was why she answered honestly. "I'm embarrassed, but I don't feel as though you pressured me. I'm quite capable of saying no when necessary."

"Are you certain?"

"Yes." Exasperation momentarily eclipsed her humiliation. "As I've already said, I am not an innocent. You haven't corrupted me."

The side of his mouth hitched before he turned the knob on the door. Light from the corridor suddenly flooded the tiny room. "I'm relieved to hear it, because this was the most arousing experience of my life. I think you might've just corrupted *me*."

Chapter Nine

Clay toed a broken bottle on the floor. Goddamn it. The police had destroyed the entire bar during the raid. Apparently, they hadn't been able to find anything illegal during their search so they'd turned their attention to smashing the liquor instead.

Those pricks.

A partnership with Big Bill notwithstanding, Clay's payments to police commissioners were supposed to prevent this sort of thing from happening. Now he had a ruined bar, thousands of dollars of spilled liquor, broken chairs and tables . . . Not to mention a night of lost revenue. Bill would regret ordering a raid on the Bronze House.

The brothel . . . Jesus, but Florence had been amazing. Unexpected. Absolutely enthralling. And he wasn't one to throw compliments around loosely. Hearing her pleasure, her cries of ecstasy as she came . . . Fuck, he'd never experienced anything like it.

He wanted to do it again. Next time, facing her. Touching her. *Helping her.*

Would she let him?

After announcing his attraction to her, he'd been resigned to keeping things impersonal between them. He'd convinced himself not to pursue anything physical with a woman like Florence. It would only make things complicated. Messy. And Clay hated both.

But having Florence naked, beneath him, could make the complication worthwhile.

"All told, not too bad," Jack said from across the room. His partner was striding around the pieces of furniture and coming toward Clay, Annabelle at his side.

"Who was it?" he asked Jack.

"Let's see. I recognized Harris and McGinnis. The others were all young, too stupid to realize what they were doing."

Clay wasn't surprised. Harris and Big Bill were of the same ilk, both on the take from every gin palace, brothel and saloon in the Tenderloin. Clay pressed his shoe deep in the carpet, which squished from all the liquid on the floor. "I honestly didn't think he was this stupid."

"Yes, well. Bill's never been known for intellect. Thinks he has you cornered and can get more."

They both knew Bill was wrong. "The question is, what do we do first? Share the evidence of his mistress with his wife or call in the note on the Brooklyn townhouse?"

"I vote mistress," Annabelle said, a gleam in her eyes. "His wife will make his life an ever-loving hell."

"Done. See that it happens, Jack, will you?"

"With pleasure. Shall we get a team of maids in here?"

Clay pointed at the mess. "Have the boys carry out the broken glass and wood first. Carpets will need to be replaced."

Jack nodded but studied Clay carefully. "Hmm. I thought you'd be angrier about all this."

"I am angry."

"Are you? I've seen you angry and this seems quite different. Or perhaps next door with Miss Greene—"

"Stop. Do not finish that sentence." Both Jack and Annabelle broke out into laughter, and Clay ground his teeth together. "Don't you both have better things to do than stand around and irritate me?"

Jack held up his hands and turned to Annabelle. "I'll leave him to you, Anna, while I try to get the club cleaned up."

"No need for you to stay, either," Clay told her.

"Nonsense," she said. "You clearly need my help."

"Do I?" He leaned down to pick up two large pieces of broken glass and set them on the bar. "Watch your feet."

She bent to carefully retrieve a broken bottle. "So you and Miss Greene."

He didn't say anything. Replying merely encouraged Anna's meddling.

"I know something happened in that tiny room tonight. You may deny it all you want."

"Perhaps it's none of your business. And why did you put us in there to begin with?"

"Because the police would never find that room should they come to search the brothel. And you're welcome." She placed another bottle on the bar. "Admit it, you both liked the show."

Florence had certainly appreciated it, but Clay didn't tell Anna that. "It was highly inappropriate."

"I figure any woman who hires you for mentoring lessons can take watching a little slap and tickle. And you do seem . . . relaxed. I think I like this woman even more."

"Me, too." Unfortunately.

"I'm glad to hear you say it. Jack did mention that your plans for the East Seventy-Ninth Street casino are moving forward. I assume you're putting off such plans for Miss Greene's benefit, considering they involve tearing down her grandmother's home."

Not ruin Duncan Greene and his family home? Clay couldn't live with himself if he didn't see this through. "Absolutely not. And my issue is with her father, not her grandmother."

"I can't imagine that distinction will matter to her."

"Nothing changes. She doesn't get a say in how I run my affairs, no matter what happens between us." Anna made a noise in her throat, one that had Clay narrowing his eyes. "You don't believe me."

"I have known you a long time, so I'm going to give you a piece of advice." She put a hand on Clay's arm. "Do not start anything with her if you are still intending to ruin her family. It's cruel, Clay. And while you are many things, you are not intentionally cruel to the innocent."

"Duncan Greene is not innocent."

"He is not his daughter, however."

"One has nothing to do with the other—and I'm not planning on courting Florence Greene. Stop worrying about her."

"Women must worry about other women," she snapped. "God knows men won't do it."

His skin heated with irritation. "I will do whatever the fuck I want with Florence Greene and my plans for her father haven't changed."

She dropped a piece of glass on the bar then dusted her hands off. "I see. Indeed, excuse me for caring. You know, if you push people away then one day your revenge will be all you have left."

An apology tried to force its way out of his throat but he swallowed it down. He'd already explained his need for revenge to Florence and it hadn't stopped her from coming here. Clearly, she wasn't concerned over her father's future. "Noted," was all he said.

Anna's face fell, anger seemingly draining right out of her. "I don't wish to fight with you. I only want to see you happy."

"I will be once I have my revenge on Duncan Greene. And I don't wish to fight, either. Other than Jack, you're my oldest friend."

"Hell, we're your only friends."

"True."

"Which is why we have noticed the differences in you since Miss Greene began visiting here. Jack told me he caught you whistling the other day as you were doing the books. Whistling!"

That was what he got for leaving his office door open after hours. "You're being ridiculous. And don't listen to Jack."

Anna shook her head as she came toward him. "I have to go. I'll just leave you with one piece of advice."

"No, thank you."

"Too bad. You're getting it anyway. Seduce the lovely Miss Greene, but be careful with her. She's young and fairly sheltered, for all her bravado. Just be honest about your intentions."

He had been. On several occasions. "Is that all?"

She sighed and started for the door. "Yes, I suppose so. Just tell her the passage is always open, should she have any questions for me. As I said, women must look out for other women—especially those who get involved with surly casino owners."

THE BRONZE HOUSE remained closed for two days after the raid. Florence was grateful for the reprieve. She spent that time going over what happened in the brothel and wondering how she would ever face Clay again.

For nearly three years, she'd led a wild and bold life, sneaking out and traveling the city. Drinking, dancing. Men. Yet, even for her, what happened during the raid had been scandalous. She'd brought herself to orgasm while in the same room with Clay. And he'd been doing the same. It was the most arousing and yet horrifying experience of her twenty-one years. Thank goodness he'd seemed to take the episode in stride, bidding her a polite good-night as she left, as if they hadn't shared something momentous.

Then a thought had occurred. What if it hadn't been momentous for him? He had round-the-clock access to the brothel, the women who worked there. Then there was the joke about her corrupting him, but that might've been for her benefit, to relax her. Those sorts of illicit rendezvous could be an everyday occurrence for him.

Did you believe you were special?

No, not to a man like Clay. He probably had a string of lovers to keep him busy. No doubt he'd forget about the closet in time, if he hadn't already. The realization actually made it easier for her to return to the casino. Now she could walk in and act as if nothing happened.

That night had been a momentary lapse in judgment, one they'd both never mention again.

But one she'd relive in her mind when she was alone in her bed.

She bit her lip and fought a smile as she entered. The man at the employee door in the back greeted her and relayed the message that she should go straight to Clay's office. Ignoring her racing heart, she removed her cloak. "Are you certain? His office?"

"Yes, miss. The floor's busier tonight than we've been in months. Everyone's come out after the raid."

Figured. The jackals in this town loved a good spectacle. She thanked him and worked her way through the inner corridors toward Clay's office. Sounds from the casino drifted through the thin walls. The men were having a grand time, it seemed. And why wouldn't they, out celebrating their wealth and privilege while wives and sisters waited dutifully at home?

Florence would change that. She'd hear the same raucous laughter and exuberance in her own casino, except the voices wouldn't be so low and gruff.

Light streaked out from Clay's open door. Wiping her damp palms on her skirt, she took a deep breath and peeked inside. *String of lovers. You aren't special.*

He was bent over his desk, pen in hand as he checked over a ledger. Black clothing, as usual. His scars were twin shadows in the gaslight and she once again wondered how he'd acquired them. Round, gold-rimmed glasses were perched on his nose, the sight of which caused her stomach to do a funny roll. *He wears glasses. And looks dashed good in them.*

Insecurity gripped her and she struggled with what to do. How should she greet him? *Good evening. No, I haven't thought at all about what you sound like when you climax.*

Which would be a lie.

He glanced up then, dark eyes framed by the metal, and his mouth kicked up on one side. "Were you planning on spying on me all night?"

"Of course not." She entered and approached his desk. "I didn't wish to interrupt."

He took off the glasses, folded them and placed them by his papers. "I heard you walking down the hall." He pointed at her feet.

"Oh. I hadn't thought of that. I suppose I'll need softer shoes when I open my casino."

"Or fewer skirts."

Now *that* reminded her of lifting her skirts the other night. Heat washed over her. Dash it. She hadn't even been here five minutes.

"You're blushing," he said, rising out of his chair. "How have I embarrassed you?"

"You know very well what I'm embarrassed about."

"Ah." He slipped his hands in his trouser pockets, his shoulders hunched but still impossibly wide. "I thought we settled that afterward."

Stop acting like a fool. You're supposed to be experienced and mature. "We did. It's settled. Ignore my fair complexion. So what shall we discuss tonight? I had questions about your accounting—"

"Yes, yes. We'll get to all that." He crossed the floor and shut the door for privacy. "First, there's something I'd like to ask while we're on the topic."

She tried to maintain her composure as nerves skittered along her spine. Was he really going to drag this out? "What is it?"

"Do you regret it?"

His expression was serious, expectant. As if the answer mattered to him. She had no choice but to speak honestly. "No."

"I'm relieved to hear it." He perched on the edge of his desk. "Would you like more experiences like that? With me, I mean."

"I . . ." God, how to answer that? "Do you?"

"Truthfully, yes. But I've made no secret of my desire for you. It's what you want that matters here."

Every impulse screamed for her to agree. But was she being hasty? This decision required thought and consideration. Clay was a man, not a bumbling youth at a society ball. Perhaps this was how these things were handled, with a clear-headed discussion between mature adults. Wasn't her family always complaining she was too rash?

And there was her purpose to keep in mind. A relationship with Clay didn't help to open her casino. However, it might help her father. Would he really continue his plans to ruin Duncan Greene if he was involved with Florence? She didn't believe so. Clay was not a cruel man, at least from what she'd seen. He could be harsh, and he didn't let anyone push him around, but he was fair.

She cleared her throat. "What would that mean? No more lessons?"

"The lessons remain a separate issue. I'm willing to mentor you for as long as you wish, regardless of what happens between us."

Well, that was a relief. "Speaking of lessons . . ." She reached into her skirt pocket for the money she'd tucked away earlier. Withdrawing the bills, she placed them on his desk. "There you go. That's everything I owe you to date."

He didn't spare the money a glance. "So?"

"I . . . don't know."

"Because there's someone else?"

"No! Goodness, no. Is there someone else . . . ?" She waved her hand to indicate him.

His mouth twitched as if he was amused. "No. There's no one. There hasn't been for quite some time."

Interesting. Annabelle wasn't his lover, then. "So like an affair?"

"Yes, I suppose, if you need to label it."

"What would you label it, then?"

"I'm not sure I should say the word in polite company."

She smirked, enjoying this playful side of him. "I thought you were no gentleman—not to mention you've already said that particular word before in front of me."

"So I have. If it helps your decision, I'm also disease-free and still in possession of all my teeth."

That caused her to laugh. Would he next brag about his stamina? "You certainly are tenacious when you want something."

"You have no idea." He straightened and closed the distance between them. "I cannot get the other night out of my head. I'm desperate for more of you. And I feel it's worth repeating that I'm a very private man. No one will ever learn of what happens between us, if anything."

She figured as much. Clay was a mystery to most New Yorkers, including his employees. Discussing his personal life seemed very uncharacteristic. Which reminded her. "Yes, you're private. So private that I hardly know you."

His dark eyes glittered as they stared down at her, a thousand secrets buried in their obsidian depths. "You know more than most anyone, save Jack and Anna. You know enough."

No, she rather thought she didn't. She stared at his mouth and wondered, could this large man be gentle with her? There was one way to find out, an idea that had her skin crawling with anticipation. But it would change everything.

Was she ready for that?

Her family thought her reckless, irresponsible—and she'd spent years trying to prove them right. Now she had a future mapped out, one that didn't include a husband or even a handsome casino owner. So what did *she* want?

Standing across from this enigmatic and rugged man, she knew the answer. Perhaps she was reckless and irresponsible because she wanted to explore whatever was happening—and she'd discuss it as directly as he had.

"Wrong. I barely know anything about you," she said. "For instance, I haven't the first clue on how well you can kiss."

He paused, but only for a second. "Are you asking for me to rectify that?" He reached out to slide his hands up her arms, past her shoulders, until rough fingers trailed under her jaw. "Because you'll find I'm very amenable to requests."

She shivered as he traced the skin of her throat with his knuckles, his gaze never dropping hers. It was as if the simple touch was a test. As if he expected her to push him away.

She didn't.

The touch had the opposite effect, the backs of his fingers mesmerizing as they swept back and forth. Tingles followed in his wake and she was quickly realizing that, yes, Clay could be quite gentle with her. And she liked it. A lot. The air grew heavy in her lungs, each breath filled with expectation, and she leaned in ever so slightly.

He bent his head, his hands shifting to cradle her jaw. She could see the whiskers on his face, the bow of his upper lip. Dark lashes that framed his eyes. Tiny lines and creases in the skin that signified a life well lived. Every inch of him was fascinating, each mark and scar another facet of his mysterious past.

His mouth hovered just above hers, their noses almost touching. "Change your mind yet?"

"No," she whispered and then his lips brushed hers, softly at first, barely a graze. Her lids swept closed and she held perfectly still, waiting. Then he was kissing her—really kissing her—and she felt herself falling, spinning as his mouth caressed her lips. He held her tight, his large frame solid and warm against her, and she clutched his shoulders, holding on, as she kissed him back.

His mouth parted and his tongue slipped past her lips to twine with hers, stroking and rubbing until she was gasping, desperate for air. It was thorough and intimate, a melding of breath and flesh, unlike anything she'd ever experienced. His mouth was inviting, soft—a sharp contrast to a body of sinew and muscle. She arched into him, straining, trying to get closer, trying to ease the ache building in her core.

Had she ever doubted his kissing abilities?

This was no young swell, with a few chin whiskers and an overzealous, sloppy tongue. No, this was a man, competent and strong. One who knew what he wanted and let nothing stand in his way. And right now he was kissing her with a single-minded thoroughness that stole her wits.

She lost track of time. It could have been minutes or hours. Days, even. Nothing existed but the two of them and the need to stay connected. When he lifted his head, she was clinging to him like a limpet, her chest heaving as if she'd swum the length of the East River. Her fingers were buried in his hair, which was silkier than it appeared. It took her a moment to reacquaint herself with reality.

"Have I proven myself?" His voice sounded harsh, deeper than normal.

"What?"

He leaned down and kissed the edge of her mouth. "You were uncertain of my kissing abilities. I hope I've cleared that up."

"I—I think we may safely put that concern to rest."

His rugged face filled her vision, his imposing features gentled after the kiss. She brought a hand to his cheek, helpless not to touch him. With a fingertip, she traced the scar through his brow. He inhaled sharply but said nothing as she stroked him. The raised skin was smooth, a testament to his perseverance. "How did you get this scar?"

"Fighting. There was a time when I would do almost anything for money."

"Was this when you worked in your uncle's saloon?"

"It was. So your answer is yes, then? You'll sleep with me?"

The change of topic was not lost on her. This decision had to be made with a clear head, so she dragged in a lungful of air and stepped back. "When? *Now?*"

"No, not necessarily." He shoved his hands in his trouser pockets. "Whenever you like. Tonight, tomorrow. The offer is open."

"Oh."

He cocked his head and studied her. "I cannot tell whether you are relieved or disappointed."

"I'm not certain myself."

"I had many decisions taken away from me as a child. I don't like to cajole or force others into doing what I want. It's better if everyone agrees on a course of action."

"Then no one may complain later on."

"That's right," he said with a nod. "Balance. An eye for an eye."

She squinted, certain she'd misunderstood, and waited for him to laugh. Only, he didn't. "I'm lost. Are we discussing revenge or sexual congress?"

"Both."

That reminded her of Clay's plan to ruin her father. She had hoped, over time, during her association with Clay, to convince him that Duncan Greene was a good man. Could she sleep with a person determined to harm her family?

"If we do this, will you abandon your plans of revenge against my father?"

"No."

One word, said with such finality that her stomach sank. There would be no changing his mind. "Then I cannot. I would never forgive myself for being intimate with someone intending to hurt my family."

"One has nothing to do with the other."

Did he honestly believe such nonsense? "That's absurd. Of course they do."

He crossed his arms over his chest, the black topcoat pulling across his shoulders and biceps. "If you think to push me into a corner, Florence, I have to tell you, I will not be pushed."

"I am not pushing you. I am merely expressing my opinion. And I won't sleep with a man attempting to ruin my family."

"I am not trying to ruin your family. Only your father."

"Now you're splitting hairs."

He growled deep in his throat and stalked to the fireplace, where he propped an elbow on the mantel. The fire popped and hissed as the moment stretched. They were at an impasse, and Florence had no intention of bending on this. How could she? While she might occasionally engage in reckless behavior, she loved her family.

"Does it help if I tell you that it's not life threatening or physically harming? That I don't plan on ruining him financially?"

Hmm. Yes, she did find that somewhat reassuring. Not enough to drop the subject, however. "So why not tell me what you're planning?"

"Because I won't. It's a risk I am unwilling to take."

She drew herself up. "Then sleeping with you is a risk *I* am unwilling to take."

His eyes narrowed, the scars on his face twisting in his displeasure. "I don't care for games, Florence."

"Funny, coming from a man who owns a casino. And I am not playing a game. I am being honest with you, mister eye-for-an-eye."

"Not entirely honest. You want to sleep with me."

"I never denied that. But intimacy is about trust, which we do not yet have."

"Don't we?" He pushed away from the fireplace and thrust his hands on his hips. "Do you have any idea of the trust I've placed in you? I've told you and shown you things hardly anyone knows. People would kill for the knowledge you've gained in this club."

She hadn't thought of their lessons in such a way but she supposed he was right. "Fine. You trust me, but I do not trust you."

His mouth tightened, his expression darkening into something fierce and ugly. "Then I believe our lessons are done for the night, Miss Greene. The door is behind you."

Chapter Ten

Though his lips were still tingling from kissing her, Clay tried not to be hurt. He'd had much worse things said to him over the years, insults he'd hardly registered. Yet, this one sentence from an uptown debutante had twisted his insides and set them on fire.

You trust me, but I do not trust you.

Fucking ridiculous. He'd looked out for her since the moment she had crossed the threshold of this club. Had rescued her from that saloon when she'd been accused of cheating. Hid her during the raid. Christ, he'd done nothing but keep that woman safe and give her total honesty.

He'd even informed her of his hatred toward her father.

Yet, despite all that, she didn't trust him.

He waited for her to say something, to apologize, anything. Yet, she merely stared at him with blazing eyes and stiff shoulders. "You cannot bully me into trusting you."

"Kissing you is not bullying you."

"No, I'm talking about the way you are scowling at me."

Was he scowling?

"It's my face, Florence. And unless you're ready to admit you trust me, then we're done for the night."

Fury sparked in her eyes, her nostrils flaring ever so slightly as she stood taller. A warrior queen, a woman afraid of nothing. The sight impressed him, even if he was equally angry with her.

A quick rap on the door sounded before Jack poked his head inside. "Clay, you have a visitor. Are you free?"

"I was just leaving," Florence said, her chin raised high. "Some people in this room are acting in an unreasonable manner."

"I see," Jack murmured, his gaze darting between Clay and Florence.

Clay didn't try to stop her. She didn't trust him. There wasn't much more to say at the moment. "Come in, Jack."

Jack pushed open the door and stepped aside to let the newcomer enter. Richard Crain appeared. Crain was a barrel-chested man who'd come up through the Tammany political ranks with their current mayor, Hugh Grant. As the city's chamberlain, he held considerable power, serving basically as the mayor's deputy. Clay had known him for years and Crain had proven invaluable on many occasions.

"Madden." Crain entered the room then stopped as he noticed Florence. "Am I interrupting?"

"Not at all," he said. "Have a seat."

Florence gave Clay a smile that was all teeth before turning toward the door. "Yes, we are definitely finished here." She sailed past Jack and out the door, disappearing into the corridor. Clay gave Jack a pointed look and his partner disappeared. Jack would follow Florence to ensure she was safely seen off in a hansom.

Clay forced himself to relax and shook Crain's hand. "Welcome, Richard. This is unexpected. Would you care for a drink?"

"No, that's not necessary." Crain dropped into a chair and crossed one leg over his opposite knee. "I came to update you."

And collect his fee, no doubt. "On?"

"Things are progressing on all fronts. Your architect's plans have been approved."

"That is excellent news." He should feel elated at this, but he was still preoccupied with Florence. Why was she so difficult?

And why did he want her so desperately?

"You know I am personally looking out for your interests," Crain said when Clay fell silent. "Come hell or high water you'll get what you want."

"Exactly what I wish to hear. Appreciate it, Crain."

"Though I should point out that Duncan Greene has many powerful friends in this city. Are you prepared for the storm these plans will unleash?"

Clay ground his molars together and tried not to react. Goddamn Duncan Greene. Had those powerful friends any idea of how Greene had kicked several families out of their homes just to build an office building? That man deserved all the retribution Clay had planned, and then some.

Reclining in his chair, he said, "Thank you for the warning, but I will be ready for whatever storm is unleashed."

Jack reappeared and came inside Clay's office. He dipped his chin, reaffirming that Florence had been seen off. Clay was both relieved and enraged at her departure. More than anything, he wanted to be alone with his thoughts. And a bottle of bourbon.

He withdrew a fat package wrapped in brown paper from his desk drawer and handed it directly to Crain. "There you go."

Crain smiled, a slick grin of avarice and entitlement that would turn Clay's stomach if he hadn't seen it countless times on different men in this city. Unfortunately, success here meant playing by their rules, which meant paying out stacks of money to corrupt officials.

"Pleasure doing business with you, Madden." The package disappeared inside Crain's jacket pocket, then he patted the bulge in the cloth. "I'll pass along your regards to our esteemed mayor."

"Appreciate it, Crain. Would you like to stay and play downstairs? Jack can set you up with some chips."

Crain rubbed his jaw, probably thinking about playing poker, his one true weakness. Clay knew this about the official but hadn't yet used the information to his advantage. He merely filed the bit away, in case he needed it one day.

"I suppose I have a few minutes," the chamberlain said as he rose. "Very generous of you, Madden."

"I am always obliged to accommodate one of our city's fine civil servants." Clay stood, as well, and nodded at Jack, who led the other man out into the corridor. Jack would set up Crain with some house chips downstairs. As Crain was a terrible poker player, he'd undoubtedly lose that amount within the hour. Then he'd dip into that fat stack of cash Clay had just handed him . . . and the money would come right back into Clay's pockets.

He'd smile if he wasn't in such a shit mood.

Jack strolled inside the office a moment later, just as Clay was pouring a drink. "Why do I dislike that man so much?"

"He's harmless, if you don't mind gutter snakes who would rob their own mothers."

Jack took the seat Crain had vacated. "Miss Greene got off safely."

"Yes, I received that message before." He dropped into his chair and cradled the glass of bourbon.

"Planning to drown your sorrows?" Jack asked.

"Fuck off."

Jack merely laughed. "Would you care to discuss your lovers' tiff with Florence Greene?"

"There was no tiff and we are not lovers," he growled. "Furthermore, I don't need managing, Jack. You should attend to the floor. We're probably being robbed blind down there."

"Tell me what happened."

"God, no. Talking is the last thing I want to do. In fact, if you plan on making noise at any point in the next two hours then you may leave now."

"There are other women."

"I'm aware of that." He took a long drink, enjoying the burn of the liquor as it traveled to his belly. Yes, there were other women, but they weren't Florence Greene. She had captured his full attention.

"I do have a piece of good news, if you're interested."

"For God's sake, please."

Jack smirked and reached into the humidor on Clay's desk to select a cigar. "Bill's wife has kicked him out of the house. He's now living with the mistress over on West Thirty-Seventh Street."

"Good. Let's call in the banknote on his house. I want to take away anything attached to his name. I want to destroy him." That would teach men on Clay's bankroll not to betray him.

Jack whistled. "You are in a mood. All right, if you're sure."

"I'm sure." He downed the remaining whiskey in his glass. "We need to send a message to the Metropolitan Police Department. No one crosses me without paying a steep price."

FLORENCE SIPPED HER coffee and stared at the flames jumping in the fireplace. The Greenes had gathered in the parlor for dessert and coffee, as was their usual habit when it was just the family for dinner. Justine sat at the piano, working on a new piece she was learning, while everyone else chatted. Voices carried on around her but Florence couldn't stop thinking about three nights ago, when Clay had kicked her out of the Bronze House.

Do you have any idea of the trust I've placed in you? People would kill for the knowledge you've gained in this club.

Yet, he hadn't trusted her enough to talk about why he hated her father. How could she consider sleeping with a man who kept such a secret?

Still, she missed him. Terribly. It was awful, wondering what he was doing, what was happening at the club. She had convinced herself that her frequent visits were only about learning as much as possible . . . but that was a lie. Clay was the reason she couldn't stay away. He treated her like an equal, not like a silly woman. And she was wildly attracted to him, her heart fluttering every time he was in the vicinity. While his enterprise might be illegal, he was a good man. An honorable man who lived by his own code.

But must that code include revenge against Duncan Greene?

Her father sat on the other sofa next to their mother, smiling at something she was saying. Duncan doted on their mother. On all of them, really. Yes, he could be fearsome when angry—which was often with Florence—but he had a huge heart. Whatever he'd done to cross Clay couldn't have been on purpose. There had to be some misunderstanding. If Clay would just confide in her—

"You have certainly been quiet tonight." Mamie dropped onto the sofa next to Florence. "Is something bothering you?"

"Do you really want to know?"

"What kind of a question is that? Of course I want to know."

"I didn't mean it that way. Sometimes not knowing is better where I'm concerned."

Mamie held her coffee cup in front of her mouth. "Is this about Clayton Madden?"

Florence did the same, shielding her lips from prying eyes. "Yes."

"Have you slept with him?"

"Mamie!"

Their parents both looked over, concern on their faces. Florence waved her hand. "She ruined my new dress."

Mama frowned. "The one with the green brocade skirt? Oh, Mamie, that's just arrived from Paris."

"I'm sorry, Mama. I'll take the dress to a dressmaker and have it repaired."

"Take it to Lord and Taylor. They do excellent work."

"I will. I promise."

When their mother's attention returned to their father, Mamie murmured, "I swear, I don't know how you think of lies so quickly."

Florence lifted a shoulder. "It's a gift."

"Now, tell me what is going on with Mr. Madden." When Florence didn't immediately answer, Mamie added, "I know you're fond of him. It's written all over your face."

That was a lie. Florence had played enough poker that she knew how to school her features. "Stop. You're digging."

"Fine, I am. But please tell me what's troubling you. That will at least take my mind off my own troubles."

She lifted her porcelain cup in front of her face again. "He wants to sleep with me."

Mamie covered her mouth with her cup. "Of course he does. He'd be a fool not to. You're stunning and smart."

"Thank you," Florence said honestly, flattered by her sister's praise. They were normally sniping after one another, not complimenting. "I've told him no."

"Good for you. So you're not attracted to him."

She thought about the night of the raid. "No, I am. Desperately so."

"Oh. Then you're worried about getting caught?"

"We're often alone at the casino. I don't think we'd have any problems with privacy."

Mamie paused and refilled her coffee cup from the pot on the table. When she sat back, she lifted her cup to hide her mouth. "You told me you and Chester had already . . . you know, at the Astor Place. If you need me to explain how these things work, however—"

"No, no. Not that. It's not the mechanics of it. I hardly know the man. How can I sleep with a man I don't trust?"

"Don't trust? Florence, you're practically putting your life in his hands every single time you go in there."

Hmm. She hadn't thought of that. She must trust him *a little.* She decided to tell Mamie the rest. "He hates Daddy. He readily admits it and says he is plotting some revenge scheme against our father. How can I sleep with a man who will do that?"

"Has he told you what this scheme involves?"

"He refuses."

"Take it from me. You cannot let Daddy come between you and another man."

Florence remembered about Mamie and Frank Tripp, Daddy's attorney. Frank had resisted any relationship with Mamie in fear of risking their father's wrath. "In this case, Clay is hoping to hurt Daddy."

"Physically?"

"No, Madden says it's nothing physical and won't ruin him financially."

"Embarrassment, do you think?"

"I cannot fathom how Madden could embarrass Daddy."

Mamie took a sip of her coffee and kept the cup aloft. "Me either. Daddy has his share of enemies, yet no one has been able to touch him. Clayton Madden wouldn't be the first to try and fail."

"You think I'm concerned over nothing?"

"I think Daddy is capable of taking care of himself. Sleep with Clay—or don't—but do it for the right reasons. It's not as if you're going to marry the man. We're talking about a few hours of pleasure, not a wedding."

Florence considered this. "I don't know if I trust him."

"Has he ever lied to you?"

"No." Quite the opposite, actually. "He's hard to read sometimes but he hasn't lied that I know of."

"Why not ask Daddy if he knows Clay? Perhaps you could get the story from the other end."

"And how am I supposed to do that? 'Daddy, I've been spending a lot of time with Clayton Madden down at the Bronze House and I'm wondering if you two have ever shared a cigar or brandy at the club?' He'd disown me on the spot."

"Give yourself a little more credit, Florence. I think you'll come up with something. Just hint at it."

"That is the stupidest idea you've—"

"What are you two whispering about over there?"

They both jerked slightly at the sound of their father's voice. Coffee sloshed out of Mamie's cup and onto her evening gown. "Dash it," she said.

"Marion," their mother exclaimed on a gasp. "Language, please."

"I apologize, Mama. I had best go and take this off straightaway." She put her cup down. "Perhaps you'd come and help me?"

"I am a bit tired," their mother said before leaning over to kiss Duncan's cheek. "I'll see you in a little while, darling. Florence, please get some sleep tonight. There are bags under your eyes."

Mamie snickered and added under her breath, "Yes, please stop sneaking out until all hours. Now, ask him."

Soon Florence was alone with her father, except for Justine still tinkering at the piano. Her father reached for a book on the table by his elbow and Florence tried not to be hurt that he'd rather read than talk to her. She tried to sound casual as she refilled her coffee cup. "Did you see the evening edition, Daddy?"

"No. Why? Were you mentioned in the gossip columns again?"

"Nothing like that." She took a deep breath and forged ahead. "There was a mention about some problems in the Tenderloin. A casino there, I think."

He grunted in response, clearly not interested, then reached for his book and began thumbing through the pages.

"The name was . . . the Bronze House. Yes, that was it. Have you ever visited it?"

"No, I've never been one for gambling. You know that." He looked up from his book. "Florence, why on earth are you asking me about the Bronze House?"

"Curiosity. The newspaper said all the wealthiest men of the city frequented there. I thought maybe you'd visited or knew the owner, Clayton Madden."

"Well, I haven't been there and I don't know this Madden person. Moreover, you should steer clear of any young man who does. Those places are filled with the worst types. They are cesspools of degenerate behavior. I wish you would find a proper fellow, like Mamie's Chauncey. He's from a good, decent family—not like these slick rascals you seem to favor."

Fabulous. Another lecture when she was merely trying to dig for information. Irritation burned in her chest and she put her coffee cup down with a snap. "Chauncey is no prince, Daddy."

"And what does that mean, young lady?"

Her sister's almost-fiancé was a bore. Self-absorbed. Vapid. Florence wouldn't be surprised to hear he carried on conversations with himself in an empty room. He knew nothing of hard work or survival. Everything had been handed to him since birth. He would make Mamie a terrible husband. "It means I don't wish to marry a man like Chauncey."

"Then what type of man would you like to marry? I would really like to know, because if you think I'll approve of a match between you and some two-bit ruffian, you are sorely mistaken."

She instantly wanted to protest that some two-bit ruffians were fifty times the man Chauncey could ever be—not that she and Clay would ever marry. But the idea that her father wouldn't approve of it rankled. "Perhaps I'll never marry. Perhaps I have no interest in coddling some overgrown toddler-man who expects me to do his every bidding."

"Yet, you prickled at marrying an older man, such as Mr. Connors." He tossed his book on the table and stood. "I've stopped trying to understand you. You don't want young, you don't want old. You don't want a man like Chauncey but you don't want someone mature and responsible, either. Hear me now, Florence. You had best choose *someone* because you cannot live in this house indefinitely." He strode out of the parlor without another word.

She rubbed her eyes with her fingers. That had not gone as expected. But then, when did any conversation with her father begin and end reasonably?

"He doesn't mean that," Justine said gently as she sat on the sofa next to Florence.

Actually, Florence had forgotten her younger sister was in the room. She laid her head on Justine's shoulder and sighed. "Yes, I rather think he does."

Her father's patience was running out for unmarried daughters, which was why Florence had to get her own future secured—fast.

Chapter Eleven

Clay paused, his pencil hovering over the ledger. Numbers blurred in front of him as he waited, unmoving. There it was. Another faint thump sounded directly above him. That made no sense. No one was allowed up there. The entire third floor was Clay's private space, his sanctuary inside the club.

Yet, someone was definitely moving around upstairs.

He threw down his pencil and pushed away from the desk. It wasn't Jack. The club was full tonight and would remain so for another three or four hours. Until they closed, Jack would stay on the main floor, watching and managing, while Clay did the day's books. That meant a maid or club employee had dared to wander into Clay's domain.

He nearly rubbed his hands together as he moved silently up the stairs. At least this would give him the opportunity to vent some of his frustration at someone. Three nights' worth of frustration, to be exact.

I will not think about her. I will not remember her tracing my face with her fingertip.

No woman had ever touched his scars before. His face was not soft and boyish; it was fearsome and blunt. The sensation of her reverently touching his injury, her gaze full of appreciation rather than pity, had nearly caused his knees to buckle.

But it needed to stop. He'd become too preoccupied with her. Had foolishly let her overshadow everything else in his life. He wouldn't make that same mistake again, if she decided to return. Lessons and nothing more.

At the door, he withdrew his key, silently placed it into the lock and turned gently. After a slight click, he entered his apartments. All appeared as it should, with his practical and worn furniture spread around. He waited a moment for his eyes to adjust to the semidarkness before continuing on.

There weren't many places to hide. The floor was composed of four large rooms, mostly open. He checked behind the sofa and in the small kitchen. That left the washroom and the bedroom. His hands fisted as he ghosted across the floor and into his most private space. Whoever had broken in would live to regret it.

Silhouetted against the open window was a slight figure. Definitely a woman. Her back was to the room as she stared out into the night. Who in God's name . . . ?

He threw the switch and the overhead gasolier brightened. The woman gasped and turned.

Florence.

All the breath emptied from his lungs in a rush. She was here. In his bedroom. Looking so damn beautiful, like a perfect angel. How in blazes had she gotten up here?

Then he remembered their conversation a few nights ago and felt the familiar anger tighten in his chest. He quashed any excitement over seeing her. She didn't want *him*. She merely wanted his knowledge.

He crossed his arms and leaned against the door frame. "What are you doing?" It came out more harshly than he'd intended but he didn't take it back or apologize.

"Waiting on you."

"I was working in my office, which you must've realized, considering the club is still open. So why not come there instead?"

"Because I didn't come here for lessons."

He blinked, focusing intently on her face, as his brain tripped over those words. Hope flared but he smothered it. She'd made her position perfectly clear the last time they saw one another. And he wasn't a man who begged or cajoled.

So why was she here?

Needing to see her better, he moved toward the window. "What have you come for, then?"

"Isn't it obvious?"

"Not to me." She wouldn't meet his eyes, her cheeks tinged with color. He wished he knew why. "Are you embarrassed?"

"I shouldn't be," she said with a small laugh. "It's not as if I'm . . ." She sighed and tilted her head back to stare at the ceiling. "This is so much easier for men."

"Not true. At the moment I'm confused and twisted inside out with possibility. You know how I feel about ambiguity."

She dropped her chin and stared right into his eyes. "I'm here to sleep with you."

Heat rushed through his veins and centered in his groin at the unexpected and entirely arousing declaration. She'd changed her mind about screwing him. Why?

Don't question your good fortune, man. Go on and kiss her before she reconsiders.

No, he had to be certain. Clay did nothing without careful and methodical evaluation. He deserved an explanation, even if his body was suddenly as eager as a young teen. "What changed your mind about trusting me?"

"I realized I do trust you. I've trusted you to teach me, to take me seriously. I've trusted you to keep me safe and protect my anonymity here. I've trusted you enough to kiss you and pleasure myself while you're in the same room. I *do* trust you."

A crack opened in the stone that used to be his heart, and a feeling he hadn't experienced in a long time welled up to warm him. *Tenderness.*

He fought to shove it back down. Buttoned it up. This was not about feelings and emotion. She was here for danger and excitement, a colorful break from the monotony of her beige uptown existence. Not for a grand love affair with a criminal. He was not a long-term choice, merely a short-term diversion.

So . . . danger and excitement. That he could do. "You want me to fuck you?"

Her lips parted on a sharp inhale. Then her gaze darkened, almost glowing in the dim light. "Yes."

Ah, the power in that single word. He stepped toward her, closing the distance between them, his body alert and ready. A thief stalking his mark. Anticipation crawled through him as she watched, unmoving, color still high on her cheeks. When he was within reach, he cupped her face and bent his head. He dragged his nose alongside hers, breathing her in. Everything blurred, his vision filled with this gorgeous creature.

"Sweet Florence, I am not one of your pampered and vacuous uptown men. I won't give you timid or soft." He sank his teeth into the skin of her neck, biting down gently. She whimpered and grabbed his arms to steady herself. He nearly smiled. Yes, he knew how this was going to go. "You want a bit of trouble, princess? Here I am. And I promise I'll give it to you anytime you like."

He placed a kiss on the edge of her mouth, teasing them both, drawing out the anticipation. He was almost fully hard, his shaft pulsing as need rushed through him. The depth of his craving for this woman scared him, not that he'd ever admit it.

Then she tilted her head and sealed her mouth to his, her lips moving eagerly, and he forgot how to think. There was only *her*. With kisses that were bold and thorough, her hands gripping him tight. She didn't wait for him to coax a response from her; she was an equal, demanding a response from him with her clever lips and slick tongue.

He loved it.

The kiss deepened, their hands gliding and groping in haste. He wasted no time and kissed her hard, urgently, and all the desperation he'd stored the past few weeks resurfaced to burn him alive. His tongue caressed and worshipped, telling her without words how much he'd suffered in wanting her. Her mouth was wet, a glorious haven. He could sink into it and die a happy man.

They stumbled a bit until her back landed against the wall, and she wrapped her arms around his neck and pressed closer, his cock grinding into her corseted belly. It wasn't enough. He needed her soft flesh, the friction of her channel gripping him. He needed her naked underneath him.

He needed everything.

Breaking off their kiss, he propped his hands on the wall above her head. His chest heaved with the effort to breathe. "I want to undress you."

"Good, because I want to undress you." Her hands traced his shoulders and chest and she licked her lips. He worked to maintain his size and strength—intimidation was his currency, after all—yet he'd never been more grateful for that effort than right now. For some reason Florence wasn't scared away by his size or his scars.

Danger and excitement, remember?

Already coatless, he began unbuttoning his vest while she watched. His fingers worked fast and soon the piece dropped to the floor. Then he lowered his suspenders, removed his shirt collar. Next, the shirt buttons. When enough had been unfastened, he yanked the fabric out of his waistband and whipped the shirt over his head. Her attention never wavered, her gaze heavy-lidded and intent, her body slumped against the wall.

He kept going. After toeing off his leather shoes, he flicked open his trousers and pushed the cloth over his hips. He stepped out of the legs and kicked the garment aside along with his socks. That left him in a thin cotton undergarment, which hid absolutely nothing. Quite the opposite, actually. The fabric cupped his cock and balls indecently.

She looked him up and down. He didn't wait for a reaction, however. In another few seconds he had the undergarment off and stood naked in front of her. Her chest rose and fell quickly, her breasts pushed high into the neckline of her emerald-colored evening dress as she took in the sight of his bare body.

This is who I am, he wanted to tell her. *Scarred, big and imperfect.* He was not one of those pampered swells with soft hands and an aversion to work. Clay was rough and unforgiving. He'd done little to be proud of in this life thus far. She'd be wise to leave and never come back.

"Change your mind yet?" He held perfectly still and awaited her answer. He hadn't felt this vulnerable since he got pinched at the age of sixteen for running an illegal dice game in the Bowery.

"Absolutely not." She lifted her hands to her hair and pulled on the combs securing her chignon. Silky blond tresses fell around her shoulders, a halo around her stunning face. "You're glorious, Clay."

The compliment was a lance through his chest, destroying the thin thread he'd had on his self-control. He couldn't wait a second longer to touch and taste her. He gripped her face and captured her mouth in a deep, powerful kiss. Her palms slid over his shoulders and down his chest, her touch light but unafraid, and so arousing he worried for his stamina. Their tongues battled and his cock throbbed between their bodies. *Idiot. Why didn't I undress her first?*

He reached for the ties of her skirt. She broke off from the kiss and moved his hand away. "It'll go faster if I do it."

Nodding, he kissed her temple, then her cheek. He moved his lips over the curve of her jaw until he reached the smooth skin of her throat. She was soft and delicate, so different than her bold and daring personality. Her fingers brushed his stomach as she unfastened her bodice. When the fabric parted, he drove his hand inside to cup her breast, the mounds tantalizingly displayed by the corset. Florence twisted to shove the heavy material off her arms so he bent his head and kissed the tops of her breasts. He nibbled and sucked, drawing her flesh into his mouth as she worked on her skirts.

"You're not making this easy," she panted.

"You picked the wrong man for easy," he said and focused on the tiny buttons of her corset cover. When that was removed, his fingers popped open the clasps on her corset, one by one. Soon, it joined the other pieces on the floor, along with her skirts and bustle, until she was left in her shift, drawers and stockings.

Grasping the backs of her thighs, he lifted her. "Wrap your legs around my waist," he growled into her throat.

She did, her arms and legs clinging to him, and his mouth found hers once more. Spinning, he carried her to the bed and laid her down, his body following atop hers, weight supported by his elbows. His hips landed in the cradle of her thighs, his shaft lined up directly atop her pubic bone. Unable to help himself, he rolled his pelvis. She threw her head back, eyes closed in surrender, and they both groaned.

God, that sight. *Fuck.* He'd never be able to forget the image of her here, her blond hair spread out on his bedclothes, her pale skin flushed with arousal. He hoped the smell of her lingered here for years to come.

She tilted her hips and the heat of her core met the skin of his cock. Oh, God, she was so wet and hot. If she kept that up he wouldn't last ten minutes. If he was a religious man he would've started praying to stave off his climax.

"Please, Clay," she whispered and moved against him once more.

He cursed. In all the times he'd imagined being with her—and there had been plenty—it had progressed as a slow seduction. Where he'd remained firmly in control. That was not happening here. She wasn't allowing him to go at his own pace, more demanding than his fantasy.

Not that his body seemed to mind. Every sigh, every touch, drove him wilder. But he had to slow down. Otherwise, she wouldn't be ready for him.

"Wait, I should—"

Another roll of her pelvis and the tip of his cock met her entrance. He paused, his muscles clenched in agony as he remained perfectly still. *Oh, Christ. Oh, God. Oh, shit.* Each cell in his body screamed for him to thrust, to drive, to stroke. No, he couldn't. *She's experienced but not that experienced. Don't hurt her.*

"Now, please." She breathed the words into his throat just as her nails clawed into his buttocks. The sting was like a shock to his system, causing his hips to flex and his cock to slam into her sheath.

She gasped—and not in a pleasurable way. He could hear the pain in the sound. Glancing down, he saw her eyes screwed shut, her face pale. Goddamn it.

He pushed off her and withdrew, coming up on his knees. Her lids flew open. "What are you doing? Don't stop now."

"Florence, it was causing you pain."

The confusion in her expression only deepened. "And?"

He frowned. "And that's bad."

"Oh, I'm sorry. I'm usually better at hiding the hurt until it goes away."

Hiding the hurt? Jesus. Hadn't her other lovers bothered to prepare her? Did she assume sex to be painful?

You didn't prepare her, either, you selfish bastard.

He stared at this magnificent woman, a lusty and audacious creature, and cursed any man who hadn't properly pleasured her, including himself. Clay meant to rectify that right now.

He slid his hands along her calves and drew down her stockings. Then he untied her drawers and slid them off. When he pushed her shift up her torso, she lifted off the mattress to help. At last, she was bare, spread out before him like a feast. Small, perfectly round breasts. Creamy skin. Slightly rounded stomach and flared hips. Her slit was glistening and swollen, begging for his mouth.

Good God, she was sheer perfection.

He didn't deserve to fuck her. He was a black-hearted criminal who valued money more than morals. His hands had committed violence and theft for as long as he could remember. And now he had one of the city's most desired debutantes in his bed, naked.

But he was no fool, either.

He might not deserve her, but he wasn't going to stop—not without showing her true pleasure. The kind he knew her uptown boys were too selfish to give.

When he began sliding down the bed, she rose up on her elbows. "Wait, what are you doing?"

"Lie back, Florence. You're about to receive another lesson."

Another lesson?

She had no idea what Clay was talking about. Worse, she felt foolish. She'd whimpered from the pain of his invasion and caused him to stop.

Why hadn't she bitten her lip or a pillow instead?

The pain never lasted more than a minute or two. Then the tingles returned and it would start to feel good again. If only she'd convinced Clay to keep going . . .

And what was he doing now? He was moving down the bed, his head between her spread thighs, his face directly *there*. Then she remembered the couple from the brothel—

His fingers touched her folds, separating them, just before he leaned in and . . . Oh, sweet heaven. He'd *licked* her. From the entrance to the tiny button on top. Her limbs twitched in surprised ecstasy as his groan reverberated throughout the entire room.

"God, your taste," he muttered. "I'll never get enough."

He dipped once more, his eyes closed, and his tongue swiped over her flesh. The feeling was indescribable. Unlike anything she'd imagined, with a toe-curling rush of sparks centered in that spot. She held her breath, silently begging him to do it again. When he did, her arms gave out on her and she dropped back on the bed, her body ready and willing for whatever he had in mind.

Apparently, he had more of the same in mind. His tongue licked and swirled, his mouth sucking and kissing. She panted and clutched the coverlet, trying to remain grounded as the earth shifted beneath her. He left no part of her unexplored, as thorough as when she'd seen him examine the night's books. The hard bundle of nerves atop her folds received the most attention, and each swipe and suck caused her insides to wind tighter. Perspiration dotted her forehead. Her legs started shaking, her muscles twitching. The pleasure built as she climbed higher. He seemed to realize this because he sped up, drawing her clitoris between his lips, nursing on it, until her back bowed.

Just when she thought she couldn't take any more, he pushed a finger inside her. She cried out, the delicious fullness pushing her over the edge. White-hot pulses of pure bliss obliterated all thought and reason. She could only lie there and let the feeling envelop her. It went on and on, wave after wave, until she was limp. Utterly spent.

As she floated back to herself, she marveled over what had just happened. It had been more intense than any orgasm she'd given herself to date. Perhaps she wasn't trying hard enough? Or was Clay just that talented?

A lesson, indeed.

He nuzzled her entrance gently, still tasting her. "Did you enjoy that?"

"You knew I would."

A rumble of pure male satisfaction sounded in his throat. "It's a crying shame that no one's taken the time to properly love this cunt."

She'd never heard the word spoken aloud, had only read it in books she hid under her bed, and she could feel her skin heating. Everything about him aroused her, even the way he talked. He was so real and raw, unpolished steel in a world full of fake gilding.

Another finger joined the one already inside her, stretching her farther. She sucked in a breath.

Not from pain, but from the heavenly drag against her sensitive tissues. She was so wet, her moisture coating his fingers as he pumped them in and out of her. Each movement felt better than the last, until her hips were rising up to meet his hand.

"It shouldn't hurt," he murmured and kissed her thigh. "Not even for a few seconds. It should only feel good."

She barely comprehended the words because he'd added yet another finger. Her walls gripped the digits as her body chased the pleasure again. When he circled her clitoris with his tongue, her hands clasped his head, holding him in place. "Oh, God, Clay."

Suddenly, he was crawling over her, the muscles in his arms flexing as he drew closer. "Come here, you delectable creature." Sliding her legs wider with his thighs, he took his shaft in his hand and notched it to her entrance. "Changed your mind yet?"

She smiled at this familiar question. "Do you ever expect the answer to be yes?"

The side of his mouth hitched, but he said nothing as he pushed the crown of his penis inside. He concentrated intently on where their bodies were joining, while she watched his face. The angles were sharper but no less beautiful. He was remarkable to look at, really. Strong shoulders, flat stomach. A powerful chest dusted with dark hair. A beautiful specimen of a man, even with the scars and a nose almost too big for his face.

He was perfectly imperfect, and she found him fascinating.

There was no pain this time, only pressure from his wide shaft spreading her open. Filling her. He seemed in no hurry, his bulk easily supported by his arms, with the pace agonizingly slow. No doubt this was for her benefit, to not hurt her again, and the consideration surprised her. Other lovers had rushed their encounters, her enjoyment not a concern.

Until now, she'd believed that normal. Goodness, she'd missed out on quite a lot.

His dark gaze peered at her face. "All right?"

She nodded, not sure she was capable of words at the moment. He was so deep inside her, his heat and strength a part of her, and it strangely wasn't enough. She trembled with the need for more. Her hands found his shoulders and gripped hard.

"You're tight," he gritted out just before withdrawing a tiny amount. He slid back in and then grunted. "Damn, Florence."

His mouth covered hers in a fierce kiss, his tongue sliding to find hers, their breath mingling as he began to roll his hips. She could smell and taste herself on his skin, the spicy wetness he'd licked like ice cream. It was brash and earthy, much more sensual than she'd imagined. She clung to him as he worked his shaft in and out of her body, dragging the hard flesh over the walls of her channel, making her light-headed. Everything inside her strained toward him, her body desperate and hungry for more.

Breaking off from her mouth, he kissed her cheek, her jaw. He dragged her earlobe between his teeth. Then he pressed hot, openmouthed kisses along her neck, sucking on the skin, tasting her. Biting her. It was like he wanted to *devour* her. She panted as pleasure streaked through her, building. Careening toward the precipice.

Then he used a hand to lift the mound of her breast, catching the tip between his lips. He sucked, drawing the nipple into the lush, wet heat of his mouth, as he ground his pelvis against her clitoris. She gasped and her back arched off the bed. The drawing suction was similar to what he'd done between her legs earlier and it only increased her craving. She was burning, aching. Mindless and needy, an animal in heat. "Oh, God," she breathed and rocked up to meet him.

He released her and began thrusting with more force than before. "*Christ.* I am so close." Covering her with his body, he moved quicker, their hands threaded together, his breath hot in her ear. She loved the weight of him, the ferocity with which he worked. The whole time he whispered a stream of compliments about how good she felt, how hot, how perfect. When his teeth sank into the skin between her neck and shoulder, the world disappeared. A climax burned through her veins, searing her. She shook and cried out, dimly aware of Clay's own grunts as the pleasure turned her inside out.

Before she'd even stopped trembling, Clay jerked away. Ropes of thick semen landed on her stomach as his hand flew over his shaft, milking it, the lines of his face pulled taut as if he was in pain. One last groan and he finished, her skin coated in his spend.

Harsh exhalations cut the silence, their bodies sweaty and shaken. It was like nothing she'd expected, beyond her wildest dreams. The other times . . . Well, they paled in comparison. Had those men been clumsy lovers? Or did her respect and fondness for Clay make the experience better?

She couldn't say. But if she had her way, this would not be the last time she and Clay slept together.

Clay's eyes opened and he winced as his gaze took in her stomach. "Shit," he muttered before pinching the bridge of his nose with two fingers. "God, I'm sorry, Florence." Without looking at her, he slid off the bed. "Don't move."

Chapter Twelve

Oh, he'd . . . apologized. That was unexpected.

Florence tried not to feel disappointed as cool air rushed over her naked skin. The erotic novels she read talked about cuddling after the act. Snuggles and soft kisses in the warm afterglow. To date, however, such tenderness hadn't been her experience at all. Chester had barely bothered to remove his shoes during their encounters—and Clay had just rushed out as if the room were on fire.

Perhaps she was overromanticizing these interludes. Men supposedly viewed sex as strictly for physical pleasure, not for any emotional connection with a partner. Somehow, she'd scared both her lovers into hurrying through the rendezvous.

You're not happy unless you're causing a stir or the center of everyone's attention.

A lump formed in her throat at the memory of her father's words. Was that how everyone saw her, desperate for affection? Craving the limelight like some stage actress feeding her vanity?

She stared at the closed washroom door and swallowed all these ridiculous feelings and doubts bubbling up inside her. There was no reason to believe any of this was her fault. She'd done nothing wrong. In fact, he was the one who'd left her here, naked and vulnerable, in his bed.

So what was she waiting for, a man to come and save her?

Grabbing the bedclothes, she wiped her skin clean. This was why she must become independent. Relying on others was a foolhardy mistake and guaranteed to fail. Lord knew how long he would leave her here before he returned.

Rising off the bed, she gathered her things and began dressing. She would find a way to put this right. They would return to their business arrangement, and she would prove this changed nothing between them. She could act just as a man would in this situation.

The washroom door finally opened. Now wearing trousers, Clay emerged with a wet cloth in his hand. He frowned at the sight of her and apprehension slithered across her cold skin.

He stopped and ran a hand through his hair. "Should I help you dress, or . . . ?"

She pulled her shift over her head. "I am able to manage."

While she struggled with her corset, he stood frozen, staring off at nothing. His jaw was hard, his eyes vacant. She had no idea of what he was thinking, but she had to get him back on level footing. "Shall we spend an hour on your accounting practices? I have questions about—"

"No."

The word was sharp, final. She blinked at him, her grip on the corset strings tightening. "If you're too busy tonight I could return tomorrow."

"No, not tomorrow. Not next week. You cannot come back."

Cannot come back? Surely he didn't mean it. Her mouth dried out and her tongue grew thick. Still, she forced out, "I don't understand."

"I can't give you any more lessons. This"—he motioned toward the bed—"was a mistake."

"Is this about trust again? Because I thought I explained myself."

"This isn't about trust. It's about you. And me. What happened tonight was a mistake."

She fought the embarrassment currently gathering like a storm in her chest. "You keep saying tonight was a mistake. But you aren't saying *why*."

He dragged a hand down his face, the muscles in his chest and arms bunching. Clay normally appeared so cool and controlled. This was the most rattled she'd ever seen him. "I don't need to provide reasons, Florence. We screwed. It was good. Really good. Now it's over and we shouldn't repeat it."

She sucked in a breath, the pain lancing her insides. Anger was there, too, and she grabbed on to the emotion with both hands, unwilling to let him see the hurt. "Is this how you act with all of your conquests? Treat them like dirt afterward and kick them out?"

He winced. "I don't mean to be cruel. I am trying to explain this to the best of my ability."

"Well, you are doing a terrible job at it."

"I . . ." He blew out a long breath and finally met her eyes. What she saw there surprised her. *Panic.* Clay was . . . scared. Of what? She was about to ask when he said, "When I first agreed to give you lessons, I thought it would be amusing to help Duncan Greene's daughter descend into the darkness of New York's underbelly. I was attracted to you but never thought anything would come of it. Women like you, those of your station, aren't raised for casual liaisons. And I am interested exclusively in casual."

Had she given Clay the impression she wanted a lifelong commitment? Was that why he'd left her in bed? "I am not asking for marriage, Clay."

"I realize that. Even if you were, we both know it's impossible. You're not made for men like me."

Why must you be different? Why can't you fit in?

The familiar questions resurfaced at Clay's rejection. How many times had her mother and father asked her this over the years?

She pushed her disappointment aside for a moment to focus on the future. "What does this have to do with teaching me how to operate a casino? Can't the lessons continue even if our personal relationship does not?"

"No, they can't. You are a distraction I don't need."

A distraction. He saw her as a *distraction*. Not a partner or a colleague. Not a mentee. Not a lover or even a friend. She was a nuisance, a bother.

God, why did that hurt so badly? Her lungs burned with unshed tears, the lump in her throat so large it was hard to breathe. She had always been the outcast, never quite fitting in with her family, but she thought she'd finally found someone who understood her. A place where she'd gained acceptance.

She'd been wrong, apparently. She didn't fit in here, either.

Bending over, she collected more of her clothing off the floor and struggled not to cry.

Poor little society princess.

It was what Justine, her younger sister, said every time Florence complained about feeling like an outsider. *There are people in this city with real problems, life-and-death struggles,* Justine liked to say, *not just hurt feelings.* In other words, keep perspective on what really mattered and *do* something about whatever is bothering you.

Fine. If Clay didn't want her then she wouldn't chase him. She had her pride. Never mind what had occurred in his apartments tonight. She would forget about it—and about him, in time. There were other casinos in the city, other men who were experts on how to operate outside the law. She'd find one and continue on with her plans.

Because she was in charge of her own future. No one else.

She drew on that strength, nurtured it, until her armor was back in place. Straightening, she faced him. "Don't let me keep you. I am able to find my way out."

"No, I should . . ." He looked around as if just realizing where they were. "Help you into a hansom."

"I'd rather you didn't. One of the guards at the door will see me off. I don't need your help any longer."

He bent to snatch his shirt off the floor and threw it over his head. "I know you're angry and I'm sorry. Trust me, you'll thank me later on."

"Trust you?" She gave a bitter laugh as she crossed to the washroom. "Indeed, I'd rather not. I tried it once and didn't care for the results." When she reached the washroom door, she paused. "Please be gone when I come out of here."

And fifteen minutes later, the bedroom was empty.

CLAY SLAPPED THE stack of papers in his palm and narrowed his eyes on the deliveryman. "You shorted me fifteen bottles this week."

The young man, probably not older than twenty or twenty-one, started visibly shaking. "No, Mr. Madden. That can't be right. I double-checked the order myself. Everything was accounted for."

"And yet," Clay said with icy detachment, "we are missing five bottles of rye, four bottles of whiskey, three bottles of burgundy and three bottles of brandy."

"I—I don't know what to say." The young man began backing up toward the door they used as a loading dock. "Bald Jack himself counted it when it came off the truck."

"Is that so? You watched him count every bottle?"

The man's throat worked as he swallowed, his skin gone pale. "No, I didn't but I'd never try to cheat you. Neither would my employer."

"Someone cheated me—and I hate cheaters."

"Whoa, what's going on here?" Jack was now at Clay's side. He reached over and began dragging Clay away from the delivery boy. "No one cheated anyone. There's no reason to get upset."

Clay gritted his teeth. "We are fifteen bottles short."

Jack tossed an envelope of cash to the delivery boy. "We're fine. Thank you for your hard work. We'll see you next week."

"Thank you, Mr. Jack." The young man scurried for his cart, not sparing Clay another look.

"What the hell?" Clay asked.

Jack retreated a few steps and frowned. "Anna needed more booze this week. I gave her the bottles and forgot to mark it down. And I should be asking you what the hell. You just caused that boy to piss his pants in fear."

Frustration and remorse throbbed in his temples. Damn this eternal headache. "Send him an extra fifty with my apologies. I didn't know about Anna."

"That's the last time I let you handle deliveries, at least until Florence Greene returns."

Clay didn't comment, merely turned on his heel and started for the stairs. Heavy footsteps behind him signaled he wasn't alone. Jesus. He hurried in the hopes Jack would give up.

"She is going to return, isn't she?" Jack asked. "It's only been three nights but your mood is worse than a wounded bear's. Not sure how much more we can take around here."

"I don't want to talk about it." At the landing, he headed for his office. His empty office, without delivery boys and nosy partners.

"Too fucking bad. The deliveryman was the last straw. Tell me what's going on with you."

Clay tried to shut the door on Jack, but his friend was quick for a man over two hundred pounds. "Don't bother trying to outrun me," Jack said as he pushed right through. "You should know better by now."

"I have a headache. Can't I drink alone?"

"No." Jack grabbed a bottle from the sideboard along with two glasses. He slapped everything on Clay's desk right before dropping into a chair. "Talk."

Clay sighed and sat down. He hadn't slept since that night with Florence and exhaustion weighed heavily in each part of his body. *You were a prick to her. You hurt her, you goddamn coward.*

Yes, a coward.

Because fucking Florence Greene hadn't been anything like he'd expected. His usual encounters were fun, mutually satisfying. A release and nothing more. But with Florence, he'd actually *felt* something for her. Something deeper, meaningful. A connection no other woman had ever triggered inside him.

And it had scared the ever-loving shit out of him.

He reached for the bourbon. It was his favorite, from a tiny distillery in the mountains of Kentucky. He normally savored it, but not tonight. By the time he was done pouring, the glass was nearly full.

"Why bother with a glass?" Jack muttered.

Clay ignored him and took a long swallow. Perhaps if he drank himself into a stupor, he'd get some rest. Too bad he hated the loss of control that came with being drunk. Plus, overimbibing never solved anything.

Might as well spill the news. "She isn't coming back."

Jack's dark brows rose and he studied Clay's face. "Did something happen?"

Clay tapped his foot on the floor, unable to stay still. With his notoriously soft heart, Jack would be furious over how Clay had treated Florence, even if there was a very good reason for Clay's actions. He'd dodged Jack for two full days to avoid this very conversation.

It hadn't done any good. Clay was on the edge of losing his mind. Perhaps admitting the truth might ease the boulder of guilt lodged between his shoulder blades and allow him to get some sleep.

Trust you? Indeed, I'd rather not. I tried it once and didn't care for the results.

He downed more bourbon. "She snuck into my apartments the other night."

"Yes, I am aware. I'm the one who told Red to open the door for her."

Ah, that explained how she'd gained access to his private quarters. Red was Jack's favorite errand boy at the casino. "Why in the hell did you do that?"

"Because she asked me."

"You know I don't want anyone in there. Ever."

"Did you kick her out?"

"No."

"I see."

"Obviously you don't. I slept with her."

Jack's brows knitted, as if he couldn't understand why Clay was being obtuse. "Yes, that's what I assumed. Though I had thought it would improve your mood."

"Does it seem like it's improved my mood?"

"No. You look like you haven't slept in a week."

Three nights . . . but who was counting? "I told her not to come back."

"Why? I know you hold affection for her. It's obvious whenever she's around."

Clay clenched his jaw. *Affection.* That was a tame word for what he felt for Florence. More like crippling need. Or obsession. Absolutely gobsmacked. He'd stared into her greenish-brown eyes as he slid inside her and something had unlocked in his chest. Emotions he'd thought long burned and buried had come rushing forth, and all he'd been able to think was, *Mine.*

He had to have her again. And again.

He'd never get enough of her.

There was just one problem. She was not the woman for a man like him. Criminals, even wildly successful ones, did not end up with high-society ladies. Though she was rebellious at heart, Florence couldn't change the circumstances of her birth, no more than Clay could change his own. Duncan Greene would slice Clay's throat with a dull, rusty blade before allowing Clay to have Florence.

Years ago, Clay swore never to allow anyone to take his choices away from him. He would remain in control, no one else.

When his family's house was bought out from under them? When they were forced to move into a tenement, thanks to Duncan Greene? Those things had been out of Clay's control. As had been his brother's death, as well as his father's up and leaving one day. Clay would never allow himself to be powerless again.

So, yes. Florence had to stay away. As much as he longed to see her smile, to hear her laugh or to kiss her mouth once more . . . he couldn't. He refused to want something he could never have. It was an exercise in madness.

He looked at Jack, who was watching Clay's internal debate with great interest. "Whatever I feel for her is not the issue. She doesn't belong here."

"Seemed to me like she fit in just fine. And you aren't worried about her reputation. You've never cared for that nonsense. So what really happened?"

"I just told you. I slept with her then ordered her not to come back."

Jack's jaw dropped open, astonishment and disappointment washing over his features. "In that order? Jesus, Clay. Not one for tenderness after the fact, are you?"

Clay poured himself another glass of bourbon, just as tall as the first. "No, I'm not, which is what I'm trying to explain. Women like her, they want promises and jewelry. Rides in the park. Can you actually picture me in a carriage during the fashionable hour?" He snorted.

"Yes, I could see that. You're more comfortable here in the club, that's obvious to anyone, but you won't catch fire in the daylight. And what makes you so certain she wants promises and jewelry? Did you ask her?"

"I don't have to. You know her father, her family's privilege and wealth. We could not be more ill-suited, even for a short-term affair. I'm one slim step ahead of the police, and only because I pay them so well."

Jack scratched his jaw while he appeared to consider his answer. Clay suspected he wouldn't like it, but he valued Jack's counsel. Always had. Jack's life hadn't been an easy one, but he was intelligent and levelheaded. He wasn't good with numbers, but he was excellent at reading people and knowing how to look at a problem from all sides. It was what made them successful partners.

"You think you aren't good enough for her."

"That's absurd," Clay said weakly. He rubbed his eyes. He couldn't even compose a proper argument, he was so dashed tired.

"No, that's it. You believe you're a black-hearted criminal and she's an uptown angel. You've placed the two of you in those ledger columns of yours and come to the conclusion they don't add up."

"Are you saying we do? The idea is ridiculous."

"I'm saying you're underestimating her. She's trying to open a casino, Clay. She's more criminal than society princess. And you have your ambitions beyond the Bronze House and our enterprise. People are not one thing or another. People are layered. They also change, adapt. Not to mention, you've made a lot of assumptions about her. Something tells me Florence wouldn't care for your conclusions."

No, Jack was wrong. Fundamentally, people remained the same. Though Florence wished to open a casino, she was a lady underneath the rebellion, along with the trappings that went with her status. Clay wasn't a gentleman, hadn't the first clue on what that entailed. He lived in a world of intimidation and revenge, pain and bribery.

"Furthermore," Jack said, "you're acting as if she wanted to marry you. Did she say something to imply it was more than the one night?"

Clay shook his head. "But you know how women like her think—"

"I'm hearing you say what she thinks, but that's guesswork on our parts. I'd rather hear why you needed to push her away."

"I just explained why. Were you not listening?"

"Oh, indeed. I was listening. What I heard was a handful of excuses, not the truth." Jack leaned over and poured bourbon into his glass. Picking up the crystal, he rose and stared down at Clay. "Which leads me to conclude that Miss Greene has gotten under your skin, so far under your skin it scared you. Am I right?"

Yes. "Do not try to romanticize this."

Jack lifted his glass in a toast. "Why would I bother, when you're doing such a damn fine job of it yourself?" With that, Jack started out of the room, whistling the whole way.

Chapter Thirteen

Florence handed a stack of coins to the driver, who took the money and glanced around, his eyes darting nervously. She understood. Her nerves were dancing, as well. There was a chance this would be the stupidest thing she'd ever done.

But she had no choice.

You are a distraction I don't need.

She swallowed the lump threatening to choke her. Clay didn't want her around and she had to move on, find someone else to help her. She wasn't giving up on her dreams merely because a surly casino owner no longer wished to help her.

Another man in New York City could teach her. One who ran as many, if not more, casinos, poolrooms and policy shops than Clayton Madden. Granted, most were on the rough side, places where violence occurred nightly. But this man ran gaming establishments and could answer all her questions. If she could convince him to see her, of course.

"Miss, I don't feel right leaving you in this neighborhood at this hour," the driver said. "Maybe you should let me take you back uptown."

"I appreciate the concern, sir," she said. "But I'll be fine. I am not going far, just down that street." She pointed.

"But, miss," the driver whispered. "That's where—"

"I know all about it. I swear, I'll be careful. Thank you for the concern." She slipped him an extra coin. "Good night."

Lifting her skirts, she stepped around the horse and off the curb. A dead animal lay in the middle of the street, rolled over by some cart or carriage, and she gave it a wide berth. Night had long fallen in the city, the revelry downtown in full swing. Taverns and saloons were crammed with sailors and dockworkers, tradesmen and students. They would drink all night, fights and liaisons spilling into the streets in the wee hours.

Florence wasn't headed to a tavern or a saloon, however. Her destination was the New Belfast Athletic Club, Mr. Mulligan's headquarters.

Mulligan owned Donnelly's saloon and gaming operation, the place that had accused Florence of cheating. *He's likely the only person in the city who knows as much about gaming as I do.* High praise coming from Clay, who wasn't one to pay false compliments. No, he was more likely to bed you then send you packing.

She shoved all those memories aside, far down into the dark pit with all her other unpleasant thoughts. There were more important things right now. Like convincing Mulligan to help her.

Two guards flanked the door to the club, their expressions grim in the yellow gaslight. They eyed her warily as she approached, her head covered by a thick cloak. She hadn't worn expensive fabrics tonight, but her outfit wasn't shabby, either. No doubt she stood out as a curiosity in the gloom.

"Good evening." She came to a stop in front of the doors. "I wish to see Mr. Mulligan."

One guard snorted and returned his gaze to the street. The other guard frowned heavily at her. "He's got no need of servicing tonight. Move along, dove."

Servicing? They thought she was . . . ? *Oh.* "No, you misunderstand. I wish to hire him."

Both men snickered. "I bet you do. He don't do it for money, either. Now, get out of here or—"

"This is not related to sexual favors," she snapped, and both young men straightened, their brows shooting high. Unclear whether the words or her tone surprised them, but at least she had their attention now. "Tell him I'm the one Donnelly accused of cheating the other night. He'll know who I am." She prayed that was true. After all, Bald Jack had sent Clay's regards on to Mulligan. Surely the message had been passed along, right?

The guards exchanged looks. Probably deciding if she was telling the truth or not. One finally nodded and crossed his arms. The other guard slid between the doors and disappeared inside the club.

Florence checked over her shoulders. She hadn't expected to be left standing on the stoop, exposed, while awaiting an audience with the kingpin. Thank goodness she kept a pistol in her tiny handbag for sojourns downtown. To date, she'd never had to use it, but carrying the weapon gave her a small bit of reassurance.

Sooner than expected the other guard returned. He held open the door. "Come along, miss."

Ignoring the fluttering in her belly, she climbed up the small steps and entered the club. The inside was huge, much larger than it appeared from the outside. Noise assaulted her, from the jeers and calls of the men watching a boxing match, to the music and laughter coming from the rear of the building. Was there a dance hall back there?

The guard veered away from that noise and led her to a staircase off to the side. They climbed two sets of ornate stairs, the walls decorated with green-and-white-striped paper. Eastern carpets lined the floors, cushioning her footfalls. Brass sconces on the walls and a fancy gasolier overhead lit the way. Quite a contrast to the Bronze House's sparse inner sanctum.

The young man arrived at an oak door. He knocked twice.

"Enter!" a deep voice called from within.

The guard flung open the door, then stood aside to let her pass. Gripping her hands tightly, she entered the room, unsure of what she might find. What did a criminal kingpin look like? Did he have a desk resting on illegal stacks of money? Or was it worn and practical, like Clay's?

Stop thinking about Clay.

A man rose from behind a huge ornate desk littered with papers. Not overly tall, he was sharply dressed, with a bespoke navy suit and green silk vest that had to cost a fortune. Gold watch fob and polished shoes. Goodness, he was handsome, with wavy dark hair and blue eyes. And young. Was he even over thirty?

She hadn't expected any of this. By reputation, Mulligan was a hardened criminal who ate enemies for breakfast. The man in front of her could pay afternoon calls on Fifth Avenue.

She lowered the hood of her cloak. The young guard sucked in a breath and Mulligan seemed to freeze in his tracks. She patted her cheeks and smoothed her hair. Was there something wrong with her appearance?

Mulligan quickly recovered and approached. "I understand you are the woman caught counting cards inside Donnelly's saloon the other night."

"I was not counting cards."

Mulligan jerked his chin to the guard, who tipped his derby and disappeared. The door clicked shut. Florence focused on her breathing, trying not to show her trepidation.

Show no fear until you feel no fear.

He bowed at the waist. "Enchanté, Miss Greene."

Her jaw dropped. "You know who I am." And he spoke French?

"I make it a habit to know things. May I?" He held out his hand, ready to escort her, as his other hand gestured toward the chair.

She placed her hand in his and he assisted her to the empty seat. When she was settled, he walked around his desk and dropped into the wide leather chair.

Who was this criminal with the manners of a courtier and the looks of an Adonis?

Shaking off her thoughts, she said, "But I never told them my name."

"Do you honestly believe I wouldn't try to learn the name of the uptown beauty being tutored by Clayton Madden? That is like dangling a red cape in front of a bull, Miss Greene."

"Then you might as well call me Florence."

The edge of his mouth hitched, softening his features, and she knew that smile must drive the ladies out of their minds. "Florence it is. Most people just call me Mulligan." He folded his hands. "Would you care for a drink?"

"No, thank you." She had no idea where to start. He reclined in his chair and waited patiently, seeming as if he had all the time in the world. She cleared her throat. "I appreciate you seeing me."

"Curiosity is one of my weaknesses. I can't imagine why a woman such as yourself would come down to my club in the middle of the night, especially seeing as how you usually spend your time at the Bronze House."

She took a deep breath for courage. "I wish to hire you."

"Yes, the boys mentioned as much. May I ask for what?"

Did anything rattle this man? He reminded her of Clay, both calm and methodical men. *Stop thinking of Clay.* "I wish to open a casino. For ladies.

And I need someone to help me learn the business side of things."

Mulligan's eyes sparkled as if he was amused. "Hence why Clayton Madden was tutoring you. May I ask what happened?"

"What do you mean?"

"With Clay. I realize he's a prickly bastard, generally hates people and likes to be alone. But I cannot imagine he hated you."

Wrong. He hadn't wanted her around. However, she couldn't tell Mulligan that. "It seemed he was too busy and couldn't spare the time."

Mulligan's brows knitted as he studied her. "Are you pulling my leg? He couldn't spare the time for *you*?"

"So it seems. Now, I'd be willing to pay you for your time—"

Mulligan sat forward and waved his hand. "I have more money than I'll ever spend. Clayton said what, exactly?"

"That I was a distraction he didn't need." Why was Mulligan hammering the point home? She felt terrible enough after Clay's dismissal. "It's understandable. I learned quite a lot from him, but it was time for the arrangement to end." Because he'd acted like a prickly bastard, as Mulligan had described.

Except . . . there had been a point when he hadn't acted prickly at all. He'd been tender. And sweet.

You want a bit of trouble, princess? Here I am. And I promise I'll give it to you anytime you like.

What a lie.

He'd practically run out the door to get away from her. And he'd *apologized.* The whole thing was utterly mortifying and infuriating.

Mulligan watched her with a strange expression on his face, as if he could see every thought in her head. She shifted in her chair. "Clayton taught me about the games and how to spot cheaters. Now I'm mostly interested in the accounting side of things."

"Were you there the night he was raided?"

"Um, yes. I was there." Why was Mulligan interested in the raid?

"He's got the tunnel going under his club to the brothel, correct? He got the idea from me. There's a system of tunnels in this part of town. Places where the coppers can't go. That didn't scare you off? The raid, I mean."

"No." She thought back to the brothel and how uninhibited she'd been with Clay, how erotic the experience had been. Her skin heated, a condition Mulligan couldn't have missed thanks to her pale skin. "Why would it?"

"Interesting. I think you're tougher than you appear, Florence Greene." He leaned forward and folded his arms on the desk. "And I'll help you for however long you wish."

CLAY HANDED HIS ticket to the attendant and pushed through the turnstile. The Polo Grounds had been finished only last year, replacing the old stadium that now sat directly behind it. A gorgeous ballpark, the Polo Grounds was home to the New York Giants.

Baseball had been one of the few pleasures during Clay's boyhood. In those days kids hung around and watched games without a ticket. The young boys gathered on the hills around the Union Grounds in Brooklyn and peered down at those fast and powerful men on the field while screaming and cheering for their favorite teams.

Clay had taken bets on the games, of course. He'd never been one to pass up an opportunity for a buck. The majority of his youth consisted of hustling to make money, to keep a roof over his and his mother's head. Lying, cheating, stealing . . . Any scruples he'd been born with were quickly shed when they lost everything.

Nowadays, he rarely left the Bronze House, except for the occasional baseball game. A bonus? The crowded public setting happened to make for excellent meeting spots in neutral territory. Some vermin were too diseased to cross the Bronze House's threshold.

Today's game promised to be a corker. Men hurried toward their seats, anxious to see the action on the field as the play had started moments ago. Clay took his time. He loved the atmosphere of the park, the gathering of hometown residents to cheer on their team. The sense of belonging to something greater than yourself. It gave one hope in mankind.

He wondered if Florence had ever been to a game.

Is this how you act with all of your conquests? Treat them like dirt afterward and kick them out?

She now wanted nothing to do with him, which was by design. He'd pushed her away, told her not to come back. So her absence should've come as a relief. The extra time had been devoted to work, and the enterprise's bookkeeping had never been in better shape.

Except he was miserable. Sitting at his desk like a machine, calculating and writing, a damn ache in his chest that wouldn't go away. Almost a week and he still looked up at the office door each time it opened, hoping that she'd returned.

Wasn't distance supposed to help? Shouldn't his dreams center on someone else now that she'd left? He hoped these emotions ended soon. Not sure how much longer he could take missing her.

You're glorious, Clay.

He swallowed hard. They couldn't have a relationship. The idea was ludicrous. She was bright and pure, a sheltered angel that needn't associate with downtown scum such as himself. Someday she'd thank him for setting her on a different path.

He purchased a bag of peanuts and made his way to his seat along the first-base side. A large pair of shoulders blocked his view. "Peanut?"

Big Bill turned around, his mustached lip curled into a snarl. "You're late."

"Game's just started."

"I've been waiting almost thirty minutes on you."

He didn't owe Bill an explanation. He didn't owe this man a damn thing. "What do you want, Bill?"

"I want you to call off the bank. I can't lose my house. My wife and kids live there, Madden. My *mother.*"

"I heard the wife kicked you out. Tough break."

"All your doing, you bastard," Bill snarled. "You have ruined my life, all because I dared to get what was mine."

"Wrong. You tried to blackmail me then had my club raided. You crossed a line. Your chance to negotiate is over."

"You have no proof I was involved in that raid."

"I don't need proof. I know the coppers involved, all guys under you. They didn't stay long, just busted up the place and ran."

"You've made enemies, Madden. Any number of people could've been responsible."

True, but in this case only Bill was responsible. "I'm going to bury you, Bill. So deep that a patrolman in Queens will think twice before breathing my name."

"You can't do that," Bill sputtered. "I am the second-in-command. You cannot take me down. Every copper in the city'll have it out for you."

One of the Giants hit a single up the middle and the crowd roared its approval. Clay cracked another shell and popped the raw peanut into his mouth. Maybe he'd get some popcorn next.

"Did you hear what I said?" Bill shifted in his seat. "If you try to hurt me, you won't get away with it."

"Maybe, maybe not. However, I'm not the only one with enemies in this town. I don't think many would shed a tear over your downfall."

"Speaking of enemies, I wonder what Duncan Greene would think about what you've been doing with his daughter."

Clay froze, though he tried not to give any outward reaction. How had Bill learned of Florence's visits to the Bronze House? "You're mistaken. I've had no contact with any of Greene's daughters."

"You're a bad liar, Madden. Word's already gotten around about you and the middle daughter. Your staff has been talking."

Not a chance in hell. The staff was unfailingly loyal. He would bet his life that Bill had bribed someone to watch the door to see who went in and out of the club, the prick. Besides, Florence was never returning to the Bronze House. "You're going to look like a clown if you try to sell Greene on that story."

"We'll see about that." Bill hefted his large frame out of the chair. "Call off the bank . . . or I'll pay a visit to Duncan Greene myself."

Clay tossed an empty peanut shell on the ground. "Good luck with the move."

"Fuck you," Bill growled and stomped up the stands.

Ten minutes later, Jack slid into the seat next to Clay. "How'd it go?"

Clay handed over the half-eaten bag of nuts. "As expected."

Jack chuckled and reached in the bag for a handful of peanuts. "That must've been fun."

"He knows about Florence. Visiting the club, I mean. Threatened to tell Greene."

"Jesus. Think he'll follow through?"

Bill may have insinuated something between Florence and Clay but he didn't have proof. Still, no one ever said Bill was smart. "Hard to say."

The crowd cheered as a third strike ended the inning. Clay put two fingers to his mouth and whistled loudly. When the stadium quieted, he said, "Doesn't matter. Florence isn't coming back to the Bronze House. Any talk is speculation. There's no evidence she's ever been inside."

"True. Even if he's having the place watched, the witness could've been mistaken."

"Exactly. I told him he was cracked."

"It's sweet that you're still trying to protect her."

Clay grunted but didn't deny it. He crushed another shell. "Didn't we talk about romanticizing this?"

"We did, but I didn't listen. Good thing, because if I hadn't romanticized it then I wouldn't be able to tell you who she's now approached for lessons."

Clay's entire body locked up as his muscles seized in surprise. Florence had gone to someone else for lessons? *Christ Almighty.* The news was like a punch to the gut. "Who?" Jack paused for effect, his lips pursed. He was enjoying this. Clay leaned in. "Tell me now or I swear—"

"Word is that she's gone to Mulligan."

Clay shot to his feet, the bag of peanuts forgotten on the ground. He was out of the row and climbing the steps toward the exit in a flash. Had she lost her mind? She could be killed merely walking down the street to Mulligan's club, let alone what might happen after she crossed the threshold.

"Wait up," Jack called. "You can't mean to go and see him alone."

"I don't need a nanny." He reached the corridor and started for the turnstiles. "Mulligan won't hurt me."

"I wish I shared your confidence. You two haven't always seen eye to eye."

"That was business. This is personal."

"Which makes it worse." Jack grabbed Clay's arm and pulled him to a stop. "Clay, think. Mulligan isn't just going to hand her over. He'll demand something in exchange."

Clay swallowed. Jack was right but Clay didn't care. "Then I'll give him whatever he wants. Anything to get her out of there."

A smile spread over Jack's face. "Go and get her."

Chapter Fourteen

The carriage ride took forever. Clay was nearly frothing at the mouth by the time he reached Great Jones Street. The sun had just fallen behind the buildings as he started toward Mulligan's club, the long shadows giving cover to illicit activities of all sorts along the way.

The two guards at the door perked up at his approach. They were babes, no more than twenty, likely armed. Clay paid them absolutely no mind as he started up the steps. "Wait," one of the guards called. "You can't just—"

Clay brushed by him and flung open the door. The other guard reached out to grab his arm but Clay shook him off. What was Mulligan thinking, putting puppies on guard duty?

He'd been to the New Belfast Athletic Club a few times. Always at night and never for more than a quick meeting with Mulligan. Their business had overlapped in various places over the past decade, and it was a constant push-pull to stay in each other's good graces. Clay had ceded most of the downtown gaming to Mulligan in the past two years, as he preferred to fleece fancy uptown patrons instead.

He took the stairs to Mulligan's office two at a time. The guards were hot on his heels, calling after him and shouting for additional help. No doubt some men from the boxing area were joining the fun.

They wouldn't catch Clay, not before he made it to Mulligan's office.

He threw open the heavy oak door protecting Mulligan's inner sanctum. A pistol greeted him on the other side, the barrel pointed directly in his face.

Halting, he waited, his chest heaving. Mulligan's hard expression quickly turned to one of amusement and he lowered the pistol. "I've been expecting you, Clayton. Come in."

A group of young men skidded and careened into the doorway like hounds on a foxhunt. Voices barked out in unison. "Sir!" "Mulligan." "Ho!"

Mulligan put up a hand. "It's all right, boys. I've been expecting him."

The hounds cast disapproving glances at Clay. They drifted off, grumbling. One of the guards from the front door lingered, however. "Want me to stay?"

Mulligan walked over and clapped the boy on the shoulder. "I'll be fine. Clay and I have business to discuss. Try to stop anyone else from getting past you, eh?"

The guard apologized and left, but Clay was too agitated to pay attention. He dropped into the chair opposite Mulligan's desk and removed his derby. Irritation echoed in every part of his body.

"Evening, Clay. You're looking well. May I offer you a drink?"

Clay wanted to shake the other man, to demand every bit of information regarding Florence, but that wasn't how these things were done. Though they were thugs to the outside world, from the inside their meetings were very civilized. "Bourbon, if you have it."

"Of course."

Sounds of glasses and pouring followed, and soon Mulligan was handing Clay a drink. "Thank you," Clay murmured.

"How are things uptown?" Mulligan dropped into his large leather chair, a glass of beer in his hand. "I hear business is good."

"Indeed, it is. You'd be amazed at how easily some of those fools risk their inheritances." He forced himself to sip the bourbon, when he wanted to throw the glass against the wall. "I've heard you're expanding into the beer business." He tipped his chin at the pilsner in Mulligan's hand.

"I am. Found a damn good brewer. He's a genius with malt and hops. You should take some of it with you for the club."

"Thank you. I'd like that."

Mulligan sipped his beer then placed the glass on a tiny metal platter. "My pleasure. Now, tell me what brings you downtown on such a fine spring night."

"You know why I'm here."

"Yes, but I would love to hear you say it."

Clay stared at the other man and struggled for calm. He had to act reasonably. No one could ever suspect what Florence meant to him. "I understand you've met Miss Greene."

"I have had the pleasure." Mulligan leaned back in his chair. "Remarkable young lady. I predict big things ahead for her."

"How long has she been coming here?"

"Let's see. She showed up three nights ago and has been visiting every evening since then. What can I say? We seemed to hit it off."

Clay's hands curled into fists. Seemed to hit it off? The idea of Florence and Mulligan together made Clay want to smash something. What was Florence thinking? Mulligan didn't have her best interests at heart. He wouldn't protect her and teach her. He wouldn't care for her.

He wouldn't hurt her feelings, either.

True, but Clay would apologize for that the first chance he got.

"I want her back."

Mulligan smiled, not even bothering to hide his amusement. "She's not a toy or a piece of property, Clay. We are talking about a strong-minded woman who has an uncanny ability with cards."

"Let me rephrase that, then. I want you to stop tutoring her."

"Don't see why I should. She's amusing, easy on the eyes. Livens up the place."

The back of Clay's neck tingled, anger sweeping over him. Mulligan was obviously baiting him, but Clay couldn't stop from fantasizing about flipping this desk and punching the other man in the jaw. It would be so fucking satisfying. "You've taken her into the club?"

"Of course. Some of us actually leave our offices. Tonight I plan to take her to a little place I own on Mott Street—"

"Absolutely not," Clay snapped. "The only thing you're going to do is tell her you can't tutor her any longer."

A hard edge crept into Mulligan's gaze, the blue of his irises turning to ice. "Not many have the stones to come into my office and order me around. You may wish to rethink your approach."

Clay exhaled slowly and tried to reclaim some of his sanity. He couldn't outmuscle Mulligan, not on the man's own turf. No, he had to negotiate logically, with a clear head. "What do you want in exchange?"

Mulligan lifted his glass and sipped his beer. "What are you offering?"

"I'll buy a hundred barrels of that beer for the club."

Mulligan snorted. "Don't insult me. By the way, I really like her perfume. It's . . . orange and some spice I can't quite place. Lingers for hours after she—"

"I'll give you the policy shop on Canal."

"The one Paddy O'Murphy runs?"

"Yes."

Mulligan stroked his jaw, his lips twitching. "You must really have your knickers in a bunch over this girl. How low the mighty have fallen."

Clay shoved to his feet. "Don't be a prick. The only reason you agreed to help her was to antagonize me. I am trying to be civil about this."

"Wrong, and you are being a sanctimonious bastard. You ran her off, told her she was a distraction and now you don't like that she's gone to someone else. Too fucking bad, Clayton."

Florence had told Mulligan about her last conversation with Clay? What else did Mulligan know?

"I shouldn't have said that," Clay muttered and ran a hand through his hair. This was humiliating, coming to his rival and having to grovel for access to a woman who'd probably never speak to him again. And Mulligan was loving every minute of it.

"Not certain the girl will care. She seems perfectly happy here, helping me with my books and learning the trade. I have plans for her. And, now that we know she likes men on the rough end of town, I'm going to see if she's amenable—"

Clay didn't think. Fury twisted his brain and he launched himself over the desk at Mulligan. Before the other man could react, Clay had his hands around Mulligan's throat. "Don't you dare touch her," he snarled.

Mulligan sat perfectly still, his expression like granite. "One shout from me brings ten men through that door who will rip you apart. Be very careful in what you do next, Clayton."

"Hard to shout after I tear your throat out," he growled.

Mulligan's features softened, his mouth hitching. "I'll give her back, but I also want to buy into that casino you're building on the east side."

Clay blinked, his grip loosening in his surprise. Mulligan pried Clay's fingers off his neck and smoothed his vest, while Clay dropped down into his chair. "How did you—?" He bit off the idiotic question. Of course Mulligan had learned of Clay's plans for Seventy-Ninth Street.

"I don't want much," Mulligan said. "I'd be an investor, of course."

Clay pinched the bridge of his nose with two fingers. Agreeing to this meant he was giving Mulligan a foothold uptown. Mulligan would use it to try to take over, expand his empire north of Forty-Second Street. Run Clay out of business.

The possibility sat between his shoulder blades like a boulder, pressing down on his spine. Goddamn this city. It was crawling with grifters and thieves, a cesspool of filth and crime from which there was no escape.

Was Clay really expected to go into business with Mulligan and risk his enterprise in return?

He knew the answer. For Florence, yes. He would sell his soul to the devil to get her free of Mulligan. He didn't like it, but what choice did he have?

He shoved aside his frustration and hopelessness. "Fine. It's still a few years off, however."

"I can wait." Mulligan folded his hands behind his head and rocked back in his chair. "You've really got a thing for this girl, haven't you?"

"Don't be ridiculous. I don't want her hurt. It's dangerous for her down here and the last thing any of us needs is Duncan Greene whipping up the police against us as retribution for his daughter."

"Hmm." Mulligan sounded like he didn't believe that, but didn't argue. He stood and came around the desk. Putting his hands in his pockets, he faced Clay. "Seems to me, the last time that woman was hurt was when she was with you. I'll let you speak to her, but the ultimate decision will be hers. If she doesn't wish to go with you, then you'll respect her wishes."

"Fair enough." Clay could convince her. Florence was reckless and pushy, but not unreasonable. "Send a note the next time she returns and I'll come down."

"No need. Give me a few minutes and I'll send her in."

"Wait, she's *here*?" Dark had just fallen. Florence normally hadn't visited the Bronze House until the middle of the night. What was she doing in the Bowery at suppertime?

"She seems to like the place, Clay. Especially the girls in the saloon."

"You let her . . ." He forced out a deep breath. Of course Mulligan let her. He'd given Florence free rein of the place and she'd taken full advantage, her safety be damned. "Tell me where she is."

Mulligan checked his pocket watch. "I don't think so. You stay here. I'll find her and send her up."

FLORENCE SAT IN the tiny dressing room used by the dancing girls to get ready for the stage. The space was a treasure trove of jewels and feathers, cosmetics and silk stockings. She liked to sit and chat as the girls dressed, then go into the saloon to watch the performance. The dancers were clever and funny, four beautiful and bold young women who loved the stage. There was no shame in their risqué routines or the bawdy jokes. They were well paid and protected by Mulligan's men.

All in all, it didn't seem a bad way to make a living as far as Florence could tell.

Here, no one made the girls feel as if they didn't fit in. There was no one judging them. No one saying they were an unwanted distraction.

Just women, dancing on a stage. Making people happy. There was a certain freedom in that, a necessary joy.

She tried to let some of that joy sink inside and cheer her. But it was hard when she was still angry and hurt.

It's been a week already. You have to stop moping. Get over him.

A silk scarf suddenly landed on her head. "And what are you frowning about, Miss Florence?"

Smiling, she removed the fabric and handed it back to Maeve. "Nothing important."

"Hmm. That means a *man*." Maeve sat down next to Florence. "I'm right, aren't I?"

Katie leaned toward the mirror to touch up her lip paint. "I bet he's one of those fancy uptown swells, the kind that ride their big horses in the park."

"And stare down their noses at everyone," another girl said as she rolled on her stockings.

"I never cared for fancy uptown swells," Florence said. "They're . . . boring. And vain."

"Well, you could do a lot worse than Mulligan, if that's who you have your eye on," Katie said. "He's as close to a gentleman as we've got in these parts."

"And an absolute beast in the bedroom from what I hear," another girl said, fanning herself.

"True," Katie said. "I wish he didn't have a rule against screwing the dancers. I'd love to ride him hard."

"My friend Amanda screwed him," Maeve put in. "Said he tongued her for so long that she had to ice her bits afterward. Sore for *days*."

The girls collectively groaned and sighed, a sound of both horror and longing.

"I don't have my eye on Mr. Mulligan," Florence said, stroking an ostrich feather headpiece. "He's just tutoring me."

"Yeah, I wish he'd *tutor* me," Katie said, drily. "At least three or four times a night."

Everyone laughed, including Florence. "I'm serious," she said. "Our arrangement is strictly business."

"Because your heart is already spoken for." Maeve searched Florence's expression. "I've seen that lost look in your eyes over the past few nights. Who was it?"

"Someone I cared for quite a lot, actually. But he told me I was a distraction he didn't need."

"What a rotten bastard," Katie said as she slipped on a wig of red hair. "You're better off. Men are more trouble than they're worth."

"He told me this right after we were, you know, together."

The room erupted in outrage, feminine sputters and shouts filling the air. Something about the reaction soothed Florence. These were women who understood her, women who didn't expect her to mind her manners or watch her words. It was refreshing.

Florence loved her sisters, but they had been brought up with the same Greene legacy hanging over their heads. Mamie was the heir, the one to carry on the family name. Justine was the baby, the do-gooder who was kind and sweet. That left Florence as the irresponsible, shocking one. The sister who disappointed everyone.

"Sweetheart, count your stars you escaped a man like that," Maeve said. "Bed's not even cold and he's treating you that way? Only gets worse from there. Take it from me."

One of the girls shook her head. "I had a man once ask me to get up and make him a sandwich. Sweat hadn't even dried on my skin."

Katie caught Florence's eye in the mirror. "Did you at least get an orgasm or two out of him?"

"Yes, I did." Florence's skin heated at the memory. Clay had been . . . inventive. Dirty. Fun.

"That's the best you can hope for nowadays," Maeve said. "We don't need men half as much as they think we do."

Florence wondered about Maeve's background. She sensed heartache behind the dancer's words and advice. Something they had in common, at least.

A knock sounded at the door and everyone paused. No one was allowed in the dressing room, per Mulligan's orders. He ensured that it was a safe space for the dancers, even from his own crew. "Yes?" Maeve called.

"It's Mulligan. Is Miss Greene in there? I need to speak with her."

"Lucky thing," Katie whispered to Florence before glancing at Maeve. "Please, let him come in."

"Is everyone decent?" Maeve asked around the room. When it was clear each girl was covered, she called, "You may enter."

The door cracked and Mulligan filled the doorway. Hair swept back and perfectly attired, he was quite a striking figure. Florence swore she heard a few sighs from the dancers. "Ladies, bonsoir."

The women offered greetings, while Katie leaned against the table, her robe slipping to reveal a bit of shoulder. "Mr. Mulligan. Good evening."

He ignored all the looks he received and kept his gaze fixed on Florence. "Someone's here to see you."

"Me?" Who in the blue blazes was here for her? A horrible thought occurred. "Is it my father?"

"We should discuss it in the hall."

She didn't care to wait another second to learn who'd tracked her here. Besides, the women had offered unconditional support. "It's all right. You may speak freely."

"It's Madden. He's upstairs in my office."

Maeve sucked in a breath. "Clayton Madden? Is he the one who—" Florence shot her a look and Maeve promptly closed her mouth.

Florence exhaled slowly and tried to calm her racing heart. How had Clay learned of her whereabouts? Furthermore, why was he here? He'd made his position clear the last time she was at the Bronze House. What more was there to say? "I don't wish to see him."

"I think you're going to want to hear him out."

"Why? What did he say?"

Mulligan thrust his hands in his trouser pockets. "I think he wants to apologize."

"Did he tell you that?"

He paused before he said, "Not in so many words."

In other words, no. Clay had no intention of apologizing. Undoubtedly, he'd believed her quest to learn about the casino business would end when he kicked her out. Now he'd discovered her involvement with Jack and didn't like it. Well, too dashed bad. She'd found someone else to help her. She didn't need Clayton Madden any longer. "You may send him away. I have nothing to say to him."

Maeve patted her arm, a sign of female solidarity that Florence appreciated.

"Listen," Mulligan said and held up his hands. "If you don't see him now, he'll only keep coming back, bothering me, until you do."

"You don't have to be alone with him," Katie told Florence. "I'll come with you, if you want."

"Thank you," Florence said, genuinely touched by the offer. She'd met these women only recently. "But that's not necessary. I don't plan on speaking to him ever again."

"Be reasonable, Florence," Mulligan said. "I can't have Madden darkening my doorstep. Please, for me? Hear him out and then get rid of him."

Guilt twisted Florence's stomach. Mulligan had been very kind to her. She could do this one small thing, couldn't she? She'd spend a few minutes with Clay then get rid of him.

But was she ready? Clay had caught her by surprise, coming down here and demanding to see her. Why must she jump to his tune? The great Clayton Madden asked and the world rushed to do his bidding. Well, not Florence. Not anymore.

She'd learned her lesson. She was a distraction to him. A bother. A nuisance. He could wait, as far as she was concerned. Perhaps that would teach him a lesson about how to treat people.

In fact, maybe that lesson needed to include showing him that she no longer cared what he thought. That she was happy, thriving here in Mulligan's care.

And maybe Clay needed to see what he was missing. Namely, her.

Her gaze landed on the colorful skirts hanging on the metal bar. Indeed, all those lessons were definitely in order. "Fine, I'll see him," she told Mulligan. "Tell him that I'll speak to him after the performance."

Maeve asked, "Are you saying . . . ?"

"Yes. Do you have an extra costume for me?"

Katie hooted and Maeve laughed. "Let's get her ready, girls!"

Chapter Fifteen

She needs a moment."

Clay stopped pacing to glare at Mulligan, who'd just come through the door. "What does that mean?"

Mulligan stepped inside the office and thrust his hands deep in his pockets. "She's busy right now. When she's free, you may speak with her."

"Busy doing what?"

"It won't take long. Come with me." Mulligan appeared on the verge of laughing, his mouth twitching, lips pressed together tightly.

Irritation prickled over Clay's skin, tiny bursts of annoyance. "Do I have a choice?"

"No, so stop complaining and follow me."

Mulligan left the room and Clay trailed him into the corridor. They continued toward the back of the building, where a hall led to another set of stairs. Once on the bottom floor Clay could hear the sounds of laughter and talking, the clinking of glass. Were they approaching the saloon?

"I don't have time for a drink," he told Mulligan's back.

"You do, actually."

What did that mean? Before he could ask, Mulligan threw open a door and they ended up inside the saloon. Round wooden tables dotted the floor, men clustered around each one. A stage took up the far end of the room.

"Beer?" Mulligan asked over the noise.

"It seems I have no choice."

Mulligan lifted his hand and signaled to the man behind the bar. Within seconds two glasses of beer arrived, the well-endowed server peering at Mulligan hungrily, as if he were a lobster tail slathered in butter. He didn't return her interest, merely thanked her and turned his attention to Clay. "Next show's about to start. We'll watch while you wait."

"Mulligan," Clay growled. "I want to see Florence. Now."

"Patience, Clay." He propped a shoulder against the wall. "It wouldn't hurt you to relax."

Clay couldn't relax, not while Florence Greene was somewhere on the premises. Had she any idea of the hazards inside this club? Mulligan hadn't risen atop a criminal empire by twiddling his thumbs. He had fingers in all sorts of illegal activity, all of it dangerous and organized under this roof.

Clay studied the men in the audience, the thieves and cutthroats, dockworkers and laborers that made up Mulligan's crew. Had Clay not hustled and schemed to get out of this neighborhood, he might have been one of these men, desperate for a respite from the drudgery of his life. Desperate to see beautiful women reveal their drawers on stage.

Notes from a piano started from somewhere off stage and the crowd cheered. Every eye swiveled to the front, except for Clay. He stared at the beer in his glass and debated how to apologize. She wouldn't be anxious to forgive him, no matter what he told her.

But he'd faced long odds before. He would persevere—

"You might want to look up," Mulligan muttered. "You won't want to miss this."

The girls were coming out on stage. They wore colored skirts that matched their wigs, their lips painted a bright red. Each wore a low-cut bodice with ruffles. He struggled not to sigh with impatience. This was a waste of his—

He froze. One dancer, a girl in a bright orange wig, caught his eye. The curve of her mouth, the sparkle in her eye . . . Fucking hell. He *knew* that curve and that sparkle. It couldn't be her, though. The uptown princess, dancing on stage? She wouldn't dare.

Would she?

Then he remembered this was Florence. Of course she would.

Each dancer thrust a hip out and lifted her skirts to reveal a shapely calf. The men went wild, shouting and pounding their glasses on the tables. He kept his gaze on the woman in orange, captivated by her movements. Every kick and turn, laugh and smile, heated his blood. There was no doubt she was Florence. He had studied her so long and so often, she could wear a disguise in a dark room and he would still recognize her.

Seeing her so happy and vivacious, when he missed her with a debilitating ache, wrecked him. His stomach twisted. How had he ever thought he could let her go?

The truth was he couldn't. This wasn't about rescuing her from Mulligan's clutches. This was about the two of them. He no longer cared about their differing backgrounds. Or about her father. He wanted this remarkable woman for as long as she'd have him. One day, one year . . . It didn't matter.

He wouldn't push her away again. If she forgave him, he'd enjoy whatever time they had together.

The pace picked up and the dancers began kicking in unison, skirts swinging. Florence's eyes met his and he saw the defiance there, the way she dared him to stop her. Yet, he wouldn't dream of it. Trying to control Florence Greene was like holding the wind in your hands. He'd much rather support her than smother her.

And watching her dance, her teasing and flirting, had blood pulsing in his groin, his cock growing thick. She was a surprise at every turn.

"You aren't angry?" Mulligan jerked his chin toward the stage. "I thought you'd run up there and cause a scene. Try to drag her off stage."

He imagined her reaction if he even attempted such a thing. "If you think I could then you don't know her."

"I was right. Knickers in a bunch," Mulligan muttered.

The dance ended and the girls gave the crowd their backs. After a quick flick of their skirts—showing a peek of drawers to the audience—they dashed off the stage. The men clapped wildly, and Clay whistled loudly. "I want to see her. Now."

"I assumed as much. I'll bring her up to my office."

THE DANCERS WERE crammed in the dressing space, trying to catch their breath after the performance, when someone arrived at the door.

This time Florence had expected the knock. Everyone looked at her and she nodded. The sooner she saw Clay the sooner he would leave.

"Yes?" Maeve called.

"I need Florence." It was Mulligan's voice.

"Coming." Taking a handkerchief, Florence blotted beads of sweat off her forehead. She'd never had so much fun in her life. Dancing on the stage was glorious.

And every kick, twirl and twist had been aimed at Clay's cold and bitter heart.

"Are you going to change first?" Katie asked when Florence started for the door.

Florence glanced down at herself. She liked this outfit. Furthermore, she suspected Clay would hate it. "No, I'm going just like this. If he doesn't like the way I'm dressed, then he may kiss my arse." The room broke out in laughter.

"Oh, he'll like it," Katie said.

"Did you see his face when he realized it was Florence?" one of the girls asked. "Like he'd been struck by lightning."

"I thought it was sweet. He couldn't take his eyes off her." Maeve came over and handed Florence her original gown. "Clayton Madden. I can hardly believe it. But don't take him back if he won't treat you right."

Florence smiled and placed her gown on a chair. "No need for concern. I'm not taking him back. I'll return in a moment to change."

She opened the door and found Mulligan there, his shoulder propped against the wall, a glass of beer in his hand. He took in her attire and grinned. "If he screws this up, I feel it necessary to say you are always welcome here, cara mia."

Who would have believed this gangster spoke four languages and was so well-read? Mulligan was a contradiction. Furthermore, he'd been kind to her. "Thank you. I don't intend on leaving, however."

"We'll see. Follow me."

He turned and led her to the back stairs. As they moved through the club, she concentrated on her anger, nursed the hurt, instead of entertaining any nerves over Clay's arrival. Undoubtedly, he planned to lecture her about the danger and impropriety of her presence here, a lecture she had no intention of sitting through. She did not answer to Clayton Madden.

One mistaken evening together didn't give him the right to tell her what to do. Tonight's dance should have proven that. She'd half expected him to jump up on the stage and carry her off. Surprisingly, he hadn't. Instead, his dark eyes had followed her every movement, his expression so intense that shivers had run down her spine.

Almost as if he'd liked her up there.

Which was absurd. He was stuck on her family's name and her father's importance. Status was everything to Clay. *You're not made for men like me.*

Well, she wasn't made for men like Chauncey Livingston, her sister's almost-fiancé, either. High-society men were hopelessly vain and inept. She'd experienced more pleasure in her one night with Clay than with any other man to date. In fact, her pleasure hadn't even occurred to her other partners.

So she'd avoid all men for now. Focus on her future and forget the past. Someday she'd figure out where and with whom she fit.

At the landing, Mulligan swung to the right and continued along the corridor. His office door stood at the end, and her stomach roiled with anticipation and dread. *I have no reason to be nervous. He cannot force me to do anything.*

Mulligan paused at the closed office door. "If you need me, I won't be far."

She nodded, touched at his concern. "I'll be fine." Taking a deep breath, she turned the knob and went inside.

Clay faced her, perfectly attired in his customary black suit. And, despite being prepared, she lost her breath at the sight of him. She couldn't read his expression but he didn't appear angry. His hands were shoved in his trouser pockets, his huge shoulders relaxed. A calm mountain in the middle of the room.

They stared at one another and seconds stretched as neither moved nor spoke. He was every bit as imposing and striking as she recalled, the resulting butterflies in her stomach every bit as intense. She hadn't realized how much she had missed seeing him and talking to him until now. A shame her interest hadn't been returned.

The sound of the door closing behind her jolted her into action. She stepped forward, ready to get this over with. "If you're here to talk me into leaving, you are wasting your time."

"I'm here to apologize."

So Mulligan hadn't been wrong. Still, she wasn't certain she wished to hear it. "Apology accepted. Good evening." With a nod, she spun and lunged for the knob, ready to escape.

"Wait."

The urgency in his voice gave her pause. She slowly turned. "Why?"

"I need you to listen." He raised his hands. "Please, Florence."

She leaned against the door, comforted by the solid wood behind her. "Five minutes, Clay."

"Fair enough. I'm sorry for what I said. All of it, actually. I didn't mean those things and you deserved better."

"Yes, I did. So why did you say it, then?"

"I was caught off guard. I'm not used to . . ." He sighed and ran a hand through his hair. "Not used to someone like you."

Someone like you. The words acted like the strike to a match. Fury burned her skin. They were back to this, the figurative box in which he kept her. "Not used to someone so sheltered or spoiled? Impulsive? Irresponsible? Or maybe disappointing? You may pick one. Or even two. Not to worry, I've heard them all at some point or another."

A crease formed between his brows. "I don't believe you're any of those things."

"You must. You told me to leave and never come back before I'd even dressed."

"I was unnerved, Florence. And that was my problem, not yours. I'm sorry if I made you feel otherwise."

"Unnerved? Why?"

"Sex has always been just sex, in my experience. But you were different. Better. I hadn't expected that."

Oh. He thought her better than the other women in his past. The knot in her chest eased a bit. "You have a dashed funny way of showing it."

"I realize that. At the time, I thought I was doing us both a favor."

"And now?"

"It was a mistake. I took the coward's way out."

She blinked. Something told her Clay didn't often admit to acting like a coward. Her anger dissipated like ice on a hot sidewalk. "What does this mean? You want to continue giving me lessons?"

"Yes, and continue sleeping together."

Desire unwound in her belly, twisting and turning along her veins, despite her best intentions to remain aloof. Their night together had been the best night of her life. Yet, it had also been the worst. She couldn't allow herself to be hurt again. Taking lessons from Clay was one thing; engaging in intimacies was another.

Though it made sense to work with Clay. His casino was exactly the type she wished to open, except hers would be for ladies. Mulligan, while knowledgeable, didn't run the Bronze House. Furthermore, Clay's casino was also a closer journey from her home.

Admit it, you want to spend time with him.

No, this was not personal. It was purely a business decision.

She pushed aside the little voice in her head that whispered she was lying to herself. "I'll return for lessons but nothing more. I cannot sleep with you."

His eyes roamed over her face as he studied her. "May I ask why?"

"It never should have happened in the first place. We should keep things professional between us. That way, no one gets hurt."

"I won't hurt you, Florence."

"You cannot promise that. Even if you did, I wouldn't believe it. You did hurt me, Clay. And I won't risk it a second time."

He started forward, slowly coming toward her, his mouth curved in a small smile. "I'm a man of my word. Once I give a promise, I never break it." He swept his hand under her chin, the backs of his knuckles brushing her skin. "I won't push you. If you tell me there's no hope then I'll never mention anything physical again. But I swear on my life, on everything I own, I won't run from you. I'm at your disposal, for as long as you want me."

Her brain fumbled over the words. It wasn't a proposal of marriage but it was . . . heady. He was offering himself up for whatever length of time she desired. He hadn't said it, but he must care for her. *You were different. Better. I hadn't expected that.*

Still, why didn't he say all this before? Why had it taken him a week? She'd been miserable these past seven days. "What changed your mind? Was it when you heard I'd come downtown to meet with Mulligan?"

"That was when I decided to see you, but I haven't been able to stop thinking about you since the night you left. You're everywhere I turn. Each flip of the card, every roll of the dice. I haven't even allowed them to change my sheets. They still smell of you."

Warmth suffused her body, from her toes to the roots of her hair. She slumped against the door and peeked at him through her lashes. "And here I thought you'd be angry that I danced."

"Quite the contrary. I want to keep you safe but I'm not your father. If you want to show off those spectacular gams to a roomful of strange men, then that's your choice."

"Spectacular?"

His nostrils flared and he put a hand on the wood right next to her head, his big body leaning in. "Fucking spectacular, Florence."

"Did you like my dancing?" Her voice was raspy, needy. Strange to her own ears.

"I loved it." With his free hand, he fingered an orange ringlet by her temple. "I couldn't take my eyes off you."

"I noticed."

"It's not as if I could help it. You are the most beautiful, most radiant woman in any room. Your smile could electrify every street in the city."

Goodness, this man. Her tongue was thick and awkward in her mouth. She licked her lips. "And compliments, too? I hardly know what to say."

"I merely tell the truth." His gaze flickered to her mouth. "May I kiss you?"

Instead of answering, she wrapped her hand around his necktie and pulled him toward her. His head dipped and his lips brushed hers gently once, then again, before he slipped a hand behind her neck to hold her in place. He deepened the kiss, his mouth sealing with hers, their lips drawing and sucking, and she rose up on her toes to get closer, her fingers sinking into his shoulders. Each breath, each sigh, came back at her, returned with equal fervor.

Many minutes later he rested his forehead to hers, both of them panting for breath. "So you'll think about what I said?"

She couldn't remember anything but that kiss, her brain muddled with wanting. His chest was so strong, his shoulders so wide. Her hands slid over his upper half, her fingers trailing over the slopes and ridges. She couldn't stop touching him. "About my dancing?"

"No," he said with a chuckle. "About sleeping together. You'll think it over and let me know if you are interested."

Ah, that. Now she remembered. Her heart raced at the idea, the beat echoing through her blood and centering between her legs. Slickness coated her thighs, her body more than interested.

Could she give in this soon?

"And if you hurt me, you'll hand over the deed to the Bronze House?"

His gaze narrowed, the dark depths dancing. "Is that what I said?"

"You swore on the deed to the Bronze House that you wouldn't hurt me."

"I believe I swore on everything I own that I wouldn't run from you."

"You're splitting hairs again."

He kissed her nose. "I wouldn't dream of it. Fine, the deed is yours if I hurt you."

She leaned in and scraped her teeth along his jaw. "Then what are we waiting for?"

He sucked in a harsh breath. "Now?"

"Had you other plans tonight?"

"Absolutely not." He took her hand and reached for the doorknob.

"I'll meet you downstairs. I need to change first."

He paused then dragged his gaze down her neck and over her bodice. "I like this look. If you're asking me, I'd prefer you leave it on."

"Fancy sleeping with a chorus girl this evening?"

He pulled open the door and tugged her into the corridor. "Only if that chorus girl is you."

Chapter Sixteen

He walked her in the front door.

The Bronze House was already busy. Gentlemen crowded the tables, where chips and dice were flying. Clay led the bewigged Florence into the midst of the action in the casino. No one would recognize her, and they'd reach his bedroom faster this way.

Heads turned but not for long. He knew what they saw, a woman dressed in an orange wig and matching skirt on a man's arm. They'd assume she was his for the night, and they wouldn't be wrong.

Anticipation coiled in his belly. The carriage ride had been pure torture, her body pressed against his for the entire journey. She'd laughed at his discomfort, teasing him. He had promised to make her pay for that teasing when they were alone.

Jack strode over to block their path. "What are you doing?" he snapped at Clay, his expression livid. "Have you lost your—"

"Good evenin' to ya, Jack." She'd adopted an accent, similar to what one heard downtown. Not her polished, genteel tone, but a huskier, rougher sound with longer vowels, and Clay tried to hide his smile.

Jack immediately relaxed when he recognized her features. "Ah, I see. Indeed, this is unexpected but a great relief to all of us at the Bronze House. Welcome, miss."

She looked up at Clay, mischief in her eyes. "A great relief, is it?"

"Don't listen to him," he said. Then he glanced at his partner. "I'm unavailable for the rest of the night."

"Ooo, lucky me," Florence said in her fake voice as she snuggled closer to Clay's side.

"Take good care of her," Jack warned before bowing to Florence. "Enjoy your evening, miss."

Clay took her hand and crossed the floor. The inner corridors of the house were empty, the staff either working in the casino or the kitchens. He and Florence moved quickly, up the stairs and along the halls, until they reached his private sanctum. Withdrawing a key, he unlocked the door to his apartments and ushered her inside.

The fire had been lit, the soft glow leaving enough light for him to see the way to the bedroom. He bent and picked her up, and her arms wound around his neck. "Clay," she sighed against his temple. "Hurry."

Seconds later, he placed her on his bed, coming down atop her. He couldn't be bothered to undress or remove his shoes. He needed to kiss her, right now.

She met his mouth eagerly, her lips parting to wind her tongue with his. He'd never tire of this, of her slick heat and taste, like mint and oranges. He devoured her, the kiss hard and deep. Rough and raw.

Kissing had previously felt like a tame prelude to other activities, a stepping-stone on the way toward getting to a woman's pussy. Florence was different. Kissing her felt necessary, a connection that filled something inside him. He loved the sounds she made, the greedy pulls of her mouth, the bold swipes of her tongue. Her breath against his skin. The way they fit together.

She was absolute perfection.

Her hands skimmed his shoulders, his chest, anywhere she could reach, each gentle sweep like fire on his skin. He was burning for her, his cock aching and hard against the cradle of her thighs, separated from her sex by layers and layers of cloth. Christ, he could weep for all the fabric that must be dealt with before he could fuck her properly. He still wore his coat, for God's sake.

Frustrated, he ripped his mouth from hers. "I might die if I don't get inside you soon." She nipped his jaw with her teeth and slid her hand between them. Then she gave his shaft a squeeze. A shudder went through him as his lids fell closed. "Have mercy, Florence."

She pushed on his shoulder and rolled him onto his back. "Relax. Perhaps I can help you."

With her assistance, he removed his coat. When he tried to get atop her again, she held him down. "Stay there. Or don't you want my help?"

A list of ways she could help at the moment rolled through his mind, none of them suitable for a lady's ear. His conscience wouldn't permit him to corrupt her further. "With my clothes?"

"No, with what's under your clothes." She moved down the bed and reached for his trouser fastenings.

Lust raced through his blood, his cock twitching at the idea of her mouth taking him deep. Distracted at the mental image, he was slow to react as she opened his trousers. "Wait, you don't have to do this. It's not proper for . . ."

The words died on his lips at the withering glare she sent him. "Not proper for your chorus girl?"

He swallowed his complaints. Florence knew her own mind, knew what was best for her. It wasn't an easy thing for him to admit, but he didn't wish to anger her again. He folded his hands behind his head. "Not proper for me to be wearing so much clothing," he said absently as she started on the buttons of his undergarment.

"I see. You could help, you know." She flicked her eyes to his vest.

His fingers flew along the black buttons. He tossed the silk vest to the floor just as she reached into his undergarment to grasp his penis. The touch of her skin to his, hers cool on his burning hot flesh, caused him to groan. He rocked his hips, pressing upward. Begging.

She laughed quietly as she curled over him. He held his breath, muscles locked, as the tip of her tongue touched the smooth head of his cock, licking him. Gasping, he screwed his eyes shut. He'd never last if he watched her.

"It would help," she said, the sultry air from her mouth gusting over his skin, "if you told me what you like. I've never . . . I mean, there's not much opportunity to practice these skills with the other dancers."

Had she done this before? God, the idea that his cock would be the first one inside her mouth made him crazed, like a lunatic on Blackwell's Island. It was barbaric, this sense of possession, but the animal side of his brain relished it. Craved it.

Requesting this was wrong, but he would not treat her like a fragile princess. If she wanted to proceed with this, he only knew how to be himself.

"Suck me," he growled. "Take me in your mouth as deep as you can. Use your tongue, your hand, your lips . . . use them all on my cock."

She apparently liked the words because her gaze went hooded, dark with desire. Was it the power of controlling his pleasure . . . or the way he spoke to her? Those inept uptown lovers had likely used silly euphemisms like "love stick" or "mizzen mast." Loads of "please" and "thank you," along with fumbling in the dark.

Clay had been raised in the streets. Knew every curse word invented, and some others he'd come up with on his own. If a woman didn't care for dirty talk, she was better off bedding a different man.

Florence wrapped her hand around his shaft and angled it toward her mouth. "Yeah, that's it," he encouraged. He thought she might ease into it, tease him a little. Work up the nerve to really get going.

He should have known better.

She opened wide and took him deep on the first pass. Wet, tight heat enveloped him and he threw his head back. "Oh, *fuck*." His legs locked to keep from thrusting into that slick heaven, pleasure coursing through him like sparks. "Christ Jesus, woman."

His reaction must have satisfied her because her eyes were dancing when he regained the ability to focus. She set to her task, sucking and licking him from root to tip, her painted lips working his flesh to perfection. The sight of her bobbing over him, the ridiculous orange wig so out of place, her cheeks hollowing as she moved, was damn erotic. He didn't hurry her, not even when he felt his orgasm gathering steam.

Except, he didn't wish to finish this way.

He levered up and reached for her. In one smooth motion he lifted her on top of him so that her knees straddled his hips. "There's plenty of time later for that. Right now I want inside you."

Moving her skirts out of the way, he found the part in her drawers. She was drenched and hot, ready for him. He inserted a finger into her channel to stretch her. "Show me your breasts," he rasped.

She unfastened the tight, ruffled bodice. When it fell away, she was left in a corset and her shift. He pushed in another finger and she gasped, her hands coming up to cover the mounds of her breasts.

"Keep going, Florence."

She popped open the corset to reveal more skin to his hungry gaze. *I need her now.* He licked the thumb on his free hand and worked it under her skirts until he found her clitoris. The bud was swollen and ripe, and he stroked and circled until she rocked on his fingers, seeking.

"Lift up." He shoved fabric out of the way, positioned her over his cock. Tossing the corset to the ground, she gathered her skirts in her fists and began lowering herself down. He couldn't look away from the sight of her body swallowing the head of his shaft. Gripping him. Squeezing him.

It was torture, the pace at which she took him. He gritted his teeth and dug deep for patience. Her sheath was every bit as snug as he remembered, those slippery walls clamping down on him like a vise. When their hips met, they both moaned, their chests heaving. He couldn't ever remember feeling this vulnerable and powerful with a woman at the same time.

"Oh, God," she wheezed. "It's too much."

He froze. "Am I hurting you?"

She shook her head. "No, I think I'm on the verge of . . ."

Coming? Sweet Mother of God, he was close, as well. Grasping her hips, he showed her how to move to rub that spot high inside her. Her lids fell and she braced her hands on his stomach, rolling her pelvis over his. The friction made him dizzy, her walls surrounding him, massaging him. When she started moving faster, he rubbed her clitoris again, desperate for her to climax first.

Her rhythm soon faltered, so he began thrusting upward, keeping up the pressure, until she quivered around his shaft. Nails dug into his stomach and her body trembled. He watched her face through it all, this flawless creature who humbled him with her adventurous spirit and bold nature. He needed to make her come a thousand more times just to see if her expression changed for each orgasm.

The pressure on his cock overwhelmed him. He was coming then, too, the world exploding in colors all around him, a sky of warmth and light that bathed him in contentment. A respite from his bleak and gloomy thoughts.

She dropped onto his chest and burrowed closer. He was still inside her, his body clinging to the tiny aftershocks of serenity. Real life would intrude soon enough. For now, he had her in his bed and that was all that mattered.

"Happy birthday, my dearest granddaughter."

Florence hugged her grandmother. This evening the entire Greene family was gathering for Easter dinner. They had spent the morning at church then joined nearly all of society in a promenade along Fifth Avenue. It was an excuse for ladies to show off their new hats and Easter dresses, the men their top hats and tails. The tradition was Mama's favorite, one her three daughters were not allowed to miss. "Granny, my birthday is in two days."

"True, but it's never too early to shower my favorite grandchild with love."

"You shouldn't say that. Mamie and Justine may overhear you."

Granny pulled back and patted Florence's cheek. "I would hate to hurt their feelings, though I don't think either of them would be surprised should they learn of my preference."

Probably not. Linking her arm with her grandmother's, Florence started down the corridor. The rest of the family had already settled in the grand salon used for more formal occasions. Florence liked to enjoy a quiet moment with just her grandmother.

The past week had been a flurry of lessons with Clay, sleeping with Clay, lying to her parents and thinking about Clay. In other words, quite busy. "When you first met Grandfather, did you believe your marriage would turn out happily?"

"Heavens, no. The betrothal was arranged by my father and I cried for two days. I fancied myself in love with someone else."

Florence gasped. "I've never heard this story. Who was this young swell thrown aside for Grandfather?"

Granny paused by an oil painting of an English garden. Some renowned artist had painted it but Florence couldn't recall who. "A passing fancy," Granny said. "We would have been miserable together. I never brought it up because I wouldn't like for you girls to fear your own matches. Why do you ask? Has your father set up—?"

"Goodness, no," Florence rushed out. "You know I won't marry any man Daddy finds. If I ever decide to marry I shall find my own husband."

"Yes, so you've said. But there comes an age where the opportunity for marriage passes you by. You shouldn't wait that long. Not to mention your father's patience won't last forever."

A fact she was painfully aware of. To realize her dream, however, she needed Granny's help. Taking a deep breath, she said, "What if I didn't want to get married? What if I wanted to do something else instead?"

Granny's brows dipped as her lips pursed. It was the same perplexed stare she gave to debutantes who didn't know the dance steps. Florence didn't wither or fidget, though. Those were qualities both she and Granny despised. Instead, she waited, her expression patient and calm.

"Like what?"

The time wasn't right. Not here in the corridor with their family milling about. She needed to tell Granny when they were alone and had time to discuss the idea. "I promise I'll come by and tell you one day soon."

"You'd better, seeing as my curiosity is piqued."

Florence leaned over and kissed her grandmother's cheek. "Thank you."

"Now, let's hurry or they'll be worried we got lost."

Smiling, Florence followed her grandmother into the grand salon. Aunts, uncles and cousins relaxed on various pieces of French furniture, while the servants served champagne on silver trays. She hurried to snatch a glass of bubbly before it disappeared.

"There you are," Daddy's voice boomed. "Mother, have a seat. While we have the whole family here tonight, I thought I'd best give everyone some news."

Florence dropped onto the sofa next to Mamie. Her older sister cast her a worried glance just as their grandmother said, "What is this regarding, Duncan?"

"The houses on this block." When the room quieted down he said, "As you've all likely seen tonight, many of the neighboring houses have been purchased and demolished."

"Hard to miss," Uncle Thomas muttered. "Why is this important?"

"I am curious myself, as I've told them I won't sell," Granny said. "What have you learned?"

"A developer has bought up the entire block. Plans have been filed for a club to be built here."

"A club?" Mama asked. "Where, on the corner?"

"No," Duncan said. "They plan to use the entire block."

"That's impossible. I've refused to sell."

"They are planning to build around this house."

Florence's jaw fell open and she heard Mamie suck in a breath. Build around this house? What did that mean?

Everyone began shouting questions and observations, but Florence sat perfectly still, wondering how they planned to accomplish such a feat. This house had been her oasis away from the pressure and conformity of her own family home. And someday it would belong to her.

With a club surrounding it?

Duncan held up his hand. "Quiet down. Thomas, to answer your question, I have a contact at City Hall who told me of the plans."

"Are they able to do that?" Mama asked. "Doesn't your mother or the city have some way to prevent it?"

"Unlikely. There is nothing in the zoning laws to prevent it. In addition, the homeowners on this block have already sold and many have left, so there's no way to pool our resources. This house is the only one remaining."

"This is ridiculous." Granny placed her glass on the side table with a thump, her bracelets clinking together. "They cannot mean to wrap another building around this house like a fur stole. The idea is ludicrous."

"Ludicrous or not," their father said, "the developer is bound and determined to build here. It makes no sense but it's clearly a land grab for someone."

"Who is this developer?" Uncle Thomas asked. "Perhaps we should speak to him."

"I am in the process of discovering the name or names of the people behind the project. You'd best believe I will be paying everyone involved a visit."

"Daddy, your lawyer, Mr. Tripp," Mamie said. "He might be able to come up with a way out of this."

Florence snorted softly. "You could not be more obvious," she muttered. Her sister was in love with Frank Tripp but trying to keep it hidden from the family.

"Shut up," Mamie said out of the side of her mouth.

"I plan to consult him, Marion," her father replied. "We should prepare ourselves for the worst, however."

"Meaning I either live surrounded by some club, with hooligans coming and going at all hours, or lose my home?" Granny practically screeched. "Is that what you are saying?"

"Mother, I'll do everything in my power to prevent it," Duncan said.

Considering her father's indomitable will, Florence thought it likely he would succeed. No one went against Duncan Greene and came out unscathed.

She wondered for the hundredth time this week why Clay hated her father. *What had possibly happened between them?* Clay didn't even know Duncan Greene. Her father had been raised uptown, in this house, in wealth and privilege. Clay had grown up on Delancey Street, which was far downtown. Under no circumstances would their paths have crossed at any point, especially considering her father didn't gamble.

Granny pushed to her feet, the lines in her face deep and tired. "I would like to go up and lie down. You all carry on dinner without me."

"Are you certain, Mother?" Uncle Thomas came forward and took Granny's arm. "Why don't I help you upstairs?"

"I am not infirm, Tom. You may stay here. I'll see myself upstairs." Lifting her skirts, she glided across the floor and over the threshold, where she disappeared into the corridor.

Florence's heart ached for her grandmother. For her family. Not to mention for herself, as this was the loss of a piece of her future. She'd been so quick to dismiss marriage because this house would give her a home, husband or not. If her father couldn't prevent the construction, her plans were even riskier.

"Duncan, what are we going to do?" Mama asked. "Your mother loves this home."

"Our father built this home for her," Thomas said. "We were all raised here. We cannot let anyone take it away from her."

Duncan held up his hand in that way of his that Florence knew meant *stop talking.* "I am aware. I will handle it."

"I almost feel sorry for whoever is behind this development plan," Mamie said under her breath.

Florence couldn't agree more. "Indeed. Whoever he is, he has no idea of the hell he's just unleashed."

Chapter Seventeen

Much later that night Florence lounged against Clay in the bath. Clay's apartments in the Bronze House were humble, clearly a functional space in which he spent little time. His bathroom, however, was decadent in comparison. Designed with white-and-blue tile, the space had gold accents and Italian marble. The rain shower was in a corner of the room, while a huge marble bathtub filled out the center. Florence couldn't imagine the amount of water it took to fill a tub this size, but who was she to complain? It was like floating in a heated clear lake, with a large naked man at her back.

In other words, heaven.

He'd summoned champagne and two glasses from downstairs, as well as some food from the kitchen. At some point she would return home, but at the moment she had everything she needed.

"What were you like as a boy?" she asked. He was such a fascinating man, yet she had no idea about his upbringing. "Other than working in your uncle's saloon."

"There's not much to know. I wasn't that interesting."

"I beg to differ. I bet you were fascinating." She stroked his calf with her bare toes. "For example, do you have siblings? Parents still alive? There's so much about you I don't know."

Muscles shifted as he took a drink of champagne. "No living siblings. My younger brother died of cholera when I was twelve."

"Oh, Clay. I'm sorry."

He pressed a kiss to the top of her head. "Me, too."

"You said you moved to Delancey Street?"

"Yes, when I was almost eleven. Before then we lived on East Seventh Street."

"You and your parents?"

"Yes."

"And are they both alive?"

"Presumably."

She angled back to see his face. "Are you deliberately being vague?"

"I don't like discussing my past. It was a far cry from yours, that's for certain."

"Because my father is wealthy."

"To start with, yes." He dragged a fingertip over the slope of her breast, dipping below the surface to circle her areola. She gave a slight shiver at the gentle touch, her nipple puckering.

"And?"

"And you're from one of the most prestigious families. Servants, cooks, drivers. You're welcomed in the best homes at the most exclusive parties."

While that was all true, there were expectations and pressures to accompany those circumstances. "You make it sound so easy and grand. In reality, it's stifling and boring."

He snorted, his chest pushing her forward. "Nearly everyone in this city would kill to be so bored."

"Not me. I am dying to get out."

"From all of it? I assumed you'd open your ladies' casino but remain behind the scenes. Run it anonymously."

She had considered that option, of course. Owning any business, let alone a casino, would not endear her to the smart set in the city. Even if older society ladies patronized said casino, they would look down on *her* for operating it.

Running the casino anonymously, however, felt wrong. Like she was embarrassed about the endeavor, which she most decidedly was not. And the constant worry of being exposed as the owner would wear her down over time.

She'd still be pretending, trying to fit in.

"I won't hide it," she said. "If people snub me as a result then that is a risk I am willing to take."

"Probably for the best. Keeping the secret would be setting yourself up for a blackmail scheme."

Hmm, she hadn't thought of that. "Spoken like a man who thinks like a criminal."

"Darling, I am a criminal."

"Not in the traditional sense of the word. Besides, gambling should be legal. If people are willing to risk their hard-earned money on games of chance, why are you the one in the wrong?"

"But it is illegal, which means I could go to prison."

"Have you ever been arrested?"

"Plenty of times."

Good God. She leaned out to see his face. "You have?"

"Sure. I've been doing this a long time. If the coppers didn't find you on the streets, the other boys turned you in just to get your racket."

"How did you amass all this, then?" She gestured to the lavish washroom.

"I learned to run fast."

She chuckled and nestled her back into his chest once more. "You make it sound easy."

"Far from it. Nothing about my life has been easy."

She thought about the differences in their backgrounds as she moved her hand in the water and stared at the ripples on the surface. Tiny movements that grew bigger, amplified, every wave connected to the one ahead of it and the one behind it. It reminded her of the choices one makes along their journey that then affect everything else. "Money doesn't automatically provide an easy life."

"Spoken like a woman who has always had it."

"You almost sound resentful."

He exhaled, his breath teasing the back of her neck. "Not of you. Your circumstances are not of your own making. But money does provide comforts and choices. For example, I worked and hustled nearly twenty years of my life to build the Bronze House. You plan to study for a few weeks, perhaps months, and then open your own similar casino. A luxury you can afford, thanks to your father."

"Do you honestly believe my father would back my casino?"

"I assumed you had a trust fund."

"I gain access to the trust fund only when I turn thirty or when I marry."

"Oh." He cupped water in his palm and dribbled it over her shoulders. Tingles followed the path of the droplets on her skin. "How will you afford it, then?" he asked.

"I plan to ask my grandmother for the money. I have to wait, however. Now is not exactly an ideal time to ask."

"Why? Is she ill?"

"No." She hesitated, not wishing to unload her problems on him. But she trusted him. They'd grown close since the night she'd danced on Jack Mulligan's stage. Whatever was happening between them was big and terrifying, but he'd promised not to hurt her and she had to believe that. "There's a chance she may have to sell her home."

"I imagine she has others." The tone of his voice was bored, yet there was something underneath. An unexpected hardness. Was it resentment over her family's wealth?

"She does, but not like this home. My grandfather built it for her when they married. My father and uncle grew up there. She's quite sentimental about it."

"No doubt the money from the sale will soothe any sentimental attachment. The property value must have tripled since it was built."

She frowned. To Clay, everything was about money. But this was more than dollars and cents.

She had to make him understand, to see that life was more than a balance sheet.

Shifting in the water, she angled to see his face. "She wouldn't sell it for a king's ransom, if she had her way. She misses my grandfather and the house reminds her of him daily. Also, she has promised to give the house to me when she passes on."

"To you?"

"It sounds silly, but I've loved that house since I was a child. I spent more time there than my sisters and it became a refuge for me." A place far away from her father's disappointment and her mother's expectations. "I don't know what I would have done without Granny and that big, rambling house."

He said nothing for a moment, then took her shoulders and settled her back against his chest. His arms wound around her, holding her tight. "Won't you marry and find a home with your husband?"

"God, no. I'd rather have my own business than a husband. And if I'm living in my grandmother's house, I can use my trust fund for the casino's operating expenses."

"I had no idea."

"No one does. But Granny's house is critical to my future plans. If she sells it then I will probably end up living atop my casino and becoming a surly recluse."

He grunted at the dig, his burst of air bouncing her on his chest. They sat in easy silence for a few seconds. Water lapped against the side of the tub, the steam curling toward the ceiling. She figured now was as good a time as any to ask the one question standing between them.

"Will you ever tell me the reason why you hate my father?"

"No."

Well, that response left no opening whatsoever. "He's not a bad man. A little intimidating at times but he isn't cruel."

"You'll never change my mind about him."

"Even if I regale you with stories about his support and love as a father? The various charities to which he donates? The time he saved a kitten and brought it home for my sisters and me?"

"None of that will affect the way I feel about Duncan Greene."

"How long have you known him?"

"I don't."

"Clay," she said, her voice rising in frustration. "You are deliberately—"

In one smooth motion, he lifted and twisted her until her thighs straddled his hips. He bent his head and took the tip of her breast into his mouth, and fire swept through her veins. Each suck and swirl on the taut skin caused her core to contract in the most delicious manner. "You're attempting to distract me," she murmured.

"Yes, I am. Is it working?"

His fingers dipped beneath the surface of the water to tease between her legs . . . and she forgot all her questions. For now.

DAYLIGHT BROUGHT A different mood to the Bronze House. It was less elegant, more practical.

Maids and servants bustled throughout, washing off the previous night's debauchery and battening down the hatches for the upcoming revelry. Suppliers and workers were in and out to make deliveries and conduct repairs. Clay spared no expense and paid his people well. Nothing less than the best would do for this shining jewel of vice and sin.

He generally rose at ten or eleven in the morning and dressed. Then he'd sip his coffee and walk through the various rooms of the casino, checking on every nook and cranny. He loved this place.

This morning he lingered a bit longer over his morning routine. He was tired, the late nights with Florence catching up with him. She was worth every yawn and grumble the next day, however. He couldn't get enough of her. Adventuresome and bold, she wasn't afraid of him. She challenged him in unexpected ways, like her willingness to experiment and asking questions about different preferences.

He nodded at a maid as she polished the brass on the main bar. "Good morning, Adeline."

She paused and blinked up at him. "Good morning, sir."

"Very fine work you're doing. Thank you."

"Oh." She cast a wary glance at the railing. "It's my job, sir."

A hand landed on Clay's arm. It was Jack, who'd appeared seemingly out of nowhere. "Yes, very nice work. You may carry on, Adeline." He began towing Clay across the room. When they were out of earshot, he said, "Stop being nice to the staff. It makes everyone nervous."

Clay frowned. "What does that mean?"

They came to a halt. "It means that your mood swings have everyone on tenterhooks around here. We're not used to seeing you smitten."

"I am not smitten," he scoffed. Jack made a face that communicated his skepticism on that statement. Clay decided to leave it alone. Instead, he asked, "Am I not allowed to be moderately happy for even a few days?"

"Neither of us has time for this conversation," Jack said. "Duncan Greene is upstairs in your office."

Christ. Clay's body tightened, every nerve on alert. He'd expected this, only not so soon. "And when were you going to tell me?"

"He just arrived. I was coming to tell you when I found you scaring Adeline."

"No doubt he's learned of the building plans filed with the city."

"No doubt."

If Clay hadn't been holding a china cup he would've rubbed his hands together. God Almighty, he was looking forward to this exchange. "Then I best give him the bad news."

"Want me to come along?"

"That's unnecessary. You have a lot to do and I don't expect this to last long. He'll threaten me and then storm out."

"Well, I'm not far if you need me."

Clay clapped Jack on the shoulder, grateful for this man who always had his back, and then headed for the stairs. Anticipation slithered over his skin. These plans were years in the making, so much blood and sweat. Fighting and scraping. All with one goal in mind: to get his hands on Duncan Greene's childhood home and destroy it.

How do you like having your life upended, Duncan?

It wasn't exactly an eye for an eye. Duncan had considerably more money than the Maddens had at the time they lost their home. The Greenes wouldn't be forced to live in a crowded tenement with rats, bedbugs and disease. Not to mention this wasn't even a house in which Duncan currently resided.

But taking his family home was the vow a young Clay had made all those years ago . . . and he'd be damned if he wasn't going to see it through.

Even if it meant dealing a blow to Florence's future.

Granny's house is critical to my future plans.

Regrettable, but he'd find a way to make it up to her.

He threw open his office door and stepped inside. Duncan had made himself right at home in a chair across from the desk, his large bulk settled as if he belonged there. The other man looked over his shoulder, saw Clay, and remained seated.

Very well, then. No pleasantries.

Clay smothered a smile as he closed the door and strolled toward his desk. Duncan was annoyed, which brought Clay an unbelievable amount of joy. "Mr. Greene." He lowered himself into his office chair and took a sip of his coffee. "To what do I owe the pleasure?"

Duncan's eyes were hard, his expression closed off. He was a big man with a barrel chest, well dressed. He'd spent his boyhood boxing, shooting, playing baseball and riding—basically any physical activity in which rich young men dabbled. He was the picture of wealthy entitlement in a city that rewarded such circumstances.

"You know why I am here."

Clay lifted the cup to his mouth. "Do I?"

"Tell me, Madden. Why Seventy-Ninth Street? You could build anywhere in the city. There are plenty of empty lots, not to mention swampland to be excavated. Yet, you chose this particular block in this particular neighborhood. Why?"

"Perhaps seventy-nine is my favorite number."

Duncan's face didn't change. "Try again."

Clay finished his coffee and carefully set the cup on his desk. "I cannot see how I owe you an explanation regarding my plans."

"You are attempting to build a club-slash-casino around my mother's home, so I would like to know why. Did you honestly think I wouldn't learn who was behind the plans?"

"I never really cared," Clay lied and folded his hands in his lap. "I seem to recall there was one homeowner who wouldn't sell. Was that your mother?"

"You know damn well that it was."

"Why are you here, Greene?"

"Tell me what it will take for you to abandon this plan of yours."

"You don't have enough money to stop me."

"That sounds like a challenge."

"I do relish watching you fail, however. So please, by all means. Try to prevent me."

Duncan shot out of his chair and slapped his palms on Clay's desk. "You stupid bastard. I am not some lowlife thug or two-bit thief you are able to intimidate. I can bury you with one word to the mayor's office."

The threats would have angered Clay if he wasn't enjoying all this so damn much. He slowly pushed back and rose, leaning in to drive his point home. "I own more men in the police department, mayor's office and Tammany Hall than you could ever hope to meet. Own, as in with debts those men could never repay. You cannot stop this, Greene, no more than I was able to stop an arrogant young buck from buying up an entire block on Seventh Street twenty years ago and displacing all the families living there."

Duncan rocked back on his heels slightly, his head cocked. "Seventh Street? Are you . . . Are you saying that yours was one of the families relocated after I built that office building?"

"*Relocated*. What a fancy, college-educated word. I prefer *swindled*."

"That's absurd. I paid fair market value for that land."

"You most certainly did not," Clay sneered. "The families were given a pittance with which to resettle elsewhere. My family ended up in a tenement on Delancey Street, where my younger brother soon died of cholera. So spare me your fair market value."

Duncan dragged his hands through his hair, his eyes wild. "Wait, this is all some revenge plot on your part? Against *me*?"

Clay didn't answer immediately. He retook his seat and shifted to get comfortable. "In case I haven't made myself clear, you cannot prevent me from building on this particular block. Perhaps your mother might wish to invest in some cotton to stuff in her ears. It's likely to be very loud at night."

Duncan's skin darkened to a deep red, a vein popping in his temple. "She is an old woman in her sixties, Madden. Have you no heart?"

"None, Greene. Absolutely none. It was stolen from me at the tender age of eleven when my family was uprooted and destroyed."

"You son of a bitch. If you believe for one second that you've won, you sorely underestimate me. I have more friends in this town—as well as more money—than you do."

"Friends aren't what count in this city. I have spent my life amassing the power and financial resources to destroy your family home. Nothing will stop me from seeing this through."

"You're insane."

"And you are wasting your breath and my time."

Duncan's jaw tightened, his chest heaving. "You have made a very powerful enemy today, Madden."

Clay gave the other man a dark grin. "Wrong. We've been enemies for two decades. You just didn't realize it until today."

Duncan didn't say anything else. He stomped to the door and flung it open, and Clay listened to the other man's steps as he retreated out of the club. That had been a thoroughly satisfying encounter. He had certainly enjoyed it, at least.

Even better, this wouldn't be the last time he faced down Duncan Greene. Clay could hardly wait.

Let the games begin.

Chapter Eighteen

Florence paced the length of her grandmother's petit salon. Her skirts rustled, the silk whispering over the expensive Eastern carpets. This room was one of Granny's favorites. Done in shades of blue and white, the decor was classic French with modern art on the walls. They often took tea in here when just family called.

Learning about the development plans had been hard on Granny, clearly. Easter dinner had carried on without her, though it had been a subdued affair. No one had felt much like chatting after Daddy's news. Her grandmother had already canceled this week's euchre game.

Florence had been worried, so when Granny requested a visit this morning, Florence had hurried over. Now that she was here, anxiety twisted in her chest and the wait seemed like hours. What would Granny do if Daddy couldn't fix this? Would she stay or sell the house after all?

The idea of a sale nauseated Florence. This house represented freedom, choices and opportunities that would be denied her without it. If it was torn down, her future would be altered in ways she couldn't begin to predict.

The sound of her grandmother's charm bracelets alerted Florence to the older woman's approach. She turned toward the door to find Granny sailing over the threshold. "Hello, Granny."

"Florence, there you are. You are a sight for poor, tired eyes." Granny enveloped her in a fierce hug. "I apologize for running off before Easter dinner."

"I understand." They separated and she followed her grandmother to the sofa. "How are you feeling?"

Granny set a stack of papers on the low tea table. "Sad. However, nothing lasts forever. We were one of the first families on this block, and everything has changed so much since those days. It's the march of time, I'm afraid."

"Does that mean you are going to sell?"

Granny sighed as she poured tea for them both. "I don't like the idea of it. You should have this house after I'm gone. It should stay in the family, not become rubble dumped into the harbor. However, I cannot see any alternative."

God, that was depressing. She tried to remain positive. "Daddy may find a way to prevent the project from moving forward. He knows everyone in the city."

"Yes, but even some things are out of your father's control. Though he would never admit it."

"True. He hates when I don't obey him. He says he's stopped trying to understand me."

"It is a daughter's job to give her father gray hairs."

"Then consider me a rousing success," she said drily, causing her grandmother to chuckle. "You had some wild days when you were a debutante, I bet."

Granny's lips compressed as if she might be fighting a grin. "It was different then. Before the city was so built up and organized."

Florence hummed as she sipped her tea. "I will pry those stories out of you someday."

"I shouldn't. Your father would have my head if I encouraged any more recklessness out of you girls."

Unlikely. The Greene sisters needed no encouragement whatsoever when it came to recklessness. "I won't tell him."

"Perhaps someday, then. Today we are here to discuss you. I thought you might tell me your idea, the one you wish to pursue in lieu of marriage."

Florence watched the tea leaves circle in the bottom of her cup and pondered on how to proceed. What if her grandmother said no? There was no alternative plan, so if Florence bungled this then a casino might be out of reach.

No fear. Show confidence until you feel it.

Palms gone damp, Florence set her cup on the table. "I wish to open a casino just for ladies."

Granny's brows shot up and her lips parted in surprise. Florence remained still and let the information settle. No need to rush in and overwhelm her grandmother with reasons and ideas. That would come later.

Her grandmother collected herself after a few long seconds. "A casino for women?"

"Yes."

"Gambling is illegal."

"Says the woman who hosts a weekly cutthroat euchre game for jewels."

Granny waved this off with an elegant twist of her wrist. "But those are just for friends. You are talking about going into business for yourself. As a casino owner."

"That's correct."

"Forget what your father will say, you must know what this means for your matrimonial prospects."

"I am aware. I do not expect to have any prospects, which is perfectly fine."

"You could keep your involvement in this venture a secret." Granny's shrewd gaze took in Florence's face. "But I am gathering you do not care for that idea."

"I want to do it. I think I'll be quite good at it, actually."

"But, Florence." Her grandmother set her cup down. "This means more than having a space where women can gather and play cards. This means shaking down people who owe you money and punishing the cheaters. It's not a noble profession."

"Only because gambling is illegal. If it were legal no one would look down on owning a casino."

"I think you're wrong, but let's move on from that argument. How would you even know what to do? It takes a huge amount of time to learn the various games and how to run them. Doing the books and managing employees. I cannot even begin to think of all the details—and I plan the Forsythia Ball each year. Let me tell you, there are always complications you don't foresee."

"You're right, it is a huge effort. But I've been studying for almost a year. I know all the games and how they work. And, for the past month or so, I have apprenticed with a casino owner. He's shown me—"

"Apprenticed! Goodness, you are serious."

"Very serious, Granny. I go late at night when the casino is open so that I may see how it runs."

"That must be tremendous fun. I don't suppose your father knows about this."

"No, absolutely not. He would lock me in my room if he found out."

"You are not wrong. He may never understand your reasons for wanting to do this. Are you willing to sever a relationship with him, possibly permanently?"

This was one of the things she loved about her grandmother, the ability to see things from all sides. A quality Florence wished that her father possessed. "I believe he'll come around."

Granny chuckled. "I wouldn't bet on that, pun intended."

"Wouldn't you like to have a place to go where you and your friends could play roulette or craps? That's all I am attempting to do. Why should men have all the fun?"

"Indeed, I have long said the same. Yet, our world remains conservative, despite the protests happening downtown. Are you not worried about the police or City Hall shutting you down?"

Florence thought of Clay and Big Bill. The mayor's chamberlain. "There are ways around that."

"I sense there's nothing I can say to dissuade you." Granny refilled her teacup and added sugar before stirring. "So are you interested in my blessing?"

Florence exhaled slowly. *Here we go.* "I am hoping you will come on as an investor."

Her grandmother had the most unexpected reaction: she burst out laughing. Florence tried not to fidget while she waited. Had this been the wrong approach? She'd never asked anyone for money like this before. Perhaps she should have written her plan on paper, given her grandmother some concrete figures on the amount required.

"Oh, you are too much, Florence. I hadn't expected you to ask for my help."

Florence's stomach plummeted. Her future loomed like a dark hole of living at home, attending the same society parties and balls with the same people at the same time of year. Same, same, same. How would she survive it?

No, you will find a way. Even if Granny refuses, you will find a way.

"That's fine, Granny. I understand. This is a lot to ask—"

"I never said no. You merely caught me by surprise. When are you thinking of carrying through with this plan?"

"Daddy is anxious for Mamie to marry, so once she is settled he will undoubtedly turn his attention to me. I have a short amount of time, perhaps a year. Maybe more."

"Let me think on it, then. I am neither agreeing nor am I refusing. But this does deserve more careful consideration."

"Oh, I have. Given it careful consideration, I mean."

"Yes, but I have not. So allow me to sit with my thoughts and I shall give you an answer soon." She edged forward on the sofa to retrieve the papers on the table. "Do me a favor, will you? Give these papers to your father."

Florence accepted the stack. "Of course. Are they about the building development?"

"I couldn't say. I haven't opened any of the letters sent here in the past few months that appeared remotely related to this building development. That is everything I have, so let your father sort through it. Perhaps he'll find something useful."

"All right, I will. I shall keep my fingers crossed."

"Me, too. I want to see my great-grandchildren raised in this house." Granny gave her a pointed glance. "Even if their mother runs a casino."

"I know you do. Though I don't think any of the neighbors will invite me over for tea." They both knew society would turn its back on her if she followed through on her dream.

"Good thing there are no neighbors left, then."

The grim reminder caused Florence to wince over her previous choice of words. "I'm sorry."

"No apologies necessary. We mustn't hide from the truth. Now, run along. I've got ten ladies coming in a few minutes to discuss the guest list for the ball."

Florence rose and went over to kiss her grandmother's cheek. "Thank you for hearing me out. Take heart. If you do sell the house then you may always move in with us up the street."

"Me, live with your father? I love him dearly, but no thank you."

Some days, Florence felt the same way.

CLAY STARED AT the blond head angled over the ledgers spread over his desk. He then considered other things he might soon spread over his desk, and his body reacted swiftly. Heart pumping, blood racing. His palms itched to feel her soft skin and make her moan. Florence had arrived only an hour ago and he was already thoroughly distracted with the want of her.

You're acting like a fool over this woman.

True, but it was a state he had no control over in her presence. He liked everything about Florence, from her angelic looks and heart-stopping smile to her quick wit and sharp mind. She was passionate and fearless in bed. He held nothing back from her—a first for him. With others, he'd been afraid of scaring his partners, of being too demanding. Florence made him *burn*, so hot that he lost himself in the moment. And she didn't seem to mind. Quite the opposite, in fact.

So would she hate him when she learned of what he'd done?

She couldn't blame him, could she? After all, he'd warned her. Jack had begged him to call off the plans for the Seventy-Ninth Street casino, but Clay would not be deterred. His revenge against Duncan was twenty years in the making. A few blissful weeks in bed with Duncan's daughter could not change that.

He wouldn't allow it.

Besides, nothing good lasted long, especially something this good. All he could do was bide his time and enjoy each second with her. Wring every sigh and moan out of her body until it came crashing down and she despised him. To that end, he glanced at the clock. Soon. He would have her in bed, naked, very, very soon.

Christ, he could hardly wait.

"Have you found the error?" he asked, ready to move tonight's lesson along.

"I think so." She lifted her head and blinked at him. As it nearly always did, her beauty struck him like a blow to the chest. Perfect features, slashing brows, full lips. He could stare at her for hours and never tire of it.

"Show me." He leaned over to see her work. He'd presented her with a recent problem in one of his poolrooms downtown. A puzzle he wished to see if she could solve.

She pointed at her notes. "This one location consistently has a lower revenue on Tuesday night races, when the other locations have a higher revenue that night. Tuesday is one of Sheepshead Bay's most popular days. Therefore, what is happening in this one location that no one is betting on Tuesdays?"

This woman. Damn, she was exceptional.

"You're right. So where do we begin to investigate the problem?"

"I assume they call the Tuesday night races in this poolroom."

"They do."

"The patrons could have a reason to avoid betting on races from that track, I suppose."

"Perhaps, but not over a long period of time. The crowd varies too much for that. What else?"

"Someone is skimming."

His mouth hitched in satisfaction. "All right. Who?"

"The owner?"

"Unlikely. He has the most to lose, if discovered. He knows me well enough to understand what happens if he's caught. Let's assume it's not him." Clay already knew the answer but he wanted to see if Florence could get there on her own.

"One of the workers, then. A banker."

"How do we prove it?"

She chewed her bottom lip in the way that drove him mad. "Look at who was working that night."

"Yes, we could do that but we might not be able to clearly isolate the problem by just studying their shifts."

"You could move the suspected skimmer to another night of the week, see if the revenue dips that night, as well."

Fuck, he absolutely adored her.

"Very, very good."

She beamed at him, happiness shining in those gorgeous eyes of hers. Everything inside him tightened in anticipation. He needed to get his hands on her.

"This was fun," she said.

"Stand up."

Her head cocked as she studied him. "Why?"

"Because I want your mouth on mine right now." He started around to the other side of the desk.

She tracked his approach through her lashes, her tongue darting out to lick her lips. "What of our lessons?"

"I have a different lesson in mind right now."

"Oh?"

Now in front of the chair, he pulled her to her feet. His fingers wrapped around her waist and dragged her closer. "This lesson has to do with my desk and your pleasure."

Laughing, she put a hand on his chest to stop him. "As much as I love that lesson, wait a moment. Let's not get distracted this early in the night."

"Why not?"

"I won't be here tomorrow so I need to soak in all the information I can this evening."

That news shouldn't affect him, as he'd seen her every night for the past week. Yet, he felt his chest tighten in disappointment. He was already dreading the long evening without her. "Plans?"

"Do not frown at me." She leaned up to nip at his jaw. "Tomorrow is my birthday and I am going to dinner with my family."

"Your birthday?"

"Yes. I am turning twenty-two."

He winced. Just a mere babe compared to his thirty-one. *You are too old for her.* He ignored that voice in the back of his head. There were many reasons why he was wrong for her, and age was near the bottom of the list.

Releasing her, he returned to his seat across from the desk. "Then we'd best make the most of tonight."

"Are you annoyed I won't be here tomorrow?" She remained standing, watching him curiously.

"No, of course not."

"Then what is it? Your mood went topsy-turvy on me."

She was too perceptive sometimes. "Nothing," he said.

"Liar. Is it about my birthday?" She approached, her skirts rustling as she moved, lips curved into a secret smile. "My family? Or is it about my age?"

Yes, too perceptive. "I often forget how much older I am than you."

She came in front of his chair and moved in between his knees. Placing her hands on his shoulders, she leaned down and gave him a spectacular view of the tops of her breasts. "You forget," she whispered in his ear, "because it doesn't really matter. Thirty-one isn't so old."

He caressed her waist, his hands smoothing the expensive silk covering her body. "Yes, but twenty-one is so young."

"Twenty-two tomorrow, and why are you focused on my age?" She dragged her teeth over his earlobe and he shivered. "Is this about corrupting me again?"

Yanking her forward, he brought her onto his lap. He slid a palm around her neck to cup the back of her head. "No."

It was about his wanting to keep her and knowing he couldn't.

He pressed a soft kiss on her mouth, pleased when she relaxed into him and kissed him back. He loved the way she kissed, with her entire being dedicated to the task. She didn't hold herself in check, playing prey to his hunter. No, she attacked and demanded. She met him as an equal. He never tired of it.

After a quick knock, the door opened. Clay tore his mouth from Florence's and glanced over to see Jack rushing in, the big man's eyes wide with panic. His friend exhaled at seeing Clay and Florence. "Oh, thank Christ," Jack breathed and bent at the waist to collect himself.

Clay set Florence on her feet and rose. "What is the matter? Has something happened?"

"Someone may've snuck into the building," Jack said. "I had Kid Johnny on the back door. They just found him knocked out cold, door wide open."

Clay's entire body froze, fear sinking into his bones. If someone was here to hurt him . . . He couldn't allow Florence anywhere near this place. Her safety was the only thing that mattered. "Come with me," he told her.

"Wait, where are you going?" Jack asked.

"I'll see her off in a hansom then join you in searching each room."

Delicate fingers wrapped around his forearm. "Clay, you shouldn't do that. If there's danger then let the other men look for an intruder."

He shook his head as he pried her fingers off his arm. Then he lifted her hand to his lips and kissed her knuckles. "I'll be fine. I know all the best hiding places."

"Let me help you," she said.

His gut cramped at the idea of her being harmed by some disgruntled patron or dirty copper. "Absolutely not. This is not up for discussion, Florence."

"I'll meet you in the cellar," Jack told Clay before hurrying out.

Clay began leading Florence to the door. "You're going home and you may not return until I'm certain it's safe."

"That is ridiculous. No one wants to hurt me. I can help search for whoever—"

"No." Once over the threshold he towed her down the corridor, not slowing his pace. The sooner he got her to safety, the sooner he could breathe freely again. "I won't allow it. You must leave. I will contact you to let you know when you may return."

"What if you don't find anyone? Does that mean I may return tonight?"

"Not tonight." As much as he wanted her in his bed he wouldn't chance it.

"So it could be weeks before I see you again. Is that what you are telling me?"

He stopped on the stairs and maneuvered her until her back was against the wall. Placing his forehead to hers, he cupped her jaw with both hands. "I'll not risk your safety. Not today, not ever. Don't ask it, because I cannot allow anyone to hurt you. It would destroy me."

Her jaw fell open as her chest rose and fell with her labored breath. They seemed to pause a moment while the weight of what he'd said settled between them. "Oh, Clay." She pressed up and kissed him swiftly, her lips warm and insistent, reassuring. She was here, right here, safe with him.

And it needed to stay that way. He couldn't let the dark ugliness from his life ever bleed into hers. "Come along," he said after breaking the kiss.

In a few minutes they reached the back door. Kid Johnny was on the floor, slouched against the wall with some ice on his head, a few other men gathered around. "One of you fetch a hack," Clay said to the group standing around. One of the boys nodded and took off out the back door. "You all right?" Clay asked Kid, who was actually twenty-five but looked more like sixteen.

Kid winced as he frowned up at Clay. "I'm sorry, Madden. Guy got the drop on me. I heard a noise in the alley but couldn't see anyone. I went out to investigate and he clobbered me."

"Don't worry about it," Clay said. "We'll find him. I need to see her off first. Then I'll return and get you settled at Anna's."

"Clay, what if I—" Florence started, but he held up a hand to stop whatever she was about to say.

"Answer is still no. You're going back uptown, princess."

Chapter Nineteen

Clay and Jack turned over every chair, looked in each corner. They searched cabinets and closets. Under beds and behind curtains. No room was missed, from the cellar to the attic. Yet, no intruder was found.

They had even checked the patrons on the casino floor. No strangers were present, no one who would need to fight his way inside. All were paying members.

It made no damn sense.

Clay stood on the balcony, Jack at his side, and watched the familiar throw of the dice, the twirl of the wheel. Men laughed and clapped, champagne and spirits flowing freely. All was normal in the Bronze House tonight, if one didn't consider the guard clubbed over the head two hours ago.

"He could've escaped," Jack said. The former boxer's arms were crossed over his chest, anger evident in the heavy set of his shoulders. Clay knew Jack took the security of the Bronze House seriously, and his friend was upset over the breach. "Or not even come inside. He might have attacked Kid and run off."

Clay didn't believe it. Random acts of violence were rare in this world. Most violence had a purpose, even if that purpose made sense only to the perpetrator. "Why bother?"

"Scouting the place? Finding out what our security looks like for a break-in later?"

A tactic some criminals employed. "Perhaps. Or he might've been doing something in the alley he didn't want Kid to discover."

"Doubtful, but that would explain not sticking around." Jack pounded a fist against the railing and the wood shook with the force of the blow. "I don't like the not knowing. A thief, he breaks in and we catch him. Someone sneaks onto the floor and we bounce him. The mystery of it doesn't sit well with me."

"Me either. But he's definitely not inside. And no one's been in or out in two hours." The dealers had given free chips to anyone wishing to leave during the search. That had kept the patrons happy and occupied while Clay and Jack tore the place apart.

"Do you think it's related to Bill?"

Clay had considered that, but attacking one of the Bronze House's employees didn't seem like Bill's style. "I'm not ruling it out but unlikely he'd bother. He'd rather come after me, not Kid."

"True. And everyone here knows him. He wouldn't be stupid enough to try to hurt you."

"Not to mention he threatened to tell Duncan about Florence's visits here. I'd expect that before he attacked the staff."

"A disgruntled patron, then?"

"We've had our fair share of those." Clay dragged a hand down his face. "I couldn't point to one that stands out as the culprit, however."

The sound of boot heels signaled the arrival of a female. Not the one Clay hoped, of course. Florence had been sent home directly after the discovery of Kid Johnny's injury. And Clay wouldn't allow her to return until he was certain this attack wasn't a prelude to more violence. No matter how much he ached for her.

"Did you find whoever hurt Johnny?" Anna asked as she approached.

"No," Clay said. "We didn't find anyone inside the building."

Anna came alongside them, her face pulled into a frown. "That doesn't ease my worries."

"Or mine," Jack said.

"We will remain vigilant," Clay said. "It's all we can do at this point. How's Kid?"

"Just peachy." Anna's mouth curved into a smile. "The doctor left an hour ago. Kid now has seven beautiful women fluttering around him and offering to play nurse. Don't expect him to recover anytime soon."

"Just send me all the bills."

"Oh, I will." She glanced over his shoulder. "Where is your intrepid sidekick, the lovely Miss Greene?"

"I sent her home." For her own good. He would have liked nothing more than to curl up in bed with her right now. Pleasure her until he forgot all about intruders, corrupt coppers, Duncan Greene and the other myriad worries that plagued him on a daily basis. Worse, this separation could last days. Weeks. If there were more random acts of violence within these walls, he couldn't allow her to return.

He ground his teeth together. The idea of going weeks without seeing her hurt worse than when he'd been jumped by three toughs in a Bowery gin house at the age of fourteen. They'd stolen his take for the week, a meager forty dollars, after busting several of his ribs.

Still, he'd rather face that than any stretch of time without Florence.

"Is she planning to return now that the drama is over?" Anna asked, oblivious to Clay's inner turmoil.

"No, not until the threat has passed."

Jack snorted. "That may never happen, considering."

"You can't protect her all the time, Clay," Anna said. "Besides, she's a grown woman. She knows the risks of coming here."

Clay didn't care. He'd protect her to the best of his ability, and that meant sorting out this mess first. "Thank you but I know what I'm doing."

"Does this mean you are going uptown to see her?"

Uptown? Had Anna lost her mind? A man like Clay was constantly on guard, always looking over his shoulder. Even disregarding his current problems with Bill and the Metropolitan Police, there were plenty of men who'd do him harm if given the chance. Clay would rather not give them the opportunity. "You know I prefer not to leave the club."

Anna rolled her eyes toward the ceiling. "Which is absurd. Your legion of enemies cannot track you at night in a closed carriage."

"Or even in the daylight," Jack put in. "If you recall, you attended a Giants game at the Polo Grounds not long ago."

"For a meeting. That was business."

"Your relationship with Miss Greene is also business," Anna said. "All those late-night *tutoring* sessions."

"Indeed. In his bedroom," Jack added and Anna chuckled.

While they laughed at his expense, Clay thought about what Anna had said. He could leave the club, of course. He just preferred to remain here unless absolutely necessary. It was safer that way. Hell, one of Clay's former associates had been gunned down in broad daylight three years ago in Washington Square Park. And that man had merely operated a low-level racket of policy shops.

Yet, the long evenings without Florence stretched out ahead of him like a thick gray fog. Lifeless and prosaic. An endless cycle of tedium. She'd brought light and joy to his world, even when he didn't deserve it—light and joy that would be permanently taken away when she discovered his plans for her grandmother's home.

That didn't leave him much time.

There had to be a way to see her outside of the club and keep both of them safe. He couldn't very well promenade with her in Central Park, but plenty of discreet locations existed for this sort of thing.

And wasn't tomorrow her birthday?

He glanced at his pocket watch. Actually, today was her birthday.

Surely he could think of a way to surprise her.

BIRTHDAYS WERE USUALLY fun, Florence thought as she finished the champagne in her glass. Tonight they dined in a private dining salon at Sherry's, her favorite restaurant. She'd worn her favorite dress. And she'd ordered all her favorite dishes.

So why did this year's celebration feel as though a dark cloud loomed on the horizon?

No one was particularly cheerful. Her father, with his tight jaw and distracted demeanor, was strangely subdued throughout dinner. Mamie also seemed preoccupied, lost in her thoughts and uncommunicative. For her part, Florence spent the meal worried about Clay and wondering when she'd see him again. Which left Justine and their mother to shoulder the burden of the dinner conversation.

It was clear by dessert that no one wished to prolong the evening. The plates were barely cleared when her father stood to call an end to the service. "Darling Florence, happy birthday. Now, if you all don't mind I have an early meeting. It's best if we head home."

"Daddy, you and Mama go on," Mamie said. "We'll stay here and finish the champagne."

"Are you certain?" Mama asked, her brows lowered in concern. "I don't like the idea of you three unescorted in a hansom at night."

Florence dug her nails into her palms to keep from laughing like a loon. If only her mother knew how often the two eldest Greene siblings were in hansoms, unescorted, late at night. She'd likely faint from the shock.

"We'll be fine," Mamie assured her. "I'll have the staff fetch a carriage for us in a few moments."

Mama glanced at their father. "What do you think, Duncan?"

"I think it's best if your mother and I take a hansom home instead. Then you three may stay as long as you like and George will see you home," he said, referring to their family driver.

Decision made, her parents gave their farewells and departed. Waiters bustled in and out of the salon, clearing away the dishes and glassware. When they were finally alone, Florence turned to Mamie. "You were awfully anxious to rid ourselves of them."

Mamie's mouth curved into a knowing smile, the one she wore when hiding a secret. "And you'll soon see why, little sister."

"Well, I want to know," Justine said. "What's happening?"

Mamie leaned back in her chair, champagne glass in hand. "Perhaps I wished for more time with my sisters."

"I'd sooner believe you plan to run an oyster cart in the Bowery," Florence said. "Tell me what this is about."

Instead of answering, Mamie handed Florence a note.

Make certain Florence leaves alone. I have a surprise for her.

—M

Who on earth . . . ? Then it hit her with the subtlety of three aces. *Clayton.* Was he downstairs? Excitement fizzed and popped in her veins, just like the champagne she'd been drinking all night. Goodness, how she longed to see him.

Confusion quickly overshadowed her excitement, however. Clay never left the Bronze House. It made no sense for him to come to Sherry's only to escort her home. "When did you receive this?"

"During appetizers." Mamie looked at her fingernails as if appreciating them. "And I kept your little rendezvous a secret this whole time."

"Why do I have a feeling I will owe you something for that favor?"

"Because you will. Frank is helping me with one of the tenement wives. She's been arrested and there may be stretches of time where I'll need to disappear. You will cover for me with our parents."

"Arrested!" Justine was aghast. "For what?"

"Murdering her husband," Mamie said. "Frank plans to get her acquitted. But he needs my help so—"

"I'll bet he does," Florence said under her breath, which prompted Mamie to elbow her. "Ouch! Fine, I'll make sure Daddy and Mama don't suspect a thing."

"You are the best liar in the family," Justine said to Florence. "You have a bizarre talent for thinking on your feet."

"It's not hard. All you have to do is sound like you know what you're talking about. People believe you if you speak with confidence." She pushed her chair away from the table. "Now, if you'll excuse me I need to see who is outside."

"But I thought it was Clayton Madden," Justine said, rising, as well.

"He hardly ever leaves the Bronze House," Florence explained. Now that she thought about it, the possibility of Clay waiting for her seemed far-fetched. And considering the assault of the doorman last night, whoever waited downstairs could have a nefarious purpose. "And there have been some strange happenings of late. It could be someone else hoping to trick me."

"Then we should come with you," Mamie said. "I won't allow either of my sisters to be hurt."

"Nor will I," Justine added.

Florence was touched by this show of familial solidarity. "Come along, then. We may stab any ne'er-do-wells with hatpins together."

The three sisters left the salon and descended the staircase to the main floor. The restaurant was crowded, a mix of high society, theatrical folk and political cronies. Black-coated waiters hustled about and diners carried on loud, animated conversations. Florence ignored the chaos and headed straight to the front door.

She could hardly breathe once on the sidewalk. Justine and Mamie were right behind her, but Florence didn't wait. She started walking up Fifth Avenue to search the carriages. Whoever was waiting for her would not find her trembling in a corner. *Show no fear.*

"Might I offer you a ride, miss?" a deep voice said from behind her.

Whirling, she gasped. Clay stood there, dressed in the finest black evening clothes. A silk top hat sat on his head, a walking stick in his hand. He even wore a crisp white shirt, a sharp departure from his usual all-black attire. Hell's bells, the man was sinfully attractive. He was thunder and electricity, a shock of raw heat and masculinity. The words died in her throat. All she could do was stare at him, frozen, like a painting.

They'd find her in a museum one day, the title of the work simply listed as "Woman Gob-smacked."

"I knew it was you," Justine said. Her youngest sister, unafraid of anyone or anything, came right up to Clay. "You're Clayton Madden."

"I am. You must be Miss Justine." He bowed—bowed!—over her sister's hand, and Florence felt her eyes nearly bulge from her skull. "And Miss Greene," Clay said to Mamie. "Nice to see you again."

Mamie smirked. "We didn't officially meet before."

"True, but I do keep tabs on everyone and everything in my club. It's not often a woman is nearly drugged at my roulette table."

"What are you doing here?" Florence said quietly. Her initial shock had receded, but she was having a hard time believing Clay was here on Fifth Avenue, chatting with her sisters. "Shouldn't you be at the club?"

His dark eyes sparkled with a teasing light she hadn't seen before, one that melted her insides like a hot knife through butter. "I took the evening off," he said. "I thought I might surprise you."

She could feel her skin heating, the blush undoubtedly evident to anyone in a three-block radius, thanks to her pale skin. "With a ride home?"

"Eventually. I have more than that planned, however." He faced Mamie and Justine. "Ladies, may I steal her away?"

"Please do," Mamie said. "Justine and I will take the long way home, just in case our parents are still awake."

"And we'll tell your maid you've come down with a stomach ailment," Justine added. "That'll buy you even more time."

"Thank you," Florence told them before meeting Clay's gaze. "Are you actually here?"

"Come along and I shall prove it to you. My carriage is just ahead."

Waving to her sisters, she allowed Clay to escort her to his carriage. On Fifth Avenue. Outside Sherry's. In evening clothes. It hardly seemed real.

He stopped alongside a large black closed carriage. Clearly expensive, the conveyance was no rented hack. Gold accents and pearl inlays decorated the lacquered wood. He handed her up then called for the driver to depart. When he followed her inside, he sat across from her, his bulk almost comically large for the intimate interior.

"The way you look tonight," he rasped. "You take my breath away."

The compliment burrowed under her skin and wrapped around her heart. She'd never had a man stare at her as Clay did, so intently. Hotly. Like he *burned* for her. She felt that heat in her belly, in the thrumming of her blood. "You . . ." She could barely articulate her thoughts. Her, the woman never at a loss for words. "You look quite handsome."

"Thank you."

"What happened to not playing the gentleman with me?"

The side of his mouth hitched in a roguish, playful manner. "Allowances must be made on your birthday, don't you think?"

"I wasn't sure you remembered."

"Of course. Twenty-two. Which is still too young but certainly older than you were yesterday."

She bit her lip. Who was this man? This was an entirely different side of Clayton Madden. "Where are we going? Just a ride about town?"

"Now, what kind of present would that be?"

"You bought me a present?"

"In a roundabout way. But it's a surprise."

She peeked out the window. They were heading south on Fifth Avenue, already past Thirty-Fourth Street. "Are we going to the club?"

"That would be disappointing, were I hoping to surprise you. You've already seen the club."

"So you're taking me to a place I haven't been before."

Chuckling, he shook his head. "No more questions. You'll not worm it out of me before we arrive."

She nearly bounced on her seat with excitement. She couldn't remember the last time she had this much fun. Though it was hard, she'd try to curb her curiosity for now. "Was there an intruder at the Bronze House last night?"

"No."

"And your guard, the one knocked out. How is he faring?"

"Perfectly well. Anna's girls have been seeing to his recovery. I'm told he may languish for a few weeks."

Florence laughed. "Well, that's good. So I may return tomorrow."

"No, not yet. I'd like a few more days until we know the assault was a random incident, not part of a larger plan."

"But Clay—"

"Don't argue, Florence." His hand shot out to capture her wrist. In one tug of his powerful arm, she ended up on his lap. He held her tight. "Let's enjoy your birthday and the rest of the evening. I have been dying to get my hands on you."

She relaxed into his chest, the warmth from his body like a drug, turning her limbs languid and heavy. "I missed you."

"Oh, my dear girl. Missing you doesn't come close to what I've felt." He cupped the back of her head and brought her forward, until her mouth met his. She nearly sighed at the feel of him, the hard chest and thighs underneath her. Soft, plush lips plucked at hers over and over again. Then his tongue darted out to twine with her own, swirling and stroking, driving her mad.

When they pulled apart, both were breathing hard. She laid her head on his shoulder. "I hope my birthday surprise contains more kisses like that one."

"Many, many more," he promised. "As many as you like."

"Tell me where we're going."

He dragged a fingertip along the edge of her bodice, tracing the exposed skin and making her shiver. "We're almost there."

"Hmm, so it's above Fourteenth."

"You'll never guess the location, so you might as well learn some patience."

"I bet I could guess it, if I had enough time."

"A gambler at heart." He pressed a kiss to the top of her head. "And no, you couldn't."

The wheels slowed and she peered out the window. They were on Broadway, just north of Madison Square Park. "Are we going to a hotel?" Many high-end hotels lined these few blocks, like the Fifth Avenue Hotel and Hotel Albemarle. Perhaps Clay had rented them a suite for the night.

"In a sense." He reached to throw open the door. Setting her off his lap, he climbed down to the street. "Come along."

She took his hand and descended. They were in front of the Hoffman House, one of the grandest hotels in the city. Tammany Hall used it as an unofficial headquarters, and nearly every major city decision was brokered here.

Clay took her arm and started for the doors. Only, he didn't lead them to the lobby entrance. He directed her toward the saloon. The male-only saloon. Moralists were always screaming that Hoffman House's Grand Saloon should be closed, due to a scandalous painting on the wall. Which was likely why women were not permitted inside. Fools. They thought protecting women from nudity would save society. *Instead, it taught shame and ignorance.*

"After you," he said and pulled open the taproom door.

"But women aren't allowed."

He dipped his head and put his mouth near her ear. "This particular woman is allowed just for tonight."

A thrill shot along her spine, the illicit lure of the forbidden. She stepped inside, unsure what she'd find. Elegance greeted her, a room as fine as any she'd ever come across. Mahogany panels lined the long room, which had high decorative ceilings. Thick Eastern carpets covered the floor and surrounded a carved wooden bar. French tapestries covered the walls, and marble and bronze nude statues were displayed proudly.

"Welcome, miss. Mr. Madden." A waiter approached them. Four other waiters hovered in the background. "May we show you to your table?"

It was then that Florence realized there was only one table set up in the saloon, under a red velvet canopy. A matching red drape covered the wall under the canopy, an ornate chandelier overhead.

"Thank you," Clay said and took Florence's arm.

They followed the waiter to the table. Florence's head swiveled as she struggled to take it all in. No woman had ever graced these floors, observed these walls. How had Clay talked them into allowing her to be the first?

He held out her chair and she lowered herself down. Who was this casino owner with such impeccable manners? The man was layers and layers of mystery. *One I hope to solve.*

"May I bring you both a drink?" the waiter asked when Clay had claimed the empty seat.

"Two house cocktails, please," Clay said. "And your oldest bottle of Bordeaux."

"Very good, sir."

The waiter departed and Florence narrowed her eyes playfully. "Should I not get to choose my own drink on my birthday?"

"Trust me, you should try the house cocktail. It is all the rage, apparently." He leaned in. "And how many women may lay claim to having tried it?"

She bit her lip. Was she so transparent? "This is the perfect gift, Clay. How did you know to pick something so unusual for me?"

His lips twisted into a smile, the scars on his face less obvious in his humor. "A woman who longs to open her own casino, who could possibly beat even me in a hand of cards, requires an unusual gift." He lifted her hand, brought it to his mouth and brushed his lips over her knuckles. "And you haven't even seen the best part."

Chapter Twenty

Before Florence could ask what Clay meant by that, the waiter returned with their drinks. A cocktail was placed in front of each of them, along with an empty wineglass. Another waiter began opening the bottle of Bordeaux.

Clay lifted his cocktail and waited for her to do the same. "To you. As the old saying goes, 'May your pockets be heavy and your heart be light. May good luck follow you each morning and night.'" He touched his glass to hers.

"Thank you." *Charming man.* She couldn't stop grinning as she brought the glass to her mouth and took a sip. The cocktail was strong, with gin and orange flavor, but delicious. "What is this?"

"Gin, dry vermouth and orange bitters. Do you like it?"

She nodded. "I do. I've never had anything similar before."

When their wineglasses were full, the waiter paused. "Will there be anything else?"

"No," Clay said, coming to his feet. He withdrew a wad of bills from his jacket pocket and passed them to the waiter. "If you could ensure we're not disturbed for the rest of the evening, we'd appreciate it."

"Thank you, sir. Consider it done."

The waiter led the rest of the staff out of the saloon and into the hotel. The doors snapped shut behind them, leaving Clay and Florence completely alone.

"I don't understand," she said as he sat down. "You bought out the place for the night?"

"Yes. Are you suitably impressed?"

"Very."

"So I shouldn't open that velvet curtain?" He pointed to the red cloth under the canopy on the wall in front of them.

Excitement raced through her veins, causing her to tingle. "Is that *the* painting?"

"It is. Are you certain your innocent eyes can handle it?"

"After the bedroom scene inside Anna's brothel, do you really need to ask?"

"No, I suppose I don't. And I realize this won't be quite the same but perhaps close enough." Leaning in, he kissed her cheek, and his scent—tobacco and pine—enveloped her. She closed her eyes and breathed him in. He was as potent as the cocktail in her hand.

When the cocktails were finished, he rose and made his way to the curtain strings. She marveled at how much Clay had come to mean to her. He was more than her friend and lover. More than a mentor. He was . . . everything.

The first person she wished to talk to each day.

The person she longed to kiss morning, noon and night.

The person she missed with a physical ache in her heart.

Lord above, am I falling in love with him?

Oh, no. The timing couldn't have been worse for those sorts of thoughts. Her entire future depended on remaining independent, on making her own choices. On operating her own casino. She couldn't allow anyone to take that away, not even Clay.

And it wasn't as if he'd expressed undying love for her. In fact, he'd said the exact opposite. *I am interested exclusively in casual.* He'd warned her and she hadn't listened.

So no, she wasn't foolish enough to fall for a man who would never love her back. Was she?

She set all that aside for tomorrow. Tonight was her birthday. They were here, together, and she would enjoy the evening.

Recriminations could wait until the morning.

He tugged the curtain's cord and the fabric parted. A huge painting came into view, the piece over eight feet high. It was *a lot* to take in. Brilliant light from the chandelier illuminated the considerable amount of naked flesh in front of her.

"Goodness. That is indeed something."

Instead of taking his own seat, Clay came around to her side. He tugged her up, only to slide underneath her and pull her onto his lap. She settled into his broad chest, her back to his front, and they stared at the painting together.

Four voluptuous naked women surrounded a satyr at the edge of a river. They teased him, trying to pull him into the water, but he resisted.

There were breasts and buttocks, but most of the genitals were covered. All in all, it didn't seem so scandalous. She had playing cards under her bed more erotic than this. It was beautiful, however, with both male and female strength displayed.

"It's called *Nymphs and Satyr.* Painted by a Frenchman, Bouguereau," Clay said. "Do you like it, my little voyeur?"

"It is beautiful. Not sure what the hue and cry is about, though. This painting is not as shocking as I expected."

"They never are."

"So why not let women in here to see it?"

"Perhaps they don't wish to give them any ideas." His hands stroked her waist through her clothing, almost as if he couldn't help himself.

"To capture a satyr, you mean?"

"No, of fighting back. Don't you see what is happening here?"

She studied the scene more closely. "It looks like the nymphs are trying to have their wicked way with the satyr and he's resisting them."

"Not quite. In mythology, nymphs presided over streams and woods. Satyrs are creatures of self-indulgence and male pleasure, usually depicted with erections. This satyr has been caught spying on a group of bathing nymphs. You can see the other nymphs in the background, observing. The braver ones, in the foreground, are going to pull him into the water to cool him off."

That certainly made sense. "They've joined together to punish him."

"Exactly." His hot breath teased the sensitive flesh of her throat an instant before his lips caressed the same spot. "One nymph can do nothing, while many can be an invincible force."

"Ah, that's why you think this painting will give women ideas." She sighed as his mouth trailed her skin, her entire body heating and melting.

"Does it give you ideas?" He slid a hand over her ribs and up to her chest. A palm cupped her corseted breast and she arched into his touch. Curse the amount of clothing they both wore at the moment.

His shaft had begun to thicken under her backside. She rolled her hips once just to tease him. "I think it's given you ideas."

"Hmm, indeed. But then, around you, I never cease coming up with them." He licked her throat then sank his teeth into the tender skin. "What do you think happens next in the scene?"

She gasped and gripped his forearms to steady herself as her lids fell closed. "They push the satyr in the water."

"Come now. Is that the best you can do?" He dragged a fingertip along the edge of her bodice and her breasts grew heavy under the gentle touch. Arousal beat like a drum in every part of her, centered between her legs. He nipped her earlobe. "Are the nymphs left unsatisfied or does he have his wicked way with them?"

"All of them?"

"Perhaps not all of them." Clay's mouth hovered near her ear as his hands went to her skirts. He gathered the fabric in his fingers and pulled, revealing her legs. "Perhaps there was one blonde nymph who caught his eye, one with hazel eyes and no fear whatsoever."

Oh, God. She sucked in air, nearly light-headed from the spell he was weaving. Hard to remember they were in a restaurant and not his bedroom. When her skirts came past her knees, she caught his hand. "What if the waiters return?"

"The doors are locked. No one is disturbing us. Relax, beautiful girl." Air washed over her thighs as he pushed her skirts to her waist. "Now, where were we?"

"The blonde nymph," she whispered.

"Yes, the brave nymph, unafraid of the satyr's hideous looks and lusty ways. For some strange reason she seemed to prefer him to all others." Reaching down, he placed her legs on the outside of his thighs. She was spread wide, her body displayed for him. "And she was so very beautiful that he felt unworthy of her."

That penetrated the lust fogging her brain. "That's ridiculous—"

"Hush," he said, his hand gliding between her legs to find the part in her drawers. "This is my story." Long fingers slid through the coarse hair on her mound. "Fuck, I can smell your arousal." Growling, he sank his teeth into her throat once more and she moaned.

"You were saying?"

"I apologize. This blonde nymph was clever, much smarter than the satyr." Blunt fingers traced her folds, never touching where she ached most, tormenting her. "She took him away from the other satyrs and nymphs, knowing the satyr couldn't resist her."

A fingertip glanced over her clitoris and she jumped. *More of that, please.*

He licked her throat and pressed an open-mouthed kiss there. He cupped her sex with his hand and she lifted her hips, trying to get him where she needed. "Clay—"

"And when they were alone," he continued, "the nymph was playful and wicked, the spark of joy his lonely life had been missing." One finger penetrated her, the thick digit filling her slowly.

"Oh, God," she breathed and closed her eyes, her head resting on his shoulder. She couldn't move, couldn't think; she could only *crave.* Her legs trembled, the muscles straining for *more* as he thrust a finger in her channel.

"Finally, the nymph allowed the satyr to touch her and it was the sweetest, most erotic experience of his life." He pressed his palm to her clitoris, grinding, while his soft, panting breaths brushed her ear. "The satyr was hard, so impossibly hard for her, when she spread her thighs and took him inside her body. He nearly died from the pleasure, she was so hot and tight. The walls of her cunt gripped his cock as he rode her, driving deep to touch her womb."

Clay worked another finger inside her, and her hips rose to meet him. The pressure felt so good, so *necessary.* He continued to thrust, faster now, his palm stroking her clitoris. Electricity built in her veins, a storm gathering inside her.

"The nymph came so hard and her nails raked the satyr's back. She tightened around him, her body milking his shaft for his seed. Pleased he'd serviced her, he let himself chase his own orgasm, pumping his cock until his spend shot from the tip."

Wicked words and wicked fingers did not relent, and Florence was clutching at him, mindless. Then he curled his finger high inside her and she couldn't withstand it. The orgasm rushed up and over her, taking her to the highest peak and obliterating everything else. She convulsed, her body dragging out the bliss, until she collapsed in a heap against him.

He nuzzled her neck, his kisses soft and tender despite the obvious erection he still possessed. "Happy birthday, beautiful girl," he rasped against her skin.

She made a sound that was a cross between a wheeze and a chuckle. "Thank you, Clay."

"You're welcome, though that was for me as much as it was for you." He withdrew his fingers from between her legs and brought them up to his mouth. Pushing the digits past his lips, he moaned, his face slackening as his lids fell shut. Like he was savoring her taste.

She adjusted her limbs so she could angle toward him. Color tinged his cheeks and neck, his muscles tight. He appeared like a man on the edge. Placing a hand on his chest, she dragged it toward his groin. "Should I tell you a story now?"

"No." He blew out a long breath. "I'd love nothing more were we in private at the club. But since we are in public and I cannot do all I want to your naked body then we should get you home."

"Are you certain?"

"Very." Setting her on her feet, he stood. "Besides, I wanted to spoil you on your birthday."

"Then I will return the favor on your birthday."

A strange look passed over his face, one she couldn't decipher. He lowered his head and pressed a quick kiss to her mouth. "I look forward to it. Now, let's get you back uptown."

CLAY HELPED FLORENCE to the exit. She was adorably disheveled, lips swollen from his kisses and her hair slipping out of its pins. Never had she appeared more beautiful to him. If he could keep her, have her remain at his side for all eternity, he would.

And no man deserved her less. He'd skated the edges of the city's criminal class for most his life. Had done many things he wasn't proud of in the name of survival. He presided over an empire of greed and corruption, one that hundreds depended on for their livelihoods.

Someday, once he had his revenge against her father, perhaps then he could leave the enterprise and casinos behind. Forget the policy shops and card games, the cheaters and the bookkeeping. Find a normal way of life where he wasn't looking over his shoulder all the time.

Florence would be long gone by then.

He ignored the tightness in his chest and led her to the door. Before he could open it, however, she tugged him to a halt. Her hand caressed his cheek and they stared at one another for a long moment. He'd never felt more at peace, more understood, than with this woman. A bizarre urge was mounting inside him to bundle her up, hop on the next train west and escape the life he'd created for himself.

She licked her lips, her voice rougher than before. "Clay, thank you. This was . . . It was absolutely perfect."

"I wanted you to have something unique and memorable. I hope you never forget it." *I hope you never forget me.*

Rising on her toes, she kissed him quickly on the mouth. "Impossible. I'll always remember it. You have made this the best birthday of my life."

His chest expanded at the praise, his skin growing hot. He had to get her out of here quickly—or else he'd rent them a suite and they'd never leave. Reaching for the door, he held it open and she passed through. When he moved to follow, he found her blocking the door. "Florence—"

And then he saw why she'd paused.

Duncan Greene and Big Bill were standing on the walk next to Clay's carriage, waiting. Duncan's face was twisted with rage, a fearsome thing to behold, while Bill's smirk made it clear he was enjoying this. The bastard had gone and told Duncan about Clay and Florence.

This was the end, then. Tonight ended his association with her. The realization made him want to punch something.

You knew this day was coming.

Yes, he'd known. There had never been any hope of avoiding it, really.

I wanted more time.

That thought floated into the cool Manhattan air like mist, unattainable and ethereal. He might as well have asked to sprout wings.

Clay stepped around Florence and shoved his hands in his trouser pockets. He locked eyes with Duncan. "Evening, gentlemen."

"Turn around and go back inside," Duncan said from behind gritted teeth. "I won't have this conversation on the street."

"Daddy—" Florence started, seemingly coming out of her stupor.

"Inside!" her father snapped. "Now, Florence."

Spinning, she lunged for the door and disappeared into the saloon. Clay waited, unmoving, as Bill sauntered by. "I warned you," the assistant superintendent said. "But you didn't listen."

Clay didn't bother responding. He'd deal with Bill later. Right now Duncan was more important.

Duncan stalked forward, his hands curled into fists. His body was tight and angry as he advanced on Clay. "Get inside before I break your goddamn jaw," her father snarled.

"I'd like to see you try," he taunted. "Fair warning, I don't fight by your Queensberry rules. My rules were learned on the streets of the Lower East Side, where men like you wouldn't last a fucking day."

Duncan pointed a beefy finger in Clay's face. "Inside, Madden. Or I'm having Bill arrest you right here on the street."

"For what?"

"Does it matter? He'll do whatever I ask and you'll spend a few weeks in the Tombs. Is that really what you want her last memory of you to be?"

Clay glared, unblinking, furious that Duncan had played the one card Clay couldn't refuse. *Florence.* Turning, he yanked on the door handle and went in. Florence stood in the middle of the room, her skin as pale as flour, arms wrapped around her waist. Her eyes darted between Clay and Duncan, who had just closed the door behind him.

Duncan's brows pinched as his gaze swept the saloon, taking in the intimate table for two, cocktails and wine. Any fool would know what had transpired here tonight—except for the part where Florence came on Clay's fingers.

That memory belonged to Clay, and he planned to savor it in the long nights ahead.

"Daddy, I can explain."

Duncan crossed his arms over his huge chest. "Is that so, Florence? Because I have to warn you. I am not in the mood for your lies. Again."

Her throat worked as she swallowed. She seemed to shrink in size and something in Clay's chest twisted. He shifted to block Duncan's view of her. "Be angry with me, Duncan. Not Florence."

"Oh, I am indeed very, very angry with you, Madden. *You had no right to touch my daughter!*" His voice increased in volume until he ended on a roar, his face nearly purple.

Clay remained calm, his shoulders relaxed. He had faced down enough furious men to know he needed to keep a level head. "Whatever you think this is, I promise you, it's not. I care for her."

"Liar. This is another way for you to exact revenge on me, by using my daughter. By ruining her."

"No, Daddy." Florence moved to Clay's side. "I've been going to Clay for lessons. He's been teaching me how to run a casino."

Her father flinched. "You sought out this criminal for lessons? *Have you lost your mind?"*

Clay's muscles locked and he took a step closer to Duncan. "If you yell at her one more time I will punch you in the mouth, father or not."

Duncan focused on his daughter. "Think, Florence. Don't you realize who is trying to tear down your grandmother's house so he can build another casino? Have you not put it together yet?"

"Another casino? I don't understand."

"He's using you as revenge against me."

"You think that *Clay* is trying to tear down Granny's house?" She started chuckling and looked over at Clay. "That is ridiculous."

Clay didn't join in the laughter. Instead, he merely stood there, his body braced, ready to absorb the hit. The accusations were true. Duncan hadn't lied. And everyone in the room, save Florence, knew it.

She'd soon realize he'd withheld this from her, that he was a monster. A selfish bastard. She'd learn that revenge mattered more to him than anything else. Even her.

It didn't have to be this way.

Wrong. There had never been any other outcome. So he waited, his throat burning with explanations he wouldn't give. It was too late to turn back.

And he could tell by the dawning realization on her face that he was about to lose her for good.

THE ROOM WAS silent. Too silent. The kind of silence where everyone else knew the end of the story and one poor fool was struggling to keep up.

Florence was the fool.

The truth was there in her father's disappointment and disgust. In the policeman's smug expression. In Clay's vacant eyes.

He hadn't even tried to defend himself.

Because he knows he can't.

Her stomach plummeted. The surroundings mocked her, this elegant stage of seduction and romance he'd orchestrated this evening. How could a man so tender, so loving, have schemed to steal her grandmother's home behind Florence's back? She'd told him what that house meant to her and her future. How could he have listened to her and still proceeded with this plan?

Maybe she'd misunderstood. Maybe her father was wrong. "No," she whispered with a violent shake of her head. "It can't be. My grandmother's *house*?"

Clay remained silent, his stony gaze locked on her father. Both men were engaged in a battle of wills—and Florence was caught in the middle.

She had to speak to Clay, alone. There had to be more to this than what her father believed. "Daddy, I'd like a moment alone with Clay."

Her father's expression grew hard. "Over my dead body. Get in the carriage this instant or I will carry you out of here."

"You force her over *my* dead body," Clay snapped.

"I have no problem with that outcome." Duncan started to remove his topcoat, his brows lowered over glittering angry eyes. "Perhaps I'll save everyone the trouble and strangle you right here with my bare hands."

"Daddy, stop!" Florence moved between them, her back to Clay. "Five minutes. That's all I ask."

"I will not leave you alone with him."

She hated to do it, but she had to point out the obvious. "I have been alone with him all night. A few more minutes won't change anything."

Daddy pushed the edges of his jacket back and thrust his hands on his hips. "Fine, damn it. Five minutes. But before I go, I have some choice words for you, Madden." He leaned in, his voice as menacing as Florence had ever heard it. "Seducing my daughter was low, even for you. Hear me now. If you come within ten feet of her ever again, I will stop at nothing to bury you."

Clay's lip curled into a sneer. "You tried that twenty years ago, Greene. Didn't work then and it sure as hell won't work now."

"I told you, that was not my fault!"

"Wait, what are you talking about?" Florence looked between them. "What happened twenty years ago?"

Silence descended for a long minute. Clay merely watched her father, his big body nearly vibrating with rage. "Why not tell her? No doubt she'll appreciate your benevolence."

"Stay away from her," Daddy snarled. "And stay away from my mother's home."

"Too late," Clay said with a smirk. "The plans have been filed and I expect construction to start within the month. It should become very loud and dusty on her block soon."

"I wouldn't be so sure of that." Now her father smirked, his expression full of arrogance and privilege. "Five minutes, Florence. Then I'm coming in."

Her father and Bill left, the door slamming behind them. Florence's head spun. What had just happened here?

Clasping her hands, she faced the man who'd come to mean so much to her. "It's true, isn't it? You are the one destroying all the homes on my grandmother's block so you can build a casino."

"I never lied to you," he ground out. "I never—"

"All you said was your revenge wasn't physical or financial. How does that make this better? It's my grandmother's *house*, Clay."

"It's no less than what your father deserves."

"Oh, I see. This is where you try to justify breaking my grandmother's heart and sabotaging my future."

Dark resentment roiled in the depths of his gaze. "I don't need to justify myself. Not to you. Not to anyone."

Her lips parted on a swift intake of breath. The callous words were like a blow, her body rocking with the impact.

Her reaction must have affected him because he dragged a hand through his hair and shifted on his feet. His tone softened. "I wasn't using you as part of any revenge. This plan has been in motion for years."

"How can I believe you?"

"I have never lied to you. Not once."

"Lying by omission is still lying."

"You knew more about this than anyone, save Jack. Regardless, everything that happened between us was honest."

She wasn't certain she could believe that. Before she could sort through her feelings, she had to learn what Clay and her father had been talking about. "I still don't understand what my father did twenty years ago. Tell me what was so terrible that you needed to carry out—"

"Time's up!" A fist pounded on the taproom door. "Come out now or I will break this door down."

Her father. She kept her attention on Clay. "You owe me an explanation."

"There isn't one. If you are hoping to discover I'm the hero in this melodrama, you'll be sorely disappointed."

"Right now!" her father shouted. "I'm giving you ten seconds. Ten. Nine. Eight . . ."

The countdown continued. Years of experience told her that Duncan Greene never bluffed. Her father would bust the door down as soon as he finished counting. And perhaps she'd let him if she wasn't the first woman inside the Hoffman taproom. If the place was destroyed tonight, the world would blame her. Then they'd never let another woman in, ever.

This is not done. I will have answers.

Florence started for the door. Before she turned the lock, she glanced over her shoulder at Clay. "I never asked for a hero. What I wanted was a partner." Flicking the lock, she yanked on the knob and left.

Chapter Twenty-One

"Not so high and mighty now, are you?"

Blinking in the dim light of the streetlamps, Clay turned to the voice. Bill. *Christ.* He'd almost forgotten the policeman was part of this nightmare. "Is this the part where you gloat? If so, save it."

"I told you." Bill pushed away from the brick building and stalked toward Clay. "I said you would regret it if you took my house away from me. Ruined my marriage. You deserve everything that's happened tonight."

Clay struggled to keep from lunging at the other man and strangling him. "You still won't get your house or your wife back. This did absolutely nothing to help you."

Bill thrust his stomach out, likely to take up more space. A classic intimidation tactic Clay often employed with his shoulders.

Yet, Clay would not feel intimidated, certainly not by this man.

He stood his ground and crossed his arms over his chest. "You've played your only card,

Bill. You've played it—and you lost. You have nothing over me now."

"Except arrest and jail time."

"My lawyers would have me released within an hour. It's a waste of everyone's time."

"This late at night, they'd have a hard time finding a judge to spring you. I'm tempted to do it, just because I can."

"This is fucking ridiculous." Clay was in *no* mood for this shit. Bill had cost him another evening with Florence, on her birthday no less. The evening had been so perfect—and now it was ruined. She'd never speak to him again.

It's my grandmother's house, *Clay.*

Spinning on his heel, he strode toward his carriage. At least he could get to the club and lose himself in the piles of work awaiting him.

"You made it too easy to find your weakness," Bill called. "All I had to do was create a threat at the club and she came scurrying out on your arm."

Clay drew to an immediate halt and slowly faced the assistant superintendent. "What do you mean, you created a threat at the club?"

"Your boy at the door. He never knew what hit him. You assumed there was an intruder and sent your paramour off in a carriage, protecting her from harm. That's how I knew you were screwing her."

The attack on Kid Johnny had been . . . Bill's doing? Goddamn him. There hadn't been an intruder. Bill had wanted to see if Florence was inside the casino and expose the affair.

Rage filled Clay's veins and his muscles bulged. He lunged for Bill, intent on taking him down, and they collided and crashed onto the walk. Clay's hands were fast and he got in two jabs to Bill's chin before the policeman fought back.

They struggled on the hard ground. Bill got the upper hand for a split second, and he took advantage by punching Clay's throat. Clay was stunned just long enough for Bill to roll Clay on his stomach and pin his arms.

"You assaulted me. Now I *am* arresting you."

Clay tried to break free but Bill had a bruising grip on his arms, not to mention a knee in the small of his back. "I will do more than assault you when I have the chance," he snarled. "I will—"

"Are you threatening me, as well? Because I will add that to the list of charges."

Clay roared and tried to throw Bill off, but it was halfhearted. She was gone. *Gone.* He'd imagined the scene many times, but this hurt so much worse than he could have ever predicted.

Anger withering, he stilled, which earned him a punch to the kidney. His vision wavered for a long second as the pain rolled through him. When Clay could breathe again Bill had them both on their feet.

Not letting go, Bill marched Clay toward a waiting hack. "Oh, I am going to enjoy this. The notorious Clayton Madden, spending the night in the holding cells. You'll be a bona fide celebrity."

"You pompous prick," Clay said, not bothering to put heat in the words. They could try to humiliate him, but this wasn't Clay's first arrest. Likely not his last, either. He knew how the system worked. The more noise he made, the rougher the coppers became, as they were able to justify the violence. If he stayed cool then he could send for his lawyers and get released quickly.

Though really, what was the hurry? Other than his pride, of course.

When freed, he'd return to a cold bed—a bed that would stay in that pitiful state now that Florence was gone. The Bronze House would only remind him of her mischievous smile, those laughing eyes. He'd hear her around every corner, a whisper to torment him from now until eternity. It was too depressing to contemplate.

Perhaps Bill had done him a favor. Spending the night in a cell was a hell of a lot better than trying to dodge memories of the woman he'd lost.

THE RIDE UPTOWN was made in terse silence.

Florence could practically feel her father's anger as they drove home. He stared out the window, jaw tight, silent, as the homes grew larger and more spaced out, his fury rolling off him in waves. The quiet suited Florence just fine. The last thing she needed was for her father to yell at her in this enclosed space.

It gave her time to think. Her mind whirled with questions and recriminations, going round and round every bit as fast as the carriage wheels. Anger and sadness warred inside her.

Everything that happened between us was honest.

How was that possible, when he'd been holding this secret the entire time? He hadn't deviated from his revenge, even after she'd told him what her grandmother's house meant to her. What sort of a man does that?

One who doesn't care a whit about you, that's for certain.

The back of her throat burned and she feared she might cry in front of her father.

The nymph was playful and wicked, the spark of joy his lonely life had been missing.

Lies, all lies.

Before long they were pulling under the portico alongside the Greene residence. Anxious for solitude, Florence didn't wait for the groom to open the door and set the step. She got down on her own and hurried to the entrance.

The house was quiet at this hour and she could hear her father right behind her. "Florence, a word." He didn't wait for a reply, merely turned and started toward his office.

Stomach sinking, she followed. Situated in the back of the house, the office was used exclusively by their father. He liked his solitude while working and was notoriously irritable when interrupted. Florence had spent the most amount of time there, however, seeing as he preferred to dole out lectures and reprimands from this male sanctuary.

Sigh.

The room was a tomb, dark and quiet, the ticker-tape machine frozen until the morning. A stream of white paper had collected on the floor, unchecked. She sat in one of the chairs facing the desk, while her father went around and lowered his muscular frame into the seat behind it. "In case I wasn't clear earlier, you are to stay away from Clayton Madden and the Bronze House."

She opened her mouth—and her father held up his hand. "Do not argue with me, young lady. You had no business visiting a casino in the first place, let alone getting involved with that man. Your mother would have heart failure if she knew."

"Are you planning to tell her?"

"No. It would break her heart, which is why I am ordering you to drop this business. No more sneaking around with Madden. No visiting casinos. Are we clear?"

"What happened between you and Madden twenty years ago?"

"It's none of your concern. Suffice it to say that I've found a way to thwart Madden's plans. He won't get his hands on your grandmother's home."

Well, that was a relief. "How did you manage that?"

"Those papers your grandmother gave you the other day?" When Florence nodded, her father continued. "It turns out the city wishes to build a school on that block. They will claim eminent domain on the house and the surrounding land. In fact, Mr. Crain is coming with the papers for me to sign in the morning. Madden will get nothing—and I cannot wait to see his face when I tell him."

A school? So the house would be torn down after all? "How does that help, exactly?"

"Your grandmother has already agreed. She'll move to Newport and live there. The house here goes to a charitable cause. Most important, Clayton Madden gets absolutely nothing."

"But why is that—"

"Florence, allow me to worry about why that matters. Right now we are here to discuss you and your improper and reckless behavior. From here on out no more Clayton Madden. No more gambling. No more running around the city at night God knows where."

"Daddy, no. I intend to open a casino just for women—"

"Absolutely not." His mustache twitched the way it did when he was agitated. "No daughter of mine will engage in such a low endeavor. You could get arrested, Florence!"

"The chance of an arrest is slim. There are ways around the laws."

"Yes, with bribes and kickbacks, methods no doubt employed by the likes of Clayton Madden to keep his business afloat. I forbid you to continue down this path. It's bad enough that Mamie is dragging out her betrothal to Chauncey. I cannot have another daughter flagrantly disregarding my wishes." He pointed at her. "You will do as I say, Florence."

"In other words, marry a childish, selfish man like Chauncey. Settle down and have kids, and oversee his household while I wither and die from living inside a gilded cage."

A flush worked its way over his neck. "You make it sound as if those things are abhorrent. There is no shame in having a family."

"There is when it prevents women from having choices!" Her voice rose with each word until she was shouting.

"Choices that could land you in prison!" her father shouted in return.

Frustration burned her skin. "If I were a son you would let me do whatever I wished."

"Hardly. Being a man comes with responsibilities you cannot imagine. Being a father even more. And as long as you live under my roof—"

"Then I'll move out."

His mouth flattened into a thin line. "And support yourself in what manner? Do you have any idea of the challenges of living on your own?"

"I told you I plan to open a casino."

"I will never allow that to happen, not while I am still breathing on this earth."

"Daddy, that is not fair."

"Fair?" He leaned in, his eyes narrowed. "Do you think it's fair for a policeman to come to my home and tell me my daughter is sleeping with a casino owner, a known criminal? Then I learn that she has been sneaking out at night to visit his casino. Have you any idea of the fear and worry I have experienced in the past four hours? Is that *fair*, Florence?"

"He would never hurt me."

"Are you carrying his child?"

She gasped, and the question would have knocked her off her feet had she not already been sitting. "No." In fact, she'd finished bleeding just a few days ago.

"Thank Christ for that," her father muttered. "And you can hardly act surprised that I'd ask. God knows how long this has been going on." He dragged a hand down his face. "You're going to put me in an early grave, Florence. I cannot understand why you thought any of this was a good idea."

"It's what I want, Daddy. I do not wish to marry and settle down. I want my own business. And I'm good at cards and games of chance."

He shook his head, his mouth twisting in a patronizing smile. "Besting the old ladies at your grandmother's weekly euchre game is a far cry from running a casino."

Lord, he would never understand her. "I am aware of that. If you would just give me an opportunity—"

"And have you considered the scandal? It would kill your mother. No, this conversation is over. Mr. Connors has asked to court you and I think it's a fine idea. I'll tell your mother to ask him—"

Florence couldn't take it one second longer. Shooting to her feet, she faced him down. "I'll never forgive you if you force me to marry."

He blew out a long breath. "Sometimes a parent must make decisions in a child's best interest. You'll understand when you have your own children. So if this hurts you, I am sorry. But you'll thank me one day."

"No, I absolutely will not."

Turning on her heel, she left the room, biting her lip to stem the tears threatening. Her father would never understand. He thought she was reckless and irresponsible. He wouldn't approve of anything she wanted unless it was to get married. Trying to convince him was a waste of time.

She had to do this on her own.

"What happened last night?"

The voice came from directly behind her. Florence started and put a hand to her heart as she turned. For God's sake, where had her sister come from? "Justine, you scared me to death."

Her younger sister took Florence's hand and pulled her into the shadows of the portrait gallery near the front entry. "I thought you heard me. I called your name."

"No, I didn't hear you. Why are you following me?"

"To find out what is going on. Daddy's mood at breakfast was awful and Mama said she had no idea why. I heard him leave before the two of you came home last night. So what happened?"

Florence grimaced. *Might as well come clean with it.* "Daddy found Clay and me together last night."

"Oh, no. He must have been furious."

Florence lowered herself on a settee. "It was absolutely awful. We were at the Hoffman House's saloon."

"They don't allow women inside."

"Clay arranged it. He took me to see the painting there after we left Sherry's."

"Just the two of you?"

Florence nodded. A lump formed in her throat, a tight ball of misery and embarrassment. And anger, of course. "It was romantic. He was so sweet. I thought . . ." *Never mind that.* Whatever she'd thought had been wrong.

"I saw the way he looked at you last night on the street. He's in love with you."

"Justine, he is the person behind the development on Granny's block."

Her sister blinked, confusion clouding her gaze. "Clayton Madden is the one buying all those houses and tearing them down? Good gracious, why?"

"I don't know. It has to do with revenge against Daddy."

"That is a bit extreme. Was it over a business deal or some such nonsense?"

"I have no idea. But Daddy told me I cannot open my own casino and forbade me to see Clay ever again."

"Oh, you know Daddy is full of bluster. He'll change his mind once he cools down a bit."

"I don't think so. He wants Mr. Connors to court me."

"Mr. Connors? But he's . . . old."

"Yes, he is. Don't worry, I'll run away before I let that happen. I don't wish to marry."

"Unless it's Clayton Madden."

Florence rolled her eyes toward the ceiling. Justine believed love could cure all society's ills. "I don't wish to marry Clay."

"Liar. It's clear you have feelings for him. Mamie and I both commented on it during our ride home."

Damn her sister's perceptive nature. "My feelings for Clay don't matter. He attempted to *tear down our grandmother's home."* Even saying it aloud was horrifying.

"In his defense, it's not as if she wasn't offered money to sell. Clay tried to purchase the property, as he did the others. There's nothing untoward about what happened."

"Except he intended to build a casino around her to force her to move."

"I'm not saying I approve of that idea but Granny has enough money to go anywhere she wishes. In fact, she could buy land somewhere else, have the house torn down and rebuilt brick by brick. Being wealthy solves most problems."

Justine volunteered with many charity organizations and fought for better services to aid the city's poorest residents. She was constantly reminding Florence and Mamie of the privileges they enjoyed because of their family's wealth.

"According to Daddy, the house will now be converted into a school. So Clay won't get the revenge he hoped for."

"Did you know?"

"About the revenge? Yes, Clay told me the night I met him that he planned revenge against Daddy."

"So you knew from the beginning."

"Yes, but there was no need to make me . . ." *Fall in love with him.*

"Aha! You were going to admit it, weren't you?" Justine appeared triumphant. "Have you asked Clay about any of this? Perhaps he was as caught up in you as you were in him."

"This is not a grand romance, Justine." Florence pushed off the settee and began pacing. "Clay should have told me."

"Why didn't you tell Daddy of Clay's revenge plot?"

"I thought I could stop it. That over time he'd come to care for me and realize my father was a decent man."

"So you had a plot of your own, one you didn't tell Clay about."

"Do not take his side!" Florence snapped, her irritation and frustration boiling over. "You are so naive. Life is not all candy and flowers. Some people are just awful and terrible."

Justine crossed her arms. "You think I am unaware of that? With all I've seen downtown, the disease and the starvation? Hopheads and gin holes. Children whose feet are frostbitten because they couldn't afford shoes. Women forced to sell their bodies for coin to feed their families. Cholera and syphilis and phossy jaw. I have seen the ugliness our society offers those who suffer. So please, do not tell me I'm naive."

Shame crawled across Florence's neck. How could she have forgotten? "I'm sorry. You're right. I'm just . . ." She let her arms fall uselessly at her sides. "Sad."

"He made you happy, didn't he?" When Florence nodded, Justine's expression softened. "At the very least, give Clay a chance to explain. He owes you that."

Hmm. As much as Florence didn't wish to see Clay again, her sister might be right. What had happened twenty years ago between Clay and her father? Clay would have been just a boy downtown. Florence couldn't see how he would have crossed paths with Duncan Greene.

Yet, something *had* happened. And that something had strangled her chance at a future with Clay.

"I'll consider it." She cocked her head and studied her younger sister. "How did you get so wise?"

"Watching my two older sisters get into trouble, I suppose." Justine came over and clasped Florence's hand. "Daddy and Granny are able to fend for themselves. You don't have to protect them or try to fight their battles. And while I may not think a women's casino is a good use of money or land, it's your dream. So chase your dream, Florence. We'll always be behind you, supporting you."

She squeezed Justine's hand. Mamie would've likely said the same and Florence was dashed grateful for her sisters. "Thank you. I don't know what we'd do without you."

Justine laughed. "Honestly, I don't, either."

Deep voices approached. The two sisters retreated into the shadows out of habit, one born of a lifelong curiosity of visitors to the household. "Who is it?" Justine whispered. "Perhaps Clay has come to apologize."

Florence nearly choked. She couldn't imagine Clay paying a visit to the Greene home, especially not after last night. "No, it couldn't be."

A tall man, nearly as tall as her father, appeared in the corridor, a leather satchel in his hand. Then their father was there, a huge grin on his face as both men walked toward the front entry. Who was this stranger and why did her father appear so happy?

Florence studied the guest's face as he passed and a memory nagged in the back of her brain. She hadn't met him, had she?

Williams helped the man with his things as her father hovered. "Crain, thank you again for the expediency. I think I'll take a little trip downtown this morning and deliver the good news myself."

Oh, yes. Her father had mentioned a Mr. Crain would arrive with papers to secure the city's new school. This didn't explain why Crain looked so familiar to her, however.

"You are the one doing the city a great service, Mr. Greene. This neighborhood desperately needs another school." The men shook hands and Crain departed.

Their father addressed their butler before the door even closed. "Williams, have my brougham brought around. I need to pay a call to the Bronze House."

A pang went off somewhere near Florence's heart. *Daddy is going to see Clay.* Part of her wanted to sneak down to the casino and eavesdrop on their conversation. Perhaps then she'd finally learn the history between the two men.

A strange feeling, undeniable and strong, pulled her gaze back to the closed door. Her neck prickled with the sense that something was off. She'd seen that man recently. But where? Most of her time of late had been spent with Clay at—

She stopped breathing, her muscles locked, as the answer unfolded with perfect precision.

The Bronze House. Crain had been at the Bronze House to meet with Clay.

But that made no sense. Crain worked for the city. He had brought papers for her father to sign regarding the Seventy-Ninth Street school. Why would he also have met with Clay?

Every instinct was on high alert, telling her the two were connected.

No, you're imagining things. Just a strange coincidence. Clay dealt with police and city officials all the time in his line of work.

And yet . . .

"What's wrong?" Justine murmured. "You look like you've seen a ghost."

"I'm not certain. Something is bothering me about that man."

"The one who just left?"

"Yes. I need to see Clayton and get to the bottom of all this."

"Now?"

"Right now. I'll go out through the gardens and catch a hack."

"Be careful," her sister whispered.

"I always am," Florence said and slipped out the opposite end of the portrait gallery, through the door to the dining room.

One way or another, she would have answers today.

Chapter Twenty-Two

The midday routine inside the Bronze House screeched to a halt when Clay walked in the next day. He'd been gone all night, cooped up in a cell at police headquarters.

"Jesus." Jack slammed down the crate of bottles he'd been carrying. "What the hell happened to you?"

Clay ignored his friend and turned to the nearest employee. "May I trouble you to fetch me some coffee, please? And whatever Cook has on hand to eat."

The girl nodded and hurried away, leaving Clay to gingerly lower himself into a wooden chair. Every part of his body ached. Not only from Bill's ham-handed fists but also from trying to get comfortable in a tiny cell for hours on end. He hadn't managed any sleep during his incarceration. And, despite repeated requests, he hadn't been allowed to phone his lawyers until daybreak.

He was starving and exhausted. Worse, a Florence-less future stretched out in front of him like a gauntlet of sharp metal spikes pressing into his skin at every turn. Painful, exhausting torture. It was too depressing to contemplate.

Jack dropped into the seat opposite. "I thought you were with your lady friend."

"I was in jail."

Jack's mouth fell open, his forehead wrinkled in disbelief. "You were *arrested*? What for?"

"Officially, assaulting a police officer and resisting arrest."

"Unofficially?"

"Trying to beat the shit out of Bill."

"Can't say I'm surprised. No doubt he deserved it. How'd he get the drop on you to arrest you, though?"

"Punched me in the throat."

Jack shook his head and grimaced. "You always were terrible at protecting your head and neck."

Of course Jack would say that. He'd been one of the country's best boxers for years. "Well, feel free to give me boxing lessons, but let me catch up on my sleep first."

"Want to tell me what happened?"

Clay proceeded to tell Jack the entire night, from the moment he and Florence had exited the Hoffman House saloon to this morning. "And they wouldn't let me notify my lawyers until daybreak. Otherwise, I would've been released a lot sooner."

The girl returned with a cup and saucer, along with some food, which she set on the table in front of Clay. "There you are, sir."

"Thank you, Pippa," Jack said before Clay could respond. "Would you mind giving us the room?"

She left and the other employees followed suit. When they were alone, Jack asked, "So Greene knows about you and his daughter. What does that mean for us?"

"Nothing. He'll tell her to stay away from me and that'll be that." He shoved half a roll in his mouth, barely chewing before swallowing.

"I can't imagine Greene isn't going to attempt some retribution for consorting with his daughter. Not to mention your efforts to run his mother out of her home."

"He's welcome to try. He will fail, however."

"We can't fight threats from all sides, Clay. Something has to give."

Clay sighed and drank his coffee. Jack was right, of course. An illegal business could only poke so many hives before it was swarmed and destroyed. "Florence will never speak to me again, so that's over. And the house issue is nearly finished. Bill has played his only hand and my lawyers had the charges dismissed."

"You don't think Florence will forgive you?"

"For trying to tear down her grandmother's house? I cannot imagine that to be a forgivable offense."

"Was it worth it?"

Clay couldn't meet Jack's knowing gaze. He stared at his coffee instead. "It will be once I open the casino on Seventy-Ninth Street."

"Liar. You'll miss her."

"Regardless, I knew this was coming. Her hatred was the inevitable conclusion to this little drama."

"You are a grim bastard," Jack said as he stood. "Get some sleep. You're making me tired just looking at you."

"Madden?"

Clay angled toward the doorway. Pete, the front doorman, waited. "Yes?"

"You have a man here to see you. I told him you weren't available but he said you'd want to see him."

"Who is it?"

"Mr. Duncan Greene."

Clay dragged a hand down his face. He felt a hundred years old today. No sleep. No food. Still in last night's clothing. Couldn't this wait?

Get it over with. Then you can move on and forget her.

"I'll see him."

"I'm coming with you," Jack said. "You're in no shape to engage in another round of fisticuffs. You look worse than I did after that title bout in Coney Island."

"He's not going to attack me." Clay groaned as he pushed to his feet. Christ Almighty. He was going to sleep for a week after this.

"I'm not taking any chances. If Bill could best you, then Duncan Greene has more than a fighting chance."

"Fine. Show him up to my office, Pete."

"Will do, sir."

Pete disappeared and Clay headed upstairs. His gait was stiff and he could sense Jack's impatience behind him. Jack remained silent, thank God, leaving Clay to struggle at his own pace. When they reached the office, Clay lowered himself behind the desk and Jack stood at his side.

They didn't wait long.

Wearing a satisfied smirk, Duncan entered when Pete opened the door. Florence's father carried a satchel, which he placed on the floor after he sat down. The door closed and Clay got right to the point.

"Why are you here, Greene?"

"How was the rest of your evening?" Duncan asked, looking pleased with himself. "Have a nice sojourn at police headquarters?"

"If you think a few hours in a cell bothers me, then you don't know me very well. Now, I'll ask again. Why are you here?"

"I'm here to update you regarding my mother's home and your efforts to build a casino on Seventy-Ninth Street. Fair warning, you aren't going to like it."

"Is that so?"

"You know, it didn't have to end up this way," Greene said. "If someone from your family had come to me and explained the situation, I would have made restitution."

"Really?" Clay's upper lip curled. "Because I tried to speak to you. *Twice.* I was turned away both times."

"I hardly would have engaged with an eleven-year-old boy. Your mother and father should have fought on your family's behalf."

"How do you know they didn't try?"

"Because you would have mentioned it just now."

"You have no idea what happened to my parents, my family, after you kicked us out of our home. Do not dare to say you would have cared about the displaced families under your boot heel."

"You wish to paint me as a monster, Madden, fine. But I did care about the displaced families. I was told they all received fair market value for their property."

"Then you were lied to."

"I see I am wasting my breath." Duncan reached inside the satchel on his lap, withdrawing a stack of papers. "I'll get to the point. By buying up the land around my mother's home you hoped to drive her away, whereby you could scoop up the property and build your casino. That will no longer be possible. I have sold the property to the city."

"Really." Clay forced himself to relax in his chair. "The city, you say?"

"Yes. They plan to build a public school on that block. All the property you bought on Seventy-Ninth Street will be acquired via eminent domain." Florence's father tossed the papers onto Clay's desk. "I'm afraid you lose, Madden."

Clay didn't touch the papers. "Impossible. I never lose."

Duncan made a patronizing noise in his throat, as if Clay was cracked. "If you look at the papers you'll see this issue is over. The city will use the property to build a school. No casino will exist there."

"Wrong." Clay reached into his desk drawer and held up a set of papers. "I don't need to look at those papers. I have my own matching set right here. The person representing the city, Mr. Crain? He's actually on my payroll. The school on Seventy-Ninth Street? Fake. In fact, the city has no interest in building a school there. However, they were interested in helping me get the last piece of property I needed for my casino project—for a hefty price, of course."

Duncan jerked in his seat, his hands gripping the arms of the chair. "But the contracts I signed . . ."

"Are legal and binding. The DESD, or what you thought was the Department of East Side Development, is not a real government department. It's my company."

Greene's eyes nearly bulged from his skull. "What are you saying? That I have . . ."

"I'm saying you have signed the house over to me." Satisfaction flooded his veins at the expression of horror on the other man's face. With a sinister smile, Clay continued. "I filed the architectural plans to build around her merely to create a threat. I wanted to back you into a corner, force you to consider other options. Except I made certain I was behind those other options. You played right into my hands, actually. Your mother's home now belongs to me."

YOU PLAYED RIGHT into my hands, actually. Your mother's home now belongs to me.

Florence froze, the words ringing in her ears as she watched from her hiding place, the peephole adjacent to Clay's office.

The school had been a lie. The city's involvement had been a lie. The eminent domain? Also a lie.

Clay had lied. About all of it.

Her chest constricted as her mind rapidly turned this information over. Mr. Crain. *Of course.* That explained why she saw him both at the Bronze House and at her family home.

Good Lord.

It was too much to take in. Granny's house . . . gone. Clay had known how much that house meant to her, how it impacted her future. It was more than a pile of stones to her. The home represented her independence, security to follow her dreams.

Dreams she'd have to reconsider now that the house was lost.

Florence sucked in a sharp breath and pressed a shaking hand to her stomach, reeling at the realization.

Clay's dark gaze met hers and pinned her to the spot, looking at the wall as if he could see right through it. Had he heard her gasp?

She didn't care if he knew she was here or not, dash it. Clay had used dishonest means to take her grandmother's house, her father's childhood home. Florence's future. It would be absurd if it wasn't so painful.

How could he do this?

She'd followed her father to the Bronze House, determined to get answers. The hansom driver had promised to keep pace with her father's carriage for an extra two dollars, which Florence had gladly paid. She'd hoped for a reasonable explanation from Clay, one that would reassure her he wasn't a complete monster.

Wrong. He was an absolute monster . . . and she'd been an absolute *fool.*

The walls began to close in around her, air in short supply. She leaned over and sucked in several long breaths. She had to escape. Get as far away from him and this place as possible.

The hairs on the back of her neck stood up at the idea. No, she wouldn't run. Why should she? She'd done nothing wrong. Instead, she would face him down and force him to admit the truth to her face.

Standing, she found the latch and turned it. Light in the corridor stung her eyes but she moved her feet in the direction of Clay's office. The heavy wooden door bounced off the wall as she shoved her way in. Jack jumped, straightening at the sudden noise, but then grimaced when he took in her expression.

Clay did not react, his face impassive, almost as if he'd expected her.

"Florence!" Her father shot out of the chair, his mouth falling open. "I thought I told you to stay away from here."

She paid him no attention. Indeed, her concentration remained on the man behind the desk. Somehow she managed to stand there, glaring at him while her heart lay shredded in her chest. Any hope she'd harbored that he wasn't as terrible and heartless as people said was now destroyed. No, he wasn't as terrible as his reputation. He was *worse.*

"How could you?" she forced out. "My grandmother's house, Clay. This whole time you were planning this . . . swindle."

He said nothing. Offered up no defense. His dark eyes were flat, accepting. She wanted to shake him, throw something at him. Anything to get a reaction from him. Shouldn't he apologize? Grovel? *Something?*

"Florence," her father reprimanded. "Your presence here is hardly appropriate."

"Have you nothing to say?" she asked Clay. "No explanation for your actions?"

"Every word of it is true." His deep voice was clear, the damning words cruelly enunciated. "I offer no explanation, other than this is what your father deserves. An eye for an eye."

"It's hardly the same," she snapped. "My grandfather built that house for my grandmother. She's older, not a family just starting out. You are robbing an older woman of her beloved home, not to mention me of my future."

"You're right. It's hardly the same. Your grandmother owns three other homes and has the means to buy any property she wishes. She won't be forced to live in a Lower East Side tenement."

"You are a cruel, heartless bastard," Daddy chimed in with. "Rotten to your very core. Getting what you want today certainly won't change that."

"Probably not," Clay admitted. "But it has been immensely satisfying to see you lose your family home."

Her father snatched the contracts off the desk and tore them in half, growling with the effort.

Clay lifted a shoulder. "Crain has signed copies and he's filing them with the city as we speak. Ripping up your copies accomplishes nothing."

Florence covered her mouth with a hand, too horrified to speak. Tears stung her lids, an oncoming flood of emotions that she desperately tried to stave off with a few blinks. She didn't wish to cry in front of Clay.

And to think, she'd come here in the hopes of hearing his side.

Fool.

"Florence, come on." Her father took her arm and tried to tug her toward the door.

Florence didn't move, her feet rooted to the floor. "You knew. This whole time you knew what that house represented to me, why I needed it. And you knew you were taking it all away."

Silent, Clay studied her from behind his icy reserve. None of the heat or affection she'd seen so often over the past month was evident in his expression. It was as if he'd erected a three-story barrier around himself, a fortress that refused to let any emotion escape.

God, this *hurt*.

"That's it, then," she said quietly. "I suppose you've won."

He nodded once. "Yes, I suppose I have."

She drew herself up and strode to the door, desperate to get into a carriage and away from this place. With her hand on the latch, she paused, not ready to leave without a parting shot of her own. "Congratulations, Clayton," she threw over her shoulder. "I wonder how long it will take you to figure out what you've lost."

Chapter Twenty-Three

Clay stared at the elegant four-story limestone building. The afternoon light bathed the facade in a golden glow, a rarified benediction seemingly reserved for the very best families. Families like the Greenes.

Duncan Greene's childhood home. Now it belonged to Clay.

So why didn't he feel satisfied?

He'd won. He had everything he'd ever longed for as a boy. Money, power, a casino of his own. The Greene family home would soon be destroyed. His revenge was complete.

Then why couldn't he shake this dark restlessness?

I wonder how long it will take you to figure out what you've lost.

She was wrong. He'd known all along. With every step closer to his goal he knew he'd taken one step farther away from Florence Greene. Each day had felt like borrowed time.

And now she would never forgive him.

It had been two days but he could still picture the hurt and betrayal in her eyes, the horror at realizing what truly lurked underneath his fancy suit. *This is why I always wear black.* Because his soul was as dark as midnight. Scarred and ugly, the inside matching his outside.

She was better off without him.

He knew this and had accepted it. So why couldn't he sleep at night? Why couldn't he look at the casino floor without his chest aching like an open wound? Why couldn't he take a deep breath without smelling her?

He was losing his mind.

Jack and Anna both had railed at him, begging him to reconsider. That no revenge was worth destroying his one chance at happiness. Clay disagreed. What's done was done. Florence hated him and he could not undo the past. Besides, women like Florence Greene married rich, entitled swells, the kinds with blood bluer than sapphires. Soon she'd forget the criminal she had slummed with for a few months and move on.

He, on the other hand, would always remember her. The woman had slid under his skin and clawed her way into his cold, dead heart. Something had unlocked inside him the day he met her, and he was man enough to know he'd never have that again. With anyone.

He exhaled and reconsidered this outing. A summons had arrived today from the home's current occupant, Florence's grandmother. Hell if Clay knew why he'd agreed to come. Undoubtedly, she would try to talk him out of the sale.

Too late. What's done was done.

So why was he here?

Because you're desperate for any news of her, any mention of her name.

In other words, because he was a goddamn idiot.

Stabbing his walking stick at the ground, he started up the front steps. A very proper butler answered the knock. "Mr. Madden. You are expected. Come in."

He crossed the threshold and removed his derby. The entrance was exactly what one expected of a home such as this, all elegance and understated wealth. Nothing gaudy. Tasteful art and gleaming wood. A large crystal chandelier hung overhead. This was Duncan Greene's world, built off the backs of the less privileged, people like Clay's parents.

The butler took Clay's things and showed him to a drawing room. As the butler announced him, an older woman rose from a sofa and folded her hands. *She has Florence's eyes.* The realization nearly caused Clay to stumble. He hadn't expected it, hadn't prepared himself for any resemblance between the two women. It almost felt unfair.

Yet, a punishment you deserve.

"Mrs. Greene," he said and offered a stiff bow.

"Mr. Madden. Thank you for coming to see me. May I offer you tea? Or something stronger?"

"Definitely something stronger. Bourbon, if you have it."

The butler went to the sideboard and Mrs. Greene extended a hand toward a chair. "Please, have a seat."

He lowered himself slowly into a delicate French armchair likely older than Broadway itself. For a second he wondered if it would even hold his bulk. But hold it did, and soon the butler presented him with a crystal tumbler of bourbon. Surprisingly, Mrs. Greene took the same.

"I wouldn't have assumed you a bourbon drinker," he said.

"There is much men incorrectly assume about women. And your gender underestimates mine at your peril."

He thought about Florence and the initial assumptions he'd made based on her appearance and background. How wrong he'd been. She'd proven fiercely intelligent and utterly fearless. Not to mention absolutely enthralling. "I have no doubt you are correct."

Mrs. Greene sipped her drink and studied him over the rim of her glass. "In fact, you probably assume I've brought you here to talk you out of buying my home."

"I had, actually, assumed as much."

"You would be wrong. I hold no illusions about changing your mind. My son has explained your reasons and, while I wish it were otherwise, I cannot fault the emotion that drove you to take my home."

She couldn't? Flummoxed, he took a long swallow of the best bourbon he'd ever tasted. Smooth and rich, the liquor was even better than the kind he usually stocked. "Then why have you asked to see me?"

"It's about my granddaughter."

Surprise knocked the air from his lungs. He could feel his skin heating—and he hadn't blushed since boyhood. *Christ.*

"I see I've surprised you," she said, a soft smile twisting her lips. "I am fairly direct. It can take some getting used to."

A trait she shared with Florence, who had never hesitated to speak her mind around him.

Calling on years of practice, he wiped any trace of emotion from his face. "You said something about your granddaughter?"

"She's come to me, quite upset about her role in all this. She feels guilty for befriending the enemy."

Befriending. Such a tame, useless word for what occurred between them. More like a life-altering collision. Two locomotives steaming down the tracks before they slammed into one another, forever changing the structure of their separate halves.

"And?"

She raised a gray brow. "I know my granddaughter almost as well as I know myself. And, based on her appearance and demeanor these past few days, I'm able to hear what is left unsaid. So tell me. Why is she walking around as if her heart has been broken?"

Though he was the cause of it, he hated to hear of Florence's unhappiness. *What did you expect? You stole her grandmother's home.* He cleared his throat. "Presumably you mean well, madam, but this is hardly your concern."

"We'll need to disagree, then. I understand the circumstances are less than ideal but she is my favorite granddaughter. I wish to know what happened between the two of you."

Keeping his expression completely neutral, he paused and tried to collect his thoughts. He certainly couldn't tell her the *truth*. "I am a very private person, Mrs. Greene. I'd rather not share the details of my relationship with your granddaughter."

"How do you feel about her?"

"Why?"

"Because I care about her."

So do I.

He shoved the words back down. This was not the time for sentiment. "That is not what I meant. Why would you encourage an association between your granddaughter and me?"

She lifted the crystal to her mouth for a drink, her arresting eyes never leaving his face. "I don't like you, that's true. But I love Florence and I'd like to see her happy. Let me tell you a story." Then she stared into the glass as she gently swirled the brown liquor. "When I came to New York City as a girl from Ohio, my family was shunned by society. We were wealthy, yes, but not the right kind of wealthy. The Greenes were low on money, however, and a betrothal was arranged with Florence's grandfather. After a time we fell in love and he fought for me—against his family, society, anything that stood in our way. There was nothing he wouldn't do for me. In the end, I triumphed over society, rising to its pinnacle."

She paused, looking a bit lost, as if trapped in a poignant memory, then continued. "He was a fearsome man, my husband, but loyal. Determined. Lived by his own set of rules. From what I am told you share these similar traits. We already know you'll fight tooth and nail for what you want." She waved her hand to indicate the room, the house in which they sat. "So are you planning to fight for my granddaughter?"

He blew out a breath, uncertain how to respectfully respond. Would he fight for Florence if winning her was possible? Fuck yes, he would. But this story differed wildly from the one Mrs. Greene told of her husband. More separated Clay and Florence than a pedigree. "No."

"Why not?"

"I'm a criminal, not a blue blood."

"Gambling is not a crime. Rape, murder, theft . . . those are crimes."

"Not according to the state of New York. Florence deserves better than being a criminal's wife."

"Even when she longs to own a casino herself?"

Clay rubbed his eyes with his fingers. While it appeared similar on the surface, there was a difference. "Longing to own something is not owning something."

"You think she won't follow through."

"I didn't say that. But I do believe there are factors she might not have considered yet. For example, her family will not approve of her operating a casino."

"Her family loves her without fail. They will support whatever endeavors she embarks upon."

"Even when society snubs her?"

"Oh, she hates society. She won't mind a bit if her invitations dry up, and the Greenes are too powerful to be snubbed." She paused and studied him. "Besides, wouldn't that work to your advantage? You do not move in society and you're not fond of her family. Her being outcast from both would only make it easier for you."

"I don't understand this. You cannot possibly wish for me to court your granddaughter after I bought this house."

"True, you would not be my first choice. Or even my second. But then, no one is good enough for Florence in my opinion—especially not a man who refuses to fight for her."

The dig was not lost on Clay. "Even if I wanted her, she'd never forgive me for this. She hates me."

"Hate and love are close cousins, as far as I'm concerned. And anything worth having doesn't come easy, Mr. Madden. You should know that, considering how hard you've worked for all you have. I'm told your fortune rivals my own."

"Duncan would certainly never give his blessing."

"Do you care?"

No, but Florence would miss spending time with her father. Clay leaned over and rested his elbows on his knees. Jesus, this conversation hadn't gone as expected. He almost felt . . . hopeful.

He went with the truth. "I wouldn't wish to come between Florence and her family. I know how much it hurts to lose loved ones."

Sympathy shone in eyes so much like Florence's that he winced. "As do I. However, there comes a time when one must leave the nest. Florence has been itching to do so for the past few years—on her terms, of course. And she is close, especially since I have decided to fund her casino for women."

"You have?" That was monumental. Florence must have been ecstatic.

"Yes, I have. Young women have ambition these days and I think such ambition should be rewarded. I want her to succeed."

"I do, as well."

"Do you?" She cocked her head. "Or do you just wish to feel less guilty where she is concerned?"

"Both, actually."

"Well, at least you're honest." She put down her glass and stood.

Clay also rose then shoved his hands in his pockets. He didn't know what to make of this remarkable woman, a Knickerbocker matriarch who should by all rights hate his living guts. Yet, she'd been kind and had offered advice.

It made no sense.

In Clay's world, violence begat violence. Evil was met with evil. Someone came at him, he hit back even harder. There was no forgiveness or charity. Kindness was a luxury he'd never been able to afford.

But this woman was pushing him toward her granddaughter, to fight for Florence.

While I wish it were otherwise, I cannot fault the emotion that drove you to take my home.

When was the last time someone had given him something without wanting an even exchange? Or when a stranger had shown him the least amount of kindness?

He felt humbled by her generosity, a gift he certainly didn't deserve. Closing the distance between them, he held out his hand. "Mrs. Greene, it has been a pleasure."

She placed her hand in his, the bones thin but sturdy. "I do hope I've given you a thing or two to ponder over."

"You've given me much more than that." Stepping back, he bowed. "Good afternoon, madam."

THE GREENE HOUSEHOLD was in absolute chaos.

Florence's older sister, Mamie, had just created the scandal of the year by refusing to marry her intended and taking up with their father's attorney instead. A man, incidentally, with a hidden past. Turned out Frank Tripp had been lying to Mamie the whole time.

Florence could certainly relate. It seemed both sisters had fallen in love with scoundrels.

Men were the *worst*.

Throwing open Justine's door, Florence strode inside without knocking. Her younger sister was sitting on the bed. Florence pointed to the mess of yarn on the coverlet. "What are you doing?"

"Knitting."

"Yes, I see that. But why?"

"I'm attempting to make a baby blanket for one of the mothers downtown." She shrugged. "It's the least I can do while I'm inside, doing nothing."

"May I help?" Anything would be better than sitting around *thinking*. That only led to sadness and pain. Honestly, Florence didn't think she had more tears left inside her at this point.

"Of course. Come here and hold the yarn for me."

Florence sat on the bed, took the ball of yellow yarn and unwound some string. Justine continued knitting, the needles clacking furiously.

"You're quite good at that."

"Thank you," Justine said. "It's easy once you get the hang of it. Would you like me to teach you?"

Not a chance. Mending, sewing and knitting were for other women, not her. Now that her grandmother had agreed to finance her casino for ladies, Florence would be knee-deep in ledgers, chips and dice. "Maybe some other time."

"Liar." Justine's mouth hitched in amusement. "You're humoring me, but I appreciate it. Are you still feeling glum?"

"I'm fine. Though it's funny how Mamie and I both were recently duped by men, don't you think?"

"I don't find it funny in the least. I hate that you're both hurting. Most important, you mustn't think you did something to deserve this."

Of course she had. She'd trusted the wrong man. "Let's see, there was Chauncey's attack on Mamie, combined with Frank's secret history, and Clay's swindle of Granny's home. I have concluded that all men are awful."

"Now, Florence." Justine never looked up from her knitting. "You know that's not true. There are good men out there and someday you'll find one."

"No, thank you." There was only one man she wanted . . . but he'd broken her heart. "Mamie and I have sworn off men forever."

"That's a silly thing to do. Especially when I foresee both gentlemen trying to win the two of you back."

Florence barely suppressed the urge to roll her eyes. "Justine, you aren't able to see into the future."

"No, but I do know people. You'll see. No man in his right mind would give up on either of my sisters."

At only nineteen, Justine was wise beyond her years. However, this prediction was too optimistic for Florence's tastes. She had no intention of ever forgiving Clay, even if he did try to win her back. "A waste of time in Clay's case. Besides, Granny has agreed to finance my casino and I'll be too busy for romantic endeavors."

"Have you told Daddy?"

"No. With everything else happening I haven't had a chance. Not that it matters. He believes the casino is a mistake, so he'll disapprove and lecture me about status and reputation again."

"That won't stop you."

"Indeed, it won't."

"This past week has certainly tested his beliefs of what's right for his daughters. I've never seen Daddy so upset. I think it's fair to say that he has no idea what any of us wants at this point."

"And what do you want, Tina?"

"To save the world, of course." She lifted a shoulder. "A husband and children, too, I suppose. Though later. I'm in no rush."

The needles clicked softly in a hypnotic rhythm. Florence fed the yarn and watched as the rows of the blanket took shape. It was relaxing, though she'd go batty if she had to do this every day.

"Would you take him back, if it could all be undone?"

Florence grimaced at her sister's question. It was a foolish conundrum, not worth even contemplating. "He wouldn't undo it so the exercise is pointless."

"It's not pointless. You can't see the future or what's in Clay's mind. Could you forgive him?"

"Please do not start lecturing me on the power of forgiveness. I swear, I will stab myself with one of those knitting needles first. Furthermore, he doesn't deserve forgiveness."

"No, not at the moment. But your anger will fade in the face of his apologies. Are you ready to live the rest of your life without him?"

The back of Florence's throat burned as her lungs seized. The idea of a future without Clay made her want to lie down and weep, but she'd done enough of that already. This past week her moods ranged from angry and hurt to sad and embarrassed. She was *done* with all these feelings. It was time to get her future under way.

The door opened. Her mother appeared in the doorway, her eyes alight with a wildness Florence hadn't seen before. "Florence, you must come downstairs to your father's office."

Florence's stomach clenched, dread gathering in her chest. She couldn't handle a lecture at the moment. Sitting here with Justine, listening to the needles move, was soothing and mind-numbing. Her father would only yell at her. "Must it be now?"

Mama's expression remained unchanged. "Now, Florence. Right now."

"Why?"

"Please stop asking questions and come with me."

Resigned, she put the yarn in the basket and shoved off the mattress. She followed her mother through the corridor and down the steps. She'd never seen Mama move so quickly. What was going on? "Is it Mamie? Is everything all right?"

"No, this has nothing to do with Mamie."

That meant this probably had to do with *her*. Florence bit her lip and tried to remember that her family loved her, even if they didn't understand her. At least, that's what Granny always said.

Her mother pushed open the door to the office and sailed inside. Swallowing hard, Florence followed. *You can endure another lecture. Soon you'll move out to run your own casino. Don't let them—*

She came to an abrupt halt. In a chair across from her father's desk sat *Clay*.

Here. In her family home.

What in God's name was he doing *here*?

Her gaze flicked from Clay to her father. Daddy's expression was decidedly dark, his mouth pinched as if he'd sucked on a lemon. The air in the office was thick with resentment and disapproval.

She made no effort to draw closer. "I don't understand. What is happening?"

"Florence, come sit." Daddy gestured to the chair next to Clay. "Mr. Madden has something he wishes to tell us."

Her feet started for the other side of the room, though her brain was stuck on the fact that Clay was here. The set of his wide shoulders draped in black cloth was familiar, yet she only felt pain and anger at the sight.

After she'd lowered herself into the chair her father said, "There, Madden. She's here. Now, let's get this over with."

Clay didn't look at her. He kept his gaze trained on her father, his expression unreadable. She couldn't guess as to what he was thinking or what this was about. "I am not one to prevaricate, so I'll come right to the point. I have decided to return the deed for the Seventy-Ninth Street property to your mother."

Florence's jaw fell open but her father gave no outward reaction at all. He merely stared at his adversary over the width of the walnut desk, the rise and the fall of his chest his only movement. "I don't believe you," he finally said.

"It hardly matters if you do or don't." Clay lifted a thick shoulder. "I've already returned the deed to your mother along with my apologies."

He had? A tiny part of Florence's heart rejoiced at this news. But nothing could undo the fact that he'd stolen her grandmother's home in the first place. He'd still lied to her. Returning the house didn't undo any of that.

"And what is the catch?" her father asked.

"There is none," Clay said. "I am righting a wrong. I shouldn't have taken it."

She frowned. He was doing this out of the goodness of his heart?

Understand that my motives are never pure. I'm as selfish as they come.

Those had been his words on the night they met. There had to be something he hoped to gain by giving up his revenge and returning the house. "Why?" she whispered.

Clay shifted and his eyes met hers for the first time since she'd walked in. "Because I hurt you."

Ah. He hoped to gain *her.*

Especially when I foresee both gentlemen trying to win the two of you back.

How had Justine known? Florence's chest fluttered yet she smothered the silly emotion. "While I appreciate the gesture, it is in vain. Still, you owe me answers and I mean to have them."

The edges of Clay's mouth lifted slightly. "Duncan, I'd like a few moments alone with your daughter."

"Absolutely not."

The words were said with such finality that Florence knew her father wouldn't change his mind. Still, she had to try. "Daddy, please. I want to put this all behind me, and the only way to do so is to get answers."

"Florence, let me do my best to protect you. His answers do not matter. This is not the man for you."

"Just like how Chauncey was the man for Mamie?" He winced but she didn't apologize for it. She hated to bring up her sister's situation but their father had been *wrong* in pushing Mamie to marry Chauncey, who'd turned out to be a masher of the worst sort.

"Florence," Mama said, a hint of censure in her voice. "That was unnecessary."

"I disagree," she argued. "You need to let us make our own choices, even if you and Daddy don't agree with them. Things are different now. It's not like when you were young."

"It's not that different," her father said. "We also had criminals looking to seduce innocent young ladies."

"Oh, Duncan," Mama said. "In case you haven't noticed, he's already seduced her. And, if you don't let her speak to him now she'll merely sneak out to see him later. Wouldn't you rather have her here than out on the streets after dark?"

Mama and Daddy exchanged a long look. They seemed to communicate without words, a lengthy conversation only the two of them understood. Finally, her father sighed. "Fine. But I'm leaving the door open and I won't be far."

Her parents departed and Florence was alone with Clay. She smoothed her skirts, focusing on the fabric instead of the man next to her.

"I am sorry."

Her breath caught. An apology from Clay? This was also unexpected. She shoved down the sentiment and tenderness and focused on her anger. "I meant what I said. Whatever you are attempting won't work."

"And what do you think I am attempting?"

"You think by returning my grandmother's house that I will forgive you."

"Are you saying you won't?"

"Returning the deed does not negate the fact that you stole it in the first place."

"True, but I cannot undo the past. I am trying to make amends. For you."

"Why?"

"Because I care about you. Because . . . I miss you."

His eyes were steadfast and clear, twin pools of deep chestnut that held no artifice, and the words tumbled down into her soul like pebbles, tiny ripples of joy echoing throughout her entire body. This was more than she'd dared to hope. Never in her wildest dreams had she imagined he would give up his revenge for her, that he would come to their house declaring his *feelings.*

Yet, it wasn't enough.

"Why didn't you tell me what happened twenty years ago between you and my father?"

"I didn't want you to know. If I had confessed what he'd done, you would have tried to intercede. Talk me out of my plans."

"So you lied instead. I had to eavesdrop in your office to learn the truth."

He stood and began pacing, his leather shoes thumping heavily on the carpet with each step. "I never lied. I was not forthcoming, but I never lied."

"We are back to this, I see." She sighed and pushed up out of her chair. "This is a waste of time. The little bits and pieces of you that I get aren't enough. I want someone who trusts me with the truth, who doesn't hide his motives. I want someone who didn't try to *steal my grandmother's house.*"

"You won't ever forgive me, will you?"

Despair filled her chest, her heart rendered into jagged pieces that could not be mended. The damage he'd inflicted was forever. There was no changing what had happened.

There was only the ash and rubble of what might have been.

She took a deep breath and struggled to maintain her composure. She would not show him the depth of her hurt. "You think to apologize and have it all go away, but you're stuck in the past. You cared more about a twenty-year-old grievance than you did about me. About us. I need someone who will put me first. I cannot forgive what's happened, Clay. I cannot."

His shoulders slumped ever so slightly but his eyes didn't change, almost as if he expected this result. "I see." He blew out a long breath. "I suppose that's it, then."

"I suppose so." God, why did this hurt so badly? She hadn't even known this man long, yet he'd come to mean everything to her. She bit her lip and fought back the tears.

Before she could move or speak, he came closer, and his nearness caused her muscles to lock, the air to become trapped in her lungs. What was he doing?

He leaned in and she closed her eyes, willing herself not to melt into his solid frame. His lips brushed the top of her head with a gentle kiss. "I'd give everything I own to start all over with you," he said quietly. "Goodbye, Florence."

Chapter Twenty-Four

Clay lurked in the shadows of the balcony and watched the evening's revelry. It used to bring him such joy, such satisfaction, to see his dominion full of patrons spending their money on games they'd never win.

Nothing brought him joy anymore.

It had been almost a week since he'd returned Mrs. Greene's deed and gone to see Florence. She'd appeared haunted and sad, such a contrast to the brave and audacious woman he'd met all those nights ago.

You did that to her. You made her miserable.

All for what? Revenge for something that happened when he was just a kid. He'd ruined his future because he'd been stuck in the past. Exactly as Florence had said.

He was an idiot many times over. The woman he wanted, his perfect match, had been in front of him the entire time . . . yet, he'd been too blinded by his own hurt to realize it. Too focused on Duncan Greene and an eye for an eye. Now he'd lost her.

I need someone who will put me first.

He flinched at the words. Yet, he didn't back away from the pain. He deserved this perpetual awful ache inside him. Deserved to see her ghost around every corner. Deserved to lie awake in bed for hours, replaying every moment with her, missing her touch with a feverish insanity.

He deserved the misery.

Perhaps he should move. Go to Philadelphia to be with his mother. Nothing kept him here in New York City, not now. Jack could run the club and Clay could start over in a place that didn't constantly remind him of Florence Greene.

A man down below started cheering loudly, collecting his winnings, and Clay's lip curled in disgust. He hated all of them, these swells too stupid to calculate odds. *The house always wins in the end,* he wanted to rail at them.

You didn't always feel this way. If she was here you would feel different.

Yes, but she wasn't here. She wouldn't ever be here again.

He turned to find a stiff drink when he heard heels on the wooden floor. He knew better than to give in to the hope, however. Florence wanted nothing to do with him. Which meant this could only be one person.

Anna appeared out of the darkness, her silk skirts dragging the ground as she made her way to where he stood. Clay hadn't seen her since the night of the supposed intruder. Still, he offered no greeting. He wasn't fit for company.

She studied his face, one delicate brow arched. "Hello."

He dipped his chin once but kept his gaze trained on the craps table below. Jack prowled the floor, always at the ready to solve problems and handle their members. Clay should have been in his office all night to work on the books. But his office reminded him of *her.*

"How are you doing?"

Were they really doing this? "I am not in the mood, Anna."

"I see that. You look terrible, in case you were wondering."

"I wasn't, actually."

"Jack is worried about you. *I'm* worried about you. This isn't like you, Clay."

"What isn't like me? Standing on the balcony to check on the floor? Pretty sure I do that every night."

She reached over and pinched the back of his arm through his suit. He winced but didn't pull away. "Do not deliberately provoke me," she said. "I am here to help you."

"And how do you plan to do that?"

"Badger you until you talk to me. You cannot retreat behind this thick wall you've built around yourself."

He almost laughed. The imaginary thick wall was doing a poor job at protecting him, if that was the case. "There's nothing to say, and I am not a problem that requires solving. I want to be left alone."

"We care about you too much to allow you to wallow."

"Wallow? Is that what you think I'm doing?"

"Yes, I do," she answered. "You thought she'd fall into your lap when you returned her grandmother's deed. Seeing as that one effort failed, are you really ready to give up? Jesus, you spent twenty years plotting and scheming against her father. One attempt to win her back and that's it?"

"One has nothing to do with the other. She said she couldn't forgive me for the past. She doesn't want to see me again."

"I thought you loved her."

He pressed his lips together. It was pointless to say the words now. Florence didn't want to hear them. But he could admit the truth, that he felt more than affection for her. It was bone-deep, this craving for her. All-consuming and raw. Ugly and uncompromising. Was that love? If so, he hoped never to experience it again.

Noise from the casino floor drifted up as a shoving match erupted between two patrons. Clay wished he were down there to throw punches, burn off some of the energy crackling in his veins. But to what end?

"I'm so tired," he told Anna. "I don't want to do this any longer."

"Stay awake, you mean?"

"No. This." He swept a hand toward the crowd below. "I've achieved everything I ever set out to do. The money, the power, the revenge . . ."

"Yet, it hasn't made you happy, has it?"

"No."

In fact, he was more miserable than ever before. At least in his youth he had revenge to plot as a way of distracting himself from his despair. Now he had nothing. Just regrets and heartache.

"If you want to win her back, find a way to fix it."

"There is no undoing the past, Anna. We both know that. We make choices every day that affect our future in ways we can't begin to predict."

"So true. In Akron, when I was fifteen, I never thought letting the butcher's son peek under my skirts would lead me to owning one of the most exclusive brothels in New York City. But it did."

He angled toward her, resting a shoulder on the wall. "I never heard this story. What happened?"

"My father caught us, called me a harlot and kicked me out."

"That is fucking awful, Anna. I'm sorry."

"It certainly felt awful at the time. However, I moved here and met a benefactor. He was wealthy and decent. I learned I liked sex and could make a living at it. You know the rest."

Yes, he did. Two of the city's wealthiest men had fought over her, one eventually shooting the other, and Anna had become a legend in the Tenderloin. Her bordello was one of the most popular in the city, catering to mostly upper-class men and politicians.

Clay sighed and rubbed his eyes tiredly. "I've lost her. The one good thing in my life and I ruined it."

"You've always figured out how to get what you want, from supporting your family to this casino and your revenge on Greene. So decide what you're going to do today to change your future."

Clay had no idea how to win Florence back. He hadn't ever been in a relationship before, not one with serious feelings involved. And he'd already played his best hand, the return of her grandmother's house. "What would you do if you were me?"

"Grovel."

He frowned. Words were not his strength. Writing or speaking his thoughts had always proven difficult. He was a man of action. A man of numbers. If the reconciliation relied on his conversational skills, he was doomed.

Anna must've seen something in his face. "That could also be some kind of gesture."

"I tried that already. It didn't work."

"No, that one was for her family. You need to do an act of kindness just for her."

Hmm. Another act of kindness, but just for Florence. What did she want? She had everything money could buy—soon to include her own casino for women. And she wasn't traditional in the sense of jewelry and furs. Florence was unique. He'd need to think up a gesture suited to her personality—

Then it hit him.

Yes. It was *perfect*. Even if she didn't forgive him, even if she never spoke to him again, he knew in his bones that this was what he needed to do.

Leaning over, he kissed Anna's cheek. "Thank you. For everything."

He didn't wait for a reaction, merely started for his office. "You're welcome," he heard her call out from behind him.

He didn't turn or pause. Finally, he had a plan.

And, if this failed, then he'd know that he had truly given the effort everything.

ON HER WAY toward the front door, Florence happened to glance inside the portrait gallery. A lone figure sat inside, one she hadn't expected to see there. His shoulders were slumped, almost in defeat.

Curious, she stepped closer. "Daddy?"

He dragged a hand down his face and shifted to give her his profile. "Hello, Florence."

The soft, flat tone worried her. Were his cheeks wet? She sat carefully on the other end of the sofa. "Is everything all right?"

He let out a bitter chuckle. "Oh, everything is just dandy. Mamie's in love with my attorney, the boy I almost married her off to is a cad, and you have been cavorting with a man of the criminal class. What could possibly be wrong about that?"

"I have apologized—many times—for my association with Mr. Madden. If I'd had any idea—"

"Forget what he did, Florence. I'm talking about who he is, about what you aspire to become. You could have been hurt a hundred different ways in those neighborhoods or in that casino. You never gave any thought to your safety—or what it would do to your mother and I should something happen to you."

"Nothing happened. I'm careful, Daddy."

"You cannot plan for every eventuality. Life always has a way of giving us what we least expect—like daughters who buck tradition and convention in favor of independence."

She tried to remain calm, to not get defensive. "I told you, things are starting to change now. Women have choices."

"I understand, but some of us are not ready for change. Some of us want to guide our daughters into secure futures with men who will do right by them, not break their hearts. We want to keep you safe and sound in our small little world, near us."

"Yet your version of my future would slowly smother me, day after day, until I couldn't take it any longer. That just isn't me, Daddy."

"I'm learning that. It turns out I know nothing about my daughters." He dragged in a ragged breath and reached over to clasp her hand. "When did that happen? I feel like just yesterday I was bandaging skinned knees and teaching you to ride. Where did I go so horribly wrong?"

Her throat knotted and emotion burned behind her eyelids. Daddy was the most confident, arrogant man she knew. Not once had she ever heard him doubt himself. "You did nothing wrong. In fact, you've done everything right. You and Mama have raised strong young women who know their minds and are comfortable in their own skins. Mamie is smart as a whip and Justine is the kindest, most honorable person I've ever met. Don't you see? You haven't raised girls to go along with the tide. You have raised girls who will *change* the tide."

He gave her a small smile. "Like Joan of Arc?"

"Exactly. Show no fear, remember?"

"I remember." He squeezed her hand and tugged her closer. "You know, despite what

Mamie thought, I never cared about having daughters instead of sons. You three have been the joy of my life, along with your mother."

"Even me?"

"Even you." He kissed the top of her head. "You are the most like me, you know. Stubborn, willful. Never could sit still for five minutes. I think that's why you and I disagree more often than I do with your sisters. Probably why you are Granny's favorite, as well."

She had no idea. "I always feel like I'm disappointing you."

"My father wanted me to go to Yale. I went to Harvard. He thought baseball and boxing were beneath me. After I first brought your mother to meet him, he told me later she was too plain to ever keep my interest for long."

"That's awful."

"I'm telling you this because strong-minded children often disappoint their parents. I didn't fit the mold of what he expected, but he still loved me. Just as I love you."

"Even if I drop out of society and open a casino?"

"Is there anything I could do to stop you?"

"No."

He sighed. "Then I best come to terms with it, shouldn't I? Just don't expect miracles. I'm old and set in my ways."

Chuckling, she dropped her head on his shoulder. "I love you, Daddy."

They sat in silence for a long moment until he said, "The road you are choosing for yourself is a hard one. I wish I could spare you the pain and social recriminations."

"Indeed, but the alternative is so much worse. I will be fine. I swear."

"So, you and Madden. That's done?"

She nodded against him instead of answering. The heartache was too fresh, too consuming to discuss at the moment.

"If he made you happy, then I'm sorry for it," Daddy said. "But I believe a man like Clayton Madden would have eventually crushed your spirit. He's too dark for you, too dour."

Wrong. He'd been perfect. And Clay had a lighter side, one he didn't show to many. He had been funny and sweet, a wonderful storyteller. A man who'd understood her ambition and restlessness.

If only he hadn't plotted and schemed behind her back.

The clock chimed three o'clock and Florence jerked. "Oh, goodness. I have to go." She rose and shook out her skirts.

Her father chuckled. "Always on the run. Just like I was at your age."

Grinning, she leaned down and kissed his cheek. "Love you."

"I love you, too. I don't suppose you'll tell me where you are off to?"

She just laughed and waved as she hurried to the front door. "You'd rather not know, believe me."

Not that she was traveling to a rough neighborhood—quite the opposite. She planned to speak with Mrs. Mansfield, one of the city's top architects, about designing the women's casino. They didn't have an appointment but Florence knew the architect spent every afternoon at the Mansfield Hotel's construction site. Florence was prepared to steal a few minutes of the woman's time.

Outside, she started to look for a hack when a figure stepped away from a sleek black carriage at the curb.

Bald Jack.

She was happy to see her friend, but her heart lurched at the reminder of Clay. Would this stupid ache ever go away? She walked toward the carriage, smiling at the other man.

The wariness on Jack's face eased. "Miss Greene."

"Hello, Jack. What are you doing so far uptown?"

"I came to see you."

"Oh? Why?"

"He wants to see you."

Her stomach hollowed out and dropped like a stone. "No."

"He figured you'd say that. Hold on." Turning, Jack reached inside the sleek carriage and withdrew a few sheets of paper. "Here you go. He asked me to give you this."

She stared at the stack as if it were poisonous. What was Clay sending her? Had he written her a letter? "What is it?"

"Read it."

"Jack, I cannot—"

"Florence, you've never been afraid before. Don't start now."

She inhaled a deep breath. He was right. Whatever Clay had to say would not change her mind. She would steel her heart, read whatever the papers contained then leave. Move on. He was in her past.

Holding out her hand, she accepted the papers from Jack. The tightness in her chest eased slightly when she saw it wasn't a letter. These were legal papers.

"I don't understand." She looked up at Jack, her brows pinched.

"You will. Keep reading."

Glancing down, she read the first paragraph. Then she read it again. Dear God.

No, no, no. This was unbelievable.

How could he do this?

She didn't know what to think, what to feel. Everything from disbelief to confusion to anger coursed through her, weakening her knees. A strong hand slipped under her elbow to support her. "Steady," Jack said.

Florence blinked up at Jack and forced out the words. "I have to see him. Right now."

"I thought you might say that." Jack reached behind him and opened the carriage door. "Let's go."

Chapter Twenty-Five

Curious eyes watched as Florence and Jack entered the Bronze House. She ignored them and climbed the stairs toward the third floor. Her heart pounded fiercely, taking up all the room in her chest, as she went. She wanted to throttle Clay. No, shout at him and then throttle him.

Not bothering to knock on the door to his apartments, she tried the knob. The door swung open. Disarray greeted her, with crates and trunks, canvas cloths and books every which way she turned. He was . . . packing. *What on earth?*

She flicked her wrist and let the door slam closed behind her. A second later Clay appeared at the door of his bedchamber. He looked *terrible.* Wrecked, as if he hadn't slept a wink in days. No, a month. Hair disheveled, he had several days' worth of growth on his jaw and dark circles under his eyes, the kind that came from total exhaustion and despair.

While she hated to see him like this, she was too angry to care. "I don't want it."

He shoved his hands in his pockets. "Of course you do. Anyone in their right mind would want it."

"Anyone except me, apparently. You cannot give me the Bronze House."

"I can and have. I am no longer the principal owner of the property in which you are standing. That would be you."

"This is ridiculous. I do not want your casino."

"I once swore on the deed to the Bronze House I wouldn't hurt you. I broke that promise—and I never welch on a bet."

That night at the New Belfast Athletic Club felt like a lifetime ago. "I hadn't remembered that conversation, but even if I had I would have refused. This club is yours, top to bottom, inside and out. It's a success because of *you*."

"Then you'll have an easy time stepping into my shoes to run it."

"Absolutely not." She lifted her arms then dropped them, frustrated. "I have my own shoes and I prefer to use them how I see fit."

His brows lowered as he frowned. "Wait, why are we talking about shoes?"

"I mean that I don't want to step into someone else's shoes. I will run my own casino, the way I want. Build it from the ground up, as you did. But for me and my clientele."

"Women."

"Yes, women. I refuse to own a club that wouldn't have me as a member."

Sighing, he stared at the wall, a muscle in his jaw working. "That makes sense."

"Excellent. So keep your deed." She tossed the

legal papers on the floor. "Continue swindling your swells and intimidating your cheaters."

"No, I've decided to get out. I think it's best I stick with that plan."

"Get out? What does that mean?"

Walking to the sofa, he lifted a stack of books into his arms and dropped them into an open trunk. "It means retire from the casino business. Move on. Go elsewhere."

Panic stung her throat, and she struggled to pull in a breath as her mind whirred. Was he serious? "Go elsewhere, as in leave New York?"

"My mother lives outside Philadelphia. Perhaps I'll settle there for a while."

She put a hand to her mouth, stunned. As furious as she'd been with him, she hadn't ever thought he'd *leave.* He was a part of this city, like the East River or Five Points. Anyone who'd ever held a pair of dice on the island knew his name. "What about the Bronze House?"

His big shoulders rose and fell. "Jack should have it. He'll fight me on that decision, but he deserves it. I wouldn't be anywhere close to where I am today without him."

Wrong. He was supposed to say he'd stay, that he couldn't bear to part with the club. "So that's it? You are just going to leave?"

"What would you have me do, Florence?" He flicked the lid of the trunk closed with a harsh snap that reverberated throughout the room. "I tried to win you back and I failed. There's no reason to stay here. I've been going out of my mind because I cannot stop thinking about you. I cannot seem to stop loving you and it's driving me insane."

A buzzing started in her ears, disbelief echoing through her limbs. Had he just said . . . ? "You love me?"

He laughed, a bitter, ugly sound wrenched from the depths of his chest. "I gave you my *club*, Florence. I would give you everything I own, the clothes off my back, if it would make you come back to me."

"You love me."

Expression darkening, he put his hands on his hips. "I thought we covered this. *Yes*."

"I needed to be certain I heard you correctly. Why didn't you tell me?"

"Would it have mattered?"

"Of course. I never knew how you felt about me, about us. I never considered this could be something more, that we could have true feelings for one another."

"Which I ruined by acquiring your grandmother's home."

"Acquiring," she drawled. "What a polite word for what happened. I think you mean *stealing*."

"Fine, stealing. I did apologize for that, by the way. Both to her and to you." He paused and studied her face. "You have her eyes."

Her eyes? "You met my grandmother? When?"

"She didn't tell you? It was before I came to see you and your father. She asked for a meeting and I obliged her." The edges of his mouth turned up slightly. "I thought it was so she could beg me not to take her home. But it wasn't that at all. She wanted to discuss you."

"Me?" Why hadn't Granny or her father informed her of this? "What about me?"

"She asked how I felt about you and how I planned to win you back."

Florence lowered herself into a cloth-covered armchair. Good Lord, this was astounding. How had Granny learned of a romantic attachment between Florence and Clay? Florence hadn't mentioned anything, other than Clay mentoring her at the casino. *Smart old bird.* Somehow her grandmother had figured it out.

She stared at Clay, still trying to wrap her head around the idea of him meeting with her grandmother. "What did you tell her?"

"That you hated me and you'd never forgive me. Both of which turned out to be true, incidentally."

Did she hate him? While that may have been the case hours ago, she couldn't definitively say as much any longer. She was frustrated and angry, yes. But there were many other emotions within, as well, powerful feelings she could not articulate.

He *loved* her.

This strong, intelligent man loved her. Deep in her bones she sensed the truth of it. He never pressured her to act the demure and proper lady. He had accepted her exactly as she was, flaws and all. Had supported her and protected her.

And when they were alone, the nymph was playful and wicked, the spark of joy his lonely life had been missing.

He'd been her spark of joy, as well. She'd been

in love with him for weeks, probably since the night in the brothel.

Nevertheless, how could they possibly move forward?

Instead of worrying on that, she pushed for more answers. "Is that why you returned her house, because you met her and felt guilty?"

"No." He leaned on a chair back, his huge shoulders bunching and appearing even larger. "I realized that I had everything I'd ever wanted, had achieved all I craved as a boy, yet, I was miserable. I didn't have you. Trading our potential future for my past was the biggest mistake of my life."

"Do you mean that?"

"Absolutely. You were all I needed, my perfect other half, but I was too stupid, too selfish, to realize it."

Emotion bloomed in her chest, rising, stretching, until a knot formed in her throat. His honesty certainly packed a punch. She sucked in a ragged breath. "Were?"

"Are. Now and always, Florence. No other woman brought me such happiness or understood me as you did. You didn't seem to mind my black heart or jagged scars." He shoved his fingers into his hair and pulled roughly on the disheveled strands. "Christ, without you, it's as if the whole world has gone dark. I can't breathe without missing you."

"Yet you're ready to give up. Move away."

"You can do better than me. Hell, you *should* do better than me. Your family will never accept me. Society will never accept me. A future together means turning your back on everything you know. I cannot do that to you."

"I am capable of making my own choices, Clay. Do not turn into my father and start dictating how my life will unfold."

He sighed heavily and shook his head once. "You're right. I apologize. I've told you how I feel. Now it's your turn. What do you want, Florence?"

What did she want? Other than focusing on the casino, she hadn't ceased being angry and hurt long enough to think about it. But she knew she couldn't undo the past, and she believed in looking ahead, not behind.

Are you ready to live the rest of your life without him?

Justine's words came back to her and the answer was there, as plain as day. No, she wasn't. But forgiving him was a huge leap of faith, a bet that she might end up losing. He might hurt her once more.

Then again, she might hurt him. There were no guarantees in games of chance or in matters of the heart. Everything was a gamble.

Still, the words to forgive him wouldn't come. In the past she'd made decisions quickly, decisively. From her gut and without a care for anyone else's feelings.

And that had nearly destroyed her family.

To move forward, she had to learn patience, to curb her impulsive nature. Think matters through carefully before leaping. She had to act differently this time.

Yes, Clay had given her his club and returned Granny's deed. But he'd been ready to move away, to leave the city. Leave her. She had to believe in her heart that he would be willing to do anything, scale any heights, to win her back. She needed action, not promises.

Her earlier conversation gave her an idea. It was terrible, really. Everything Clay hated.

Which made it absolutely perfect.

Exhaling, she met his steady gaze with her own. "I've always enjoyed taking a risk."

He swallowed hard, the column of his throat working. Hope lit the dark depths of his gaze for the first time since she walked in. "Is that so?"

"Yes, but you'll need to prove you mean what you say."

"I have never lied to you."

"Semantics and you know it."

"What would you have me do, then?"

She lifted her chin. "Just be ready. I'll cable you instructions tomorrow."

FROM ATOP A great brown stallion, Clay glanced at his bright green riding coat and muttered, "I feel fucking ridiculous."

"I cannot see how you are complaining," Florence's father snapped. "You have the bigger horse."

It turned out that Florence Greene had a wicked sense of humor. Or, she merely enjoyed torturing Clay. To prove his devotion to her, he had been ordered to join Duncan Greene in the park for a ride. Early in the morning. Wearing clothing of any color but black.

She was a cruel and twisted woman.

Yet, he hadn't balked. This was important to her and he would see it through, no matter the awkwardness with her father. And it had been dashed awkward.

The two men could barely tolerate one another. They hadn't made eye contact at all and only a handful of words had been spoken. That Duncan even agreed was a damn miracle.

"How did she get you to participate in this farce?" Clay asked, too curious to not raise the question.

"She didn't. I refused, but my wife convinced me. Something about young women looking up to their fathers and how forgiveness sets a good example."

Clay couldn't help it. He snickered. "Those females run roughshod over you."

"I suppose they do, but I love them all fiercely. Which brings me to another reason I'm here. If you ever hurt one hair on Florence's head, I will bury you where they'll never find the pieces."

"That is absurd. I'd never hurt her."

"See that you don't. Because I will be watching, Madden. The fact that you've given up your casino is one of the only reasons I am willing to tolerate your presence in her life."

"And the fact that you are searching for the East Seventh Street families to make proper restitution is the only reason I am willing to tolerate you."

"As I told you, I thought they would receive fair market value. I had no idea the man who handled the transaction was stealing from me."

Clay grunted and kept quiet. He wasn't here to make polite conversation. The ride was almost done and he preferred less interaction with Duncan, not more. The park had been mostly empty at this time of morning. Thank Christ. This was bad enough without adding the stares and whispers of the city's snobbish elite on top of it.

They rode in silence for the rest of the journey. When they arrived at the entrance to the park, a familiar blond beauty awaited. His heart lurched in his chest as if the organ was attempting to get to her first.

"I see you both survived," she said, her wary gaze bouncing between the two men on horseback.

"Indeed, we have." Duncan kept going, still not bothering to look at Clay. "I expect you to follow shortly, Florence."

"I will, Daddy. Thank you for today."

"Let's hope you remain grateful. Do not forget what I said, Madden."

Clay stopped the horse, slid off the saddle and dropped to the ground. Taking the reins, he led the beast to where she stood. Her eyes never left his face.

"Was it awful?"

The twinkle in her hazel depths gave her away. "You knew it would be, which was why you suggested it."

Her lips twitched as if she were fighting a grin. They began slowly walking toward the exit. "You look dashing in your green coat."

It had been the only coat he owned that was not black. "Perhaps I'll order a new wardrobe of bright colors."

"Purple?"

"If you wish it." And he meant it. He'd dress as a proper English dandy if it meant keeping her.

"I cannot believe you actually agreed to do this. You took a morning ride in the park. With my father, no less."

"I would do anything for you. *Anything.*"

"I do not doubt it. Not after this morning."

"Does this mean I passed your test?"

Her brows dipped together, as if she regretted what she'd asked of him. "I had to be certain, Clay. Too much was at risk to decide impulsively."

He stopped and faced her. She was close enough to touch but he didn't dare. Not yet. "Do not apologize. Any amount of humiliation or agony is worth another chance with you."

"Just promise to always be honest with me."

His skin tingled with anticipation as he placed a hand over his heart. "I swear on my life I'll never hide anything from you again. Not ever. I love you and I'll spend every day making you the happiest woman in Manhattan."

She stepped closer, into his space, and his body went rigid, waiting. Hoping. Anyone passing by would be scandalized by the impropriety. He didn't give a damn.

Her teeth briefly sank into her bottom lip. "I love you, as well. And I'll spend every day making you the happiest man."

Relief flooded him, his big body nearly trembling as he cupped her cheek. "Just stay by my side. Nothing could ever make me happier."

"For a man of few words, you certainly know how to use them to your advantage."

"I speak only the truth. And you should know, I will never let you go. You're mine." He bent to kiss her forehead. "I don't believe in luck, but fortune was smiling down on me the night you first walked into my club."

"We were both fortunate."

He took her arm and began leading her toward the street. "How could I ever argue with that?" He could see why the Greene women always got what they wanted. He was truly besotted and would deny her absolutely nothing.

"You cannot." She reached behind him and playfully slapped his bottom—in broad daylight. "So don't even try."

Chapter Twenty-Six

La Maison d'Argent
Eighteenth Street and Seventh Avenue
1894

The laughter never failed to make Florence smile.

She stood on the balcony, grinning, overlooking the casino floor, where scads of women were drinking, gaming and laughing with one another.

It was everything she'd ever dreamed.

One year ago they'd opened the doors and La Maison d'Argent, or the Silver House, had been an instant success. The name was a nod to the Bronze House, of course, except as Florence had told Clay, "Silver is more valuable than bronze."

Currently, La Maison had seventy-five members, all women, ranging in age and backgrounds. The club was so popular that she'd been able to pay her grandmother back after the first eight months. Now it was entirely hers.

While her parents didn't approve, they didn't actively disapprove, either. Mostly they acted as if La Maison didn't exist. That suited Florence perfectly. She lived on the top floor with Clay, which her parents did actively disapprove of, but she had no intention of marrying. Besides, neither she nor Clay had any use for society whatsoever. Occasionally, she'd encounter one of her parents' friends, who snubbed her, or moral crusaders would picket outside the club, but happiness was the best revenge against people such as that.

And she was happy. Deliriously so.

Her sisters and grandmother had all joined the club, as had many of Florence's old acquaintances. Indeed, as word spread, she'd been forced to turn women away. For a few more years membership would remain fairly small. The exclusivity would help elevate the club's status in the city, and Florence was still learning how to manage her fiefdom.

Thank goodness she had an excellent teacher.

Clay had given the Bronze House to Jack, who'd continued to build on their empire. Clay still oversaw a few minor gaming properties but had recently decided to invest in baseball. A team was being brought in to play in the city and Clay had joined as one of the owners. His keen financial sense and intuition about leisure activities made this a natural fit for him, and she was glad to see him so passionate over a project once again.

A partner in all things, he'd supported her every step of the way with La Maison, guiding but leaving the decisions up to her. He didn't interfere and only offered opinions when asked. She was incredibly lucky to have him in her life as a lover and friend.

A group of women squealed with delight at the roulette wheel. They were celebrating a birthday together, something that happened with regularity at La Maison, and the mood was festive. Which meant lighter pockets upon their exit. Florence nearly rubbed her hands together.

"Florence."

She glanced up to find her assistant, Pippa, approaching. A second cousin of Jack's, Pippa had been working in the Bronze House until Florence lured her away to come work at La Maison. Pippa was sharp and efficient, exactly what Florence needed. "Yes, Pippa?"

"Mr. Madden has asked that you meet him in the office." Her mouth twitched and Florence wondered over Pippa's reaction. The girl was normally quite serious.

"Now?"

"Yes. He said to tell you to take one night off and that if you argued he would come out and get you."

Florence bit her lip to keep from chuckling. Clay was not allowed anywhere in the casino while it was open. No men, ever. Florence couldn't make an exception for Clay, even if she loved him beyond reason. "He wouldn't dare."

"I don't know," Pippa said. "He seemed quite determined."

"I hadn't realized he would be home tonight." There had been a dinner meeting regarding the new baseball team. Was he done already?

"He was considerably anxious. I think he's fixing to surprise you."

"Oh." A surprise? Warmth slid low in her belly, deep in her core, as she contemplated all the ways Clay had surprised her over the past few years. He was creative when the mood struck. "I suppose I best go, then. Will you see that—?"

"The birthday group receives a complimentary bottle of champagne. I know." Pippa began pushing Florence toward the back corridor. "I'll take care of it."

"I have no doubt. Thank you, Pippa, for everything. This past year wouldn't have been possible without you here."

"This is the best job I ever could have imagined," Pippa said. "No men anywhere around? It's absolute heaven."

"It is nice, isn't it?" All the dealers, servers, bartenders and attendants were women, even the guards at the front door. Clay didn't like it; he maintained she needed big, intimidating men at the doors in case there was trouble. So far the only trouble had been from suppliers thinking women were too stupid to add properly. "Come find me if there are any issues."

"There won't be. See you tomorrow." Pippa waved before Florence disappeared around the corner.

The office wasn't far. La Maison had less square footage than the Bronze House, but every inch of it was elegant. Where Clay had scrimped on the personal side of his casino, Florence had given Eva Mansfield liberty to design each and every bit as she'd wished. The architect had outdone herself. The rooms had all been crafted with women in mind, from the three women's lounges, each with four water closets, to the tasteful artwork and crystal chandeliers.

Above all, Florence had wished for La Maison to be a relaxing and pleasant gathering space for women. The club was light and airy, with comfortable seats. A tearoom served repast and beverages all day long and well into the night. The casino allowed for gaming and cards, and there were bedrooms available for those who needed a place to stay. And the crowds proved that her idea had been a good one.

She turned the latch on her office door and entered. The room was dark except for a row of lit candles on the mantel and several more candles on her desk, which had been turned into a dining table. Clay stood by the desk, his hands thrust into his trouser pockets. She shut the door behind her. "What's this?"

"We're celebrating."

"Is that so?"

"Of course. Don't you remember what today is?"

"Yes, I do. I wasn't certain you remembered, however."

"One year ago you opened La Maison. How could I ever forget?" His dark eyes tracked her approach with an intensity that caused her to shiver.

She placed a hand on his massive chest. "I never could have done it without you, my love."

The edges of his mouth turned up as his hand landed on her hip. "Yes, you certainly could have."

"You're right. I could have done this alone, but I am very glad you have been here by my side."

Bending, he pressed a soft kiss to her mouth. It never failed to impress her how such a big, tough man could kiss so sweetly. "I love you," he whispered. "And I'm proud of you."

Her heart stuttered as her chest expanded. "Thank you."

"Now for your surprise." He patted her hip and then walked to the far wall, where a huge covered piece rested. Was it a portrait? Grabbing the cloth, he pulled it free, revealing a familiar erotic painting. "I bought it for you from the Hoffman House."

Nymphs and Satyr. She covered her mouth with a hand. So many memories. The image was just as provocative as before, but with deeper meaning. "I'm your nymph."

"And I, your satyr." He shifted to stand behind her, where he wrapped his arms around her and pulled her into the flat planes of his body. Heat enveloped her and she leaned into him. "We may now study this at our leisure. Forever."

"It's perfect, Clay. I love it. Thank you."

He kissed the top of her head. "How much do you love it?"

"Enough to let you lift my skirts and bend me over the desk while we look at it."

She felt the air leave his chest. "Jesus, Florence. I am the most fortunate of men."

"Yes, you are." She shifted her backside into the growing erection behind her. "And I'm never leaving you."

"God knows I'm never leaving you," he murmured as he pressed his hips forward. "Marriage or not, you're stuck with me."

"Even if I don't want children?" Though she openly used a womb veil to prevent contraception, they hadn't had this exact conversation. But she was more and more certain that motherhood was not for her.

"I don't care whether we have children or not. I've no legacy to protect, no estate to pass down. As long as you're with me I'll remain content."

She spun to see his face. "Just content?"

"Ecstatic." He kissed her throat, leaving a trail of goose bumps on her skin. "Blissfully happy. Thrilled beyond measure."

"Hmm. I'm not convinced."

"Then come along, sweet nymph, to the desk where I shall begin to prove it to you."

Acknowledgments

Gambling was illegal in New York during the Gilded Age, but it was widespread and popular. The upper classes gambled discreetly in clubs, while poolrooms and policy shops ruled downtown. I am not a gambler, so I had to learn a lot about the odds, rules and different ways to cheat, mostly from blackjackage.com. All the errors are mine.

Thank you to Diana and Michele, who read an early (and much shorter) version of this story and convinced me it wasn't terrible. Writing would be incredibly lonely without them in my life. I'm also beyond grateful for the friendship and support of Sarah, Sophie, Julie, Sonali, Lenora, Eva and Megan. You are all amazing and such inspirations to me.

Thank you to Tessa Woodward for her enthusiasm and guidance on this story. It is such a joy to work with you on my books! Thanks to the entire team at Avon/HarperCollins, especially Elle, Pam, Kayleigh and Angela. And thanks to Laura Bradford, who always looks out for me.

A shout-out to the Gilded Lilies on Facebook! Thank you for sharing my enthusiasm for this time period and loving my crazy stories.

Thanks to all the readers, bloggers and librarians for spreading the word about romance and my books. You're all superstars.

As always, thank you to my family for all their love and support.

Don't miss Jack Mulligan's story
in the next Uptown Girls romance
from Joanna Shupe,

The Devil of Downtown

On Sale Summer 2020

From Avon Books

Next month, don't miss these exciting new love stories only from Avon Books

A Hero Comes Home by Sandra Hill

After being held prisoner for three years in an Afghan prison, Jake Dawson is finally going home—except everyone, including his wife Sally and young sons, believed he was dead. As summer winds down, all the folks in Bell Cove are pulling out all the stops to get Jake and Sally together again for a Labor Day Love Re-Connection . . .

Wicked Bite by Jeaniene Frost

Veritas spent most of her life as a vampire Law Guardian. Now, she's about to break every rule by secretly hunting down the dark souls that were freed in order to save Ian. But the risks are high. For if she gets caught, she could lose her job. And catching the sinister creatures might cost Veritas her own life.

Never Kiss a Duke by Megan Frampton

Sebastian, Duke of Hasford, has discovered the only thing that truly belongs to him is his charm. An accident of birth has turned him into plain Mr. de Silva. Now, Sebastian is flummoxed as to what to do with his life—until he stumbles into a gambling den owned by Miss Ivy, a most fascinating young lady, who hires him on the spot. Working with a boss has never seemed so enticing.

Discover great authors, exclusive offers, and more at hc.com.

REL 0120